CAROLINE HANSON

Also by Caroline Hanson:

Love is Darkness

Bewitching the Werewolf

ACKNOWLEDGEMENTS

As always, a surprisingly large number of people helped to get this book done. My husband and children who deserve a home-cooked meal if we can ever find someone to make it. My parents, who helped out so that I could write and go to conferences. My friend Melissa who kept me sane and made me exercise—I like you anyway. And to Lauren, who defies description and is the best writer I know.

Also, I need to thank my writer's group, Witchy Writer's, who have read more scenes and revisions than they ever wanted to. Will I ever buy enough pancake puppies to make it up to you? Thank you Mertianna Georgia, R. A. Gates, Roxanne Price and Lauren Stewart. Laura, Melinda and Sarah, can't wait for your books too!

And finally to my first fans whose enthusiasm and willingness to give opinions has kept me going. Keren Kiesslinger, my cheerleader. Jessica Porter who gave me detailed notes and to Mandy Norrell, who not only gave feedback but made a LIF soundtrack for me.

Thank you!

PROLOGUE

AUGUST 18, 1587

Cerdewellyn, King of the Fey, smiled triumphantly at the baby's first angry cry. The sound reverberated off the thin wooden walls of the primitive shelter. He looked around in disgust. It was nothing like the opulence they had been forced to leave behind. Two tallow candles were sputtering in the room, dimly illuminating the spent woman who held her newborn child. Eleanor, the child's mother, murmured something soothing to the babe, then looked up as Cer approached.

"A girl, just like you promised," she said tiredly, but with a smile.

She doubted his word? *Yes, because no one fears the Fey any longer.* "Do you have a name for the child?" he asked, ignoring the unintended slight.

"Virginia. Virginia Dare is her name."

His black eyebrows pulled together in a frown, giving him a satanic look in the guttural light. His inky hair fell forward into his eyes and he pushed it away absently. "What is the purpose of such a name? Why did you choose it?"

"Because of the Queen, of course."

The English Queen. A mortal. More regal, more deserving of having an infant named in her honor, than the Queen of the Fey.

Of course.

He nodded, watching absently as the baby whimpered and struggled, rooting around her mother's chest.

Cer was pleased, felt a moment of gladness that this, at least, was going as it should. It was an omen for what was to come— it must be. Their lives depended upon it.

"She is strong," he said and turned to find the midwife watching him as if he was a rabid dog about to steal meat from the fire.

Her arms were crossed defensively and she made a sign at him, as though to ward away an evil spirit. As if a hand gesture could impact him in any way. Cer took a moment to study the deep crimson stains on her apron, eyeing it and her until she saw something in his expression that made her take a step back.

And she should fear me.

"It's not his place to be here," the midwife said, never taking her eyes off him. "Seeing the babe before your husband, before your father."

"Hush, Martha. His Highness has been nothing but goodness to us."

Martha shook her head and went back to Eleanor, pressing on the woman's stomach repeatedly until the afterbirth, a huge glistening organ, spilled from her onto the bed.

Cer's voice cut through the night like a blade. "You are done here. Go, Martha."

Martha looked at him, then back to Eleanor. Did she really believe Eleanor's wishes would trump his?

"You are to leave. Now. This is mine. The child is mine. Do nothing to interfere or you will regret it."

"Are you threatening me?" the woman said, her bloody hand flying to her chest as she stumbled backwards towards the door. The confusion and fear on her simple face made him want to kill her and leave. But it would distress Eleanor, and, after the service she had done his people, he felt magnanimous.

"No," he said quietly, and then waited until her beefy shoulders slumped in relief. "I threaten you, your children and your man. You leave here and speak nothing of this. Nothing of me, nor the dark birth I will take with me. One whisper, one rumor of this and all you love will perish."

"You are the devil!" she cried and backed out the door, slamming it behind her. He heard her footsteps on the dry ground as she ran to the nearby huts of the other Roanoke settlers.

He placed the afterbirth into a bucket gently, gave the mother and child a blessing, then went to the woods, ready to reclaim his world. He'd promised Eleanor Dare a daughter and a husband, promised her that her family would prosper. He'd made it happen.

I still have the power to give someone a destiny.

But the Fey never gave away anything for free. Cer had helped the woman conceive for his own purposes—moving the Fey realm, and its living portal, required a host on the perilous journey across the sea.

Eleanor Dare had carried their magic to the New World just as she carried the babe in her womb. They had fled Europe, leaving from County Norfolk for a wilderness so vast and unreachable that no one could harm them.

She'd consumed Fey magic and the essence of their land until she was near to bursting with it. Most of his people—too weak to exist outside his realm—waited for him to complete the rite that would allow them back to the mortal world. And tonight, he'd do just that.

Cer walked into the woods, feeling the night air closing in around him, as though it wanted to meet him, lift him up and return him back to his former glory.

Waiting.

How long had they been a civilization on the brink of extinction? How many had been slaughtered by Lucas over the long centuries?

When the time came, Cerdewellyn would kill him.

It was a death he imagined every waking moment. Akin to a fantasy of a woman he desired but had never taken—he would close his eyes and imagine killing *him*. He didn't care if he looked Lucas in the eyes, didn't care if he stabbed Lucas in the back, didn't even care if someone else forced the stake through his heart...so long as it was done.

He stepped into a clearing in the woods, where the trees and brush had been cut back by the settlers. The strongest of his people— those who had not needed to lock themselves away in the portal— fell to the ground, the Wolves howling in recognition. Cer could *feel* the expectation.

A fire raged in the middle of the circle, flames licking so high that they singed the nearest branches—an inferno under a witch's control.

Tonight they would be reborn, put the past behind them and start again.

His witch, Nantanya, stepped forward and took the bucket that contained the bloody after birth—and all the magic of his people—and went to the fire.

Cer looked at the remnants of the Others. A handful of Empaths, a few Witches, and all that was left of the Wolves. Many of their loved ones were trapped in Cer's dimension, never aging, nothing changing, as they waited for a way to return to the mortal world.

He made eye contact with each of them, feeling the weight of loss and ruin in their worn clothing and lean faces. The journey to the New World had been hard, and Roanoke was not as plentiful as they had hoped. But once the portal was opened, that would change.

"With this birth, our fortunes change. Our new life begins. Bonded together by death, we are no longer enemies, but kin. All of our kind forged together in a fire of despair." Cer paused, letting the men and women think about what they had left behind. How dire their situation had become. There had been only one choice.

Leave. Because Lucas and his horde had destroyed them all.

The silence gave way to the slight crackle of leaves underfoot. His Queen approached, their witch leading her by the hand. She was naked and walked forward slowly, flowers twined in her long, honey-colored hair.

The trip had been especially hard on her, and as he watched her come forward, he noticed that she was thinner than usual— her stomach concave and her breasts smaller.

He felt a moment of unease. *A true goddess is unaffected by mortal coils.* But they'd been together for hundreds of years, had dozens of children together, and as she smiled at him, all his doubts disappeared.

The witch chanted, sliced her palm with a sharp knife, her blood dripping into the fire with a hiss. She lifted the afterbirth from the bucket, holding it suspended over the fire.

The witch had cast the spell allowing their dimension to be moved, but Cer and his Queen were the ones who would break it, allowing the Fey to come and go between the two dimensions.

Nantanya knelt down and cut into the bloody mass, slicing off two small pieces before casting them into the fire. They burned with a flourish, a cascade of rainbow-colored flames sparking bright.

Cer felt the magic rise from the fire like smoke, knew the moment it touched him— thickened him, his cock pulsing in time to his heart and the witch's chant.

A breeze rustled across his skin and his Queen's hair flitted across him arm, twining around his hand. The fire crackled again and he was hard as obsidian. The urge to mate with his Queen an overwhelming need.

Magic and power flooded the night. He drew it into him, channeling it into pure desire, before throwing it into the land, aware of it touching each person in the clearing. Their sudden moans of carnal hunger, a primitive song in the night.

The witch approached, a strip of meat dangling on the edge of her blade. He inhaled, the smell of blood and power potent and intoxicating. Without question, thought or hesitation he swallowed it whole, felt it burn through him.

The magic needed an outlet. The magic was half him and half his Queen. Only their joining would make the magic whole. Cerdewellyn watched as his Queen opened her mouth, taking the flesh between her lips. She closed her eyes in bliss and raised her hand, covering her mouth as though she savored every drop. *Or as if she might retch. No, impossible.*

Women came to him from the crowd, helping him take off his clothing, stroking his body. They touched him everywhere, their passion growing as he fed his desire to them.

A woman tugged the sleeve of his shirt away, then touched his chest, her finger grazing his nipple. Another unfastened his pants, pulling the laces free, her hand touching his cock, sliding her fingers across the damp head. He was ready and full, potent and eager to mount his Queen.

With this offering, with their release, they would all be free.

His Queen closed her eyes and made a choking noise, an expression he couldn't identify scraping across her features. But it wasn't joy. Uncertainty flooded him and he shoved it away. This was their chance. Their realm hinged on this night. There was no time for uncertainty or doubt, no going back. The rite would work.

Love Is Fear

Because there was no alternative. Male hands caressed her flesh and stroked her hair. Readying her. With a cry, she swallowed, tears running down her cheeks.

He knew that pleasure: When his body was so overrun with verdant desire that he could barely function beyond the moment and his own urgency.

Cer grabbed his Queen around the waist, her back to his front, his fingers going around her body and plunging between her thighs.

She was hot and wet. A Queen built for desire. He pushed his fingers into her, opening her, making her wide for him.

No gentleness, no hesitation. It was unnecessary because she was Queen of the Fey, as ready and hot as he was. She was his equal—a mirror for his desire.

She cried out at his blunt invasion, struggling closer. He settled her on the ground, raising her hips into the air as he impaled her from behind in one, swift move.

Like a dagger plunged to the hilt.

Like the last gasp of a dying man.

That connection was everything.

Cer thrust within her, slow then pounding, feeling the magic course through him. It was building, growing.

Wrong.

He felt it even as the orgasm gathered in his cock.

He was buffeted by sex and violent urges as his followers mated around him. The men took the women hard, the wolves half-transformed, all control wiped away and fed to the magic. There were not enough women and several of the men were pleasuring each other, holding tight fists around their pricks, their motions quick and greedy.

Bodies writhed while their groans rent the air. He heard the witch chanting, felt the fire grow, consuming the very air around them, urging them towards completion.

His Queen was below him, her body milking him, fingers sunk deep into the earth.

Wrong.

Through the fire of lust he knew *this* was not right, that something was out of balance. With a hoarse yell, he pulled out of her, flipping her onto her back and sinking his face between her thighs. He kissed her and licked her, ate at her with a passion driven by the elements.

She clenched hard, exploding around him. Her taste burned him, scalded him, tasted…. *Wrong.*

He ignored it, still driven to come, to break the spell that kept the Fey trapped in another dimension. He loomed over her, looking down at her perfect face, and caught a flash of *something.*

It was as though she wasn't there. As though she'd faded and was covered head-to-toe in an illusion of death. Her skin gray and mottled, her eyes wide in her sunken flesh. The leaves she wore, dead and rotting. He blinked, and the image disappeared. His Queen was whole and beautiful before him, body lush and spread, ripe as spring, hot as summer.

She stared at him with an expression he'd never seen before. As if she didn't want him. He kissed her deeply, plunging his tongue into her mouth as he slid inside of her.

They were one.

Orgasms erupted around him, each offering of seed and honey greedily taken by the magic. He felt the first spasm within him, his essence pouring into her as he ground himself deep, the climax wrenching, as though his seed had become heavy, liquid gold.

She shifted away from him so that he slipped out of her, the final potent lashes of his seed falling to the earth.

He heard the fire roar and die—*Wrong*.

His Queen lay beside him, crying, and the whole night was as dark and still as the dead. Cerdwellyn stood, pulling her to her feet.

Her breath made a strange hitch and then she struck him, hand open, so that his head cracked to the side. "Where is the portal, Cerdewellyn? We have come so far and there is nothing!" She hissed the words at him.

Cer didn't bother to touch his face, tasting blood at the corner of his mouth. He strode away from her, towards the smoking coals and the witch who had served him for decades.

The lines on the witch's face were etched even deeper with the night's failure. She started speaking as soon as he was near. "It should have worked. The spell was perfect. You did your part. But the Queen—Did you not see it? You *hurt* her, Cerdewellyn. If she were still your equal, that would have been impossible. She is no longer the true Queen, my lord."

"She has been my Queen for time beyond measure," he said, words hollow with fear.

The witch's voice trembled. "But that doesn't mean she still is. There was another before her, and now there is another to replace her."

He shook his head in dismay, pressed his lips together hard, even as his gaze strayed to the fire and then out into the distance. Through the trees and towards the ocean. Where the barest, faintest hint of light was—and the newborn female babe conceived with all the magic of the Fey.

"And where is my Queen then?" he asked harshly, even though the answer was plain.

"You know, Sire. Surely you feel it. Affection, a shared history is irrelevant. Survival is all that matters now. The Queen will understand. She knows her duty."

"She is but a babe. It will be years before she could perform the rite as a true Queen must. If I open the portal and we go in...we cannot come out for years, not until she is old enough to perform the rite and break the spell."

He looked around at his people, cursed Lucas again for forcing them into this situation. "Tell the settlers. They come with us, to wait for Virginia Dare. If they want to live, then they must come below."

CHAPTER 1

What in God's name is Jack doing here?" It's like meeting the man of your dreams and then meeting his beautiful wife."

Jack stared at Val hard, but he didn't move away from the door frame. His arms were crossed, and he looked exhausted. Dark stubble was visible on his lean cheeks. He studied her intently, like someone he'd seen somewhere but couldn't quite place. His voice cracked like a whip and she wanted to yelp in response.

"Excuse me?" he ground out.

"Um...Alanis Morrisette. It's a line from the Ironic song." She cleared her throat. "You know, you make a decision and then the worst thing that could happen happens. Funnily enough, not a single one of those things were actually ironic. They were just bad luck. Which actually is...uh...ironic."

What the hell am I saying? And why am I saying it out loud? She collapsed against the wall soufflé-like. Sweat beaded on her forehead and she felt nauseous and sick, like the time she'd eaten that taco in Mexico and Montezuma had his revenge upon her. Nerves. That's why she was saying something so stupid.

It just wasn't fair. Jack had been in the dark about her knowing Lucas and now that it was over, Jack saw them together. *Fucking irony.*

"What is this, Valerie?" The words were a barely leashed growl, as though he'd wanted to scream, *What the fuck do you think you're doing?* , but had managed restraint.

No words came to her, no excuses or half-truths. Not even the truth! What was the truth? Val looked at the floor. Her tennis shoes had little droplets of blood along the top and sides. Maybe some brain. Shouldn't it have turned to ash? *Focus, you jackass!*

"Okay. I know you want answers, but let me take a shower first, all right?" That would give her time to think through what she *would* tell him, *should* tell him and *wouldn't* tell him on pain of death. Val stood, still not looking at him and kicked-off her shoes to the corner of the room.

Jack was quiet, but the tension was palpable, giving the air around him a soft glow. Valerie blinked and squinted. The haze didn't go away. *Great, now I'm going blind too.*

He swept forward and grabbed her by the arms, his fingers digging into her hard enough to bruise. She squeaked in pain and surprise, her eyes flying to his.

His face hard with anger. "No! He called you at the hospital, didn't he?"

Her arms were going numb. She nodded at him, dumbly.

"I asked you who it was and you wouldn't tell me. You said it was '*none of my business.* ' Really, Val? What the *fuck*?"

"Wait—" She needed to stop this conversation. This was too important for her to wing it. She needed time.

"*No*! No waiting. Tell me why you were with him. Why didn't you ask me for help? I would do *anything* for you!" His voice broke.

"You're hurting me!" she shouted, making a frantic effort to, at least, have physical control over herself before he steamrolled over her emotionally. She could hear the anguish of those words over and over again as they took up permanent space in her brain. Jack would do anything for her. *There is a special place in Hell for people like me. Above pedophiles but somewhere below petty shoplifters.*

Jack let her go abruptly and stepped backwards, his hands surrendered in the air. She rubbed her arms, trying to get the circulation going again, the pain momentarily increasing as the blood rushed back.

"It's done," she said, "Lucas is not coming back. Marion took me from the hotel to use me against Lucas, hoping she could get him to do what she wanted. It didn't work and he brought me back here."

What a stupid explanation! And why were we all over each other, you ask? We weren't. I accidently fell against his lips and erection. Plus, his hands were only on my ass for stability.

"Marion was here? Tonight?" The mere mention of Marion was like a flag before a bull.

Oh. Much more important issue than me making-out with Lucas.

"Why would she take *you* to use against Lucas?" His hands raked through his hair, so that a small section stood on end, making her want to touch him and smooth it back into place. It made him look approachable and real.

"No. Let me start at the beginning. I'll just start over. Promise me you will listen. *Please?*"

He was emoting like a statue. Christ, she had to be careful. She didn't want to lie to Jack, but she had to be strategic in what she told him. How much could he take before he snapped?

Deep Breath. "Lucas came to me in Hampstead. He told me that if I didn't help him, you and dad would get hurt. At first, it was simple. He wanted me to give you the information on Marion, knew you wanted her dead and was going to help you—"

"Why?" His voice was menacingly quiet, and Val had the unpleasant sensation of being a rabbit trapped with a rabid dog: as soon as she moved, he'd attack her in a frenzy.

"The vampires were going to revolt against him. Marion was the leader. Lucas said he wanted you to kill her, so he wouldn't have to."

Or maybe he thought Marion would kill you, so he wouldn't have to, were the words that she didn't say. Was that it? Lucas was such an underhanded bastard, treating life as a big chess game. It was entirely possible that was what he'd planned on happening. Marion had been powerful. Jack wouldn't have stood a chance of killing her. *Had Lucas intended for Jack to be dead already? Cut out the competition?*

"That file you found in my room. He gave it to me," Val said.

"You never wanted to help your father and I, did you?"

Frantically, she shook her head in disagreement and rushed to him. "I love you, Jack. I do. I was a coward to not help you before, when I could have. I thought that if I kept away from you that"—she swallowed, tried to make the emotion go down her throat—"maybe that my feelings would go away."

No, that wasn't it. "You know what it was? I thought that the only thing worse than loving you and losing you would be having you love me back and *then* losing you. Like getting to the gates of Heaven, having a look around, and then being cast out."

Her voice was trembling and she couldn't look at him as she spoke. "You want revenge more than you want me, Jack, and I always thought it was an 'either/or' situation. One was exclusive of the other. But they aren't. You can have revenge *and* my help. If you have something to come home to, maybe you'll fight harder."

There was a big pause as Val ordered herself not to cry like a big wuss.

His hand stroked her hair. "Come on, Val. Finish telling me about Lucas. We'll sort out the rest later," he said soothingly, like she was about to jump off a great, big ledge.

She'd bared her soul and gotten no encouragement in return. Had she been wrong all these years? Had he stayed away from her because he *just* didn't want her?

"All the information about every vampire that I've given you came from Lucas. He said he'd fed information to Gilbert Arthur too. But then someone killed him, so he had a job vacancy to fill.

And, lucky me, I got the position." *That sarcasm was crystal clear, right?*

His hands cupped her cheeks and he was so close his warm breath fanned her face. "Why didn't you tell me what was going on?"

Val realized he wasn't just angry but sad, too.

"I would have protected you," he said fiercely.

Val laughed miserably. "No, Jack, you would have died." She took a deep breath. "Lucas is not killable. Believe me. I watched him tear apart three-hundred-year-old vampires with his bare hands."

He stiffened in affront, his face closing down. Then he let her go, walking away from her to the other side of the room. As far from her as he could get.

"And Marion? You think I can't kill her either?"

It was as if he had Short Mortal's Complex instead of Short Man's Complex. He was going to try to take on every big, bad vamp he could just to prove that he had giant cajones.

I blame testosterone.

"Marion's gone. She lost to Lucas tonight. He put her in a box, wrapped it with chains after bleeding her dry, and took her somewhere. I don't think she'll be back in *our* lifetime. Potentially ever. She'd be dead now, but Lucas wanted her girlfriend to help him. He's good at blackmailing people into doing what he wants. Find what someone loves, shake, threaten, stir and *voila*!"

Jack was silent, thinking about what she'd said, no doubt. A look came across his face, one of intense study, like she was about to tell him the winning lottery numbers.

"Are you fucking him?" he asked.

"Gee, that's some mouth you got there."

"What? You're blushing, Val? Really? Don't dick around with this. Is it *love*? You *make love* with a vampire? *No*. If you're going to sleep with a vampire, it's fucking. At least, own your actions."

Now she was pissed. "Don't be an asshole. And no, I'm not fucking him. I've *never* fucked him. In fact, there has been no penetration of any kind." Val finished, arms crossed, knowing she looked pleased with herself. And why shouldn't she be? Lucas could set any woman's knickers on fire. Someone should throw her a parade for not boning that man!

He looked shocked, the 'you just killed my puppy on purpose' look. "Jesus Christ, it hadn't even occurred to me that you might give him blood. Did you?"

"What? Is blood worse than sex?"

He grabbed her, pulling the neck of her sweater down, examining her throat, then her wrists, looking for puncture marks.

She swatted at him. "You want to have a gander at the femoral artery too? Yank my pants off and take a peek at my girly bits? Get the hell off of me!" She was shouting as she pushed by him and went into the shower, turning on the water and taking off her clothes. "It's over. We're done." She knew

Jack was behind her, could hear his footsteps on the bathroom tile as he followed her into the small space.

"We're not done yet!"

"Fine. But I can't talk to you like this." Her voice wobbled. "I'm *covered* in blood. I almost died. I've got blood and Lucas." She blinked back tears. "He's— it's like he's here. Like he still has me." She stripped furiously, heard her clothes tear as she ripped them off. She glared at him, whipping her shirt off over her head, standing before him in a blood-stained bra.

Men usually paid for women to take their clothes off, but not Val. He backed up, finally understanding just how emotionally whacked she was. He shut the door, and she couldn't believe she was alone. *Stripping works every time. I can't even give this away.*

It was so quiet all the sudden. She got into the shower and began to scrub. Lots of shampoo, lots of soap. And lots of thoughts of Lucas. Coming towards her, wet and dripping from the shower. Desire on his face, wanting her to understand that he wanted her, and that she could have him if she made the *slightest* effort.

In a million years she couldn't believe that she'd be here. Lucas had come to her at sixteen, golden and beautiful, scary as hell. The King of the Vampires, and he'd helped her, rolled her mind to take away her fear, stood beside her and encouraged her as she killed a vampire.

She'd killed a vampire with him. It was intimate. And he saved her life. He'd also been kind to her. And then he'd left her alone, leaving a little brand on her soul. It was like a zit. No amount of concealer was going to cover up his effect on her.

When he'd come back into her life, she was a graduate student in London. He'd appeared and told her she was going to help him. He'd been scary, but hot.

In his own fucked up way, maybe he'd been courting her. But he didn't become King of the Vampires by being warm and fuzzy. He'd almost lost his throne, and she'd watched him slaughter every vampire who crossed him. Had realized just how alien he was.

How cold and unfeeling.

She'd known she was going to die and swore that, if she made it out of there, she'd find Jack and make it work. If she was going to die anyway, then she wanted it to be with Jack, the man she'd loved forever.

And just when she'd come back, determined to declare her love, he'd seen her getting groped and grop*ing* Lucas.

Gulp.

How could she keep Jack and convince him it was over with Lucas? How would she get him to believe it when she didn't believe it herself? No, it *was* true! Lucas was gone. Down the drain. If she had Jack, she wouldn't think about him anymore. Would never see him again. Lucas had said he'd wait for her to come back.

I will never go back.

She shivered. There was no going back. Her future was with Jack. Since she'd been twelve–years-old, Jack had been her knight in shining armor. Yeah, he was a little tarnished now, but she still loved him. They could make it work, right?

CHAPTER 2

The shower gave Val a chance to think, something she hadn't yet had a chance to do. Marion was gone. Her father, Nate, was gone. There was nothing to keep them going. They could walk away from hunting vampires and never look back. She finished her shower, got dressed and she was ready for round two.

Great.

"Jack, it's over. You don't have to fight vampires anymore."

"Really? How'd you get to that conclusion?" he said in a dead tone. He had his cell phone out, and he was flipping it in his hand and catching it again. He didn't even look at her, just watched the phone jump up into the air before he caught it again.

"You can't kill Marion—she's basically dead already. She's locked in a coffin that is wrapped in silver! Lucas is unkillable and he won't be giving us any more information. So, we're free."

Jack smirked, a reaction to an unpleasant joke. "No, Val. She's not dead, and Lucas is not dead. The only things that have changed are that Nate *is* dead and they are harder to get to."

Val felt the tears welling up again. "Your whole life has been revenge. If your parents were alive, what would they tell you to do now?"

He shook his head and frowned.

·"If they were alive, they'd want grandkids and want you to be happy," she said earnestly.

His eyes bore into hers. "Are you telling me you want to settle down? Have kids together and pretend the world is better than it actually is?"

Was she? *That's a big jump, Val.* Settle down. Have kids. When an hour ago, she'd been desperate to climb Lucas like a monkey and screw him blind.

Which is stupid and dangerous.

This was Jack. A future that she'd wanted her whole life. She was going to take it. Forget Lucas. Forget the attraction.

She loved Jack. He was as hot as Lucas, but even better—because he was alive and cared for her.

But settle down? That might be excessive. For all I know, you're terrible in the sack, and it won't work out. How about a vacation first, and we can see where it goes? Hawaii!" She sounded a little hysterical. Hysteria, one of the things men never looked for in a woman, according to Cosmo.

She couldn't even look at him. She felt like a used car salesman trying to convince a mechanic that a Yugo was a sound investment. "People die everywhere. Starvation, disease, bad luck, stupidity—we can't stop that either. We can't fix the world. Your goal in life was to see Marion dead, and she is."

"You said she's in a box."

"Right. A coffin. Where dead people go," she snapped.

He was looking at the ceiling. Val crossed her arms over her stomach, like he might try to kick her and she wanted to be braced for impact.

"Why did Lucas want *you*?" he asked, words slow and precise.

Nervous laughter. "Should I be offended?" He didn't think she was good-looking enough for Lucas?

"Offended about what?"

Wait, what? "What?"

She had the distinct feeling that he had all the answers, appearing smug and removed as he prepared to lead her down the garden path. "I was asking why Lucas would have you do his bidding when there are hunters all over the world. Male hunters. Female hunters. If he'd wanted dead vampires he would have used one of *them*. I can't think of any reason why he'd choose *you*."

She blushed, and he squinted at her.

"My good fashion sense?"

"So, it is you he wants." Big pause as Jack took a predatory step towards her.

Uh oh.

"But you don't want him, right?" His voice washed over her, dark as chocolate.

She shook her head.

He moved towards her slowly, silvery eyes locked on hers, his pull magnetic. "Because you want me?"

Val looked at the ground. Her hands flew to her cheeks, covering her blush. Cold compared to the heat blazing off of the rest of her. She risked a look at his face.

His eyes were intent on her lips as he crowded into her personal space. "You want to go to Hawaii?"

"What?" Was she this stupid, or was he hard to follow?

"I asked if you are really saying you want to be with me?"

That's what I thought he said. And yet it still makes no sense. "Yes! I do. Things are done with Lucas. It's always been...you know...." she trailed off.

"Actually, I don't think I do. I'm not sure I have any idea what you're going to say," he said, arms crossed over his chest.

Talking out problems, sucks. "I have...always been...in love with you."

Jack appeared to be thinking so hard she thought he might have an aneurism. Finally, he blew out a breath and then nodded. "Okay then. That's settled then."

"What? What is settled?" Val whispered.

"We'll go to Hawaii and be a happy couple." He stopped right in front of her, his finger tracing her cheek, voice husky and low. "I'll show you how good I am in the sack, and then we can see where we are." He shook his head slightly, absently. "I can't make any promises, Val."

Valerie was frozen, his words not sticking, like a wet Band-Aid. Did he just say 'yes'? Jack would give them a chance, take a break from killing, and see if he could be the white-picket-fence guy?

Shouting 'Whoot!' seemed like an insufficient response. She threw herself into his arms, and Jack grabbed her tightly, squeezing her hard against him. She gripped him back, as though holding him tight enough would mean she couldn't think about anyone else.

And yet, she had the oddest sensation that they were both feeling the same way. Both running away from something and bumping into each other to make their problem go away. But Jack didn't have a problem, did he?

Relief flooded her, desperate happiness—like a life raft just as her mouth filled with sea water.

Jack was here. She could feel him, touch him, smell him. His hand went to her neck, holding her still so that he could kiss her deeply.

His lips were soft and full, *so warm,* she thought, then hated herself for comparing Lucas and Jack in any way. She opened to him, felt his tongue surge inside then retreat, licking her lower lip lightly as though he wanted to taste every part of her mouth.

Valerie felt panicky. She wanted to kiss Jack, but the night had been too much. She was frazzled, too much had happened and she needed a break. The gore of all those bodies, the evilness of what she'd seen at the Challenge—Lucas killing all those vampires with his bare hands, the way he had reveled in it. It all clung to her like a miasma, contaminating this perfect moment with Jack.

When they were older, she wanted to look back at this moment and not have Lucas' heavy shadow intruding upon them. They would go away, learn each other, talk to each other and resolve all of this first. Then they would hit the sack. And she wouldn't leave him or the bedroom, even to eat. They'd order room service for a week.

She pulled away from him, looking into his heavily lashed eyes, looking for affirmation of what he'd said.

He gave her a small smile, rubbed his thumb lightly over her bottom lip, as though he wasn't ready to stop touching her. He stepped back and gave her a slight nod. Jack went to the door and opened it "We'll talk some more in the morning."

"Wait. What about my father?" Val asked, feeling numb and sick.

"He knew what he wanted, Val. He's going to be cremated, and then they'll send him back to us. He wants to be with your mom."

She thought of something else. "We're close to your home, right? Do you want to go there for a while first?"

He looked at the floor, shaking his head slowly as he thought about her words. "No, Val. I don't want to go back there. And if you want..." His lips turned down unhappily. He had something to say, and he was fighting it. "You don't want me to go back there, either." With a grim glance towards her, he closed the door, leaving her alone.

She heard him in the room next door, opening the wardrobe to pack his things.

Val stumbled into bed, her eyes burning with exhaustion. She pulled the sheets up over her head and slept.

Almost.

She turned over heavily. *Would* Lucas leave her alone? Could she sleep with Jack and not think of Lucas? Had she hurt Lucas' feelings? Okay, that was stupid. He was an emotionless vampire who wanted her. At best, she'd given him a bad case of blue balls.

Her and Jack were going to try to have a relationship. She didn't really believe it. After all the years she'd spent wanting to be with him, now she would.

How the hell could she sleep with Jack and not think about Lucas? No, it would be fine. Jack was the love of her life. Things with Lucas were over. Plus it wasn't like they would get there and instantly have painfully awkward sex. They would canoodle, have noodles, and get used to each other before they got to work on the mind blowing orgasms and true love crap.

Was it even possible to have a relationship with Jack—something she'd wanted for half her life—and have it be anything close to the dream?

CHAPTER 3

Jack stormed out of Valerie's hotel room and went to his own, shutting the door behind him like it was made of fragile hand-blown glass. If he shut it with even the slightest bit of force, he'd lose it.

Valerie and Lucas.

She was *fucking* him. It was obvious. She told Jack she wasn't, but she was. Had to be. Lucas had gripped her ass, pulled her up against him, and all she'd done was wiggle closer.

How *could* she? After what vampires had done to her mother? To Jack's family? Even her father. Everything she had seen and knew should have made that relationship an impossibility. He couldn't trust her. She said she hadn't slept with him and he didn't believe her.

But he knew just who to ask.

An hour later, Jack was looking up at Rachel's apartment window from the street below. She lived on the second floor in a good part of Rome. At least, it was one of her addresses.

All the curtains were open, and he could hear music coming from inside. She walked by the window, and Jack watched as she took a sip of wine, then made a gesture—like a toast—but he couldn't see who she was with.

Was someone up there with her? She'd told him she was alone.

She took another drink, and then shook her head, giving another toast. Her back was stiff, posture straight. Then she raised her arm and throw the glass, heard it shatter as she laughed harshly.

He sighed. Vampire chicks were even more fucked up than human ones.

Jack trudged up the stairs, checking his weapons as he went. Just in case she wasn't alone. *And what if she is alone? Do you need that gun then? You won't shoot her, will you?* He knocked loudly, pounding his fist against the door, so she could hear him over the music.

Rachel opened the door instantaneously and stumbled a little, like she'd moved too fast with her super-vamp-speed. Her lips were red, and she wore a white camisole that had a few drops of wine spilled down the front. Must have been a hard night. Her pupils were wide and dilated, her cheeks flushed as she breathed rapidly.

Drunk.

She took a breath and frowned. "You smell like the little hunter girl. That's odd. I'd have thought she'd be...*otherwise engaged.*" She made a motion for him to enter and wandered away, giving him her back.

"Do you know her name?" Jack asked.

Rachel gave him a coy look. "You want me to say it? Should I get a wig, too? Little Valerie Dearborn. Oh yes, I know her name. I've talked to her. We go way back."

"Has she been fucking him?" he asked, unable to wait or use any subtlety.

Rachel laughed.

"Yes or no," he growled.

She took a sip of wine. "If she came running back to you after the shit that went down tonight, then my guess is no. But honestly, I'm not surprised Lucas screwed it up."

Jack was still standing, watching her as she sat on the couch, rolling the glass of wine between her palms. He crossed his arms, unwilling to sit down or move in any direction. He just needed answers. "He's doing *something* with her."

She shot him a glance under her lashes. "Well, yeah. Have you seen him? Geez." There was a pause while she refilled her glass. "So Val came back to you? Lucas is gonna go nuts." She raised her eyebrows at him. "You better lock that down."

"Excuse me?"

"You heard me. He's a hot, hot man. With lots of experience. A bit cold, it's true. Probably not up on all the TV shows, but once they hit the sheets, you don't have a chance. If she's come back to you, you better lock that down, sew it up—do something vaguely domestic with her."

"Why hasn't he slept with her?"

Rachel made a snorting noise, then said "You men. How do you know *she* hasn't slept with *him*? Maybe she's the one stalling."

Jack scrubbed his hand across his face wearily. "I wish that were true. But that's not how it appeared. He...*fuck*...I don't think she's the one saying no. Let's just leave it at that."

She leaned forward a little and said in a conspiratorial voice, "Well, they don't actually let me into the bedroom with them, so I couldn't say. And I'm not exactly his favorite person at the moment. I don't know why he hasn't shagged her. But count your blessings and move fast."

He could feel his jaw lock in place. "What makes you think I'm going to get involved with Valerie?"

"Oh, please. The two of you? It's like that show, the one where the two of them are supposed to get together, but never do."

Despite himself he asked, "Which one?"

She scowled. "I don't know. They're *all* like that. Doesn't matter. Point is, Lucas apparently let her slip away, and she's come back to you, right?"

He nodded, forced the words past his lips. "Yeah. She's come back to me." He watched as she stood and went to the kitchen, opening cabinets, shirt pulling taut over her breasts as she stretched. She pulled down a wine glass and came back, filling it, then handed it to him and sat across from him, a coffee table between them.

"She chose you. Congrats. Let me know how that works out for you," she said tonelessly. Rachel gulped the wine.

Jack muttered, "It's going to be a fucking disaster."

"I feel like there are undercurrents to this conversation, but it's only you and me, so how about you fill me in on what I'm missing."

"I've done it. I locked her down. We're going...away. I guess."

"And where do young people go these days to be unapologetically in love? Fort Lauderdale? Tijuana?"

"Hawaii," Jack said in a dead voice.

Rachel coughed, wiped the back of her hand across her mouth and leaned closer to him. "Oh shit. You're serious. You and the little hunter girl are going to Hawaii? You have more game than I thought you did. Guess I know who to come to when I get back out into the dating world."

Jack was staring at the ground, her comments getting no reaction.

"Seriously. How is that possible?" Rachel asked.

Jack looked up, had to swallow before he could speak. "I'm honestly not sure how it happened." He took a sip of the wine. It was smooth, finishing with hints of chocolate. The whole thing seemed a bit surreal. He'd come here for a purpose and it sure as hell wasn't to tell Rachel about his love life. *Christ. What is my reason for being here?"* Do you think he'll come after her? Or me?"

Rachel looked around the room, head tilted to the side like she was thinking carefully. "No. My guess is that he will leave her alone for a while. And you? Well, shit, if you died, she'd think Lucas did it, right? You're probably safer than you ever have been." She smiled, and it chilled him.

"But if he loves her, he won't let her go."

Rachel slammed her glass down on the table and leaned forward. "Hold up! I never said love. He's not *capable* of love," she hissed the words. "He's a vampire. A really...*old*...vampire." She enunciated the words harshly. "He wants her, but he's not going to...*pine* over her, write poems about her or anything. Who knows, he might even forget all about her."

Jack briefly wondered what had gotten her so upset, but he didn't care enough to ask. "Why her?"

"She's pretty. Spunky." Rachel hedged, leaning back and wrapping her arms around her flat stomach.

"Why her?" he asked again.

"No idea. And that's the truth. He's been very hush-hush about it." She smiled at him like they were high -choolers gossiping. It made him want to shoot her. "But do you know that no one has been allowed in Northern California without his permission for years now? Isn't that where you both grew up?"

"You think it's because of her?" He felt his trigger-finger twitch.

She shrugged, swinging a leg back and forth lazily.

That was a shock. All this time? Had Lucas been interested in Val for *years*? He put the thought aside, something to torture himself with late at night and every waking hour.

"I hear Marion is in a box."

"You hear correctly." She made another toasting gesture with her wine glass.

"But she's not dead." His gaze roamed the room, then back to her, like she might strike out at him if he looked away for too long.

The place was modern. All chrome and glass. Very impersonal. Except for a stuffed animal—panda to be exact— that was sitting on the couch. And there was a fire in the fireplace. She'd been burning things.

Jack stood, walked closer, seeing half-singed papers and photos that hadn't made it all the way into the fireplace. Like she'd thrown them carelessly.

A picture of Rachel in a tux, the photo black and white, at least fifty years old was on top. She held a cane and had a top hat perched on one side of her head. It was pretty in a peculiar sort of way. Another picture was mostly charred, but he could see Marion's face, only half-destroyed. He had a visceral reaction to it. Felt sick, cold...*afraid*. As though time had slipped away from him, putting him right back to the day his parents were murdered.

"Good times, huh?" She came over to him and held out a glass of wine for him.

He took it absently and continued to look down at the burned images. "What were the papers?" he asked roughly.

"Love notes, dirty limericks, tax bills. All the normal shit one accumulates over time."

He shook his head a little. "This looks final. But she's not dead." He looked at her hard, hoping his anger and hatred were banked tightly enough that she wouldn't see it.

"She's dead-ish. There was just about nothing left when he put her in that coffin. It's like she's in a coma. And she'll die soon enough. Lucas won't let her out of there."

Jack felt oppressed, as if he was sinking in quicksand. He had to ask, didn't think about why. "What were you to her?"

A big moment of silence. Rachel looked at him from under her lashes, almost coy. "Are you armed? I don't want you to shoot me for an unpleasant answer."

"I've had a lot of bad answers tonight. I'm pretty numb to it," he said, facing her head on, absorbing every square inch of her harsh beauty.

"Yeah. So, what was I to Marion? I was her girlfriend and her keeper. Anyway, I've been alive since 1905, and Marion has been my responsibility since 1927, when Lucas gave her to me. And just so you know—the summer of whenever it was? 80-something? Italy? I wasn't there."

It was like she'd punched him in the gut. She referred to the summer Marion killed his parents casually, as if they'd almost gone to the same concert or vacation destination—something trivial rather than the defining moment of his life.

Jack wanted to kill her. But he wouldn't. He was cool. Contained. *Numb.* He'd stay that way. Everything was a lie with a hint of the truth. Rachel, Valerie, Lucas—all of them had him as their mark it seemed. As though this were some elaborate shell game. If he could just keep his eyes on the prize, watch their deceiving hands move fast enough, he might guess right.

"That's.... You were with her almost a hundred years." The numbers were boggling. A hundred years with Marion. What sort of woman did that make her? He just didn't know. Jack couldn't figure Rachel out. Heaven help him, since the night they'd first met—when she came to him offering to get him a crack at Lucas if he crashed a vampire ball—he'd tried.

"Yeah, sometimes it felt like longer, but most of the time it was pretty good."

"Why did Lucas give you to her?"

Rachel moved close to him, in his face. The perfection of her features was even worse up close. She wasn't just pretty, she was traffic-stopping beautiful. Her voice was sharp. "You misheard. Lucas gave her to *me*. If I hadn't wanted her, he would have killed her. I'll save you a question or two. I'm a witch. Very rare. Very valuable. Marion was like an offering from Lucas to me."

"Why would you try to kill him, then? If he's been so good to you?"

"It wasn't really my plan." She shrugged.

"But he left you alive."

She ran a hand through her short, straight hair. "I'm a witch. He needs me."

"Why? For what?"

He moved away from the fireplace, standing several feet away from her.

"Do sit. Hostess with the most-ess."

He shook his head and stayed where he was.

"He's got a plan. Have you heard of the Fey? Werewolves? They're real, but extinct. They've been gone for centuries. He wants to see if they're still around. It's so stupid."

"Why is it stupid?"

"He fucking killed them all! You don't apologize for that— it's cheeky," she said, which seemed to him like a bit of an understatement. He supposed that was why she said it.

"So why is he doing it?"

"No idea. He's got something going on. I don't believe it's altruism on his part, but I'll be damned if I know what it is." She gave him a mock salute and a wink. "My job is not to question, but to try to protect our asses if we find them. Now if you'll excuse me, I have some things to burn."

She put the wine down and stood, swaying towards him, walking like a femme fatale. Her gaze dipped to his lips, and she was close to him, her voice a purr. "Unless there was something you wanted? Something I can help you with?"

The bitch.

Jack closed the door behind him and Rachel watched it for an unreasonably long time. Why? In case he came back? Because she couldn't believe he'd been there? Rachel was surprised. Shocked actually. After things with Marion hadn't panned out she'd expected Jack to sever his connection with her. Or even that Jack might try to kill her. But apparently not. Things were bad if he was coming to her for information.

She needed to tell Lucas what had happened. He would want to know and she was already on his shit list. Rachel picked up the phone and called his cellphone. It rang three times before he answered.

"Rachel," Lucas said in that deep bored voice of his.

"Jack came to see me." Several moments went by while she waited for him to say something. Rachel got a dustpan and broom out of the closet so she could sweep the ash back into the fireplace.

"Why?" he finally asked.

"He wanted to know what your relationship was with Val."

"What time did he arrive?"

Rachel checked her watch, thought about it. "I don't know, twenty minutes ago, maybe half an hour."

"That would not give him a lot of time to grace her bed."

Rachel shook her head and went to stand near the window peeking out. "He didn't sleep with her. But he's going to make a move of some sort, I think. She looked like a sure thing tonight. Maybe a bit stressed out with the almost dying and all but.... how'd you mess up?"

There was another pause but this one wasn't overly long. "I miscalculated. I wanted her to make the choice. I didn't think she could walk away."

So clueless.

"If you thought to 'calculate' a woman into bed, then yeah, that is a problem. You clearly want her, why didn't you just *take* her?"

"Since you have spent the entirety of your young immortal life with the most impulsive woman who ever lived, I will ignore your incomprehension."

She almost laughed. *Poor Lucas. So hot and so out of it.*

"Rachel," his tone was silky and she became a little worried, had the urge to look behind her like she might see the threat coming. "Why would Jack come to you within moments of leaving Valerie? What sort of connection do you have with him?"

Rachel swallowed. *Careful.* "Well, he hates my ex and he hates you. He thinks Valerie has been lying to him and apparently my honesty is refreshing. When Marion hatched her scheme she thought to bring the hunters into it. Thought it would be amusing to get Jack to support her."

"Is he aware of your connection with Marion?"

"Yes. But he thinks I'm happy to be free of her."

"Because we both know that you are not. Is that correct, Rachel? I hold your loyalty because I have Marion tucked away and available to kill or resurrect at my whim?"

Rachel looked at her nails, rubbing her fingers over the smooth finish. "You know you do," she said, voice near a tremble.

"Can you seduce him?"

She sucked in a deep breath. "He'd probably kill me first."

"I do not want her with him. That relationship must end. If Jack is intrigued by you then that is something I wish for you to further."

She pursed her lips, "He's more interested in getting a stake into me than his dick. But I'll try."

The line went dead.

CHAPTER 4

The plane touched down on the tarmac and Valerie opened her eyes, exhaling quietly as they landed safely. People started chattering and Valerie turned her gaze to Jack, who was watching her with a small smile that made her knees weak.

"What?"

"I didn't know you were scared to fly. Is there anything you're not afraid of?"

"Hey!" She punched him lightly in the arm. "You're just trying to get me so irritated that I'll break first, but it's not going to happen."

And they'd decided they wouldn't talk about vampires for the first four days of the trip. There had been some flirty talk of potential punishments for the first violation.

Val knew she wouldn't lose. She also had Jack's punishment all planned out. When Jack lost, he'd be singing his little heart out. It was one of the best memories she had, Jack singing 'Take On Me' the summer before college.

People said one couldn't go home again, but she was going to give it a try.

She'd already imagined it. He'd sing, she'd think it was hot, but then—and this was the good part— she actually would get to go to bed with him.

The idea of it was so exciting that she wanted to shriek in delight. But that wasn't playing it cool, and Val could do cool. All jumping and squealing would be safely contained behind closed doors.

"Jackie my boy, you won't even make it to the end of the day. Watch, I bet we'll be sitting at dinner, the waiter will be a little pale, and the next thing I know I'll have to bail you out of jail for attempted murder."

"Har har," he said sarcastically. "Although this is Hawaii. A pale waiter is suspicious. Everyone gets a tan here, right?"

She shrugged noncommittally, watching out the window as the plane taxied down the runway towards the gate. It came to a halt, and people started shifting and rummaging around, refusing to be caged for a moment longer— common courtesy be damned.

Air travel was a dog eat dog world.

Val took down her huge tote and the man behind her almost lost an eye in the transfer. She also had a huge hat that she hadn't wanted to risk packing. It was straw and had a pretty pink   ribbon   around   the   brim.

They descended the shaky stairway onto the tarmac and Val felt the warm ocean breeze dancing across her body. Taking a deep breath, she turned to Jack, a wide smile on her face.

"You shouldn't look that happy, we haven't even been to bed yet."

She looked away, laughing nervously while he watched her, a provoking smile tugging at his lips.

"Don't you think the air smells better here?" she asked, desperate for a distraction. Jack making a comment about getting her into bed? She felt like she should giggle inanely or something.

Jack took in a deep breath, theatrically, standing up tall and puffing out his chest so that he towered over her. His broad shoulders were defined under his blue T-shirt and she watched him happily, enjoying everything about him and this moment: the breeze that ruffled his thick, dark hair, his tanned and muscular arms, even his dark wash jeans and Adidas.

"I only smell gasoline. You think it smells better, more fumey, than the gas station at home. But it doesn't. It just costs more. A simple marketing trick."

"Okay, there is a slight tang of airplane but you can smell the ocean too. Never mind. This isn't a winning argument. Wait until we get to the hotel. It will definitely smell good there."

He raised his eyebrows at her and her heart flip flopped like he'd said something audacious. *Ah, lust.*

They'd paid extra for a convertible, deciding to do it in style, but when the car turned up she checked the paperwork again. "The color is listed as Champagne," she said, looking down at the paper like the words might change.

"*Pink.* This car is pink. How cool am I going to be toodling around this island in a pink convertible? Also, it's a Sebring. They didn't have a Mustang?" Jack complained.

"Cool guys don't toodle anywhere. Let me drive and problem solved."

He dumped the bags in the trunk and waved a finger at her chidingly as he went to open the passenger door for her. "No. Hop in. My manliness will overcome it."

Val laughed, holding on to her hat as they went to the hotel. Neither the hat nor the convertible were as great as she'd hoped. Her hair was super knotted and the hat kept wanting to fly away. But the island was beautiful. Everything was warm and humid, the ocean was a vibrant blue and there wasn't a cloud in the sky.

They were on Oahu and going to stay at the Turtle Bay on the North Shore of the island. It was secluded, and every room had an ocean view and balcony.

A pineapple was in their room, cut up and waiting for them, little toothpicks to eat it with as well as a bottle of champagne.

"This is so romantic! Jack, did you do this?" This counted as hidden depths.

"I read it in a book called, '5 Easy Steps to an Easy Lay. ' How is it going so far?" he asked, popping a piece of pineapple into his mouth.

"Ask me after the champagne. That's probably step number three. Step one, find girl, Step two, ply her with alcohol, Step three—wait, why is it five steps?"

"Val. I'm kidding. I don't think there is such a book. And no offense, but when you said we could get a king size bed, I thought you were a sure thing."

"Your odds would have improved drastically, if you'd let me drive. And with a comment like that, maybe you should have spent the $7. 99. But it's only noon. You have time to redeem yourself." She stood next to him on the balcony, sipping her champagne, the bubbles making her tongue tingle before it fizzed down her throat.

She took a deep breath and shot him a sideways glance. Val did her Italian impression. "See, the air, it's better here, no?"

Resting his hands on the metal balcony, he widened his stance a little, closed his eyes and took another theatrically large breath like he'd done at the airport.

She watched him breathing deeply, and the moment before he exhaled, when his lungs were filled, she poked him hard in the stomach, forcing him to exhale sharply and making him cough a little.

Totally worth it.

"You're going to regret that." He reached for her and she tried to squirm away, back into the room, but he caught her easily, pulling her to him so that her chest was flush against his. Jack's hard arms trapped her against him. She tilted her head up to him, breath painfully short as she waited for him to kiss her.

They hadn't touched since Italy. They'd packed, made plans for her father's ashes, then flown home to San Loaran, a charged silence between them as they waited for the trip to start.

It was an unspoken agreement that they were waiting until they got here. This was not real life. And if it didn't work out, maybe it would be easier to separate out the memories, compartmentalize everything if it happened somewhere totally removed from their usual life.

At least that was the rationale she was sticking with. She also felt desperately confused about Lucas. Was he heart-broken? Was she making a huge mistake by being here with Jack?

No! There was no way that being with Jack was a mistake. She had loved him for as long as she could remember. This was *it*. If they didn't try to have a relationship now, they never would. And she couldn't let that opportunity go by just because she was still thinking of Lucas. She was meant to be with Jack. Lucas was a monster incapable of love.

Jack loved her.

So yeah, she was going to fucking do this, and she was going to love it! She smiled at Jack, refusing to think about Lucas anymore.

He smiled a little cockily. "Do you want to go swimming first?" His hands were on her back, then slid downwards slowly so they were on her waist, pulling her closer to him.

She shook her head slightly, incapable of speaking.

This is really going to happen.

She felt a little dizzy. The roller coaster feeling again. She was at the top, the tracks had stopped clicking, everything quiet for a moment, and then in a blink one is hurtling towards the ground—at 100 miles per hour.

His head moved a fraction closer to hers, torturing her with the wait, while he fixed his eyes on her lips. "What about food? Did you want to go to the restaurant?" he asked teasingly as he bent down, kissing her neck.

"Oh, shut up," she said a little breathlessly, "sure thing, remember?" and she launched herself forward so that her lips met his— maybe a little too hard, but she didn't care.

And then he deepened the kiss, like *this* kiss was going to make up for years of sexual frustration. His tongue mated with hers and she was instantly damp, his tongue mimicking what his cock would be doing to her soon.

Now, if Valerie had anything to say about it.

With a hungry murmur she gripped his arms, leaning backwards to pull him into the room and down onto the bed. Jack's weight settled on top of her— solid and delicious. But not as heavy as Lucas would be.

Don't think about him here. Because this is it. If we can't make it work in paradise, it isn't going to work anywhere.

She kissed him like a sorority pledge girl trying to impress a frat boy.

Her hands went to his face, feeling the slight stubble on his cheeks and chin, then turning his head slightly so that she could kiss him deeper, be in him just as much as he was going to be in her.

"Don't think I'm a slut, but help me take off your pants," she panted.

He laughed deeply, the sound vibrating from his chest to hers, making her nipples pebble. Her hand wiggled between them, her knuckles sliding down his soft t-shirt, enjoying the flat muscles of his muscular stomach, until she found the top button of his jeans.

His fingers met hers there, tangling with hers as he shadowed her movements, unbuttoning the button, pulling down the zipper....

She felt the hard ridge of his erection against her fingers as his hand stayed over hers.

He closed his eyes in pleasure, murmured her name and kissed her raggedly. He pulled away with a slight gasp and stood, dropping the jeans beside him and whipping the shirt off over his head in a terse move.

And there he was— naked. Hard. Looking at her with desire. The culmination of years of desire distilled down to this moment right here. She'd finally have him.

He reached for her waistband and stopped, leaning over her instead, lifting her shirt a little so he could kiss her stomach, breathing deeply as he unsnapped her shorts and pulled them down her hips until they fell to the ground behind him.

He pulled her up and his hands skated her waist, his fingers trailing up her ribs, raising goose bumps on her body as he took her top off.

Jack left her bra and panties on then knelt before her on the bed, dragging her closer to him, his large hand cupping her bottom as he settled her firmly against his erection.

She arched into him, throwing her head back in pleasure at the sensation. He kissed her neck hungrily— slow kisses, wet kisses with tongue and little nibbles, his hands grazing her bra, raking her nipples lightly through the fabric, and then palming her whole breast with his hand and squeezing gently.

She didn't want to wait anymore. This needed to happen now and she didn't want to risk an interruption or having something that could keep him from taking her as he should have done years ago. She whipped off her bra, took off her underpants and laid back, waiting for him.

"I need to get a condom. Wait a minute."

Her voice was shaky, unable to think clearly, her body aching for him. "I'm on the pill, it's okay." He paused for the briefest moment, but then stood and went to the table, opening his wallet and pulling out a condom.

His gaze met hers as he walked back to the bed.

"I've only slept with one guy Jack, and he was a virgin, too."

"Yeah, but I haven't been as circumspect as you. I'm clean Valerie, but...."

"You've slept with enough people that you're worried." It was like talking through sandpaper. *I don't want to talk about this.*

His lips firmed into a hard line and she could see him closing down in front of her. He was inches away from her, was going to do something totally intimate with her and yet she could feel the distance between them growing. How could anyone get through that control?

Was he even more emotionless than Lucas? Lucas was a vampire, his emotion tank was genuinely on empty. Jack had emotions, he just ignored them.

"Do you want to have this conversation now? I will always wear a condom Valerie, unless I'm married or it's a committed relationship, that's it."

And this isn't a committed relationship, she thought painfully, the sadness of it lurching through her.

His hands came up to her, holding her head lightly, forcing her to look to him, "If it's going to be anyone, it's going to be you, Val. But I've always done it with a condom and I don't really want to find out just how great sex is without it and then have to go back."

He rubbed her cheek with his thumb, dark eyes burning into hers as he willed her to understand. "I have always loved you. But that doesn't mean we are going to be together. We're here because we have problems. Maybe...shit, let's just go to the beach for a while, take a walk and not force it."

No! Desperately, she grabbed him, pushing him backwards again, fusing her lips to his, not wanting to stop when they were so close. *Good God, we're both naked! We can't stop now!*

Sex would change things between them, and it almost had to be for the better. It would be one less barrier between them. She wanted him and loved him. She knew he loved her too. And what was the problem, anyway? This was probably the first time a guy had to convince the girl to use a condom. It was stupid to take it personally. Her heart beat jaggedly.

His lips were hard beneath hers and then he sighed, his body relaxing, lips suddenly soft and welcoming. His tongue touched hers lightly as his hands roamed her back.

Faster.

Restlessly, he rolled her over, his body covering hers as he slid down to kiss her breasts, sucking her nipple into his mouth and flicking his tongue against her, making her breath catch in pleasure as she writhed beneath him.

Now. Don't wait. Now. She must have said it aloud because he spoke.

"Wait. Are you ready? Let me make you come first," he said, pulling back from her.

"No. I don't want to wait. I just want you inside me. Please."

Then he was over her, and she reached down to grasp his hard length, guiding it between her thighs as he thrust against her lightly.

She shifted her hips, accommodating his wide girth as he began to ease into her, stretching her pleasurably wide. His lips met hers again, kissing her slowly, absorbing her reactions. He paused, and she moaned, her legs wrapping around his hips to urge him onwards.

"Patience. Let's just take it slow."

Slow is for losers. Ignoring him utterly, she clasped him closer, jerking her hips up to his relentlessly. His eyes opened and he looked down at her, an expression of pleasure and irritation on his face. "I suppose I should just tell you to keep going, harder and faster, then you'll do the complete opposite. Slow down or else there will be quite the-" he sighed in pleasure and kissed her again before saying, "predicament."

She murmured in his ear, "The key part of that word is dic—*Oh!*"

He grasped her hip, stopping her words as he sheathed himself in her deeply, until they were totally flush, his body fused to hers, as he kissed her, held her, came in her and wiped all thought of anything else from her mind.

CHAPTER 5

Valerie took a sip of her cold chocolate and swallowed, waiting for the feeling of bliss that came with drinking her favorite drink from Café Rouge, a chain restaurant in London that she liked. And the same place Lucas had found her all those months ago.

She was still waiting. Nothing. *Nothing?* She took a larger sip and noted how tasteless the drink was.

"Food never tastes as good in a dream."

Val looked up to see Lucas standing next to the chair on the opposite side of the table. He motioned inquiringly and she nodded. Watched hungrily as he folded himself into the chair. He was so large and heavily built she was surprised it didn't squeak—or break. His blue eyes skated down her body, like he was absorbing every detail of her so he could remember her later. She knew it, because she was doing the exact same thing.

"Is this my dream?" she asked. And if so, shouldn't he be naked instead of wearing a light blue dress shirt and slacks?

"Yes."

"I dream about chocolate milk at Café Rouge? Typical." She took another sip. "Will you remember our conversation?"

"Yes."

"And I will too?"

He nodded.

"All right. Are you still waiting for me to go with you to Roanoke?"

"Indeed. My reception will be received with more sincerity if it is delivered by you."

"Why is that *exactly*?"

"You are an Empath. The Fey can read you just as you can read them. They will be able to assess my sincerity."

"Through me? I don't know if I think you're sincere! You just tell me things and manipulate me," Val said. I can be exasperated in a dream too. *Excellent.*

He sighed and put two fingers against the bridge of his nose. "Minions are wonderful because they follow orders. You don't do that and while it is generally charming... it can be quite exasperating. You should take my word for it. Believe in what I tell you. I am a king."

"Honey, you ain't my king," she said sassily and felt like she should snap her fingers or something. "And I'm not convinced you have my best interests at heart. Let's not forget that you almost let me die back at the Challenge."

"No. Let's do forget about that," he said, voice warm with anger, "For that is not what occurred. You would not have died. I knew that I would win, but if I adjusted the odds and invited more competitors to Challenge me it would have upset the odds. The safety Marion offered you was false." He leaned towards her, arms folded in front of him, the seams of his shirt pulling at the shoulders. *Is sexually assaulting someone in a dream still a crime? So many gray areas....*

Val was determined to act rationally, all thoughts of hotness wiped away by the memory of almost dying. "If you lost I would have *died*. You could have avoided that and didn't. Maybe Marion wouldn't have kept her word, I don't know. You tell me vampires are big on rules and honor so maybe she would have. If you had died I would have too. How can I trust you?"

She nervously twisted her hair into a knot. His eyes tracked her movements and she let go of her hair.

"And you trust Jack. I assume we are here because there is a hitch in your romantic tryst?"

"Are you trying to say there is a bump in the road? Things are great...." she paused, biting back the end of her sentence, *we've been fucking like rabbits thanks for asking*. That would be really bitchy. And it wasn't true.

"What does going to the Fey entail?"

He studied her carefully as though to read her change in emotion. His hand lifted off the table, running one finger down her arm to the top of her hand. His jaw was taut, lips compressed.

She turned her hand over and his fingers closed over hers. He lifted her hand to his mouth, kissing the back of it gently.

Chastely.

His lips were dry and warm, his hands cool and hard. She felt her heart give a gigantic leap as though it suddenly had to work a lot harder to circulate all the crazy lust-filled endorphins that he evoked when he touched her. Or looked at her. Or walked into a room. *Dammit.*

He shook his head, "Seeing you again, knowing you are with someone else.... It is not what I expected. But sometimes, when I am idle and thinking I see you before me, an image that is so far away and so unattainable...." The sentence trailed off.

Then he sighed, flashed her a small, almost shy, smile and said, "If I told you that you make me feel...as though I have been waiting fifteen hundred years to just sit here with you would you believe me? Could you take it at face value that at this moment I feel that sincerely?"

She didn't know. She squeezed his fingers and let him go.

"I want to be safe and happy. I want to be a teacher and have kids. And...I don't think I'm going to have that. But I *know* I won't have that with you. Ever. You can't love me. You've already said so. And anything you could feel for me, by drinking my blood, you won't do that either."

She couldn't look at him. What if he looked sad and repentant. She wouldn't be able to resist him if he was genuinely upset. Then she remembered the last time she had seen him. How he'd flaunted himself in front of her, wanting her to make a move. Was this more manipulation?" I'm with Jack. Already. So, thanks. But I have to go. I'm sorry."

Don't look at him. She squeezed her eyes tight, the only way to not give in. *What if he's sad? What if he is sincere?* She opened her eyes because she had to know. Looked first at his hand on the table, then her gaze moved upwards, over his chest, past the buttons of his shirt, to his neck, his chin—she jerked awake.

CHAPTER 6

Consciousness is a bitch. I slept with Jack. And dreamed of Lucas the moment I fell asleep.

Nice.

Classy.

Oh. God.

If there is a hell, I'm totally gonna burn. Although Lucas would probably be there too. So, that's a bonus.

She heard the hotel room door open, then the clanking of a room service cart as it was wheeled inside the room. Val snuggled under the covers a little more. She could hear the lids being lifted, caught a whiff of bacon and coffee.

Things are good. I'm not a slut.

"If you bring me coffee I'll be your best friend," she mumbled.

"Well then bestie— you're in luck."

"Great." Val sat up, watching Jack come towards her with a cup of coffee. *This makes the top ten list of surreal things that have happened in my life.* Jack was already in his swim shorts, wearing a dark t-shirt and flip-flops, and felt like she needed to blink again. "I sort of imagined you wearing jeans and shit-kickers on the beach."

He was back at the cart, a piece of bacon halfway to his mouth before turning to look at her, "What does that say about me?" he asked with a smile.

"Maybe that you've got a stick so far up your ass you don't know how to have a good time?" she said sweetly then took a sip. The coffee was strong and bitter.

Just like I like my men.

Jack put the piece of bacon down and walked towards her, smiling mischievously. "You better be careful with those stick comments."

Valerie squealed as he prowled up the bed towards her, "No way! No how! It's never going to happen, no sticks will ever be up my—"

His mouth descended, kissing her, cutting off her laugh. She set down the coffee cup blindly, sure she was putting it in the right place, but she didn't. The cup fell to the ground with a smashing sound and Jack jerked away from her, both of them peering over the edge of the bed to see the shards of broken porcelain.

"I should clean that up," she said, flushing in embarrassment. *Total accident. Nothing to do with dreaming of Lucas.*

He got off the bed and went to get a towel while Val picked up the pieces and tossed them in the trash.

She took a towel from Jack's outstretched hand. A few moments passed in silence as she carefully blotted up the liquid. *Just an accident. I really wanted to keep kissing Jack and go back to bed for more sex. Really.*

"Are you going for a swim?" she asked steadily.

There was a slight delay before he responded. "Yeah. I was thinking about it."

She nodded absently. "I need an hour or so anyway. I want to check on things for the funeral, see if anyone has emailed about coming over for it from abroad."

She heard him behind her, moving things around on the dresser. Probably looking for the room key.

"I don't know how many of the Hunters will come," he said.

"Why do you think that is?" she asked. It seemed odd to her. Someone you fight the good fight with dies, and yet they couldn't be bothered to pay their respects?

Jack sounded distracted. "What? Why don't they go to a lot of funerals? Expense? Too busy killing monsters? Maybe they don't want to think about it?"

"Those are reasons, I suppose," Val said slowly. There was nothing left to blot. Val stood and tossed the towel into the bathroom before coming back, staring at the palm frond pattern on the carpet.

Jack sat down on the bed and sighed. "You have something you want to say?"

She blinked. "No." *Yes, but no, because if I say something, the good times won't roll.*

"Fine, I can start. You shouldn't have a funeral, Valerie. You know that." He sounded exhausted. They'd slept for nine hours. *What, he's emotionally exhausted by 9 am?*

"Excuse me? I'm supposed to bury him without a goodbye?"

He fell back on the bed, hands over his eyes like he was trying to ignore her. "No. You said your goodbye at the hospital. He wouldn't have wanted a funeral. He wouldn't have wanted other people's lives to be interrupted to come see his grave. He loved you. You don't need to do this. It doesn't prove anything." The last bit was mumbled, his hands sliding down his face as he spoke.

"Don't say that," Val said quietly.

"Which part? That he loved you?"

Val didn't respond, felt the cream from the coffee curdling in her stomach. They should just go to the beach. Where was the pretend happiness she'd signed up for? *It's pretend, is it?* She wondered if the conversation was over.

"Everything he did was about keeping you safe."

Nope, this conversation is still happening. "No, it was about avenging my mother. It had nothing to do with me."

Jack blew out a breath loudly. "Look, he didn't have the greatest paternal instincts."

She couldn't help but laugh at the understatement. "Ya think? Jack we met when I shot Marion in the back as she tried to steal you away. I was nine. That is fucked up. Who needs a Barbie when you can have a Colt, right? He threw me to the vampires at sixteen. 'Good luck. Hope you survive! Jack would!'" she said, mimicking her father.

He laughed unhappily. "Don't bring me into this."

"We can't have this conversation without bringing you into it."

"Maybe we shouldn't have it at all."

No, we shouldn't, Val thought as she stepped away from him. She went out to the balcony and looked at the ocean. There was a cute little girl in a sunhat, her mom sitting next to her, reading a book as the little girl dug with her shovel. Envy snaked through her, strangling her tight.

That was normal life. Maybe the father was snorkeling or playing golf. Or on a walk with his son or daughter. At the end of the day they'd put the kids to bed, sit out on the balcony and have a glass of wine. Just another day in paradise.

Val was sure that envying thirty-year olds who spent all their time tending to little people's runny noses and filthy bottoms was a bit pathetic. *Fabulous. Jack* won't *give me that and Lucas* can't *give me that. How much is eHarmony?*

She turned to go back into the room but Jack was standing behind her.

"Oh," Val gasped in surprise.

"Alright, let's do it. We have the argument once and then it's over," he said, sounding resigned.

"Why the change of heart?" She squinted at him suspiciously.

"Because this is a problem. You're mad at me and I..." What would he say? *I don't want you to be mad at me? I want to work past it?* Either of those things and she would let it go, but she knew that wasn't it. There was a long list of moments where Jack could have done things for her, or for them, and he hadn't.

She waited, hoping that sex had somehow changed things.

"I'm pissed at you, too. So let's have it out. This relationship goes nowhere with this hanging over us."

Oh. No apologies, he was mad too. *Big let down*. Val chewed her lip. She hadn't expected that. No, she had, she just hadn't wanted it to be true. And that pissed her off even more.

"Okay, then I'll just sum it up for you so I can get down to the bar and get my Pina Colada," she said. "I loved that man, I really did. I wish I hadn't been a disappointment, that I had been tough enough to be who he wanted me to be. But I wasn't and it pisses me off that he didn't realize that. He didn't adjust his expectations based upon the person that I was, I just became a failure. I'm smart and capable, there are good things to me, but to him I was a failure. He's dead and I feel—"

"No. Stop. It's not a good idea. Let's just go downstairs and sit by the pool."

"Yeah, cause that's going to be the most romantic day ever! Sitting by the pool, having the rest of this argument in my head all day. Hell, no!"

"You should honor your parents. He tried. He loved you," Jack said, exasperated, turning away from her and stalking back to the dresser where he picked up the room key.

"Stop fucking telling me how he felt! He didn't tell me and that's what we are talking about. What he actually did for me. He's dead, and I feel sad, yes, but I'm also a little bit relieved. And that's why you want me to shut up, because I'm relieved. I won't miss him, I'll miss the idea of him." Her vision was blurry. *Shit!*

"I knew that we would work it out, that somewhere down the line we would talk and have that moment where we realize how misunderstood we've been—blah, blah, blah—but that was bullshit and it didn't fucking happen. It was never going to. And that's why I'm sad, because the hope of fixing things is gone."

She took a deep breath. He was looking at the ground hard as he slapped the key against his thigh.

"But you know what? It's almost a relief too. Knowing that he is at rest, and maybe he's with her. He was a dead man walk—"

Jack exploded, "Then what am I? I'm the same fucking guy, right? So you want me because I'm like your father? The chance to get it right?"

It was a punch in the gut.

"Go to the beach," she hissed, finality in her words. *Do it or else*, was what she didn't have to say. *Do it, or there is no chance this will ever work.*

And so he left.

Val sat down on the bed, feeling panic race through her. This wasn't going to work. This was stupid and would ruin their relationship forever. No. She could make it work. It was only an argument. She'd find him, they'd go on the snorkeling trip and everything would be fine.

This was paradise.

CHAPTER 7

Water dripped onto the floor. Val looked down, surprised to see she was in her swimsuit and wet, like she'd just stepped out of the ocean and into someone's expensive bedroom. *Snorkeling has more fish. And water. Uh oh.*

She knew this room. Lucas' bedroom. And there he was, sitting before the fire in a chair. A book was open and draped over his thigh, his hand hovering above it. Had he just put it down or was he going to pick it up? Except that he was oddly still.

Lucas in freeze frame.

She shivered and couldn't help but look at him. She'd seen him less than a week ago, heck she'd dreamed about him last night, but— and it fucked with her head to even think it— she was hungry for the sight of him. She didn't just look at him, that was too tame, too ordinary. She devoured him with her gaze. A look wouldn't be enough. She'd have to touch him.

He was beautiful, like looking at a favorite piece of artwork. Not something one can own, but something in a faraway museum, where she would have to go half way around the world, push through crowds of people, just to catch a glimpse of his unreal splendor.

And Lucas was still perfect. Still inhuman. Still a monster who could promise her nothing but pleasure and a life in danger. He was dressed in 'old' clothes again. Breeches that looked like suede, hose so white it was like snow in the sunlight. He turned and looked at her, eyes momentarily widening in what she thought was surprise.

Her whole body trembled and she began to cough.

"Valerie?" he said quietly and with a fair amount of disbelief. He was suddenly before her, holding his robe out towards her, then wrapping it around her and leading her towards the bed. She couldn't stop coughing, felt her face turning red, and became embarrassed. He was already out of her league, even without the Tuberculosis cough.

"I think I'm going to be sick," she managed to choke out.

His hands were firm on her arms as he set her down on his bed.

"Wait. What if I yack all over your bed?"

"That is not a concern. But hold and I shall get you a basin."

Basin? She hunched forward, retching hard, throat burning and then he was back, a bowl thrust under her nose. He was just in time. Val threw up, huge amounts of sea water pouring out of her mouth. Lucas leaned over her, one hand on her back, patting her gently, the other holding the bowl in place.

So humiliating.

He took the bowl away, disappearing into the bathroom and bringing her a towel and a cup of water. Her voice was scratchy and she blinked owlishly before saying, "You're a very good nurse. Color me surprised. And embarrassed. Really embarrassed."

He knelt down before her, looking up into her face, and his expression floored her. Was that how she looked when she saw him? Wonder, fear and more, chased across his face, faster than a flash of lightning. He gazed at her like she was a precious antique that had been lost.

She cleared her throat.

His hand reached up, brushing wet strands of hair from her face. His lashes were thick. A dark golden color, but so dense she was surprised they didn't get tangled together. She smiled and worried that it was wobbly. A tremble raced through her.

"What am I doing here?"

His expression changed, shutting down, but an intensity was still there, visible in the press of his lips, the tightening of his grip on hers. "What do you remember?"

Lucas stayed crouched before her, as she willed the answer to come to her. "I was with Jack."

His hand withdrew from hers and he leaned back, shifting away from her like hearing Jack's name had made him flinch. He reached up absently, going to move his hair over his shoulder, but it was gone. He'd chopped it off before the Challenge. His hand dropped down to his knee instead. Maybe he'd had long hair for centuries.

"You should not be here. You need to focus on where you were and go back. Do you understand me? Think about where you were, exactly."

She strained to think about what she'd been doing. It was like she'd woken up from a dream and each moment that passed pushed the dream further away, made it less real. "We were snorkeling." She looked around his room, like it would give her clues. "I think, I think there was a cave. And I dived down to see it, but there were a lot of rocks." She shook her head, not remembering the rest. God, his bathrobe smelled good.

Val looked at the fire. The orange flames stalled, then flickered, finally vanishing altogether, plunging the room in darkness. The only light came from Lucas, as though he was surrounded by a hundred candles. The walls of his bedroom shrank away, consumed by the dark.

"What is that?" she whispered. Blackness, like living shadows were creeping closer towards them, the light surrounding Lucas dimming.

"Valerie! Hear me. You must go back. Close your eyes and remember where you were. Think of Jack. Go to him, now!" he said, anger and desperation in every word.

Val was stunned, wanting to ask him what was going on. Cold water rushed over her feet, the whole floor suddenly awash in black seawater. Huge ropes of seaweed swayed through the rising tide like they were alive and hungry. She could hear the loud rush of water, see the room filling, feel the water's cold sharpness sweep over her legs and rise higher.

She jumped up from the bed and Lucas stood too, mirroring her movements, watching only her, as though oblivious to the huge flood that was consuming his bedroom.

"What will happen to you?" Val asked frantically.

"You cannot stay here or you will perish. This is not reality. Go to Jack. Please. Go!"

She reached out to him— for protection, for comfort, to save him too? But he stepped back, evading her grasp. Water crashed over her head, seaweed coiled up her legs, pulling her down deep into the water.

Val opened her eyes under the water. Everything was dark, only the barest flicker of light surrounded Lucas as he floated in the water, eyes closed. A corpse in suspended animation. The water carried him away from her like invisible pallbearers, his clothes waving gently, fingers and arms loose as he drifted away.

She screamed for him and the water poured inside of her, choked her and squeezed her lungs in a vice. The water wanted inside of her, aching to take her too. Val breathed in deep, felt her lungs explode in a death so heavy it felt like grief.

The grim reaper called her name. He'd taken Lucas from her, and now he called her too. He hit her in the chest, slammed her down and yelled at her over and over again until she did what he wanted, threw up again, then opened her eyes to the blinding light of day.

Jack's voice was loud and above her, his hands on her chest, forcing life inside her as he yelled at her to breathe and called her back to life. Not the grim reaper after all.

Quickly, amid shouts and the rocking of the boat, people stripped her, taking off her wetsuit and snorkeling mask. Strands of her hair were ripped out with the mask, sharp little pains that were totally subsumed by the larger shock and despair that wracked her body.

Someone was chanting, saying something over and over again, but Val didn't know what they said or why. She wished they'd shut up. They were so loud and insistent.

Jack wrapped her in a towel, and the boat shuddered to life as the captain turned the engine on. People sat down, the boat excursion over, now that a stupid tourist had almost drowned. Jack was sitting on the floor of the boat across from her, leaning against a seat, his head in his hands, shoulders hunched in against himself. She'd never seen that look on his face before.

No. She'd seen it once. When he was twelve years old, sitting next to his mother's dead body. He'd looked just like this. Tears ran down his face and she wanted to tell him not to cry, because she was alright and wouldn't die on him.

And that was when she realized she was already talking. She'd been talking since the moment she started breathing again. She was the person who wouldn't shut up. *Lucas, Lucas,* she said over and over again as Jack sat there, a look of fear and horror on his face.

CHAPTER 8

They came back to the room and waited for the hotel doctor to check Val out. He said she was fine. The seawater was out of her system and the best thing to do now was rest. *I can do that,* she thought, already half asleep.

Jack sat beside her, his hand clasping hers as though afraid she'd disappear the moment he let go. When she awoke he was gone. On his side of the bed there was a note. And yeah, it was super weird just thinking that he had a 'side of the bed.'

The note said he was in the bar. *I don't blame him. I want to be in the bar.*

Val sat up, remembering the look on his face when she kept calling out for Lucas. *Shit, we are going to have another fucking conversation.* And she had to tell him about her dream/vision of Lucas drowning right along with her.

Surely that was a dream.

Her mind had tricked her, made her see him. But, it had seemed so real. *So real and so awful.* Seeing him again, even a pretend him...her body had responded. Not just simple attraction, but more than that. She'd felt like a lamp that had been plugged in. Unnatural brightness and connectivity. She'd bet money it had something to do with her being an Empath and drinking his blood.

It was sunset and the sky was a hundred different shades of pink and orange. She'd been asleep for hours. And, even though it was wrong, she wanted to call Lucas. Just to make sure he was okay. *Of course he's okay. You can't call him, it's like an alcoholic taking a shot of Nyquil to prevent a cold.*

She looked out at the ocean, and absently watched the curtains billowing into her room from the breeze. They undulated, rippling into her room and back out again several times—Then they stopped. The sheers caught on a form, the indentation of a person standing on the balcony.

Val leaped out of bed and ran to the balcony, pulling back the sheers and almost running into a pair of crimson lips.

Oh shit. Rachel.

Her skin was like porcelain, her dark brown hair pushed behind her ears. It was short and thick. She looked different than usual. *Softer. More feminine. Less murderous.*

She wore black linen pants and a pink, silk camisole-top that showed her pale arms. Incongruously, she wore flip-flops with a pretty gold bow on them. Her toes were painted the same color red as her lips and she looked like she'd just come from a pedicure.

She looks better dead than I do alive. Bummer.

"Valerie, Lucas sent me to check on you. Don't run, it'll just make me hungry. And Lucas would kill me if something

happened to you. Come have a chat. I brought you a present."
She gave Valerie a pretty smile.

Val went to the bed first, reaching under her pillow for her stake. Lifestyle hazard. They hadn't brought guns to Hawaii, what with not wanting to be arrested and all. Plus they hadn't thought they would need them. Hopefully, that was still true.

Val went outside, making sure the stake was in plain sight. Rachel was sitting in a chair, legs crossed. A manila folder rested on her lap. Rachel looked at her carefully. From head to toe, then back again. It wasn't sexual, or even predatory, but studious.

"What, is he going to quiz you?" Val asked.

Val thought Rachel smiled for a moment, but it was fleeting. "He will want to know *everything*," she said dramatically. "Look at you, a simple human snaring the Big Bad. Well, almost human, hmm?"

"He told you?" Val asked, shocked.

"Oh, yes. Only me, though. It's not something he wants to get out."

"You stabbed me and almost killed me. You almost killed him, too! Why would he tell you anything?" Val said, incredulous.

Rachel looked unimpressed, stuck her leg out and looked at her toes, no doubt examining her recent polish job. "I'm one of Lucas' favorites. Well, probably the *only* favorite. He's really gone off vampires, in the last, what, three, four hundred years? But that's just what I hear. I'm only around a hundred, so just about everything I know is history or rumor."

"Around a hundred?"

"Yeah. I'm 106, but when vampires talk time they usually round to the nearest century."

That was bizarre. "You cannot be his favorite," she said indignantly.

Rachel actually laughed. "Oh ho! Look at you thinking you know so much about him."

Valerie gave her an are-you-fucking-crazy-look. Although, she was Marion's girlfriend, so maybe she was crazy. "He turned your girlfriend into a dried-out mummy and put her in a box before torturing you."

"Yes. And he also made me super-powerful and sent me to check up on his sweetie."

Val ran her hands through her hair. It was brittle and knotted with salt from the ocean. And she suspected it looked like the sort of tangle a small rodent would like to vacation in.

Oh man, she was so weak, and yet, she had to ask, "Why didn't he come himself?"

Rachel laughed— again. The sound so sincere and loud that a few birds dashed away from the palm tree next to her room. *Isn't she just the perkiest person.*

"Seriously? You're on some faux-honeymoon after telling him to go fuck himself and you wanted him to come after you? You can't have your cake and eat it too."

Val slumped down into a chair. "Am I a terrible person?" she asked, not really expecting an answer.

"I'm a vampire. I kill people. In my book you're fucking Mary Poppins with a slightly mischievous boy-craziness thing happening."

Was that supposed to make her feel better? *Well, it doesn't make me feel any worse.*

"Where is my present?" Val asked, changing the subject.

"Ta da!" Rachel picked up the folder and held it towards Valerie. Cautiously, Valerie reached forward and took it.

Rachel settled back in the chair, legs crossed demurely as she looked out at the ocean and waited for Valerie to do or say something. She seemed happy to be here, tilting her face up to the sky and closing her eyes.

"So, how come you won the trip to Hawaii? And why are you not burned to pieces?"

Rachel opened her eyes, her expression wary. "Too late. The sun set ten minutes ago. Oh, I almost forgot. Lucas wants you to practice containing yourself. Now that you have his blood, you are all over the place. In his dreams and memories. Frankly, he looks exhausted. You need to cut the guy a break. You dump him then haunt him. It's just not nice."

She was outraged, "I'm not trying to! What do I do to stay away from him?"

"I put a Post-It Note on that page. Some mental training stuff. Start tonight, see if you can get yourself separated from him sooner rather than later. He's not a guy you want to push, my tasty treat."

Valerie nodded, uncertain what to say or even how to feel about the fact that Lucas wanted her to stay out of his mind.

"Wait. Is he coming into my mind too?"

"Oooh. This is the question I wanted the answer too: did he drink from you? It's relevant so answer," Rachel said, tucking her legs under and leaning forward eagerly.

"No."

Rachel's eyebrows rose sky high and her cheeks hollowed out as she clucked her tongue in shock. "Not even a taste? Wow. That's some serious restraint."

"He said he wanted to but was too old. He compared it to indigestion. Or maybe I did. What does that mean?"

"Oh, look. There's Jack." Rachel said, with an odd note in her voice. Anticipation and something... dark, but Val couldn't have said what. "You know, Marion swore that if she'd known how cute he'd be, she would have kept him. I always thought she said it just to piss me off. Now I'm not so sure."

Jack was a long ways away, coming up a cut rock path from the restaurant down the beach. Men in hotel uniforms were lighting tiki lights, while little kids were being hustled back to their rooms by sunburned parents.

They both watched Jack walk for a moment, his tall, graceful form eating up the distance before him. Rachel shifted her chair, moving it into the shadows so that if he looked up he wouldn't see her.

"So, before I leave here. Anything you want me to pass on?" Rachel asked.

"Well, he's okay, right? I almost drowned and I thought he was there. It was like he died, too." She imagined it again—him dead, floating away from her and she couldn't help him. Couldn't save him. She blinked tears from her eyes.

Rachel worried her lip, a dainty, pearly white fang visible. "Look, Lucas is old. He disappears and kind of retreats. When you saw him last you were in his mind. Not with him physically. He's been gone a lot lately. Physically present, but mentally...hibernating? I don't know. It's kind of taboo. Everyone knows about it but doesn't really want to talk about it. I guess it's a bit worrying or something."

"Does it have a name? Is it a condition or illness?"

Rachel shrugged, "We don't talk about it so how the hell can it have a name? Pay attention."

"People don't like to talk about death but it has a name," Val said sharply.

Rachel huffed and waved her hand around airily. "I guess the people you hang out with don't talk about it, but man death is *all* I talk about. My death, Marion's death, your death, Lucas' death. The Fey, the wolves...dead, dead, dead."

"What about the wolves and the Fey? Roanoke, when is he going?"

Rachel stood and brushed at her pants absently, taking a long moment like she was deciding what she wanted to say. "I think he's going to wait a little longer for you."

Valerie shook her head emphatically, "No, I'm not helping him anymore. He knows that."

"Look, I could really go either way on you, but I'll do you a favor here, so listen up— you don't fuck with vampires. Don't think you are a step ahead of them. You will never outsmart them, nor will you survive them. You're a distraction, a means to an end, an object, maybe even a cherished one, but there is always an agenda. Lucas has big game afoot and he needs you to pull it off. He's going to find a way to make sure you help him. See you soon. Get a tan for me."

And with a snap of her fingers, she was gone.

CHAPTER 9

Jack waited for the elevator, staring fixedly at the orange light on the up button. What the hell was he going to do about Val? She'd almost died. And then she'd called for Lucas like that fucker was oxygen. As though Lucas was her entire world. Would she die for him?

He remembered. Waiting in her hotel room for her to show up, the slow build-up of panic as he wondered where the hell she was. He'd seen Lucas before. Once. When his parents had died. He'd been there, at his parents' hotel before Marion killed everyone.

To see Lucas again, his body wrapped around Valerie protectively and...casually. As though he'd held her before and would do so again. The tension between them had been there. Heavy and hot.

"Penny for your thoughts." The words were sultry, right next to his ear, raising every hair on the back of his neck. He knew that voice. His heart kicked out a staccato rhythm. His hand fisted, like he was gripping a stake.

"Why are you here, Rachel?" A rough growl, a threat of violence leaking out.

The elevator chirped and opened, but he stood there frozen, waiting for her to respond. She sauntered past him, her arm brushing his as she went into the elevator, leaning against the brass rail as if she'd wait all night for him. She was like a cat: she appeared calm but if she'd had a tail it would be swishing.

He met her gaze, warm and knowing. He felt it reach through him, like a hand around his shaft. The day would come and he'd kill her. On his life, he swore he'd kill her the moment he didn't need her anymore.

She was a monster but she would play nicely with him if he wanted her too.

I don't.

Forcefully, he willed his body to relax, and followed her into the elevator. The doors shut behind them and she reached past him, pushing the stop button so the elevator wouldn't rise or open. It was just the two of them now, trapped in the enclosed space. He moved to the opposite side, putting distance between them.

It made her smile, as if she was happy at the thought that he wanted to put space between them. As though he might not trust himself with her. This irritated him, but he didn't let it show. She could think whatever she wanted. He didn't need to stand close enough to be killed for no other reason than pride.

"I've been sent on a humanitarian mission," Rachel said.

He raised an eyebrow.

"You're human... I'm here...a mission. Humanitarian. No? Not funny? Yeah, you're right. It was stupid," she said dismissively.

He felt his jaw lock down tight, and was surprised his teeth didn't break in half. She was always so casual with him. As if she didn't think he could kill her. *As if she doesn't care.*

"I'm here to give Val some info. Lucas sent me to make sure she was alright."

Jack felt himself stand a little straighter, come to attention. "Why wouldn't she be?" Did Lucas know Val had almost drowned? How?

"Because she almost drowned when you two were snorkeling."

Fuck. "She called him?" Jack said.

"No. If it makes it better she hasn't talked to him, but if it makes it worse, she doesn't need to. They have a telepathic connection. So he knew she was on the verge of death."

"Why? How?"

She made a strange expression, almost like a grimace. "Blood. His. She drank a lot of it a while back."

Her words overwhelmed him, made him want to give up and just slink to the ground in defeat. How the fuck could he save her or help her when this was going on? Why hadn't she told him?

"What's he want with her?" he croaked, trying to keep the pain and betrayal locked tight.

"Why are you asking me? Go ask your girlfriend."

He bit back the automatic response—*she's not my girlfriend.*

Rachel gave a slow nod as she looked down at the ground, saying softly. "You can't trust her? You can sleep with her but you know she's lying to you. Letting you inside her body but not her heart."

"I have her heart," he growled.

"You have half her heart and none of her thoughts. You're asking me instead of her."

Jack rushed her and she didn't move out of the way or defend herself. It was the total opposite. She went limp so that as he reached her and pushed her back, her body was close to his, like they were dancing. Just for the barest moment.

Her back hit the wall of the elevator and he crowded in close to her, fuelled by anger. So close. Even closer. He saw her eyes widen, didn't flatter himself enough to think it was fear.

"Because you'll tell me. Why is that? Could you kill me? Do you want to? Tell me the truth!" He shook her like a rag-doll. "Look at me when you tell me," he said savagely, dragging her closer, holding her tighter with each word.

She struggled a little, voice breathy. "I could kill you. I could hurt you and I'd enjoy it." She stopped struggling but her voice was ragged. "Don't get distracted. You've got enough girl problems. Lucas wants to find the Fey and he needs Valerie to go with him."

"Why?" What could he do to make her answer him?

For a moment, he thought he saw some expression cross her face, like sadness or regret, sorrow, then it was gone. *A trick.*

"You need to talk to her," Rachel said.

"Fine," he said, rapidly losing patience.

"You want to know what's going on with Lucas and Valerie, you need to see them together. You want Lucas dead, so do the

Fey and the Werewolves—if they are alive. The vampires tried to kill Lucas to stop him from going after them."

"Why didn't he kill you?"

"Why does everyone assume Lucas will kill me? I am *really* charming."

Jack couldn't help but laugh. "Sweetheart, I'll be damned if your charm is enough to keep you alive."

She pouted and took a step closer to him. He wanted to throw his hands out, keep her back. "I can be very charming. I can be sweet too," she said, purring the words and it raised the hair on his arms. "Or cruel. Innocent. Damaged. All you have to do is tell me. Tell me what you want me to be and let's see if I can do it. Do you want to know what Marion liked me to be? *Everything*. I was her mother, her daughter, her lover, her keeper, her abuser. I should have won a fucking golden globe I was so good."

"I don't care what you were to her. Why are you here?" Everything was imploding around him.

"Lucas sent me. Obviously."

"I want him to stay away from Valerie."

"I want a tan, doesn't mean it's going to happen. He wants her bad. He's going to have her, Jack. Don't force him to kill you. He will. Right now, he's being indulgent. He's letting her have her freedom because he thinks she'll choose him."

"Is he stupid? She's loved me her whole life. He will never have her." He needed to hit something. Wanted to hit her to shut her up. *Hit her. Do it. You'll feel better and she'll probably like it. It's not like you can hurt her.*

Rachel's smile was almost sad. "Jack—"

"No! Don't pretend you're good, or trying to help me. You take me for a fool? If Marion was evil, you're the one who's fucked up enough to love her. You encouraged her and helped her survive. She was a one note monstrous bitch. I don't know what the hell you are. But maybe when I sink a stake into you, I'll figure it out."

Rachel stood straighter, her back rigid, a tight smile on her face. She came close to him, pushing her body forward so that a bare millimeter separated them. *Don't hit her. Don't flinch.*

"Hold up Casanova. Why threaten me? I've been good to you, haven't I? I don't have to be. I don't have to help you at all. In fact, if you're not nice to me I could make things really, really...*hard* for you, Jack. Think about that when you're with her."

"I will hurt you if you don't go right now."

He could smell her perfume, see the flecks of glitter in her lip-gloss because she was so close. She whispered, but it was loud enough, "You'll hurt me, Jackie? Go back upstairs and take her wrists in your hands, put them above her head and hold her down tight. Take her hard, Jack. So hard that you don't see anything else but her. And she'll be with you all the way, fucking you just as hard, giving in, desperate to see you when all she's seeing is—"

He snarled at her and struck out, his hand a fist. She let him hit her, the punch throwing her backwards so that blood dribbled down her chin and onto her silky top.

She dabbed her lip carefully. "Feel better? Keep practicing or you'll never get that thing into me." She pushed the button and the doors opened. Sauntering out, she turned and looked at him, a rakish smile on her slightly swollen lip. The bleeding had stopped and it was almost healed already, "You won't stake me either."

Jack was frozen in murderous desire.

"This was fun. Have a great trip," she said and gave him a pinky wave, her blood shiny and wet on her finger as the doors closed behind her.

CHAPTER 10

Jack walked back to the hotel room wearily. His encounter with Rachel hadn't pumped him up or left him feeling like he needed a fight, it had exhausted him.

Everyone wanted things from him. Nate had wanted him to be the perfect fighter, dedicated, and without flaw. Valerie expected even more. She admired him. In a way even put him on a pedestal, needing him to be strong and heroic, even as she begged him to give up the fighting and be Joe Normal.

And right now, he wondered why he didn't just give up. He couldn't kill all the vampires. He spent every damned day being one step behind. That wasn't the way the winning side worked. It was how the losing side worked. As he was backing away, pulling reinforcements away from the front lines, trying to set traps, the victors marched forward.

It's a lost cause.

That didn't mean he'd quit, but sometimes he got worn down. He'd look at Valerie, all she was offering, what she wanted and what he wanted *for* her, and he was tempted.

The tiredness would pass. It always did. His goal couldn't be about killing every vampire or winning outright, it had to be about saving one person at a time. And he'd save Valerie from Lucas if it killed him.

When the weariness passed, he'd feel like himself again. The rage would come back— so bright and hot that it could rival the sun. His desire for revenge, desire to wipe out the monsters hotter and fiercer than his love for anything or anyone.

Even Valerie.

He pulled the keycard out of his pocket, hand poised over the key slot. He couldn't go in yet. If he did, he'd yell at her, scream at her, ask her if what Rachel said was true— was she fucking him while thinking of Lucas? Was that the reason for the desperation?

Think of me when you're fucking her. He heard her say it over and over again. The words repeating on loop inside his head. Telling him how to take her, who to think of.

Jesus Christ. Jack might be confused on some things but he knew for a fact that Rachel wasn't one of them.

He rolled his shoulders, stretched his neck and swiped the key. Val was waiting.

CHAPTER 11

Valerie looked at Jack, her face slightly pale, lips drawn into a worried line. Beside her was the folder from Rachel. Her hands were folded on top of it, gripping tightly. She opened her mouth to speak, but he stopped her with a shake of his head. "Let's go eat. We can talk about it there."

"All right." She walked past him and into the bathroom, brushed her hair and put on some perfume. It was something floral and woodsy. It wasn't soft or delicate, but memorable. *That's her.*

Jack leaned against the door, propping it open with his weight as she put on her sandals.

"You're feeling better?"

"Yes. Thank you," she said, sounding almost shy.

She passed by him and waited for him in the hall. Jack wondered if he should have kissed her. Did she even want him to? *Shit, do I want to?*

They walked into the restaurant and sat down, managing to do it without saying a word, touching, or even looking at each other.

He wanted her. He loved her. He did. But...he'd never expected to *have* her. And looking at her now, as she studied the menu like it was the most important thing in the world, he wondered if maybe she didn't know what the hell to do with him, either.

Val wanted to throw up. Tonight was the night. She needed to talk to Jack and tell him what was going on. It wasn't fair to either of them. Her whole life she'd wanted him but not like this. With secrets and tension.

Spotlights were set up outside, strategically placed so that one could see the ocean waves crashing at night. The silence was uncomfortable as they looked at their menus and waited for their order to be taken.

She tried to rally herself for the coming conversation. *Is this what people mean when they say they are girding their loins? Whatever.* "Rachel was here, she brought me a folder from Lucas."

A muscle jumped in his jaw. "Yeah, I know."

Her palm cradled her face, elbow propped on the table. "How?"

"She told me. Came to see me after dropping it off with you."

"Did you— kill her?"

Jack gave her an insincere smile, one corner of his mouth turning up. "No."

Val wanted to ask him why not. And yet, she didn't want to know and suspected he wouldn't tell her. "What did she say?"

He leaned forward, so they were no more than six inches apart. Face as close as a lover, but his expression was filled with anger. "Why don't you go first. Be honest with me and we'll see if your stories match."

Val jerked back in her seat, knotting her fists under the table. "You'd believe *her* over me?"

"Just fucking talk to me, Val. You know I love you. I'm not your father. Just...tell me what the hell is going on." He sounded so tired, so betrayed that she wanted to reach across the table and touch him. Apologize. *Anything.*

But he wanted the truth. She owed it to him anyway. "There is something...between Lucas and I. He's attracted to me and it's because I'm an Empath."

Jack blew out a breath. "What?"

"Okay, I didn't start at the right part. There are vampires but that's not all. There used to be Werewolves, Fey, Witches and Empaths. But they're gone. Extinct. Except for me."

"How'd you win the supernatural lottery? And how does he know you're an Empath?"

Val worried the napkin in her lap. "Um. Well, he told me and the way we react to each other is...not... normal."

"Just because you want to fuck his brains out, does not mean you're an Empath."

She felt blood rushing to her face and stared at the crisp, white tablecloth. "It's more than that. I know desire and lust. It's not that. It's not love either. It's...worse." *Is that a good enough explanation? Cause this conversation blows.*

Jack closed his eyes for a moment, rubbed his hand across his jaw. "Okay. What does an Empath do?"

"Well, I think that's why the folder is upstairs. So I can get a better idea. Apparently I'm only part Empath. An Empath senses emotions and for a vampire or a werewolf an Empath can...help with their emotions. Soothe an angry wolf or make a vampire sad or happy."

"How?" Here his voice was tense, as though he'd guessed the answer, but was waiting for confirmation.

Val gulped. "Through blood."

"I asked you before if he drank your blood. You told me no." Low, angry words, torn from him.

"He hasn't. He's told me before that he won't." She didn't think she should tell Jack how much Lucas wanted to. That was part of the attraction between them—he wanted her blood more than anything and she wanted to give it to him. It was a dangerous balancing act and now that she had his blood it was worse. She *needed* to get her blood into him.

Sometimes she fantasized about it. As she lay in bed, the dark surrounding her and no one to see or know... that was her fantasy now. Lucas giving in. Her breathing picked up and she crossed her legs, just thinking of him drinking her down, how that might change things, excited her. It would shift the balance of power between them. She'd be stronger, different if it happened. She knew it instinctively.

"Something happened. You called his name Valerie. You almost died today and the first thing you did was ask for *him.*" Jack blinked and looked around, reached for his glass of wine and took a slow sip as though buying time to get his emotions under control. *Isn't that my move?*

"I drank from him. That night dad died. I was in Rome too. Marion and Rachel almost killed me trying to take power from Lucas. He gave me his blood to save me." She took a sip of her water and crunched an ice cube.

"What a fucking hero."

Val shrugged. She wasn't going to defend Lucas to Jack. It had been Lucas' fault she was there anyway. "Since then, there has been a connection between us. I see some of his memories, sometimes we are in each other's dreams. I was in the water, drowning, and he was there with me." She stared at the candle, watching the flame twist and burn. "He died with me." Saying it felt like a premonition.

A long moment passed. "So you're lying in bed with me but dreaming about him?"

That cut like a knife. "No! I'm with you. I told him no."

"Why are you here?" Jack asked.

Val gasped, uncertain what he meant. Did he want her to leave? Was he breaking it off? They couldn't make it more than a few days?

"Why has he let you go?"

She scowled. "I told him I didn't want him. That I wanted you. He let me go."

Jack laughed unhappily. "Really? What's his endgame?"

Val flushed and wanted to slide under the table and hide. "He thinks I'll come back."

Jack stared at her intently, trying to read her face for any clue of her feelings. "Will you?" he asked quietly.

"No, I won't," she said, wishing he could know how sincere she was.

"But you are dreaming about him?"

"Rachel says I can stop. It's only because I don't know my own abilities that we are sharing dreams. I'll get control over it and poof, he's gone."

"You don't believe it's that simple." It wasn't a question.

The waiter came and put the food before them. They both ordered Mahi Mahi fish tacos.

"You said the Fey and Werewolves are real? Where are they? How do they fit in?" He looked down at his food and she wondered if he wanted to eat. If he felt as likely to heave as she did. He took a big bite of his taco.

The bastard.

"I think they're gone, but Lucas isn't sure. That was part of the reason he wanted my help. Empaths used to be mediators between the groups, and he wanted me to try to find them. See if they exist and get them to come back to the world or declare themselves."

"Why?"

"Because vampires are evil and he says they've become worse since the Other races disappeared. He said vampires used to be more...human, not as evil but now they don't have emotions, and they're murderous because killing is the only pleasure they get. If the Fey and wolves came back, there would be balance."

"He killed them all. Now he's changed his mind? I don't believe it," Jack said, before eating the last bite of a taco. "So, Werewolves and the Fey. Why would they restore the balance?"

"From what I can tell, Werewolves are good. People, basically, but preternaturally strong and they can kill vampires. Back in the days of yore, if the vamps got greedy and killed too many people, the wolves would kill them. I think they all fought a lot. So the vampires were more secretive and hidden, as well as being better behaved because they had to watch their backs."

"And he wants to return to the good old days? That's what happens when you date an old man. They always talk about how good it was back in the day. How long ago was that? Before toilet paper? Before dentistry?"

"Yeah, and there is a possibility that some of the wolves and the Fey are still alive. Last seen Roanoke, North Carolina."

"When? You'd think we'd hear something about wolves or faeries wandering around."

"Uh, they were last seen in the sixteenth century."

His eyebrows rose and he stopped chewing. Then swallowed. "You're kidding."

"Nope. That was what I was supposed to do next. Go to North Carolina and figure out if they've been really, really quiet for the last 400 years".

"What are you going to do, hit up Pet Smart for some Snausages and go trolling through the woods on a full moon?"

"Cute. I don't know. He didn't say. It was a need to know basis. And I really never needed to know."

Jack grunted. She watched his eyes scanning the back of the restaurant.

"Thank God. Here's dessert," he said.

Val looked down at her full plate. She felt like she was being interrogated. And that wasn't conducive to eating. "Do Empaths have any effect on humans?"

Valerie blinked in surprise. "I don't think so."

Jack multi-tasked, keeping an eye on Valerie while shoveling chocolate into his mouth at the same time. "The vampires—except Lucas—the guy who led the charge in wiping them out—don't want the Fey or the wolves back, right?"

"Right."

"So if they're around and he can find them, more vampires will die?"

"Yeah." She crushed her lips together, biting back the words that were swirling around in her mind. She knew what he was going to say. How could he?

"Then let's do it. Let's go to Roanoke and see if Peter Pan is still flying around," Jack said, recklessly.

"This isn't a joke. It could be dangerous. If you put me in the same room with Lucas—" She wanted to scream. Keeping herself from saying what she wanted to say was so hard.

"I'll be there. We'll go together. Rachel says it's a terrible idea. She thinks they'll kill every vampire they meet, especially Lucas." And the way he said it, told her how much he liked that idea.

"Alright, Jack. Here is the end of the line. The buck stops here. This is the big moment. I want to go back to London and go to school. I want to pretend Lucas was a bad dream. I don't want to risk my life for some supernatural BS." Now she leaned forward, staring at him hard so that he'd know how serious she was. She said clearly, "If I'm with him, something will happen between him and I. And I honestly believe that if we go to Roanoke it will put my life and yours in danger. Now, here is the million dollar question. Do you *really* want me to go?"

She prayed that he might say what she needed him to say. *He's not the guy. He won't put me first.* She held her breath.

"So what, we do nothing? Stay here and hide because something might be dangerous? That's how you do things. You run away. That's not me. If I see a chance to help I'm going to take it. Yeah, I think we should go. Because—"

Val pushed back her chair, not bothering to listen to whatever lame-ass reasoning he was going to give her. "Well, Jack. It's been a good trip."

"Wait." He stood too, voice loud and angry.

"No. I'm going to get another room for the night and tomorrow I'm going home. I'm going to dad's funeral and then...shit, I don't know what I'm doing then. I'll pack up my stuff in the morning."

She turned to go, rushing out of the restaurant. He caught her at the exit, his arms wrapping around her, his voice low in her ear. She couldn't see him. Her heart was breaking, her eyes filling with tears. *That is it. Things with Jack are over. Jesus! The relationship could be counted in hours.*

"They took everyone from us, Val. My parents and yours. If we can make a difference," his voice wobbled, sounded rough, like he might cry too. Maybe he was, but that wasn't enough.

She pushed away from him, hot tears coursing down her cheek. She threw the words at him violently, wanting to hurt him, make him get it. "I want him Jack. Not in a pretty romantic way, but I want to... *own* him. Claim him and mark him. I want him in me and I want every secret that he has. It's *sick—*"

"*No!*" he cut in, "You just don't do it. It's not hard. You put others above yourself, look at the big picture and do what you ought to, rather than what makes you happy. You just keep your legs closed and don't fuck the monster. That's what we're talking about, right? You'd let people die because you're worried you'd be his whore?"

For a moment she was speechless, couldn't think beyond breathing. "You say these things to me...just throw them at me. Do you know how much they hurt? Do you care? I catch glimpses of you, Jack. Of the boy I grew up with and...he's not you. You're harder, colder. You've built up a huge wall around yourself and I thought I could get through it. That it would be me who you loved.... I thought maybe sex would get us there. Form that final connection where you would let me in and maybe want something else. But you don't. You're with me, you look me in the eyes, and yet...I know, *know*, that I'm not enough. "

She took a step back from him, ready to turn and flee.

"Don't put all these fucking words in my mouth. How dare you talk like you know me. You are in my heart. I would die for you. You know that!"

She threw her hands up in the air. "I'm not asking you to die for me! I'm asking you to compromise for me. And you can't. I know you don't respect me and the decisions that I have made."

His hands fisted in his hair and he looked up at the ceiling. "There is nothing else for me. I'm sorry. I'm sorry I did this. Sorry I brought you here...I thought I was doing the right thing. Being with you so you wouldn't be with him."

Her throat was choked with tears and she had to wipe her nose on her hand, she was crying so hard. People passed by them, staring and then looking away the moment they got close.

"Oh God, Jack. Really? The only reason you're here with me is to keep me from him?" she said and felt like she was choking. She backed away and left him behind.

CHAPTER 12

She'd left him two days ago. Jack could feel himself sneer in self-loathing. Self-hate that reached into his gut, grabbed a hold of his nuts and left him feeling like, shit, who knew what the hell he felt like, he just needed another fucking drink.

No, he was a shit. He glared down the bar at the bartender, who squinted back at him, leaving Jack to wonder if he might get cut off soon if he wasn't careful.

There were always more bars. Always more drinks. Always more vampires. But only one Val. And one person left in his family. Unfortunately, it was the same one person.

Jack wasn't quite sure how things had gotten so messed up. One moment they'd been having a conversation and while he wasn't happy about it, he knew he was keeping his cool. Being methodical and practical.

And then...then he told Val to keep her legs closed.

California was six hours away by plane, but it felt like another lifetime. He wished he could go back in time and change things. The bartender finally came down and gave him a refill. Whisky. He didn't care what kind. Whether it was cheap or expensive. Single or double. He just wanted it to burn. And to keep on coming.

She might never forgive him. And why should she? He'd been an asshole. In fact, he'd probably accomplished the one thing he didn't want to. His whole agenda for coming here had been to keep her out of that fanger's bed. One goal. And she was probably fucking him right now.

How could she make such a piss-poor decision?

"Buy a girl a drink?" He exhaled sharply.

"You know, I didn't think this night could get any worse," Jack said.

He heard her make a noise, like a petulant growl, before saying, "Don't be that way, Jackie. You may have girl problems, but it's not me that's the trouble."

He turned on the seat, arm on the bar and hunched over slightly, looking at Rachel over his glass as he swallowed his drink. "Am I dead? Are you the welcoming committee from hell?"

She waved her fingers at the bartender and he hurried over. "I want what he's having—" she flashed Jack an inscrutable look, "—and so does he, his glass is empty."

The bartender scowled at Jack. "He's had plenty."

Rachel leaned forward and Jack saw the moment it happened, when the barkeep looked into her eyes and got trapped in her gaze.

"Give him a drink," she said in her husky voice and the man filled up Jack's glass without complaining.

The bartender walked away and Jack grabbed her arm, fingers biting into her cool flesh. "Don't fucking do that. You hurt anyone else and I'll kill you."

"That train has sailed, my friend." She took a sip. "I was killable by you and your—"she looked at him insolently, gaze raking him from head to foot, lingering on the center of his body before she made eye contact again, "—little stick, but now, let's just say I got promoted. You can try to get it in me, but—"

Jack stood, pulled out his wallet and found his cash, throwing fifty dollars down on the bar before walking out the door. He remembered meeting Rachel at the elevator and didn't want to go that way, so he pushed out a side door instead, heard the pounding of the ocean, could feel the spray on his cheeks as he stalked out into the night.

He looked at the sky. No stars. Too many clouds. The night was warm and he was glad, happy to be alone. After a few minutes he hit the dark of the beach, all the lights fading behind him. A woman was sitting out there all alone.

"Jesus fucking Christ! Take a god damned hint!A guy ditches you at the bar, it means he's not interested. Leave now, or else."

She snorted. "Or else what? You punch like a girl."

"Don't. Don't push me."

There was a huge, empty moment where she didn't say anything and the only sounds were the ocean waves crashing against the rocks. It was almost like he heard her though, promising to push him. As if he had spoken a dare, and all she wanted was to push every button he had.

Rachel stood, dusted the sand from her palms. "Yeah, the surliness just won't work with me. I know you've had a rough few days, but I'm not your bitch. Not your whipping boy. Not your girlfriend. Geez, you didn't even buy me a drink. Ask me what I want and then I'll leave you to sulk. Or is it a pout. What's the status of your lower lip? If it's jutting out, then you're pouting."

His fist flashed out of the night, close to her jaw. She turned her head a little. As if meeting him for a kiss on the cheek. *She let me hit her. Why?* She pushed back, lightly, using just enough force to make him lose ground.

Her low laugh washed over him. She was happy. Pleased that he had lost control and punched her. *God. How could I do that? She's a woman. No, you fucking moron she's a vampire bitch who deserves to die.* One he seemed unable to kill. *No. Once the timing is right, I'll do it.*

"Punch me again and we'll have this out Jack. Is that what you're looking for?"

Jack stopped. His breathing was harsh, and she could feel the warm puffs of his breath on her face, smell the alcohol on his—blood.

She could smell his blood.

He must have caught his knuckle on her earring. The physical reaction to the smell of his blood was worse than any punch. His scent. The vitality of him. Her desire for him assaulted her, ripped her defenses down, stripped her bare.

If he told her to kneel, she'd do it.

If he told her to lick it off of him and suck him dry she would.

She didn't breathe. Didn't dare. Didn't look down at his hand, either because she couldn't bear to see his shiny essence glinting at her in the night.

So fucking weak. Don't step back. Don't give him a clue. Stay still. She took a step back.

He didn't seem to notice.

"I need a favor," Rachel said, and stood a little straighter. She sounded calm, collected.

Good.

Jack laughed, like he'd found out he'd won the lottery and been diagnosed with incurable cancer in the same breath. "Oh God. That can't be good."

"You'll probably get to kill something," she said.

"Who? What? Why me? Shit, let's just go for all five—who, what, where, when, why?" He sat down on a nearby rock, moving carefully like the truly inebriated do.

"Some evil people. Monsters. San Jose. Soon. Because."

He gave her a look of disgust. She could see it even in the dark, might have felt it even without her heightened senses.

"Why me?" Jack asked, extending one leg out and leaning back on both arms.

"I need backup."

"Get Lucas to help you."

"No. I owe him enough. I don't want him involved."

"Real friends wouldn't use it as leverage later," he said snidely.

She chuckled. "Lucas isn't a real friend. He is my Lord and Maker. Big difference."

"Lord and Maker. Creepy. He's your best chance at success if you need firepower. Ask him."

She looked down, kicking her foot on the ground. Her words were quiet. "He can't know. It's too important and I want to keep her away from him."

"Her? New girlfriend?" He asked and couldn't stop the unhappy laugh that came out.

"No. Niece, actually."

He grunted. "Niece? How is that possible?"

"Witches are long lived. It's my sister's daughter. I want to get her out of the coven."

"Why?" He shifted, resting his hands on the rock behind him.

"People don't know witches. They are not like their image. None of this granola-eating, white-magic, love-the-earth, blessed-be, crap. They're evil. Like Wicked Witch of the West after she ate Toto for breakfast, evil."

"Hmm," he said, brows drawn together. "And you want to save one of them? And you think I'll help?" He looked at her oddly, like he couldn't believe he was hearing her correctly.

"She's still little. Her powers have not manifested yet. But the witches, if she stays with them, they'll have her start doing magic early, trying to bring her powers on. And that would turn her evil. Like serial killer, evil."

He visibly recoiled. "How old is she?"

"Ten."

"And they'd have her...killing people?"

She nodded, looking at the ocean and away from him. he didn't answer. She'd have to say something else. She could feel him staring at her in the dark. Shit, she didn't have anything else to say that might convince him.

"Is that what you did?" he asked, too calmly.

"For a little while. Witches have to use their power. And it's dark. You can't do it without causing a certain amount of pain. But that doesn't mean she has to be a killer. Lucas got me out at twelve, and by then, I'd done a lot."

"Why did he save you?"

She smiled at him a little oddly. "I'm a witch."

"Yeah, but.... Why didn't he take someone else or—"

"What are you fishing for?" she said, sounding impatient.

"What does Lucas say about why he saved you and what he wants from you?"

"I haven't asked him."

"Why?" He burst out, "How could you not want to know?"

"Because it's the nicest thing anyone has ever done for me, and I don't think he did it out of the kindness of his heart. He's of the heart-two-sizes-too-small-variety. I don't want to know that the best thing that's ever happened to me wasn't done because he—" she swallowed hard, "—okay, you know what, I didn't come here for therapy. I'm going to go in and kill some bitches. They are murderers and fucking evil. I need help getting my niece out and you can do that."

He leaned forward. "What is your plan, exactly, and why me?"

"Any other vampire would use it as blackmail. Witches are supposed to be extinct. She's valuable. I need someone who'd be willing to protect her...someone good."

He shook his head and blew out a huge breath. "Good. I'm the good guy." He laughed.

"Have you seen the crowd I run around with? You're *totally* a good guy. Always will be."

He looked at her for a long moment, his hands going up to his hair, raking through it in agitation. "What will you do with her?"

"I've got a home for her. And assuming I survive this fucking quest for the Fey, I'll help her out, "

"You?"

She chuckled and it was so...pretty that it made him want to smile. "Yeah, me. Maternal instincts. No, seriously, she's a witch. Witches need to do evil things. Need to harm and hurt to give their magic an outlet. You can't take energy, use it for gain, without paying a price. But that doesn't mean she needs to kill kittens and toddlers."

The enormity of what she was saying and asking finally hit him. His voice was quiet. "Wait. So she really is evil. Why would I want to save her at all?"

"She's powerful. She can kill vampires. What if we find the Fey? They're scared ofwitches. You want a balance where evil is encouraged to play by the rules. And they only do that if they have something to fear. They'll fear *her*."

"But she's evil. You just told me that! *I'll* fucking fear her. It's like getting Kujo because you're afraid of a German Shepard."

"She is not inherently evil. Her magic is dark, that doesn't mean she's evil. We can make her be good. If she's involved in the human world, goes to school, grows up with someone who loves her, she'll want to protect people. She'll know the value of life."

"That's a pretty speech. What, she'll be like you? What's your kill count?"

"Are you going to help me or not?" she asked heavily.

"No," he said without hesitation and stood up, ready to go back to the hotel.

"Mother fucker!" she yelled at him. "Fine. You want the fucking truth? I have never killed anyone who wasn't scum of the earth bad. If I could stop Marion, I did. I stayed with her for eighty fucking years because she liked what I did to her. With Marion, I couldn't cut deep enough. There was *never* enough blood."

She crowded in close to him, almost eye to eye she was so tall, her chest heaving, anger so high and close that it was like a pulse in the air. He'd back up if he had to, stake her if had to. "Everything I needed, she gave willingly—no, happily. Do you know what it's like to be evil, to do monstrous things and then have your victim *thank you?* To know that you have made their day? It's beyond fucked up, but I needed her and she gave me peace. I can save Molly, give her a life beyond murder. But I can't do it alone and if you won't go with me I can't ask anyone else."

"If I don't go, you'll go in alone?" he asked. She jerked back a step, like she was scared of his voice.

She was breathing hard, quiet for a long while. "Yeah. I think so. I might ask Lucas, after all. He's in a weird head space anyway. Who knows, maybe he'll die before he gets a chance to blackmail me."

"That's bullshit."

"What? Lucas? He's on the way out. I'd bet my life on it. He's tried to die, you know. I think that's why we're going for the Fey. If anyone has a weapon to kill him, they'll be the ones to make it."

He blew out a breath. "Okay, one thing at a time. You're saying that if we rescue this girl now, she won't hurt anyone for a decade, maybe more?"

"Yes."

"I have something else I want to know."

"Yeah. I bet. What?"

"Marion is gone. Who are you torturing now?" His voice was silky soft and she knew why he wanted to know. Felt the threat in the air.

"You'd still kill me after this bonding session? You're a cold cat, Jack. Don't fash yourself, as my mother would say. The S and M scene in New York is wild these days. I can always find someone. Unless you're offering?"

"Don't fuck with me," he said flatly and with total disgust. Revulsion clear on his face.

"So your answer is a '*no*'?" she asked exaggeratedly.

He came closer to her and all the air seemed to flow towards him. There was nothing left to breathe. No matter how many breaths she took she'd still need air. He'd always have the upper hand with her. It was a fucking problem. And if he figured out the power he had over her—

"Valerie. If she's with Lucas I want to know. If she goes with him to the Fey, I want to be there. You tell me what the hell is going on and if he makes a move on her. She doesn't even want to be there and...she was worried about being alone with him."

"I bet she was. Emotionless vampire and a gal whose got more pleasure in the tip of her little finger than a box full of uppers. Yeah, everyone should be worried."

He looked at her murderously. She sneered at him. "You humans never want honesty."

"I want to be there. Every step of the way. To keep her from him. You want my help, you have to take me along."

She looked at him for an endless moment. "Deal." She looked up at the sky, hands on her hips and then shook her head. "Why do I feel like I just made a deal with the devil?" she asked, then turned and sauntered away down the beach. "Well, thanks. I'll take you out for a burger after."

"Let's be clear," Jack said, voice caressing her like a lover, "No, you won't buy me a burger, go anywhere with me...." An endless silence where she waited in dread for what he might say. The thought was there, the words seemed to be stuck in his throat and when he spoke his voice was gruff, "or do anything with me. This is a job. And if I find out you have been killing people—and let me tell you right now, I'm waiting for it—then I'll kill you. Really easily."

Death was in his eyes. He'd kill her and not even think twice about it. He'd do it and be fine with it. Maybe even be proud of it.

Yeah, I got it.

CHAPTER 13

Cerdewellyn unbuttoned his jacket, the warm summer air stifling. Virginia threw him a look that was far older than her sixteen years and drew her dress over her head, carelessly tossing it onto the grass before running towards the water in her shift.

Her hair fanned out behind her, the undergarment's material almost transparent. He could see the outline of her hips, her smooth back. She turned back and looked at him, beckoning him towards the water.

He shook his head slowly, unable to help the smile he knew was on his lips. Her precociousness and innocence were enchanting. In truth, she was a woman now, and his followers were becoming impatient. Her breasts were developed and full, her body ripe and ready for womanly pleasures.

But he was still waiting.

Laughing, she went into the water, running all the way in, and then squealing that it was cold. He laughed with her and went to the water's edge, looking down at her as she shivered, watching the gooseflesh rise on her pale arms.

"Why do you go in if it is so cold?" he asked, squatting down near a rocky ledge so he could see her face.

"I want to get it over with. I think that if I waited on the shore and inched my way in, I would never go. So I do it all in a run, just don't stop and then—it is too late, I am in!" She splashed him. He ignored the droplets that clung to his clothing and dripped down his cheek.

"It is good to see you in such a happy mood. Recently, you have seemed...." He shook his head and let the sentence hang there, knowing she would fill it in.

Virginia looked at her hands in the water, settling them on the surface and holding them still, like they were pressed against a pane of glass. "Won't you come in?" Her head was down, not meeting his gaze as she asked, her voice a siren's call, and he felt his body react.

"No. I shall only sit here and speak with you. No more."

"You *used* to go swimming with me."

"Yes. And after we are joined, we can go swimming together again."

"Well... why not now?" Her glance speared him. So direct. She looked at his coat, like she wanted to touch it. "Why wait? I am old enough. You are my destiny, Cerdewellyn, and I am ready for it."

Cer sighed and rubbed his forehead, squeezing his eyes shut, unwilling to look at her. She moved a little closer, so half of her body was out of the water, the material of her fine garment now doing nothing to hide her. Her pebbled nipples and the pink areolas, her flat stomach, and even the shadowed juncture of her thighs.

"Virginie," he said, using his pet name for her. "I know what it's like to be young. To think you are more grown-up than you are."

"Are you calling me a child?" Her voice rose dangerously.

"No. I am saying that I want things to be perfect between us. Not just for you and I, but for our subjects. And for that, we need to wait."

She stepped towards him, out of the water, droplets falling off of her hair and fingers. "I see the way the Queen watches me." A lengthy pause. "The world could be ours. We could be together, and yet, you hesitate."

Virginia dropped to her knees beside him, bringing her chilled face close to his. "I want you. I know you want me." Her hand reached out, touching his full lips, stroking her finger across them.

Cer leaned back from her and grabbed her hand, hard enough to get her attention. "You are still a young girl. Now you are pretending to be a woman. What we do will remake the world. Herald our return and cause a reckoning. And yet, you are being impatient. I will be your husband—ever your King. Even when you rule all others, I will still rule you. And I say we wait."

Maybe he had been too harsh. Her mouth was frowning angrily, but her eyes were watering with tears. "I know you are mature, and perhaps you are ready. But, it does us no harm to give you a little more time to prepare. We have one chance,

Virginie. Only one. And you must be strong and secure in your magic to help me open the portal."

Her lower lip trembled. "She'll kill me, I know it."

His first instinct was to laugh. "Who? The Queen? No, she will not. What good would it serve her? She knows her duty. These are her people, too. She wants what is best for them."

"She does not put anyone above herself. I feel it in my heart, Cerdewellyn. If she can kill me she will, no matter the consequences." She wrapped her fingers hard around his, like she'd force him to listen this time. "They all bow to *me* now. I am already Queen to everyone but you."

Cerdewellyn made a tsking noise in the back of his throat, partly scolding her for her ridiculous fears and partly scolding himself because he was going to kiss her. She looked up at him, an expression of trust and innocence—anticipation that had nothing to do with being a girl but a woman. He could indulge her with a kiss.

Her lips were cold, but the moment he touched her she exhaled, warm breath contrasting with the coolness of her skin, and he moved closer, wanting more of her. He pressed firmly, his tongue licking along the seam of her lips, and she opened her mouth and met him greedily. He wanted to laugh again, because she was so endearing, thinking this was her chance and she would make full use of it. His Virginia was always daring, always ready.

As though she could never have been anything else but his Queen.

He wondered at the perfection of the moment—her lips and the life that lay before them. Opening the portal, returning to the world. And one day, when their numbers had grown, he would have his revenge.

His tongue slid into her mouth, tasting her, craving her so much, that at first, he didn't even feel the arrow that pierced his heart.

Finally. Finally! Virginia thought with fierce exultation. Cerdewellyn kissed her, and she wouldn't give him the chance to stop, would kiss him so ardently that he would be driven by desire to claim her and make her his. She opened her mouth, letting him inside, arching closer with a moan, disbelieving that he was finally kissing her.

Cerdewellyn, King of the Fey, would finally be hers. So tall and imposing with his dark curling hair and black eyes. Eyes that looked as if they had seen everything since the moment time began. A king of beauty and life.

She tilted her head, felt her body responding, opening, wanting, needing him. And then there was a slight noise, a combination of a woosh and a thud.

A shadow loomed over them. She pulled back and Cerdewellyn was gazing down, his hand flat to his chest, over his heart, staring dumbly at the heavy, red flow of heart-blood soaking through his white shirt.

Virginia cried out and stood, looking everywhere around them, searching for the danger. A shimmer of yellow cloth glided out from the trees. The Queen came closer, her once beautiful hair dull in the light, her skin flushed. Her guards were with her, one holding a bow, the other an axe.

"He is not dead," the Queen said. "He is a deity. They do not die so easily. Look."

Her heart thundering, Virginia looked back, saw that Cer's chest still rose and fell. He lay on his back, staring at the ground, but where the arrow pierced his heart, vines were growing. They were snaking out of his chest and twining up the wooden shafts, stretching over his body, coiling over his legs, even towards her, forcing her to scramble away.

"He is healing. That is what it means to be immortal." Here, she smiled at Virginia. "The same cannot be said for you."

The Queen pulled out a short sword from her tunic and advanced. Virginia looked to the guards, half-men and half-abomination, creatures the Queen had created with her darkest magic and Virginia saw their empty minds gazing back at her. They would not help her. She looked around wildly. Saw no one to aid her.

She screamed.

"Virginia, Virginia, did you think I would let you take him? My king. My crown. My people and *my* land. They all bow to you. You cast me glances, Every day you look at me like I am a fool. As if I will *take* it. As if being a Queen was your destiny. And now you have none. You are a fate that never was."

Virginia felt a hand in her hair, a guard grabbing her from behind, pulling her neck taut. She threw herself backwards, trying to think of *anything* she could do to escape. She kicked and screamed, struck out with her hands, raking her nails down the guards hand and arm, feeling skin come away because she dug so deep into his flesh. *Delay the moment. Fight. Someone will come.*

She looked at Cer, met his gaze as he begged her to keep fighting. Tears filled her eyes, clogged her throat as she fought the guard who held her. The Queen moved closer but Cer moved his arms, almost able to stand and save her. *Another moment and he'll save me, one more, just one—*

The blade sliced her throat, slipping across her jugular cleanly. Delicately. A small, insignificant line across her throat. Her life pulsed out in huge liquid gasps. Her vision narrowing down to the pond in front of her, to Cerdewellyn on the ground, still covered in snaking vines. The final blow came, severing her head from her neck, and she didn't feel a thing.

The queen worked quickly, kicking the girl's head out of the way and turning her attention back to Cerdewellyn. His eyes were blinking, the vines receding. Where the arrow had been, there was now only a fine pile of mulch. The arrow devoured and composted, returned to its natural state. Cerdewellyn breathed deeply and coughed, looking up into his Queen's familiar blue eyes.

She shook her head sadly at him. "You lost, Cerdewellyn. You lost to Lucas because you were too late to act. You lost your people because you were too weak to open the portal. And now you have lost her, too. So blind to the treachery around you."

She stabbed him in the chest, pinning him to the earth with her blade, and then snapped her fingers to the waiting guards. "You'll be as close to dead as I can get you, here in your realm."

The guards worked quickly, hacking Cerdewellyn into pieces: feet, legs, arms, then his head and torso. But the *heart*—*his* heart she took for herself. She clenched it in her fist. The part of him that he'd once given to her and then taken away, she now had again. She alone would dispose of *this* piece.

He would have killed her. Replaced her with Virginia Dare. Did he think her a fool? There had been a queen before her too. She knew that her death was required for Virginia Dare to rise. And Cerdewellyn, an antiquated man from another time, had assumed she would behave honorably. Put their people first, let him kill her and transfer her magic to Virginia Dare.

Lucas had won because he was aggressive. Before anyone could scream for help, he had already acted. That was something she had learned from the vampires. Something Cerdewellyn had never comprehended.

The victor always strikes first.

CHAPTER 14

Valerie picked up the phone and exhaled deeply. Took another breath in. Another breath out. Looked at the phone and imagined a hundred different ways this conversation could quality as the 'worst phone call ever. '

She was being ridiculous. There was no reason to get flustered. She'd just stay focused on the goal. *Call Lucas, tell him I will go to Roanoke. Skip lots of painfully awkward questions and emotional upheaval, maybe talk about the weather instead. Will I need a coat in Roanoke?*

Argh!

She tried to remember their last conversation. The one where he'd stripped down and flaunted his body like a waiter with a stacked dessert cart, hoping she'd lunge over and shove her face into his huge...piece of cake.

'*When you come back, this changes. '* Wasn't that what he'd said? Man, someone really needed to tape record those big moments. They always seemed hard to remember in retrospect.

She shivered at the memory of his words, the look on his face. The general shirtlessness.

What a slut! Her relationship with Jack had *just* fallen apart, and she was ready to jump on Lucas' bandwagon? No, all she was doing was calling him to tell him that she was ready to go to Roanoke. She had no intentions of doing anything shirtless.

Who was she kidding? Intentions, inshmensions. She'd probably be flat on her back the moment she saw him. They might as well just bury her in a Y shaped coffin. Jack's words came back to her—'*Just keep your legs closed.* '

She'd never forgive him or forget the look of disgust on his face. The fact that he wouldn't listen to her. He'd made her feel ashamed and stupid. Her actions *were* stupid, she knew that! That was why she'd brought it up! He was supposed to listen to the words, not just assume she *liked* being coffin bait.

Frankly, she never wanted to see Jack again. But Jack would be back. When would he track her down? Tomorrow? A week from now? And he'd demand she find the Fey. So fuck it. She'd do the right thing, but she wouldn't bring Jack. If she wanted Jack to come out of this alive, she had to make sure they didn't meet.

Maybe she shouldn't call Lucas yet. She'd just buried her father. Some of her laundry from Hawaii was still sitting in the corner of her room. Waiting sounded like a wonderful idea. She only needed a decade or two.

But if she waited, Jack would show up again and demand to go with them to Roanoke. Talk about disaster. Jack and Lucas looking daggers at each other. Jack trying to kill Lucas, her hoping Lucas was feeling magnanimous enough to not kill Jack.

She'd get it over with. Go to Roanoke, figure out that faeries existed only in Disneyland, and then she'd ditch them both.

Maybe look up Ian, see if he was still on the hunt for an issue-laden American.

Her palms were sweaty, and she had that twisty feeling in her stomach where she thought she might dash to the bathroom and have to decide if it was a sit-or-stand situation.

She looked around her room for a moment, still stalling. Her pretty, pink room that her mother had decorated for her. Before she was killed by a vampire. And now Val was going to call Lucas, King of the Vampires, and tell him she was willing to help him. *And probably bone him.*

Oh shit.

She dialed the number quickly, heard it ring, and had her voice-message all planned out. He'd never answered before. In fact, there was probably nothing to be worried about. Not at all. She almost wondered if he *ever* answered the ph—

"Hello?"

Oh fuck! Her mouth hung open as she tried to remember the English language. "Lucas, it's me. Umm... Valerie," she said feeling like someone should congratulate her for remembering her name. She knew, even with that one word that it was Lucas. She knew because her nipples pebbled, her breathing hitched, and she plopped back onto the bed bonelessly.

"What's wrong?" he said, voice clipped.

Her chest went tight, and her lower lip felt like trembling. She wanted to say things to him, tell him what was wrong because... he'd listen? He cared? He made it seem like her problems were something she'd move beyond? She tried to think what to say. She'd expected voice mail! She must have waited too long because he spoke again.

"Are you in danger? Shall I come to you?" His tone was distant and hard, like she meant nothing to him.

"No. I'm fine." She swallowed. "You know where I am?"

A lengthy pause. "No."

How come she couldn't choose a guy who used lots of words and explained himself? Val sighed, staring at her bedspread, picking at a pink flower whose edge was coming up. "I'll help you find the Fey."

Another long pause. Maybe he didn't want her help anymore. Why would he? What the hell was *she* going to do anyway? She was half-convinced the whole thing had just been a ploy to get into her panties in the first place.

She wasn't 'super' anything. Not 'super' powerful, 'super' tough. Crap, she wasn't even 'super' hot, smart or thin. *Oh wait. I'm 'super.' 'Super' ordinary.*

But then she'd rejected him, ditched him for another guy and was now crawling back. She could hear it, feel it in her marrow—he was done with her. He didn't want her anymore.

"What has happened?" he said impatiently.

"Nothing." More lower lip trembling. She heard breathing over the phone. *Oh no, it's mine!* Val shifted the phone, flushing. She'd sounded like an asthmatic Pug, panting down the line.

"You would come with me to Roanoke? Meet me there?"

"Yeah. Sure. Umm...but...Jack wants to come, too." Her eyes were squeezed shut as she said it, like that would somehow lessen the blow. Why the hell had she said it anyway? She didn't want Jack to go. Was it to try and provoke Lucas, get some indication that he might be jealous? *That was stupid, Valerie.* She hadn't meant to mention Jack. But she'd gotten flustered.

Big silence. "No."

"Lucas—" She heard him exhale, and it raised goose bumps on her skin.

"Valerie, I want to have this conversation in person. Is Jack there now?"

"No," she said a little sullenly.

The line disconnected, and she went to hit redial again.

Her doorbell rang and she squealed like a thirteen year-old with Justin Bieber at the door. Val's heart began to pound and she went into frantic panic mode.

She looked in the mirror. *Yikes!Don't do that again.* Why hadn't she put on makeup? Why hadn't she done her hair, or in any way anticipated that he might show up?

Val brushed her hair, put on lipstick and dashed downstairs. She opened the door and there on the porch, leaning against the wooden porch rail, arms crossed, was Lucas. In the flesh.

Oh, that flesh.

He looked very modern. Black jeans and a black t-shirt that was beautifully tight and showcased the hard muscles of his arms. And his hair, still with a hint of curl, was disheveled in a way that she wouldn't have thought happened naturally. Did he spend a lot of time on his hair?

"Hey." *That was dumb.*

"Hey," he said back, but the way he said it sounded more ironic and had a soft accent in the undercurrent. Made even that crappy, inferior little word sound sexy.

Man am I in trouble now. She scowled. *Modern language. Modern look. WTF?*

"Would you like to discuss this somewhere else? We could have dinner? New York? Paris? Tell me where you would like to go."

She was going to say no, but then stopped. He could, and would, take her to dinner anywhere in the world? *Wow. That's fracking hot.* "Do something jerk-like," she grumbled.

"Excuse me?"

Her shoulders slumped. "No, don't take me anywhere...nice. Just come in—"

"No. Do not invite me in." He'd thrown out a hand towards her like he could stop her speaking with a gesture.

"Okay. I hadn't thought that would pose a problem. Sorry," she said, oddly discombobulated.

Lucas came closer to her, didn't touch her, just looked at her carefully, like she was somehow different than he expected. He came close enough that she would have had to tilt her head up to keep eye contact. She couldn't help it—she shifted back a little, keeping an extra few inches between them. The hollow of his throat was right in front of her face.

Lip level.

She stared at his mouth and his the carefully neutral expression. She wanted to make him smile, frown, press his lips together like he was flustered, too. If she kissed him, she could wipe that bland expression from him.

"I want to talk about what has happened. And you should never invite a vampire into your home." He sounded paternal and distant.

She shooed him away, and he stepped back, watching as she closed the door behind her and came outside. "Fine, we can go on a walk around the block."

He nodded and turned away from her, gliding down the steps gracefully, his tread light. Lucas paused on the walkway and looked back at her, fingers opening like he was going to help her down the steps, but then stopped and faced away from her, clasping his hands behind his back instead. He actually shook his head like he was disgusted.

At me.

God, this was awkward. Cold sweat, a stomach in knots. And him! He seemed almost... uncertain now. And while she was happy to confess that she'd had many a fantasy of him being as wrong footed as she was, now that she was experiencing it... it sucked. It didn't make her happy at all. She liked his ego and swagger.

Did I do that to him? She couldn't believe she had that kind of power. *Make up your mind, moron—did you crush him or does he not care?*

"So, how have you been?" she asked, desperate for some connection. She couldn't feel what he was thinking at all. If she tried to reach for him in that vague magicky way, it was like groping a rock. He was inert. They made it to the end of the sidewalk in front of her house, and she watched him hungrily as he looked at everything around him—everything except her. Lucas didn't stare at her like she stared at him.

He doesn't care. That's which one it is.

It was dark outside. The trees appeared black and she could see the big dipper up in the sky twinkling down at her. She heard a dog barking down the street, the sound of a car driving by, and it was like normal life.

He put his hands into the back pockets of his jeans, stood ramrod straight and looked bored. It expanded his chest, stretched the material a little bit, and she knew she was ogling him as he looked away from her.

Was he doing it on purpose? Giving her a chance to see the goods and all that she'd passed up, because he knew how much she wanted him?

His voice cut through the night, startling her. "After all my years, you would think I would have patience, but I do not. Speak what you mean to say. Do not attempt to spare my feelings or drag this out. Why have you changed your mind about Roanoke so soon?"

He crossed his arms again, his gaze resting on her face for a moment as he adjusted his stance. Setting his feet slightly apart while he waited. It made him a little shorter, now her eye level was his lips, not the hollow of his neck. Not actually that helpful. Just easier to reach.

She crossed her arms and realized they were mimicking each other. Some seriously closed-off posturing.

Lucas stared at the ground for a moment, and then his light blue eyes, which looked dark in the nighttime, came back to hers. Sliced her open from sternum to stomach, the look was so sharp.

She couldn't look at him. "Finding the Fey will help humans, right? Keep the vampires in check?"

"If they are alive, yes."

"That's important. So, let's do it."

"This is not your idea," he said flatly.

"How the hell do you know?" *Defensive much?* But he was right—it wasn't her idea.

"*He* wants you to do this. Where is he? Why is he not here with you? I find it odd he would let you meet with me alone," Lucas said, a warmth to his words that was far from sexual. She flushed and hoped he couldn't see it. "Jack doesn't know. He's out tonight."

Lucas looked away from her, brought his arms up, lacing his fingers behind his head. It made him taller, stretched his form out, lifting just the edge of his shirt so that a small amount of flesh was exposed.

She could see the very top of his hip bones, that pale, smooth skin, his stomach muscles that rippled and jutted out in cut lines. That gap was so small, and yet her reaction was huge. Her stomach fluttered, her hands opened, ready to reach out and touch him. Desire coiled through her, pooling in her core, making her damp. Ready. Wet.

Her desire to touch him was totally out of proportion to what—and how much—of him was exposed.

She wanted to strip him bare. Be with him here and now. *You're in the middle of the damned street, you horny moron.*

God, she wanted him. Oh, to put her palms on his waist. She'd heard his voice and her breath had been short. She'd seen him and she'd felt wet. But now, now that he was here and his body was on display, she needed him inside of her. It was a question of sanity, a fix for her addiction.

She took a step closer to him, and he took a step back, voice controlled but dark, scraping over her harshly. "You do not get us both. Is that why you wait until he is away?"

She jerked upright, desire put on simmer. "No!"

"Then what? Explain." He really didn't sound like he wanted to hear what she had to say.

She started walking. Wouldn't have this conversation while staring into his eyes and feeling horrifyingly vulnerable. She'd walk down the street feeling horribly vulnerable instead. "It's over between Jack and me. We tried but he—" She couldn't speak. It was so embarrassing. So humiliating how quickly things had fallen apart. She blinked back tears.

"He is sending you to the Fey."

She nodded.

"And so it is done?"

She nodded again. "It's so stupid, but no one wants me for *me*. No one will put me first. My safety or my happiness. I've got two stupidly hot guys who want my body, but that's not enough. I couldn't even get the tiniest violin to play a pity song for me because I'm so pathetic."

They had been walking slowly down the street. And it was only fitting that her feet should stop, rooted to the ground in misery, right in front of this one particular house. It wasn't grand. It was quaint. Four bedrooms, a doggy door, and a green lawn the husband was probably militant about.

It had a big backyard and a pool. "I used to babysit for them—the people who live in this house." She inclined her head towards the house, saw him turn to look at it. "I used to envy them. After I put the kids to bed, they'd come home...and they were so happy. It was so different than what I had. And I always wondered...if my mom had lived, if that's how my life would have been."

Val sat down on the curb, her head in her hands, feeling overwhelmed with sadness and despair. But she wanted him to know and understand. *Why? So he knows what you are giving up every time you see him? In hopes that he will leave you alone and go live his cold emotionless existence somewhere else?*

"My father...he took down all her pictures after she died. They were gone for years. When I found them again and saw what she looked like, I was surprised that she didn't look like the lady I babysat for. I hung one up in the dining room, and my dad—when he's home...I mean, when he *was* home—" There was a deep, painful sob lurking in her chest. It felt like a baseball shoved in her throat, and she tried to keep it inside, swallowing it back. "He wouldn't even look at it."

Valerie stood, ready to keep going, keep walking. Walk away from this house, from all the memories and do what she ought to do. Go with him to find the Fey. Shut the door on the life she had always wanted. That was a fantasy. People didn't get their fantasies. She needed to grow a pair and get over it.

And then Lucas was in front of her, his large body blocking out her view of the house, the street, the night. He was so close, she couldn't see anything else besides him. His hands were flush along her jaw, thumbs stroking her cheek, tilting her to look up into his eyes. She could feel his heat, smell his cologne. The space between them was charged, like that little space between magnets, forced close together. The very molecules between them buzzing.

His words were guttural and thick, like he was just as in the moment as she was. Wanted her just as much as she wanted him. And like he wanted her to remember this moment and him.

"*I* can keep you safe. I can give you more than any man ever could." His mouth was close to hers, each word bringing him a little closer. If she leaned forward at all, he'd be kissing her.

She felt his pause and restraint. *What is he waiting for?* She wanted him to kiss her, take her away from that house and what she couldn't have, give her something else to make everything worthwhile.

"Pleasure and lust...but not love," she said softly. It broke her heart.

"I can do this:I can make you happy. I will be attentive, cherish you and take care of you. I will put no one above you. These are not trivial things."

"I know." Tears slid down her cheeks, and his face dipped in, kissing them away. He made a sound deep in his chest that felt so sincere and honest she wanted to drop every hesitation and give in to him. She pulled back a little, stepping away, but he followed her, didn't let her go.

"But I will love you," she said. "That's the real problem. I will fall in love with you, and *every* day I'll know you're not in love with me."

He kissed her chastely on the lips. Then again and again. Each time a little longer, a little harder, his body moving closer and closer to hers. "I'm sorry. Truly I am," he said, so close their noses touched.

She could smell mint on his breath and, in a way, that made it worse—because it told her he knew how this was going to end. No objection of hers would sway him. He was going to kiss her.

He looked at her fiercely, the words barely above a heavy whisper. "I told you I would not let you go. You have come back, and now you are *mine*." His hand fisted into her hair at the nape of her neck.

A sign of his possession. It also reminded her how easy it would be for him to hurt her. Physically. Emotionally.

He can hurt me anytime he wants to. That's what love is, her mind whispered as though it were a coy secret. *Love is passion. Love is fear. Love is darkness.*

She'd throw everything away for him if she wasn't careful. No family, no white picket fence, just a destructive love that would end in death. Nothing was forever. Not even vampires, no matter what they claimed. Maybe that was what love was.

Mortal.

"How do you know it will not be love?" he said. "I will do everything I can, and it will be so close to love, you will never know the difference."

He was suddenly blurry as tears swamped her eyes. Val kept her eyes closed, like this was her last chance to keep herself together, keep pieces of herself just for *her*. He'd take everything he could see and, if he could see into her eyes, he'd take her soul too. So she squeezed them tight, but felt her body collapse under the weight of...what? Fate? Stupidity? An error so large it would be her death warrant?

"I do not make the same mistake twice, my Valkyrie," he said, his voice a mixture of lust and triumph.

His mouth was on hers instantly, demanding she open to him. And she did, twining her arms around his neck, relaxing every part of her, letting him take her weight and keep her safe. He held her flush against his chest, and she felt the world shimmer, as he took them somewhere else.

She opened her eyes—his bedroom.

His tongue met hers, lightly, gently. And then he picked her up, wrapping her legs around his waist effortlessly, still kissing her with such slow, sweet passion that she couldn't even think about fighting or stopping.

With a hand on her back, he lowered them to his bed, his heavy body settling over her. His elbows were next to her head, and he was watching his hand smooth her hair away from her temple. He wasn't smiling, didn't look triumphant, more contemplative more than anything. And she felt... everything.

His head lowered to hers, eyes open, almost daring her to look away from him. It was predatory, determined, the focus more than a man who's about to have sex...this was primal. He was going to make his mark on her.

"You will go nowhere else. You will *want* no one else." He pressed her close to him, making sure she felt the hard ridge of his erection through her clothes. "When I am done with you, you will be ruined for other men." Lucas kissed her slowly, his tongue in her mouth, his hand sliding down her side to her hip, gripping it and then the span of flesh on her upper thigh, where her skin was sensitive, hardwired to the core of her body. From a long way away, she heard herself cry out in need—and she didn't care.

His hand came back up to her chest, not touching her breast, but settling firmly underneath it, along her ribcage, almost burning a hole through her clothing.

It built her expectation—that hand settled on her as she waited for what would come next. What he would do next. His patience drove her crazy, the feel of his body on top of hers and the slow kiss as his tongue fucked hers. Every move was gentle and languid while her body wanted faster, more, everything.

Her breathing changed, body becoming restless, and she made a noise, urging him onwards and needing him to move. Her arms tightened around his neck, trying to bring him closer. Lucas shifted, hips pressing more firmly between her legs, so that all she felt was the steady throb and pulse of her core against his cock.

He surrounded her: his heavy weight on hers, that large hand that he wouldn't move, his taste and smell. There was nothing beyond him. He kissed her endlessly, and with each exhale she climbed higher, wound tighter.

And somewhere in the midst of her growing need she recognized the deliberateness of his actions. That with each exhale he was a little closer, increasing the pressure of his erection against her center minutely, so that she was closer and closer to the edge of orgasm—without him doing much of anything.

In some distant part of her, she knew that he was teaching her a lesson, proving to her that he could make her come, with only the barest touch of his body on hers. Even now he was scheming, ensuring she understood how much pleasure he could give her. More than any mortal man ever could.

Jerk!

She trembled and gasped into his mouth. Dimly aware that she should protest, maybe even slap him because he was so damned egotistical. But she was so *close*. One more breath, and she'd be there.

Val arched her hips against him and froze. A series of sweet, sharp bursts resonating through her as she cried out beneath him and came. His mouth slanted over hers, claiming everything, including the sound of her release. She felt him around her, could smell his cologne and clean skin, feel the slight abrasion of his chin against hers. Everything crystallized, the fog of lust that had gripped her from the moment he'd twined his hand in her hair, receding a little.

Damn him! It worked!

His lips were slightly swollen from kissing. His look was beyond knowing—it was the expression a predator shows its prey before batting it around a little. Was that the look he wore before he killed someone? A look that made a promise—that if she gave in, he'd make it good.

Make the death so sweet, she might beg him for it.

He pushed away from her, so that he stood next to the bed. He took off his shirt, and she looked at his chest. Smooth, pale and muscled. He still wore his jeans—the outline of his erection huge, hard and ready. She needed it, and him, inside of her now.

Always.

Lucas leaned forward and unsnapped her jeans, pulling them off of her, leaving her underwear on. Then he extended his hand, and she took it, let him pull her up a little as he pulled her shirt over her head, tossing it to the ground beside them. Val sat there, in Lucas' bedroom, clad only in her pink bra and underpants while he looked at her intently.

"I am going to make you come again," he said, and his hands settled on her raised knees, slid along the tops of her thighs to her inner thighs. His words sizzled over her, her inner muscles clenching, the empty feeling inside of her becoming an ache. He pushed her legs open, leaving her underwear on, his weight over her again as he settled between her legs, notching deep into the vee of her legs.

"I need you inside me," she said, near whimpering.

His body was taut, every inch of him like satin over steel. She moved under him, her body open and ready. She tilted her hips, wanting him to feel how soft and wet she was, like he'd feel it even through the layers of clothing. She kissed his neck, and then opened her mouth over his jugular as though she was going to bite down on him. Val knew he liked that, had done it to him once before, and it had almost made him lose control.

This time she'd make it happen. He wanted to make a demonstration of her desire? That he could make her come with a touch? Fine. She could do it too. She'd break his will right back.

She bit down, felt a shudder run through him, and gasped against his flesh. Her hands slid along his jaw, hands grabbing his head, forcing a kiss on him as she cried out his name, pouring the words into his mouth: "Take me, I need you. Please, Lucas. Please." Her hands slid down to his buttocks. The muscles bunched under her fingers and she tried to urge him closer still.

His brows drew down into a harsh expression, and he moaned in response. He palmed her hip, thrusting against her, his erection sliding over her clitoris. Her hands were between them, and she grabbed his cock through his clothing, then fumbled with the buttons of his jeans.

He jerked away from her, taking off the rest of his clothing. His cock was huge and hard, flush against his stomach as he settled back over her.

"My underwear," she said.

Lucas smiled slightly and, with the barest tug, he ripped them off of her, tossing them aside. He was over her, breathing hard, looking into her eyes as he took her hand between both their bodies, wrapped it around his cock, his fingers and the velvet slide of his shaft poised at the gate of her body. It was intimate and surreal, doing this together, focusing on the fact that they were both invested in the pleasure that was to come.

She felt the strain in his muscles and in her own as they lingered in that moment before they did something irrevocable. He pushed against her gently, giving her time to get used to his width.

He kissed her again, and then said, lips still on her mouth, "I want to bury myself in you. One hard thrust and sink home, so you know that you are mine."

His nostrils flared as he worked his way into her slowly. Too slowly. She wrapped her legs around his waist and drove her hips up to meet him, felt him lodge tight within her, and then he was moving, fast and hard, his forehead pressed to hers. He kissed her jaw, down the column of her throat, her collarbone. He moved faster, harder into her as she felt his breath on her pulse.

Val squeezed her thighs tight around his hips, clinging to him. She felt his lips kiss the flutter of her neck, his tongue lick her, and then he stopped, leaned back as though he was about to get off of her.

"No, stay," she said, and it felt like black smoke coiling through her as she shut her eyes in pleasure and expectation. That part of her—what she thought of as the Empath part of her reached outwards—needing him to bite her.

Eager for him to take her inside of him. Claim him just like he'd been claiming her. She tried to compel him with her body, moving under him, wanting to drive him higher, force him to do it.

She twisted her head, bared her neck to him. Slowly, so slowly, he descended that final inch, lips against her neck, a sound of the deepest pain coming from deep in his throat. His hair fell against her cheek.

The press of his lips on her neck affected her, making her beg him in a broken whisper, "Please, please. Bite me. Take me. Why can't I be in you, too? Come on. Come on."

And then the world turned around as he flipped them. She was on top, straddling him while he lay below her, eyes closed, head turned away, gathering himself. His stomach muscles bunched and released as he breathed.

She leaned down, her nipples grazing his chest, then kissed him hard, almost angrily—part of her unhappy that he still had that much control left, that he wouldn't give her what she wanted on a primal level. But more than that, the Empath in her wanted it. He was denying her, controlling himself and this— every move, kiss and release would be at his direction. Val wanted to give up, give in, let him position her, touch her and bring her anyway he wanted, but then what? If he controlled this too, there would be nothing left of her, *for* her.

He looked back at her, voice soft and intimate, slightly ragged, features as soft as they were ever going to be, passion making his skin flushed. Almost, but never quite human. "I could hurt you?" The words were slow, a question, like he couldn't remember the reason for not biting her either. "You think it's because I don't want you. I do. Heaven help us, I do."

He brought his hands up to her breasts, cupping them gently, thumbs sliding over the hardened peaks. She rose up on her knees, so his shaft was almost out of her completely. His hips lifted, chasing the wet heat of her body, pulling her back down as he pumped into her.

She shook her head and lifted up again. "You tell me I'm your weakness, but you're not weak."

"You can have anything else you want. I cannot let us do that." His hand slipped between her legs, finding her wet and hot, soaking. He flicked her, stroked her, worked on bringing her again.

His voice was a low scrape of sound, a vulgar whisper in the dark. "I know why you want it. I want that too. I want to drink you down and feel you burn through me. Then I could make you mine in every way. Have you here with my cock." He pulled her down onto him, sinking deep, and she cried out at the pleasure, writhing against him. "And here." His hand came up, cupping her neck, his thumb brushing her collarbone. "I want to mark you, take you. It is not only you that feels denied. There is an emptiness in me, too, and you could fill it."

He licked his lips. "The Others have always been thieves—vampires take lives, the Fey take happiness, Witches take from the elements. But an Empath takes emotion. That is their delight and torment. To take pleasure and pain, all the variations therein, and play with them." His eyes were on her neck again.

He shook his head almost sadly, and then he held her face gently in his hands as he moved under her, grinding the base of his cock against her core. "But you can tell me." He smiled at her, no teeth, a scornful smile. The smile of a villain. "Tell me what would happen to me if I drank you down."

She rocked forward, and he groaned, eyes closing and flashing open to hers. Her fingers sought his, twining with them. "I'd own you," she breathed, pressing her breasts flush to his chest, enjoying the rightness of the words.

Lucas laughed, an unfamiliar and peculiarly happy sound. Then he looked at her steadily. "That is something I will never deny."

"I want more." Val said, eyes already tracing his body, feeling wet, ready and expectant.

He smiled.

CHAPTER 15

His lips felt numb and his whole body was slightly...off. He licked his lips, felt how she watched him. Her gaze snapping to his mouth. It made his heart pound, sent blood rushing to his cock. Her expression changed from satisfaction to hunger. Lucas closed his eyes, needed a moment. He could still hear her cries echoing in his ears, still felt the slight tremors of her body milking his shaft.

Every piece of him felt different. His heart seemed to beat differently, every nerve is his body was *warm*. And his skin...he felt the bed sheets in places that he never had before. The way it wrapped around his leg, brushing the back of his knee. How had he never noticed?

Lucas wondered if he should tell her that even her kisses affected him. She thought she was getting nothing from him, that he was not compromising. But every kiss and lick, every fuck, every time he tasted her, part of her seeped into him.

It wasn't a lot. Like trying to survive on raindrops in the jungle—it prolonged the inevitable.

A slower way to die.

But it had been *so long* since he had felt anything that the slightest difference was near to overwhelming. Should he tell her? His Valkyrie would like that. She would like to know she impacted him. Had power over him.

Valhalla. He needed time. Time to think. He heard her make the slightest noise, like a purr, and then she was up on her elbow looking down at him. Her lips were swollen from kissing, her face flushed, her sweet pulse jack-hammering under her skin. Want slammed into him. Want that was worse than before. Every time he saw her, it was worse.

"I'm not done. I want more," she said, and her hand slid down his body, grabbed his cock. The smell of her and sex...They would never be done. Her fingers wrapped around him, and he thrust lightly into her palm. He was still wet from her come and his. She began to stroke him, up and down with a firm grip, the slide easy and warm.

She was rubbing herself into him. And even that would alter him. Her fingers swept over the tip of his cock and he jerked her over him, settling her on top of him, chest to chest, her sex open, surrounding him. He exhaled sharply wondered if she felt the slight tremor in his limbs. Would she know how foreign it was for him to want, no, *need*, anything this badly? He could go long periods without food, sleep, even companionship. And now he needed something. The slick heat of her body and the taste of her mouth, her soft flesh twined around his.

He murmured *something*, hands on her ass as he slid her silken flesh against him. That wasn't enough. Lucas rolled her over, desperate to be inside of her and in control. He wrapped his hand around his cock, nudged at her almost blindly. He

CAROLINE HANSON

143

needed to wait, had to slow down. And then the head of his shaft sank inside of her.

"Yes," he groaned and began to move within her. Hard strokes, pounding into her so hard she threw her hands above her head and braced herself on the wall. *Was he insane? How mortifying.* But he couldn't stop pumping into her. Instead he moved his arm, wedging his forearm behind her head and stopping their momentum with his arm.

"I'm sorry," he gasped.

She opened her eyes, seemed to have no idea what he was talking about. What he would be apologizing for. *Because this is not the plan. The plan is to make you come so hard, and for so long, that you do not leave. You go nowhere else.* Something sharp and jagged knifed through him, but he had no idea what the emotion might be. Jealousy? Possessiveness? That desperate feeling when one knows loss is looming before them?

Unchangeable and unavoidable.

Her thighs were like satin. He pulled her wider, lifting her leg so that her ankle rested on his shoulders, thrusting home, seeking an extra fraction of an inch, wanting to be deeper inside of her.

Deeper, more. No man would ever take her so deeply. *No one but me.* She tilted her hips, and there it was. His cock ached and he felt the climax there, ready to overwhelm him.

Her fingers gripped his ass, hard, like she wanted him to be deeper, too, and that was it. With a hoarse cry, he came, pumping into her endlessly. She kept moving, seeking her own release. His cock was so sensitive it hurt. *Irrelevant.* He would keep going, get her there. He had wanted her to come first. How had he gotten so distracted from his purpose?

This is sex for a reason, to bind her to me.

He pulled free from her and slid down her body, keeping her legs wide open and took her swollen clit into his mouth, tonguing it, sealing his lips around the flesh, giving just the right amount of suction to bring her hard and fast.

She screamed in pleasure, her body rigid. He felt her contractions on his tongue and felt a satisfaction, a smugness in knowing that he could bring her so quickly. She undid him, unmanned him. But he would take her with him.

"Don't stop," she said.

Never

He had made her spend over and over again. And yet she still needed more. He wanted to press her down into the bed, pin her, hold her still with his hand in her hair, his fangs in her neck, his cock in her core. Make her take it. He had made her come, would make her come all night, and he knew she was feeling that emptiness still.

Because she was an Empath. She would not be satisfied until he drank her blood.

He had been with enough empaths over the centuries to know that, no matter how satisfied she was, without blood she would still want more. He grinded his teeth together and flipped her over, pulling her ass into the air, plunging into her slick heat from behind. Taking her like a savage. Her fingers clawed into the mattress. On a moan she begged him to take her harder, little sobs of pleasure coming from her. He bent closer, weight on one arm while he used his other hand to stroke her in tight, fast circles.

"Oh god, I'm going to come," she whispered, and then she did. He felt it in his cock, and he came again, his movements disjointed as he lost his rhythm.

Thirsty. He was so unbelievably thirsty. He wanted her blood. Nothing else would do. But he could not. He must not do that. He turned her back over, and she made a small oomph as her back hit the sheets—again. They were both covered in sweat, a small bead of it at the hollow of her throat.

Do not, he commanded himself, even as his head lowered to her throat, sucking that drop of moisture off of her with an open-mouthed kiss. It burned him, ratcheting up his need higher.

She threw a leg over his thigh, then ground against him like she felt it, too. What if she had? What if there was just enough of *her* in him, that she could feel his desperation? He could not think. How many times had he tasted her and kissed her? Her lips, her core, her sweat, every inch of her body.

He would kiss her again, take her one more time, and that was it. "You will need my blood," he said, the impact of the words racing through him, dragging his balls up tight to his body.

"You will be sore if you do not." Time had passed. It could have been hours, days, weeks. He didn't know. Enough time so that he was a different creature than he had been before they entered this room.

She shook her head, touched his jaw with the palm of her hand. "No, keep going. I won't." Her words were slurred. She had no idea what this was, that her Empathic side would keep going, keep *wanting* until she had his blood. But she was tired. So tired, he could see it on her face. One more orgasm, and she would sleep. Her desire to have her blood within him would be manageable in the morning. One last time and then, if he had to, he would compel her to sleep.

Her eyes flashed open suddenly, languid need gone as her body tensed—not in arousal but *more*.

Dangerous. The thought skidded through his mind, beating through the lust and the haze. He pushed back on his arms, away from her, getting off the bed and holding a hand out. She didn't take it. Cocked her head to the side in question. "Shower. Then food," he said, noticing his words were fast.

"For who? For me or you?" she said, sounding intoxicated.

"We need a break. This is...time has passed."

She raised her eyebrows at him. "Is this how it is? With a vampire," she asked, voice slow, words slow, eyes half-lidded.

He didn't know what to say. How much to tell her. Would the day ever come where he wouldn't think through all the ramifications of what to tell her? She slid her foot up his thigh, leg open, his gaze instantly focused on how wet she was.

"You need blood and food," he said.

She looked at him for a very long moment, the words having an impact on her that he didn't understand. But all the things they had done, the small licks and tastes of her that he'd had, coiled through him, made his veins feel hot, like they flowed with lava. He looked at his hand—it was fisted. Every part of him was rigid with tension. He blinked, took a deep breath, released it and heard it. The faintest sound of shakiness, of stress, coursing through his body.

He felt panicked, like he needed to get up and move. He needed blood. He wanted hers. But more than anything, he wanted to go and find a room full of humans to slaughter. Twenty, maybe thirty of them, fill himself so full of blood that every hint of her that was inside of him would get crowded out. Bring back his cold, emotionless existence.

Really? That is what you want? Lie.

Lying to oneself was dangerous. Led to death and over-estimation of one's self. The truth of what he wanted was enough to make him weep or cower in fear. The image of his desire was perfectly clear in his mind: He would scrape his fangs over her pulse, pierce her lovely neck and have her feed him, remake him into someone else. His heart would beat for her and his existence would revolve around her and the feelings she gave him.

He wanted to slide down her body, lock his lips on the inside of her thigh that wasslick with passion and experience the taste of her blood mixed with the taste of their bodies as he fed from her.

He needed to end this before he did something stupid. Fear skidded up his spine. Fear that he might make a wrong decision after all the care he had taken with her. *What care?* He had left her to her own devices for years, just to avoid this moment. The moment where he lost control and made mistakes.

Five hundred years of numbness was being chipped away. Emotions hammered at him, only one of them clear as the night sky—fear. He pushed back from her, jerked his gaze away. Helplessly, looked back.

She had a smile on her face. The thought came again: *Dangerous.* He was unstable. She was determined. This interlude needed to end immediately.

"What are you going to give me, Lucas? This isn't normal, is it? This *want.* This *ache.* It's not just sex. It's sexual, but it's more and it's worse. The ache is everywhere inside of me. You need to fix it. You have to help me."

"My blood will calm you. You will eat, and then I can compel you to sleep. In the morning, when the hunger has left you, we will discuss this like rational beings."

"I don't want to take your blood. You know what I want. I need it to happen," she said, staring at his mouth. He pressed his lips into a flat line.

She laughed and rolled up on the bed, her look making him hard. A look that said she wouldn't stop, wasn't going to relent, and that she knew him better than he knew himself.

He doubted that.

He knew what he was capable of. For her, this was a game. He gave an ugly laugh, and she cocked her head at him, surprised.

"It's funny? Lucas, you can't just give, you have to take, as well. I'm me and I'm an Empath. That's what this is about. That's why I can't stop, isn't it? How much of me do you want? Just half of me? Just the easy part, and then you'll leave me frustrated and wanting...magic unfulfilled?" Anger crept into her voice, and it raised his own, like a tinny echo.

"You play with things you do not understand," he said, low and hard. But not harder than him.

She reached out a hand, twining their fingers together, pressing her palm flush against his. Val gave a light tug, pulling him back to the bed. She may as well have been tugging on his shaft, the way he gave in. He returned to the bed, one knee on it.

"Sit down," she said, and he did, giving her his back, feet on the floor. His hands were flat on his thighs.

Get out of this.

And then she was in front of him, standing between his legs, arms twining around his neck. She reeked of sex, and he tried to close down, reached for that dark hole inside of him that ate every scrap of light in the universe and tried to become *that*.

And nothing more.

Tonight, there was nothing but chaos inside of him. His hands lifted, settled on her thighs and he pulled her on him, over him, her warm folds sliding over the head of his cock, and he moaned hoarsely at the contact. He had tried to find his internal strength, but there was nothing left inside of him beyond desire. The need to take her again. To become nothing more than sex. So it was all he'd taste, smell and feel.

His cock ached, his heart hurt. *In her, just get* inside *of her. Come in her so hard, you empty everything out. All emotion and every thought.*

His hands swept along her body from her breasts, which he cupped and lifted, and then down, dragging his fingers down her waist and cutting in towards the vee of her legs. It felt like he was dragging her emotions, even her desire, to her sex.

"I understand," she whispered, and then she kissed him slowly and thoroughly. He opened his mouth for her, let her inside, wanting her to take him piece by piece and put him back together however she wanted.

She spoke softly, "In Café Rouge, I touched you. In my dorm room, I reached out. In Italy. I always come to *you*. *I'm* the one who can't resist, while you watch and wait. You take what I give, tell me when to stop, and offer me nothing in return." Her hands were in his hair, slid down to the base of his neck, nails trailing down him like silken claws.

"I'm giving you something," he said harshly and pushed her down, seating himself to the hilt inside of her body. He gasped at the sensation, felt a tremor inside of him, his cock harder.

Deeper. Get deeper.

She whispered in his ear, and the sensation tickled down his spine. "You give me this because you were forced to. You gave me the information about being an Empath because I was in your dreams. You don't give me *anything* voluntarily. And you won't take my blood either. And this—" She slid up and down his shaft. Leaving. Taking herself away.

Stay still, it does not matter. This is a game. Be patient. He put his hands on the bed, marked the passing of time in seconds. This was important, the pounding of his cock overrode everything, told him what he needed to do was take her, do what she wanted...but something was happening here.

Slow down.

No. He wanted to throw her on the bed. Instead, he fisted his hands in the sheets. Every muscle in his body locked into place as he held himself still. *Don't give in. Don't move. Voluntarily. What do I give voluntarily? What could she possibly mean?*

His heart was pounding, each beat sending more blood into his overstuffed cock. He lifted a hand an inch off the bed. He was going to give it to her. There was no question about that. He needed to...*wait.*

Do not touch her, do not grab her hip, or sink home. She was so wet. *So close.* He could feel the entrance of her body as she stayed poised above him, expectant. He wanted to look down and see how close his cock actually was to her. It felt a million miles away. But her heat was there. She dipped down onto the crown of him, and he closed his eyes. Had to. Lucas bit the inside of his lip to keep from yelling, praying she would not notice the betraying gesture.

She slid down onto him and he groaned. She rose back up and he wanted to beg for her to stay. The fact that he wanted it made him hesitate. The hot wetness of her....

Think.

"I'm not satisfied, Lucas. I need more than this. I need—"

He tilted his head up so his lips were beneath hers, eyes so close—as if he really was about to beg her. "Are you giving me an ultimatum? Already, you tell me you will...." *What? Go to another? Leave? Hate him? Force him?* He couldn't think. Didn't *know.*

What was he supposed to say? Someone needed to tell him what he was supposed to say. His chest felt tight in panic, he felt the need to come in every fiber of his being, the urge to drink her down and watch her swallow his blood. She was in him already. Didn't she know? Wasn't that enough? Couldn't she see the panic and the fear in him? Couldn't she feel it? He'd compromised!

"What are you saying? You'll leave me if I don't do what you want?" His voice was cold, as blinding as the Arctic. *Stay cold.*

"I'm telling you how I feel," she said.

She was lying. This was a threat. "I'm a King and a man—I offer you that." *I'm thirsty and empty. I need to possess you and keep you. I'll tie you to the bed and make sure you never leave if you force it.* He had to get distance, get out of here, or she'd know what a wreck he was.

This was awful. He felt like he'd woken from a bad dream. Couldn't remember what it was, knew that there was nothing to be scared of but terror pulsed through him.

No change in expression. Nothing altered. Lucas kept his breathing the same, clutched hard for shards of his broken control. *I will do this.*

She squeezed his biceps. "You know what I mean. Does it bother you to think that I might leave you? You say it like you don't care if I leave here right now and never came back."

Val hoped she sounded tougher than she felt. Could she convince him she'd leave him? Even though she was so filled with his cock, so exhausted from hours of multiple orgasms that she could barely move, let alone walk out the door.

His gaze narrowed and his nostrils flared as he shifted her, forcing her to lean back on his braced forearm, exposing her body so he could slip his hand between them. Without the slightest hesitation, he began pushing her towards another orgasm. It was almost relentless, felt disconnected somehow, like he'd closed down and was looking outside of himself at the both of them.

"You'd leave me?" he said fiercely, "leave what I can give you?" And, by the end of the question, she was on the edge—so close. His words were a hazy blur, but she got them. She heard the message. *You won't leave me. Only I can give you this. Where else would you go? I'll make you a slave to your own desires.*

She grabbed his wrist as hard as she could, felt her nails digging into his flesh as she forced him to stop touching her.

"Yes, I *will*," she said defiantly. He needed to know she was more than this. More than her body and need. The Empath part of her was new and foreign. She was still the same person she was before. She had already left him once, and she could do it again.

"No, my Valkyrie, I am made for you. Just as you are made for me." He looked down her body, at her heaving breasts, at her hand that shook, being so close, and yet so far away from satisfaction. "You won't." And then he twisted out of her grip, and his hand was back between her legs, his mouth kissing her breast.

He was right. It didn't matter.

No! It did. "Dammit," she said, her fist hard in his hair to pull him away from her while she again grabbed his wrist, pulling him from her body. The hardest thing she'd ever done.

"If you want me to stay and choose you, you have to give me something too," she said and sank down on him. "You're a king, but you won't be able to keep me." She kissed him, pulled back, spoke the words into his mouth, so that he would take them into his lungs, feel them slide through his veins. "I'll leave you, Lucas. I will."

"You take my cock inside you, bring me to climax again and again. Even now, you slide up and down my shaft to make your point. Now you will change tactics? Accuse me of being a coward?" His words were getting quieter and quieter as he spoke, more intense and meaningful.

This emotion in him was a fire, and his words came out, burned down low. "And *none* of that matters." His words were angry. He grabbed her hips, impaled himself within her. "The only thing that matters to me is keeping you. I have warned you and told you but..." He shook his head angrily, stood in a smooth motion, his hand on her ass, keeping her fused to his body before he turned back to the bed and lifted her off of him, tossing her back onto the mattress. His intensity was almost tangible, like a soft glow around him.

Yes! She thought with a dark, almost-malevolent pleasure, and she wondered if she'd said it aloud and not noticed because his eyes widened and, for the briefest moment, he checked himself. Stood still. Uninvolved, uncaring, inhuman.

Her legs fell open, wide as she could, watching hungrily as her movements jerked him into action, made him utter some noise halfway between a growl and a sign of frustration. He prowled up her body, took his cock in hand, and she watched him stroke it, his long, artistic fingers stroking himself from base to tip.

"All right. You have done it. You have called my bluff. I will not let you go. I will do anything to keep you with me. But believe me when I say that the day will come when we both regret it."

And then he moved, grabbed her hips and shoved himself inside of her in one exquisite move. She cried out in ecstasy. His hand was back in her hair, a hard fist as he ground her mouth against his. Hard. Lips pressed to bruise.

He sucked her lower lip into his mouth. His whole body was on edge, alive, shaking. The whole world stopped. The moment she would remember for the rest of her life as the day everything changed again.

Life had changed when her mother died. Life had changed when Lucas came to her and saved her. Changed when she chose Jack. And now, it was changing again—for the final time— not just a decision, but an irrevocable, final, ending point.

His fang pierced her, just the lightest prick. The faintest hint of copper filled her mouth. Barely a drop. The tiniest amount, but she *understood* the moment it touched him.

It was impact. Something that seared and scorched.

A perfect moment like praying in church, asking for a miracle and opening one's eyes to find sun streaming through the stained glass, illuminating the world in a new and profound way.

She was two people—herself and that tiny sparkle of blood that trembled on his tongue. And then he swallowed, the cords of his neck moving, his gaze locked on hers.

He licked his lips again and watched her. It ran through him, exploded into his veins, and she closed her eyes as feeling swamped her. She could see him behind her eyelids, as if his image was now burned in her brain. That little drop of blood, just the faintest piece, and she knew its progress, felt it warming him like striking flint in a snowstorm. So small, yet essential.

One of them would die without it.

This was what she was made for. Lucas was suddenly on her, in her, almost savage in his need for her. They were the same now—her gasps were his, his cries echoed in her. She felt him thrusting inside of her, felt the climax building behind her pelvic bone, each shudder a ricochet to her core and beyond. This time it would be enough, this time would be different than all the ones before. He called her name, his hand on her jaw, forcing her to look at him as he pumped into her.

"Come. Come for me. Come *with* me."

And she did. The last thought she had before she slept, as he pulled her close, wrapped his arms around her and shielded her with his body, was that she wanted him to do it again. One day, she would have to know what it would be like if it was more. If he drank and drank and drank until there was nothing left.

CHAPTER 16

Jack's steps slowed as he approached his apartment building. Rachel was sitting on the steps, and he barely managed to bite back a curse. She looked up and gave him an overly-cheerful smile. Her hair was cut in a choppy way, almost grazing the shoulders of her black leather jacket. She had jeans on and black boots, as if she was ready to spend an evening bar-hopping.

He put the key in the lock and opened the door, holding it open so she could follow him in. She stood there, looking at him for a long moment. He supposed one of them should say something.

"You want a written invitation?" he said unhappily, getting a slightly better grip on the door she had yet to walk through.

"Are you inviting me in?"

"Sure." He looked at her flatly.

"Why, Jack. I don't know if I should be flattered that you trust me not to kill you or offended because you trust me not to kill you." Her smile was bright and artless. A happy, vacant sort of smile he might associate with a cheerleader. Or, in her case, a hooker.

Expression blank. "In or out."

"Oh, *in*," she said, sauntering past him, a cloud of perfume in her wake, the words suggestive.

He stomped past her, up the landing to his door, opening that, too. She followed him inside, watching as he set a grocery bag on the table. His apartment was Spartan. Not even a picture on the wall. The paint was old and peeling.

"So, how long have you lived on Lucas' doorstep?" she asked.

"He's miles away," Jack said, taking beer out of the bag and walking into the miniscule kitchen.

"The Czech Republic is his. You're in Prague. You're pissing on his doorstep."

"Well, I'd rather *kill* him on his doorstep than piss on him, so I think I'm being quite civilized," he said, shutting the fridge door.

She blew out a breath, waiting impatiently while he used a bottle opener on his beer. "Where is Valerie these days?"

Jack took a sip, swallowed and waited. Rachel would tell him eventually. He refused to ask her.

A small smile formed on her lips, conveying a lot. *I can wait too*, the smile said. And she did. There was a clock somewhere nearby, and it was ticking.

Eventually, she sighed and spoke first. "Okay, I'll cut to the chase. Get your stuff, and let's go," Rachel said, shrugging her shoulders.

"Now?" he asked, voice rising in surprise.

"Yeah. I hate to tell you, Jack, but you're behind on this one. He's bagged and tagged her. They're going to Roanoke tonight. In about twenty minutes, actually. So if you want in...."

For a moment he thought the beer would come back up. "Tell me you're lying." His words were a whisper

"No. I'm not." The barest pause. The sort of pause someone gave when they had to give bad news, but didn't want to be the one to do it. "Sorry, Jack, but she's already with Lucas. She told him she'd help him, and Lucas wants me there tonight."

"When?" he asked, angrily.

"When what?"

"How long ago did she contact him?"

"Uh. Not sure. My guess would be recently," she said, not looking at him, staring fixedly at the worn-looking couch.

"Why?"

"If you're coming, go get your stuff. But keep in mind, no weapons," she said, giving him a don't-try-to-pull-any-crap expression.

"I'm not going without weapons," he said.

She rolled her shoulders. "I can't take you to my King and have you be armed. We both know you want to kill him. And I can't help you with that."

"You don't trust him. He's hurt you. Why do you care if I try to kill him? Christ, *you've* tried to kill him."

"Maybe I do and maybe I don't. But if you want to try to kill him, leave me out of it. Do it on your own time. I won't bring you armed."

"You'd let me go in there defenseless?" He was studying her carefully.

She looked him over for a moment, like she was trying to read him. And suddenly anger blossomed inside of her, like a bullet that explodes on impact. "Why wouldn't I, Jack? You're a means to an end. We *both* have an agenda. You don't like me. You don't trust me. You hate me. You'd rather kill me than look at me. So stop dicking around with this act like we're buddies, or are on the same side. I'm out for me. And you're doing this for you and for her." She shook her head, dragging her fingers through her hair. "But you can bring a knife or two," she grumbled after a moment.

"Why are you letting me bring a knife?"

She blew out a breath. "Because you'd be just as likely to kill him with a knife as you would with a crayon. Fuck, Jack. Tell me you're smarter than this. Tell me you have some sense of self-preservation. He will kill you if he can justify it. You can't let him do it out of self-defense."

"She'd never forgive him."

"Oh, dear. That sounded perilously close to suicide talk—which is just pathetic."

"No, it isn't. I *will* kill him. And I may die doing it. But I will choose my moment," he said, voice deep with promise.

"God save us from religious fruitcakes. That's what you sound like right now. Like this is some kind of jihad or kamikaze trip. Jack, listen"—she stepped closer to him—"if we find the Fey, they will do everything they can to kill Lucas. Everything. Your best chance is with them. And let's not forget your real prize. Marion is your real prize. Don't make a move on Lucas until the Fey bullshit is done. Wait until I get Molly out from the witches. If you can wait, I swear, I'll get you Marion myself."

She wanted to hit him, cover herself away, anything so he'd stop looking at her like that—like if he kept looking he'd see into the heart of her.

"I heard you cried when it happened," Jack said. It caught her unawares—a slap from the dark.

"And I heard you were terrible in the sack. That doesn't mean it's true."

"Just because *one* thing is a lie, doesn't mean the other is," he said, ignoring the jibe. Why was she offering him Marion?

"You're right—you can be terrible in the sack. That's all yours."

"Did you cry?" he asked, and this time he took a step closer.

"Who *cares*? What does it matter?"

"I can't believe you'd give me Marion. I don't. But I know Lucas could kill me without trying. I'm not an idiot. Give me five minutes to get my things."

"Wait." She rolled her eyes then said, "I don't want to keep having this conversation—this heart-to-heart bullshit really wears me out. So, let me give you the idiot's guide – *me* vampire, *you* tasty. Our goals are the same for a small window of time. That's it."

"Then, you did cry," he said slowly, trying to make the pieces fit. Was she lying to him and would save Marion the moment she could? Had she burned Marion's picture and celebrated because she knew he was coming over? Where was the lie? Did she love Marion or not?

"Who *fucking* cares? Yeah, I cried. That doesn't mean you know my motivations. I had to get Lucas off my back, and he needed to think I was invested in getting her out. *Or*, I really *do* care about Marion and my plan went wrong. In which case, I'm gonna bust Marion out of the clink the first chance I get. My crying tells you *nothing*," she snarled and grabbed the bottle of beer out of his hand, taking a drink of it before going to his couch and sitting down, giving him her back.

"I'm leaving in five. Lucas will be pissed if I'm late."

CHAPTER 17

Roanoke wasn't what Val expected. She'd looked on the internet, knew the land was owned by the state, that people came to visit and have a look at the place where one of the first English colonies was set up. And, of course, the most interesting part was the enduring mystery of what had happened to the colonists all those centuries ago. But seeing it was different.

It felt sad, somehow. She could believe a tragedy had happened here. Val stood at the edge of the water and looked out, trying to guess where the colony might have been, how far underwater it might be—assuming anything was left after four-hundred years.

The sun was setting, the late afternoon fading to night. Val was cold, a chill suddenly crossing her skin. She shivered, and Lucas wrapped an arm around her waist, moving into her so that his body blocked the wind.

He rested his chin on top of her head, his hands clasped in front of her, and she snuggled into his sweater, enjoying how warm he was. The solidity of his body. The moment was just so...normal.

Being this close to him, and knowing how they had spent the previous night, turned her on. Made her want to leave here and go back to bed.

He tilted her chin up and looked down at her, a small smile on his lips. "This will not take long. And then we can go."

Her heart fluttered as he bent down to kiss her. He kissed her slowly, the barest slide of his tongue across the seam of her lips. His grip tightened, as if holding on to her would keep him from doing more. And then he stopped, raised his head, looked back out at the water. Reluctantly, she followed his gaze.

"The shore has eroded a thousand feet since 1850," Lucas said. "The settlers built their fort 300 years before that. The original settlement is long gone." A pause. "Their things are probably still on the bottom of the ocean."

"What things?" Val asked.

Lucas let her go, took a step away from her, glaring at something behind her. "Why is he here?" His voice snapped out like a long, leather whip, and Val looked behind her, trying to figure out who Lucas was talking to.

Rachel was coming toward them, Jack walking beside her. Jack looked murderous. Val looked at Lucas. He looked murderous, too.

Oh, fuck!

"You didn't tell me it was invitation-only," Rachel said with a brittle smile. She bit her lip and looked to the ground, almost hunching-in on herself—she'd made a mistake. She knew it, and there would be repercussions. And frankly, Val was glad.

In addition to the monstrous black mark of almost killing her, bringing Jack here to Lucas, like two dogs and one bone, was not only super uncomfortable and distracting, but it wouldn't end well. Like body-bag-bad.

"What are you doing?" Val said to Rachel, moving towards her. "Are you *trying* to get him killed?"

All Rachel did was stir the pot and try to get Val, and the people she loved, killed. Rachel looked a bit stunned, but didn't respond, appealing to Lucas for help.

"No!" Val snarled at her angrily. "*I'm* talking to you. What are you doing? Why would you bring him here?" She was going towards Rachel like a hurricane—though, Lord only knew what she'd do when she got there. Tug her hair? Have a catfight? And Rachel took a step back, hands raised, mouth slightly open in shock.

If she says something about me being a kitten with claws, I'll deck the bitch. Val reached down and grabbed a large rock in her hand as she advanced towards Rachel. Was she really going to hit her with a rock?

"I won't touch her," Rachel said, still moving away from Val until Jack crossed in front of her, two feet from Val's face. Val jerked to a halt like there was an invisible barrier between her and Jack.

"Valerie. I want to talk to you. *Alone*," Jack said, voice cold with fury.

"*That* is not happening," Lucas said darkly, and Val jumped, shocked that his voice was so close behind her.

Val whirled around and poked Lucas hard in his invincible and gorgeously-ripped stomach. He made a slight 'oomph' sound, which she knew he only did for her benefit, since it didn't hurt. If he had wanted to, he could have made his flesh so hard she would have broken a nail.

"Don't you tell me what I can and can't do!" Val said and poked him again. He was right behind her, no doubt would have stopped her before she could get within scratching distance of Rachel.

He looked down at her, a small frown of confusion on his face. As though she were a terrier nipping at his shoes, and he wasn't sure if he should kick her away or wait until she got sick of gnawing on him.

"And you!" She turned back to Jack. "I don't want to talk to you, anyway."

"Val, don't be petty. This is serious," Jack said.

Rachel winced at Jack's words and put a hand out towards him.

"Petty? Me? After the crap you said to me? I want you out of here. I want you gone! I may never want to speak to you again."

"You heard her, take him back to where you found him," Lucas said to Rachel. Val heard the smug triumph in his voice. Rachel stared at Lucas for a moment, oddly indecisive.

Jack looked at Val entreatingly. "Look, we both said things we regret. That's what happens. We're family. This could be life or death. If something happens to you...*you know*. You know I would—"

Valerie wanted to kill him. "You always play that card with me. What *my* death would do to *you*. Why do I care? You don't give a shit what your death will do to *me*. You think he won't kill you? He makes Hitler look like a guy who just had a bad hobby!" She was shouting.

Jack turned away, and it seemed like it cost him. He was biting back some vicious comment, and she just knew it was along the lines of 'then how the hell can you fuck him? ' He stalked away from her, a dozen feet, maybe a little more.

Val put her hands in her hair, fisting them tightly like she would rip her hair out, feeling like a petulant child. "Fine. Then don't talk to me. And leave Lucas alone. Don't provoke him. And, for the record, if anyone calls me something pet-like or baby-like, I'm gonna lose it!"

"Well, we would not wish to wave a flag before the bull. Let us go," Lucas said. Jack cast a deadly look at Lucas, and then back to Val. The question was there, on his face: *Did you fuck him?*

Val turned away in disgust, already knowing she'd made the wrong decision, staring out at the water where the Roanoke settlement might be moldering away at the bottom of the ocean even as they stood here and argued.

There was a part of her that wanted to hurt Jack, tell him she'd screwed Lucas and wasso dehydrated and sore, she thought she wouldn't pee for a week. No, she'd say she *had* been in his bed for a week! Ugh. There was a lot of pain there. She was sick of him hurting her and knowing she could hurt him, too.

That was the trouble with family. They knew exactly how to tear each other down. They could rip out each other's hearts faster than a vampire, so long as they chose the rightly-wrong words.

Rachel said something, then cleared her throat and tried again. "Let's go that way. I can feel something over there," she said and pointed into the surrounding forest. Rachelstarted walking, and Jack went with her.

Val turned, finding Lucas staring at her, a look more cold and forbidding than anything she had ever seen. It was like they were back at the Challenge—he was unapproachable and untouchable.

Oooh, I just compared him to Hitler. And Hitler had been the nice guy. No nookie for me tonight. He turned and walked away, leaving her behind. How the hell was she going to apologize to him? Flowers? Candy? A blow job?

What could she say to him? They were here trying to find the handful of Others who he hadn't managed to slaughter. He'd done evil things—there was no erasing that. She couldn't ignore it. And he hadn't reformed. He hadn't even offered to reform, and frankly, she had not asked him to. *Because he wouldn't?*

At some point between his saving her life and giving her a capital 'O', she'd made the decision that *she* was an exception. He might kill everyone else. But not her. *Reality meet Valerie Dearborn.* Lucas was a monster! Wasn't he? Could she have slept with him if she really thought he was evil? She just didn't know.

This day couldn't get any worse, she thought, as she miserably trailed behind them.

CHAPTER 18

They walked into the forest, through the trees, Rachel in the lead, looking for some sort of psychic clue. At least that was the impression Val gathered. No one was particularly forthcoming. She tried to calm down, feeling jittery from...everything. Her confrontation with Jack just now. Seeing him again after their disastrous trip to Hawaii. From the knowledge that she and Lucas had to have some sort of conversation about what she'd said—which may or may not be fixable by oral sex.

And finally, because Lucas and Jack were on a collision course. It was unavoidable. And the outcome was a problem. No bookie in the world would bet on Jack. The odds weren't even a million to one. David and Goliath, the tortoise and the hare—all that was bullshit. In real life, the tortoise got turned into a hairbrush and David got squished, just like Jack would.

Could she prevent it somehow?

There would be no dissuading Jack. He had never listened to her. That wasn't how their relationship worked. There was no equal footing between them. He had a mission and he pursued it. Yeah, every now-and-again, Val got in the way, and they had a romantic interlude, but really, Jack had his mission, and there was no wavering.

Lucas would just have to be magnanimous enough to keep Jack alive. *So I'm gonna be on my knees forever.* The truth was that she'd forgotten her problems for a little while. The post-orgasmic glow had made everything seem farther away. *I'm a fucking idiot, and my life just got more complicated than ever.*

Leaves crackled underfoot, and she had to step around patches of mud, all that remained from the last winter storm.

Lucas said, "When the settlers were here, they arrived in the worst drought the area had experienced in 800 years. Their food supplies were gone. They did not get along well with the natives, and no further ships came from England for three years. Famine is a terrible thing." Val wanted to know more, but Rachel jumped in, saying to Val, "If you were up on your abilities, you'd be able to help"—slight pause—"probably."

"Thanks for the caveat. Really?" Val asked, allowing herself to be distracted. It'd be kind of cool to be in 'the know. ' *For once.*

Rachel stopped in a clearing and looked around. They all fell silent while Rachel walked around the area. It was a large space, maybe a hundred yards of bare earth. Trees surrounded them on all sides, but there were no rocks or even grass in the clearing. Just dirt and mud.

"How come *you're* doing this and not Lucas?" Val asked, curious.

Rachel smiled at her. "Because I'm the witch."

Valerie's mouth dropped open. "You're a witch?" *You mean W instead of B?*

Lucas raised an eyebrow and said lazily, "Why else would she be alive after the trouble she's caused?"

Her mouth went dry. "I thought...." Val felt sick at her probable misunderstanding. "I thought it was affection. That you let her live because you liked or... maybe even cared for her," Val said.

Lucas stared at Valerie with a blank expression, as though the words hadn't even registered. As though love had a definition he had never been able to comprehend. She'd called him Hitler, and, at first, he'd looked a little irritated. She'd wondered if she'd hurt his feelings, but now it was clear— she hadn't. Emotionally, there was no one home.

I better be wrong, or else I just boned a soulless monster.

Her ribcage seemed to contract, like a giant fist squeezing tight. Val hadn't realized what a cornerstone his not killing Rachel had been. Sure, he'd said it was for leverage over Marion, but she'd thought it was something real. A sign of his humanity.

Nope. No sign.

"There should be trees in this clearing," Lucas said. "There once was. And look at the pattern. The precise circle. This is not a natural formation. Nor is it recent."

Rachel tilted her head side to side. "Yeah...there is something here. But it's funky."

"Could you be more specific?" Val asked. It was getting cold. The night, her heart, everything beginning to freeze.

"Give her a minute," Jack snapped.

Val wanted to kill him. He did *not* just take Rachel's side over hers. "Her girlfriend killed your parents! She almost killed *me*. And you're going to defend her? Are you fucking high?" she yelled, totally at the end of her patience.

Jack stared at her, all expression wiped off his face. "She's not the most dangerous person here. Not by a long shot."

"Neither are you. But that doesn't mean you can *trust* her. Why the fuck do you keep going to her?"

"And I'm supposed to trust you? This *all* goes back to him. And here you are...canoodling with the fucker! We were supposed to do this together." He took a step closer to her.

"Yeah, I think we discussed that rightbefore you called me a whore. Believe it or not, that didn't make me want to spend more time with you."

Lucas appeared between them, moving so fast she could feel a slight breeze as he displaced the air around them. "Say another word, and I shall take you from here myself, Jack. We can leave here and forget all about the Fey in ten minutes, depending upon what we learn."

Jack shook his head, then turned and stalked away from them.

Rachel raised her brows and started talking to Lucas, kicking the dirt at the same time. "There was definitely a spell done here. A big one. And it was of the...more *elemental* variety shall we say."

"Fey," Lucas said flatly. "Cerdewellyn, perhaps."

"Who's he, and what does 'elemental' mean?" Jack asked.

"Cerdewellyn was the King of the Fey. He should be dead. But one never knows with the Fey. And 'elemental' is a tactful way of saying there was sex involved in the ritual. And blood," he said 'blood' tonelessly. So tonelessly, it reminded Val that he was a vampire and liked to have a splash of it on his cereal. Assuming he ate cereal.

Note to self, don't go to breakfast with Lucas.

"If you think he's dead, how could he have done it?" Val asked.

He turned and approached her, so she had to look up at him. Maybe making sure she really heard him. "I killed him. Chopped off his head and ran him through the heart with a sword. That is typically permanent for one of the Others. But he was old. Far older than I and, at one time, much more powerful. But as the centuries passed, the Fey weakened. When I slew him, I had expected it to be permanent. Only later was I told that he survived. Someone saw him."

Her heart was pounding. He was making a point. But damned if she knew what it was. That he liked chopping off heads?

Curiosity got the best of her. "Who saw him?"

Lucas turned to look at her, not at Jack, focused only on her. "Marion."

God damn it. How did I let myself sleep with him?

Rachel turned around and looked back at them, hands on her hips. "Marion hooked up with the Fey King? I didn't know that. Good for her." She sounded genuinely pleased.

"You don't care that your ex was with someone else?" Jack asked her, staring at Valerie. He'd ignored Marion's name, as though it hadn't been said. Val didn't trust his disinterest for a moment.

Rachel gave him a huge smile and looked pointedly at Val then Lucas, "No. Do *you*? I told you, I'm done with the mommy set. She was hard work. If she managed to get someone like him to look after her for a while, kudos to her."

"Marion was not with Cerdewellyn, but his queen."

Rachel snorted. "A lesbian to the very end. Once she went 'chick', she never wanted—"

"*What* have you found?" Lucas said.

Rachel cleared her throat rather theatrically. "Something went seriously wrong with the spell. There was a lot of magic here. There still is, actually. It's dormant, though. Get the right trigger and something big will happen. It's like we're walking over a minefield of magic out here. I don't know whose fault it was... but my money is on the witch."

Lucas walked close to her, looking from Rachel to the tree line and back again. "Why?"

"Because the magic *feels* Fey. The witch created the spell, like building a lock. The Fey should have had a key. But *their* magic, the key, is here. So, it didn't fucking fit. That's probably why nothing is growing here. It's like a magical Chernobyl."

"So, are they dead?" Jack asked blandly, like if she said yes he could leave here and go get a drink.

Rachel tsked. "Don't know. Maybe. I could try to check."

Lucas nodded slowly at Rachel, clearly thinking something through. "What is your guess? No matter how unlikely. We know the Fey were here. We know they did a spell, and it failed. And we know that they are now gone. What about their belongings and their dead? Would they all be at the bottom of the ocean?"

"I suspect it would have been a spell to establish this as their new home. Open a gateway into the Fey world. But it's not open."

"Then they would all be trapped?" Lucas said.

"Do you want me to check?" Rachel asked, then continued in a sing-song voice, "It's just a teensy drop. And I promise not to taste." She winked at Val.

It reminded her of the night Rachel almost killed her. Val took a step back, heart pounding in sudden fear. *I shouldn't be playing with the big boys.*

Lucas walked away, into the clearing, looking up at the trees and pivoting slowly in a circle like he was taking-in the view. "Rachel would need your blood, Valerie. Yours and hers, to do a re-creation spell. That would give her a vision of what happened." If he were human, this would be the spot where he took a deep breath, but he wasn't. So, this was the small break when he made like a momentary statue. "I do not want your blood spilled."

"I'll do it," Jack said.

"Your blood would be useless. It must be from an Other. And not a vampire. As with most of these things, it takes a pair. One person to make the offering another to perform the magic." Lucas looked at Jack superiorly, and Val knew Jack wanted to shank him.

"How much blood are we talking about here?" Val asked unhappily. A vision of blood gushing all over the ground made her feel a little sick. She really hated the sight of blood.

Especially mine. Plus, this was blood spilled in a really non-sexy way.

"A few drops. That's all," Rachel said and began to come closer.

Jack took a step towards Val, blocking her from Rachel. "Don't even think you're going near her with a blade."

Lucas was standing painfully still, watching Val from fifteen feet away. Watching how she had moved to stand behind Jack for protection when Rachel took a step towards her. Was Lucas irritated she hadn't gone to him for protection instead?

She hadn't done it on purpose. It was habit. Jack had always protected her. Lucas, well, he was just happy being in her pants. He'd protect her for that reason, but Jack did it because he loved her.

How many egos was she going to have to stroke on this little adventure? She moved away from all of them, walking to the edge of the clearing and hanging out under a giant tree.

Lucas looked to Rachel and said something in a foreign language. Rachel shrugged and said something equally unintelligible back. The back and forth went on for a few minutes while she and Jack watched in growing agitation.

Then they were done, and Rachel switched to English. "Right. He's going to go wait...somewhere out of bloodshot—in case the mere scent of your blood sends him into a frenzy—"

"What?" Jack said, in a deadly tone.

"The cliff notes? He wants her blood bad, but is abstaining. He's gotta watch the figure. I know I watch his figure."

"Rachel. You do not need to be given such a long leash," Lucas said.

Rachel turned to Lucas, the picture of abject apology. "I'm sorry. You're right."

Val rubbed her eyes, and when she opened them Lucas was gone, leaving her alone with Jack and Rachel in the middle of nowhere, ready to spill her blood.

BEST. DAY. EVER.

CHAPTER 19

"Is it going to hurt?" Val asked.

Rachel looked at her distractedly, opening up a black backpack and taking out some herbs and a couple of stained wooden bowls. "Do you want it to?"

Rachel laughed at Valerie's disgusted look.

"No, Val, it probably won't hurt. Magic is funny that way. It's one of those pleasure/pain things. It's either going to feel really good, or it's going to hurt. And that's up to you. If you're uptight and resistant, if you fight it, then it might hurt. But if you lay back and let it happen... well, you just might like it, little girl," Rachel said distractedly. Like the comment was an afterthought.

But still.... *Ewww*.

Val wanted to change the subject. "So, how long have you been a witch?"

Rachel looked through the twenty or so, Ziploc baggies of herbs she had spread out on the ground. "I was born a witch. Raised a witch," she said, holding one bag up so she could see the contents clearly in the fading light.

"Well, that's succinct. Um, is that marijuana?" Val asked.

"No. Mongolian Moss. Lucas found me. Took me from the coven and gave me a life. Then he gave me Marion. I'll always be grateful to him."

Valerie held back a startled noise. "Grateful? He took you from your family and gave you to a monster, and you're happy about it? That's what you're saying?"

"Um, *no*, that's what *you're* saying. You don't know witches. They were burned at the stake for a reason. Nasty, evil women. I was very talented, and when Lucas took me away... I was on a dark path. I needed a witch-based After School Special." Rachel was looking at the ground as she said in a deep, narrator-style tone, "Just say no."

"But now you're a white witch? Gray witch? Glenda?" Val said sarcastically. Rachel had been Marion's sweetie—no amount of bleach was going to make her white.

"There is no such thing as a white witch. All magic is steeped in darkness. All power comes from death and harm."

"Enchanting." Valerie felt goose bumps rise on her arms.

Rachel held herself stiffly, spoke too confidently...like whatever she'd done had been so bad she had to hold herself perfectly still, or it would come and get her.

"Witches are tied to the earth. They force the earth to give up its strength and power, or they take it from people and animals. Pain and death charge our batteries. It's like splitting apart an atom—the energy released is something quantifiable, something we can take and channel. And I'm strong. But there are less invasive ways to take power, and that's what Lucas gave me. The freedom to not need a death for my magic. Marion...

she was a twisted woman. The years had not been kind to her. She was a little bit broken. That's what happens to vampires. We shouldn't live as long as we do. It warps us, makes us odd. Marion was almost childlike in her wonder and pleasure. But *normal* things didn't bring her pleasure. Violence, pain—those are the things that she liked. And those were the things I needed to survive." Rachel shrugged like it was no big deal. Herbody language at odds to the intensity of her words.

Val's voice was quiet. "So you *did* love her."

"That *does* seem to be the topic people want to ask about," Rachel muttered. "She was my first love. My *only* love. As twisted as she was, she looked upon me with joy. I was a fucking *revelation* to her. The darkness I need to thrive, she craved. Whatever I needed to do to sustain myself, she welcomed. Isn't that love? To find that *one* person who can take our darkest selves and cherish them? Look at our pain and awfulness without flinching?"

"No," Val said hesitantly, thinking the statement through. "I don't think that's love. I think that's taking someone down with you. Love is knowing that someone wants more for you, wants you for yourself and the best possible *version* of yourself that you can be. And that even though we might stumble, or fail at being good, they love us and know we'll get there eventually. It's support."

Rachel laughed darkly. "I think we are speaking of the same thing, Valerie. That's why Lucas is drawn to you. You cast love in terms of lightness and goodness because that's what you are. I cast it in darkness because that's the creature I am. Whether I want to be or not. And when it was going to break me—the killing and the torturing—when I could do it no longer without succumbing utterly to evil? *That's* when Lucas found me. He gave me shelter, tied me to Marion. He gave me a gift."

Rachel was walking a circle, sprinkling the moss on the ground as she talked.

"That's fucking poetic," Val said, feeling like Rachel was putting her on. "Then how could you turn on him? Marion tried to kill him."

"Lucas is a big boy. And make no mistake, it wasn't just the two of us who revolted—lots more would have, but they knew it was hopeless. Besides, Marion wasn't going to beat Lucas."

"They why did she try?" Valerie asked.

"Because Marion was bat-shit crazy, that's why. Do you know who can kill Lucas? The Fey. The wolves. They can kill him. And they probably will. And, if we live, we can say we were there. Look for the upside, right? Now let's do this spell. We can bond later over margaritas."

"I don't want to get to know you. Why are you telling me all this, anyway?" Val was genuinely confused.

Rachel looked at her, an earnest expression on her face. "Because the game has changed, Valerie. You're my boss's girlfriend. And I *like* being alive." Her grin was wolfish.

"So now you'll be nice to me? You can't just betray someone and then be forgiven."

"Really? I think you can. If you're valuable enough, like say, the only witch a vamp has had on the payroll for 200 years. Then, yeah, I can get a free pass or two on betrayal."

Val sat down on the ground, pulling her knees up to her chest. "I can't believe he trusts you."

Rachel laughed harshly. "Lucas doesn't t*rust* anyone. If you haven't figured that out by now, then you're in deep shit. He makes people obey him because, if they don't, he'll kill them. Brute force doesn't need trust. It only needs the occasional reminder of who is in charge. Like the Challenge, for example."

Talking to Rachel was like talking to the mad hatter or Jar Jar Binks—hard fucking work. "That makes it sound like he wanted a Challenge."

Rachel shrugged non-commitally.

"No. If he had wanted a Challenge to—what—purge the ranks or see who was still loyal, then he manipulated you, too and got you to do what he wanted."

"Or?" Rachel asked, dusting her hands, and then putting all her plants back in the backpack.

"Or...you were in on it the whole time? Which you were not." *Right?*

Rachel came towards her, knife in her hand, holding it hilt-out to Valerie. She crouched down before her, her shiny, chin-length hair swinging into her face. "I've led you down the garden path, Valerie. I've told you stuff and tried to help you out. Don't forget it."

The knife was warm, the handle a dark, worn leather so old, it was black. *Or it's stained with vampire blood.* "How have you helped me? You've talked in riddles, tried to kill me, and now you've left me super-confused. Everything is conjecture—you haven't given me a single straight answer."

She smiled at her. "Confused might keep you alive. Trust is what will get you killed. I don't charge by the hour or anything, so no worries."

Jack had been deadly silent, so far away she had to turn and look for him. His arms were crossed, and he was leaning against a tree like he was bored out of his mind and not paying any attention at all.

Sure.

CHAPTER 20

Valerie watched her blood drip into the bowl Rachel held. "I'm bleeding because of you. Again. We have to stop meeting this way," Val said, hearing a dull ringing in her ears. *Please don't faint.*

"Bind it up tightly, all right? Here's a Band-Aid. It's a small cut, but you don't want to drip any. Got it?" Rachel said dismissively.

Just looking at the cut made Val a little woozy. *What a wuss.*

Rachel set the bowl on the ground and squatted down next to it, raising the knife to her own hand.

"Whoa! Hold up. Are you going to cut yourself?"

Rachel looked up at her, a wide smile on her face as she said sarcastically, "What part of *blood magic* did you not get? Your blood is the offering, mine is the conduit for the spell. I'm going to mix them."

"I get it, but seriously, hold up. I'm going to... go over there and sit down," Val said weakly.

Rachel frowned at her. "You're *still* yucky around blood? How is that possible? There is a lot of blood involved when dating a vampire."

"She's not dating him," Jack growled, and both Valerie and Rachel jumped.

"Jesus, forgot you were there," Rachel said.

Val decided to be the bigger person and ignore Jack's comment. "Well, maybe I would be over my fear if it wasn't *my* blood that kept getting spilled or someone wasn't getting their heads ripped off or heart ripped out in front of me. I've always got a front-row seat." Breathing deeply she walked into the woods a little, heard Rachel begin to chant and could only imagine what was going on – blood, that was what was going on.

She walked a little further into the clearing and sat down on the ground. Once upon a time, someone had told her that it was impossible to faint if one was lying down. Val hoped that was true. Ignoring the sticks that poked her in the ass and back, she lay flat on the ground, resting her arms at her sides.

She took a few breaths, listening to the sounds of the forest around her. Her bloody hand felt hot, as though it was infected. Dirt from the forest floor clung to the cut where she must have brushed it on the ground. She could hear the shushing of her blood pumping around her body, felt her muscles relax.

The forest grew quiet, hushed. *Something is coming.* The birds knew it and they quieted. The trees became still. Anticipation.

She felt her heartbeat stop.

CHAPTER 21

Val was running. Her breathing was even, steady, and she knew her lungs would never burn, her muscles wouldn't tire. Her feet flew over the dirt path before her, as though she had angels guiding her way.

The sun streamed through the branches overhead, little pockets of light that she passed through and around. The smell of trees and fresh air filled her lungs. Heady and invasive.

Keep running.

Keep going.

He will tell you when to stop.

Her long, gray dress was kicked out in front of her, then billowed out in back as she sped through the trees.

And then the forest was gone, and she was in a meadow filled with flowers of all the colors of the rainbow. It was almost too bright.

Manic color.

The flowers came to her shins, the blossoms all open and at that perfect moment of bloom where they were all life without a hint of brown decay.

A light breeze ruffled her hair, made the flowers shift in a wave, and she felt a moment of lightness. Like she could spread her arms and fly away. A moment of perfect happiness.

She heard steps, the slight springing of undergrowth as it was trampled, and she turned to find a man coming towards her.

An inhumanly-beautiful man. Her urge was to run to him, throw her arms around him, and clasp him close.

Clasp him? I'm not much of a clasper.

She watched him approach. The breeze caught his wavy black hair and tossed it onto his forehead. As if the wind itself wanted to touch him. He wore black breeches and white hose, a crisp, white shirt with a spill of fabric down the front. A black coat molded to his body, like a riding coat. He looked up, his eyes brown, lashes thick, skin tanned, as though he spent most of his life outdoors in the sun—and the sun loved him, the plants loved him. Even the trees were leaning towards him. If Lucas was death, he was life.

Who is he?

The wind sighed the answer, carrying it to her in a soft tone, light and sad—*Cerdewellyn.*

He stopped next to her, and she looked up into his dark gaze, his eyes the color of wet earth. His lips were full, his jaw square. He had a Roman-look to him, which seemed a bit odd.

"I thought the Fey were Irish?"

"We started elsewhere. The Fey. We've had many forms over the centuries. Many locations where we dwelled." When he spoke, he sounded like he was from Europe, somewhere between the East and the West, but not Irish after all.

She nodded like she understood.

"Where did these come from?" Val asked him, looking down at her hand and the flowers that she was holding onto tightly. She'd been picking them absently. She'd run and run, until a flower would catch her eye and she'd feel compelled to take it.

He smiled at her, a closed-lip smile, like he was indulgent and secretive at once. "You gathered them. You have five. There are seven left." He held out his hand.

She gave them to him without hesitation.

"You are making good progress, and I thank you. Now come here."

"Why?" Val asked, even as she moved closer.

"This is a secret. It's our secret. Do you understand?"

"Yes." *No.*

"And so I must make sure it stays a secret."

He touched her, stroked a hand down her cheek. "Forget all about this, Valerie. Forget, until we meet again."

Val opened her eyes, examined her bleeding hand that was covered in dirt, and couldn't believe she'd fainted. What the hell was she doing hanging around with vampires when she fainted at the sight of blood?

She stood and went back to the clearing.

CHAPTER 22

Lucas stalked through the forest. This had been a mistake. He had wanted to see her with Jack. See how she interacted with him—now that she and Lucas had been intimate. He had told Rachel to bring Jack here so he could see the reality of their feud.

What on earth had possessed him? *Jealousy.* One drop of her glorious, Empathic blood, and he had given in to human emotion.

He had waited too long. Saving her at sixteen, rescuing her and then leaving her to live a life while he waited, patiently, like a spider hoping she'd wander into his web. That had been a foolish decision. Apparently, he had waited just long enough to make sure she loved another.

Irrevocably.

A young love that would mark her soul for all eternity. He had stayed away out of self-preservation, and then had failed, drawn to her like a moth to a flame.

She was a weakness. *His* weakness. If he were a smarter man, as ruthless as he had been centuries ago, she'd be dead right now.

What she represented—excitement, feeling, passion, joy and despair—were things he craved. He was honest enough with himself to admit it was his weakness.

She had told him that she would fall in love with him. *So honest.* And all he had thought was '*good.*' In the darkest corner of his black heart, that had been the moment he had exulted. Known without a doubt that he had won. She would love him if she came to his bed.

His Valkyrie was not a casual lover. Just like the Valkyries of legend, she chose her warriors, and would take his soul if she could. She could not simply 'scratch an itch,' let a man into her body, without engaging her heart.

There had been a plan: make love to her, seduce her, fuck her, take her in every way until she breathed, ate, and came only for him. Physically, he had been there, ready to be just as seduced by her flesh as he intended her to be with his. Had wanted to taste her, and claim her in every possible way a man could.

It had been so easy.

Until she had given him the ultimatum. Drink her blood, or she would not love him. As if that was possible. As if she would be able to hold herself back from love. But a tiny part of him had feared that she could do it—leave him just like she had left Jack.

He was always careful. And yet, he had given in. Her passion, kisses, and heat had all infected him, altered him just enough so that he chose poorly. It was his age. Someone younger, like Rachel, wouldn't have been affected by making love to an Empath.

But he had been. Valerie had disconnected him from his cold shell, made him feel panicky, desperate, overwhelmed and hungry. She had not offered anything he did not want. Her blood was something he would kill for. One momentary lapse, his slight confusion, and she had won.

Pure, blinding panic had made him believe her. Otherwise, he would not have given in. *I did not want to say no.* Because she and her blood were the only things in all the world that were left for him to want.

How would he keep saying 'no' to her when all he wanted, with every dead fiber of his being, was to say 'yes? ' When he was deep inside her body, her breasts flush to his, her tongue in his mouth, how would he say no?

What if you harm her? Kill the Golden Goose in your lust? He imagined drinking her dry, feeling her blood pound through him until he felt like every pore would explode from the pressure. For years, he had only to think of it, and it had made him hard as stone.

And now. Now that he knew her, now that he had tasted one measly drop of her rare blood, he felt—

He heard a shout in the forest. Jack. Calling for Valerie. Lucas swore and, using his preternatural speed, raced to find her.

CHAPTER 23

One moment Jack was scanning the trees looking for Val and the next Lucas was in front of him. That cold fucker looked like he'd just come from the pub, he was so smooth and unruffled.

"Where is she?" Lucas asked in that bored tone.

Jack looked the other man up and down. Had an almost impossible urge to shoot him, but he couldn't. He'd see Lucas dead but he'd only get one chance to do it and by god he wasn't going to fuck it up. But that didn't mean he'd pretend to like him. "If I knew where the fuck she was, why would I call her?" Jack snarled.

Lucas didn't change expression, his gaze scanning the area briefly before returning to Jack, so much time having passed that Jack was about ready to move away and go searching deeper into the woods when Lucas finally spoke in that same dispassionate way, "Well then, where the *fuck* did you lose her?" he said, mimicking Jack 's words. The peculiar delivery of the words, as though he'd never said fuck before, took Jack aback.

How could Valerie feel anything for this monster? Let alone want to sleep with him? Jack felt like he was as hetero as they came, but he could understand that certain men had an appeal, but this guy was so...*wrong*.

Lucas cut into his thoughts, "We are in a Fey forest. She could be in grave danger. Tell me what happened. Now."

Jack felt a chill down his spine at Lucas' killing look. "I thought she was on a bathroom break. So you've decided the Fey are alive? What changed?"

"Answer the question or I will force it from you. I want her unharmed." Lucas called for Rachel and she instantly appeared beside him, slightly out of breath.

"Where is Valerie?"

Rachel grimaced and bit her lip worriedly. "She donated blood for the spell. I cut myself and it made her squeamish so she backed out of the circle. I had a vision, and when I came to, she was just gone."

Lucas frowned and stared hard at Rachel, "Are the Fey alive then?"

"They were. But the spell didn't work, the portal didn't open. Cerdewellyn was there and he took everyone, all the colonists and the Fey, some wolves, even a witch into the Fey dimension."

Jack watched as Lucas turned around in a circle, scanning all directions for her. "If we do not find her in five minutes we must assume she has been taken. You will do a spell and open a portal. Go get what you will need and return—"

Rachel and Lucas suddenly turned, looking in the same direction like a hound spotting its prey. A moment later Jack heard a branch snap. Then Valerie came through the trees and Jack felt his heart squeeze in relief.

He went forward, wrapping her in his arms for a brief moment, felt her body go rigid as she tried to pull away from him.

"Where did you go?" Lucas asked, the words a hard slap.

"Nowhere. I just wandered around a little. I don't like the sight of blood.

"You will not do that again. You cannot leave the group. No, I amend that, you *cannot* leave my side."

A look of disgust crossed Val's face. "You're the one who chickened out at the sight of blood first. Mr. One-drop-will-turn-me-into-a-crazed-killer."

"They called for you. Why did you not respond?" Lucas asked, suddenly next to her. He put a hand on her face, cupping it gently and then pulled her to her, hugging her. He was warm and strong and she felt lust spiral through her again.

I *just* walked away! I didn't *go* anywhere. I've been right over there the whole time," she said, talking into his sweater. He moved back a ways and kissed her gently on the lips—a promise of what was to come. She could almost forget that Jack and Rachel were there, she wanted him so much.

He frowned and said to Rachel. "What did you see?"

"The Fey were here. They tried to open up their realm and it didn't work. Their witch believed it was because the Fey had changed Queens. So they went into the portal and—for whatever reason, they've never come out.

"Who was the witch?"

"Nantanya? Heard of her. But she wasn't my blood line so I'm not sure what exactly she would have done. I'd have to research it."

"So they are trapped?" Lucas asked.

Rachel shrugged. "I don't know. What do you want to do? Try to open the portal, see if anyone is still around over there? Maybe they want to be hidden. Truthfully, I'd give up. What's the point?"

Lucas stared at Valerie in a serious way. Looking from her head, travelling down her body to her feet. His face was grim. "I do not know. I want time to think about it. I had not expected this sort of problem. Honestly, I had assumed they were gone."

"Then why are we looking for them?" Val asked. "Why bring us here and not follow through in finding them? You never wanted to find them, did you?" Val guessed. *Then what did he want?* Not a person. What's left? He had commented about their stuff being underwater. She'd thought he was just being a little macabre. Maybe not.

There was that Fey ring he had planned on wearing to the ball. The I-want-to-shred-you-and-make-hot-monkey-love-with-you ring. "Is that it? It's an object you want?"

Rachel piped in, "The Fey use glamour and illusion. Their magic is from the earth and based in life. It's not compatible with vampires. Plus most of their magic is gone, right? Marion had a few Fey trinkets and would talk about the things they'd once made. But that was centuries ago, I thought the power of their stuff had diminished—what with the extinction and all." She looked at Lucas like from a certain angle he had two heads.

Lucas ignored them both. Stared hard at Valerie like she had the answer. Was the answer. He looked the same, she knew there was no visible sign of his feelings, but he was coming for her now, she could feel it.

"We will meet you later and discuss it," Lucas said over his shoulder and then he wrapped his arm around her, standing stiff and proud, like he didn't want to touch her at all and took her away from the forest, transporting them back to his room.

The moment they were in his bedroom she took a step back. "What's the deal? What do you want with the Fey?"

He ignored her, seemed calm but she could feel the intensity in him. And right along with it, like the two emotions fuelled each other, was lust.

His hands were on her instantly as he unbuttoned her coat and threw it to the corner of the room. And then he pulled her shirt up, making her lift her arms so she didn't get tangled in her clothing. Val squeaked in protest.

"What are you doing?" she asked.

"Have you forgotten so soon? That is an unacceptable oversight on my part." And then his shirt was gone. He slipped off his shoes and his hands came back to her skirt, lingered at the buttons along the waistband.

He was breathing faster, his brow furrowed in a frown, lips slightly parted. And then he shook his head, mumbling to her or him she didn't know which. "No, I like this. Keep the skirt on. The skirt and the boots."

Val waited in a moment of overwhelming lust and suspense as she stood before him. She looked at his scarred hands, his beautiful fingers, and everything fell away. Even the impending doom and her distrust of him as she was consumed with lust. She always wanted him.

He entered a room and she was stunned, like one of those animals that gets clubbed over the head and then doesn't protest as it's dragged off to become dinner. But now, seeing him as befuddled by desire for her as she was for him? It wasn't just arousing, she felt like she was drowning in want.

His hands were under her skirt and she felt her underwear tear again as he ripped the seams of it, pulling it off. Cool air hit her flesh, her skirt raised in the back as his hands palmed, then kneaded her ass.

His head descended, kissing her, demanding she open her mouth for his kiss. Her lips parted and his tongue was instantly in her mouth, kissing her, tasting her and she couldn't help but moan. She felt him take another breath, like he was devouring her passion. As if he had to take *something* from her since he wouldn't be taking her blood.

She walked backwards towards the bed and he followed, crowding close, a noise like a growl coming from his lips as he kissed her jaw and then the area behind her ear. He was almost frantic, his heavy hand hiking up her skirt as soon as her back hit the mattress. His fingers were on her, between her legs, his touch surprisingly gentle considering that he was almost trembling with... *something*.

"If I could kill him, I would. If I thought I could do it without losing you, I would wipe him from the earth. You are mine, Valerie. Do you understand that? I will not share you, will not allow you to go back to him, there will *never* be anyone else," he said, commanding her.

Lucas slipped down her body, urging her to open her legs, then settling between her thighs, spreading open her soft flesh to his hungry gaze. And then he kissed her, open mouthed, as though he could make her obey him, wipe Jack from her mind and body with his touch.

She was instantly arching under him, grinding closer, felt his hands move to her hips as he pulled her infinitesimally closer. Held her how he wanted her. Her hands fisted in his hair, pulling him closer, her thighs locking on his head. And then she was coming, long and hard, with a cry.

Waves of pleasure rippled through her, she was still coming when he was suddenly on top of her, his hand lifting her thigh, opening her as he sank into her in one powerful thrust. The power of it, the pleasure of him stretching her wide stole her breath. He was so large that if she hadn't been aroused and made to spend first, it would have hurt. Instead it was just right, almost profound.

He pounded inside of her, thrusting in hard, fast strokes, claiming her. "Tell me, Valerie. Tell me you are mine," he said in a harsh whisper.

She looked into his eyes, shocked to see the emotion there. It wasn't love. It wasn't human or pretty but it was an emotion and he was drowning in it. She could see it in the set of his mouth, feel it in the possessive grip he had on her and the way he kept her close even as he ruthlessly sought his own release in the depths of her body.

"My name. You will call my name as you come. Do you understand me?" His hand slipped between their bodies, his fingers rubbing her, stroking her again. She almost told him she wouldn't be able to, that it was too soon after the last climax to come again, but then she felt it building within her.

She closed her eyes and met him thrust for thrust, hands on his shoulders, nails embedded in his back. He hissed in pleasure, thrust faster and she felt the orgasm winding tight within her like a wave pulling back from the shore.

"Say it, my Valkyrie." She opened her eyes, almost as if he'd compelled her to look again, to keep that connection between them. She could see the slightest flecks of green in his pale blue eyes and she tried to see deep inside of him, past the surface.

Maybe she was searching for more than was there. More than there ever was to him. The man he might have once been. The man who had been a husband and a father. Who had loved fiercely and walked in the daylight.

"Lucas, Lucas," she said quietly, over and over again like a promise. His forehead dipped to hers and he kissed her, like he was taking the taste of his name on her lips into himself.

She came, even more intensely than the time before. Sharper, a sensation closer to the sweetest torture. She felt him come, his loss of momentum, the halt of his indrawn breath as his body froze over hers, the heavy pulsing of his cock as he came deep inside her.

Moments passed and he kissed her again, slowly, maybe a kiss as close to love as she would ever get from him—possessive and jealous instead of kindness and love.

And the sadness of that threatened to overwhelm her. That she wouldn't be able to see him as the monster he was from now on. A tiny part of her would always see him as what she wanted more than anything else in the world and something that she could never have.

She felt him shift, ready to move off of her but she wrapped her legs tighter around his waist, her arms hard around his neck. "No, stay."

"I am not too heavy?" he said, looking down at her with a slight smile.

Yes, you're much too heavy. "No."

Lucas shifted very slightly to the side so he could see her body, touch her softly from her breast to her hip. She touched him back. Leisurely, like they had all the time in the world and nothing else mattered. It was just the two of them and they could stay that way forever and he'd never let her go.

And for now it was enough. It had to be.

CHAPTER 24

Val was back in the meadow holding a fist full of flowers, enjoying the sun on her face. A deep voice spoke from behind her. She whirled to face him, so surprised she made a small yipping noise.

"What are you doing here?" Lucas asked.

"You're in my dream. What are *you* doing here?"

He reached for her hand, frowning. His gaze stuck on the flowers she held. "Where did you get these?"

The wind rose, making her long, gray dress snap. His fingers were slightly rough as he tried to uncurl her hand from the stems.

"No," Val said and took a step back, clutching the bouquet to her chest.

"Do you know where you are?" he asked her.

"No. Where am I?"

"This is the land of the Fey."

"It's beautiful. It's like ours but...*more*. Eloquent, huh?" She smiled.

Lucas didn't smile. If anything, his expression became even more grim. "Valerie. Why are you dreaming of this place?"

"It's just a meadow. We could be anywhere." But even as she spoke, she knew he was right. He'd said it was the land of the Fey, and she'd felt it shiver down her spine like a hot breath on her back. A resonance that poured through her.

He closed his eyes. "I ask you again. Where did the flowers come from? What is the purpose of them?"

"I've been gathering them," she said, aware that her explanation sounded peculiar.

"To what end?" he said louder and gripped her by the arms, bending his legs so that he could peer into her eyes.

She shook her head.

"Give them to me."

"No," she said, the response instant, her body awash in fear. Like he was a murderer trying to take away her child. She clutched the flowers tight. Tried to step back. Suspected she was moments away from panicking.

She could see him thinking. "Just hand them to me. I will give them back. I will not harm them."

She shook her head. "Let go of me. If you want them, let me go," she said, hearing the protectiveness in her tone.

He released her and she took a step back. Val had the urge to run away from him. "I can't give them to you," she whispered.

He hesitated, like he was dealing with a crazy person holding a gun. "All right." His gaze flashed down to her hand then back up. "I will not touch them. Put them down on the ground instead. Just for a moment."

"Why?" Her heart pounded just thinking about it.

Val bent down, ready to lay the flowers on the ground, but stopped. She didn't want to. No, it was worse. She *couldn't*. "I don't want to let him go."

His jaw hardened. "Who?" Lucas asked softly.

"Who what?"

"Whom do you not want to let go?"

"I don't know what you're talking about."

"This is more than a dream. Put the flowers down, Valerie." The way he said it made her think he was running out of patience.

"I can't."

He bent down, kneeling, then reached into his Jacket pocket and withdrew a knife. Val backed away with a gasp. Lucas rolled up his sleeve then dragged the blade across his arm lightly, a faint line of blood appearing. Then he picked some grass and rubbed it onto the wound. He made a noise as though it hurt.

"What the hell are you doing?" she asked.

"I want to see if the wound is there when we awake."

"This is a dream. That's not possible."

"We shall see."

His head tilted to the side. "You must give them to me, my Valkyrie, or I will take them from you."

Lucas doesn't belong here.

She turned and ran, which was stupid. She couldn't outrun a one-legged vampire, let alone the King of them all. But her heart kept pounding, telling her to leave him behind.

It seemed like she ran for hours, tirelessly, without the barest stumble. Finally, she stopped and turned around, almost expecting him to say 'boo' and scare the crap out of her. But she was alone. Lucas was gone.

She was on top of a hill, the long grass waving against her legs with a gentle shushing noise, a slight rustle of leaves in the trees, and, beyond that, nothing. The silence drew her attention because it was so unusual, so different than what she was used to.

A huge pond was in front of her. Lily pads dotted the surface, and it had a certain Pride and Prejudice quality to it, like Mr. Darcy might swim out at any moment.

She wanted to go into the water.

Val walked forward, undoing the laces of her dress as she moved. *Wait. Laces?* She looked down and noticed her peculiar outfit. Like she was going to a Henry VIII costume party after this.

Ignore it.

She kept walking, stripped off her clothes down to her chemise, a thin cotton undergarment that was like a slip. Nothing would stop her from going into the water. In the middle of the pond was an island with a red Orchid in full-bloom. The flower got caught up in the breeze, swaying gently as though it wanted to make sure she saw it. As though it was begging for her touch.

"Stop."

"Lucas. You're back." She didn't look away from the flower on the island, but knew he was behind her.

"There is magic here, Valerie. Do you feel it?"

"No." She needed to get to that island.

He needs to leave.

"You must not do anything else until we know what's going on. We must talk to Rachel."

Val waded into the water. Lucas cursed, the splash of his footsteps audible as he followed her into the water. She dove, swimming frantically in hopes of avoiding him and getting to the last flower.

To Cerdewellyn.

Lucas pulled her ankle and yanked her up, his hard arm wrapping around her waist.

"No. *No.* You cannot!" he growled at her, hauling her back towards the shore.

She screeched and tried to pull away from him, kicking him hard in the leg. He grunted and continued to drag her out of the water. The weather changed, a storm coming in from the east, covering the land and them, rain soaking through her and chilling her to the bone within moments.

She kicked out again, and Lucas dropped her to the ground. His hair was plastered around his face, highlighting his harsh cheekbones and the severity of his features. "Wake up, Valerie. Wake up now!"

Val woke with a cry to find Lucas over her, shaking her hard.

"Let go. I'm fine. I'm fine," she said. Even to her, it sounded like a lie.

CHAPTER 25

There was a knock at the door, and Rachel came in wearing a red silk robe, her hair tousled and free of makeup. It made her look young and innocent, like the makeup turned her into someone else and the real her was a lot more vulnerable than one would expect.

"You rang?" Rachel said.

"She is dreaming of the Fey and is compelled to pick flowers," Lucas said quickly. He was wearing jeans, having dressed in haste a moment ago, the top button still undone. He put his hands on his hips and waited for Rachel to speak.

Rachel pursed her lips. "Forced to pick flowers, you say. Sounds like something serious to me. Even your dreams are boring. Christ, all I ever dreamed about was sex and death, but you—"

Lucas grabbed Rachel around the throat and slammed her against the wall, her words choked off in a gurgle.

"Do *not* belittle what I say. What can it mean that she sees these things? She is performing a task for the Fey. You must see how dangerous this is? Someone knows of her, is using her for something. I want that connection severed." His words were deadly. The threat in them, his willingness to harm Rachel shocked Val, made her pull the sheet up higher on her body and wrap it close.

He dropped her and stepped back. Rachel coughed and shot him a look under her lashes. "Okay. Well, the Fey used to be able to come to people they had a connection with. So how did you get a connection with the Fey? In legends it was eating an apple or drinking something, even making them a promise. Did you do anything like that?"

"No," Val said.

"What happened to the blood from the spell?" Lucas asked Rachel.

"I burned it," she said without hesitation.

"Was any blood spilled?"

Rachel shook her head. "I was careful."

"Were you careful?" Lucas asked Val. Meeting his gaze was like bumping into an electrical force-field.

"With what?" Val asked, confused.

Lucas asked the words tightly, like he'd shout if he wasn't careful. "Did you spill any blood while we were searching for the Fey?"

"Probably. I *was* dripping blood," Val said.

Lucas put his head back, thunking it lightly against the wall. "I assume you must know what I know, that things which are second nature to me would be obvious to all...." He took a deep breath, actually closing his eyes in agitation before speaking, "Here is your lesson then. And you must listen well. Do not *ever* let an Other of any kind have something of yours. Be it blood, hair, even clothing. All of these things contain your essence.

Curses can be made, your will manipulated. And they can find you. As you now know. If you bleed, wipe it up, keep the handkerchief until you can incinerate it."

"So what, from now on if I have a cold or a bloody nose, I have to put soggy tissues in my pocket until I can have a little bonfire in my wastebasket?"

Lucas shot her a look she couldn't interpret. "Yes."

He was apparently done with Val, because he addressed Rachel. "I want that connection gone, immediately. What do you need to make that happen?" Lucas said, picking up Val's clothes off the ground and throwing them at her.

"I can be ready by sundown."

"And we meet back at the clearing?" Lucas asked.

"Yes."

"Fine. I have something to take care of and then we will be there."

Rachel bowed rather insolently, then left.

Lucas went to his closet and pulled out a green cashmere sweater, pulling it on over his head as he walked back to her. "You will be fine. We will fix this. But, do not go back to sleep."

Val wasn't sure how afraid she should be. But Rachel had been spooked, Lucas seemed in panic mode—which meant he was moving and talking like a normal person—so she knew she should be worried. "Don't go back to sleep? That's your advice? And where are you going? You're not going to stay with me?"

"I'll be back as soon as I can," he said softly.

"Where are you going?" she asked, suddenly feeling like her stomach was full of curdled milk.

"I will not go to the Fey without being at full strength. I must feed. I will be back as soon as I may."

She tried to bite the words back, but failed. "Who is it?" she couldn't help but ask.

He turned back, his expression stern and distant. "It does not even matter. I could not give you a name if I wanted to. I do not ask. I do not care. The only thing that I am thinking now is that I have to keep you safe. Do not ask me to jeopardize that."

She could feel his eagerness to leave. "What if I did?"

He shook his head. A warning.

"What if I did?" she repeated.

"What would you ask? That I never feed again? That I drink only from males or in a cup? It is only as important as you make it. It means *nothing*."

"It does mean something, because you won't drink from me when you know how much I want it. How much you want it!"

"Want is irrelevant. You wanted Jack. You wanted me. Now you want me to drink your blood, when before the idea disgusted you. We all want things, more so when we cannot have them."

"But—"

"Do not." And then he was out the door, the conversation over and Val was alone, in his bed, with no underwear and the desperate urge to hit something.

CHAPTER 26

Jack and Rachel were at the edge of the forest when they arrived. Jack had come over and handed her a Kit-Kat bar. It was her favorite, and he knew she had a weakness for them.

"You think this is going to be enough to make me let you stay?" Val asked.

"It's a King size."

Good point. "I don't think this is a good—"

Jack cut her off. "I know what you are going to say, and I promise not to do anything stupid. I got you into this."

"Lucas will make Rachel take you back. Look, there they go," she said, watching as Rachel and Lucas stepped away from them, presumably so that Lucas could bitch Rachel out about bringing Jack.

Rachel had her arms crossed and was looking at the ground. Lucas was tall and imposing, wearing a green cashmere sweater and black jeans. He gestured to the forest around them with one hand and then towards where Val and Jack stood.

"Uh-oh he gestured at her. He must be pretty riled up," Val murmured.

"I can't tell if you're kidding or not," Jack said and she knew he was scowling.

Val shrugged. "I don't know if I'm kidding or not! The man is elusive. Who knows what agesture might mean? But I'll tell you what I do know. I know he will want you gone."

"Yes, but he wants to get into your pants more. Tell him it's alright with you if I stay. I'll behave. Besides, we should be out of here in ten minutes. That's what Rachel said, anyway."

She gave him a long searching look. Then he gave her the puppy dog expression. *Dammit.* "Don't do anything stupid!" Val said, stepping closer to him and sticking a finger in his face.

"Deal." He stepped around her and started walking back to Rachel and Lucas. Val followed him, noting how Lucas and Rachel instantly stopped talking and took a step back from each other. As if they were the cool kids and wouldn't say anything around her and Jack cause they were lame.

She really hoped Lucas would punish Rachel. But only after she got Val out of this Fey business, though. Maybe that really was the reason Rachel got away with so much backtalk and attempted murder: if you need a witch, who you gonna call? Rachel. And Lucas couldn't call her if she was dead. Still. One of these days, she was going to get her comeuppance.

Hopefully.

The birds were plentiful, squawking and calling to each other as they walked back to the clearing. They were almost there, no more than a hundred feet away when Val noticed a subtle change. At first, she wasn't sure what it was. If it was a different sound, smell, temperature or what. It was just...odd.

Wait. It was the sound of their *shoes* that was different. Almost like they echoed differently, more muffled, as if the ground was softer.

She turned back and looked at Lucas, who was a few steps behind her. His gaze locked on hers with laser-like precision, and she shivered. Goosebumps raced up her spine, and she didn't know if it was him or the cold. Over his shoulder, the way they had come, was in shadow as if the sun was setting on that space. She looked at her watch. 5:30 pm. *What the hell?*

She studied the road behind them again. It was definitely darker. And the trees were a deeper green, a slight shimmer on the leaves in front of them.

"What is that?" Jack said, pointing.

Val was surprised when Lucas took Jack seriously, instantly scanning the area and on the alert.

"What do you see?" Lucas asked Jack, quiet intensity lacing his words as he moved closer to her, as if he was ready to protect her should the need arise.

"I see shadows. Like this path is brighter, and the one behind us is darker. It's almost like it's farther—"

"Grab him and run," Lucas said harshly, before picking Val up in his arms, carrying her fireman-style and running, inhumanly fast so that the trees were a blur. Behind her, she saw Rachel had taken Jack 's arm and was propelling him along, lending him speed.

Lucas pushed harder, ducking, weaving like an animal racing over his territory. And then all the forest looked the same, uniform and she wondered if it had just been a trick of the light.

He stopped and put her down before walking in a small, agitated circle. "Let's go back. They'll be just down the path, I imagine." He began to walk, and she followed him, looking behind her once more. Everything looked the same now.

The day was sunny again, but then she realized the differences. Their feet didn't crunch on the ground, and the birds were silent. They were in the same forest, but it felt empty.

Dead.

Jack and Rachel were suddenly before them, one moment out of distance, the next visible like a camera lens going from blurry to sharp in a quick twist. Jack stopped, hands on hips, breathing hard.

"What the fuck?" he gasped.

Val shot a glare at Jack. "Really? You can't even get out a whole sentence?"

"You know what I mean. Fine. What the fuck is going on?"

Rachel was staring at Lucas and shaking her head slightly, a look of fear on her face. She'd seen Rachel afraid once before. When Lucas was deciding whether or not he'd kill her after she and her uber-murderous girlfriend had tried to kill him. Now she was worried again? *This is bad.*

"Welcome to the world of the Fey," Lucas said quietly.

"Go on," Jack said, like he was trying to hold on to his temper.

"Someone has brought us here. Carefully, as well. They shifted us out of our time subtly, so we did not notice."

Rachel bent down, touching the dirt, taking some in her hands and spilling it between her fingers. "That's pretty damned impressive. I should have felt something. And if not me, I would have thought you would," Rachel said casually. But the set of her shoulders and the way her attention was focused on the small task in front of her, made Valerie think that Rachel was anything but relaxed.

"Indeed, vampires are not immune to Fey Glamour. Typically we are more susceptible. It was part of the reason we hunted them in the first place. There is no reason to tolerate an enemy," Lucas said tightly.

"Are you talking about me?" Jack said.

"You flatter yourself." The words held no inflection.

Valerie stepped between them. Wasn't it supposed to be hot to have two guys fight over her? It wasn't hot. She felt guilty, clammy and petrified. "This is bullshit. There are more important things going on than your petty insults!" Val was happy with her word choice. She'd wanted to make some comment about them having a pissing contest or seeing who had the bigger penis, but managed some tact.

After a beat, Jack nodded, then said, "So, who is it and what do they want?"

"I do appreciate your pragmatism, Jack." Lucas said, his tone indicating he didn't like anything about Jack.

"You don't need to appreciate fuck all about me."

"We will need shelter immediately," Lucas said, scanning the dense forest all around them. It all looked the same to Val.

Trees. More trees. Lots more trees. And, undoubtedly, a huge number of bugs who would gnosh on her.

"You want to find shelter? We need to get out of here, not set up house," Jack said.

Rachel turned to Jack, dropping the dirt from her hands and wiping them together. "I feel magic because I'm a witch. Unless someone is incredibly powerful, I should have felt the shift when we left our reality and entered the Fey World. At the very least, I should have been aware of something, even if I couldn't see it. I didn't notice a thing. Do you notice it now? It's almost like the...*quality* of the world is different. This world is almost heavier. At least that's how it feels to me."

"And you can feel it now?" Lucas asked Rachel.

She nodded unhappily. "Yeah, I feel it."

"Whoever has brought us here has dispensed with subtlety, then. They dropped the magic that kept you from noticing."

Val bit her lip. "Wait. Do you see it?" she asked Lucas.

He gave her a haughty look and didn't answer.

"What does that mean?" Jack said.

"It means we're in deep shit," Rachel said.

Lucas ignored her comment. "Whoever has done this knew we were in Roanoke and brought us to them intentionally. So they can open the portal, take people, but cannot leave themselves." It was clear he wasn't looking for an answer.

He continued, "After the incident with the Lost Colony, there are no known incidents of people disappearing over the last few centuries. No mysterious circumstances surrounding kidnapped people occurring in the woods. Either something has changed, or the Fey felt no need to take anyone." His gaze landed heavily on Valerie. "Perhaps there was no one interesting enough to take. Until now."

Valerie looked up at Lucas, arms crossed, shoulders hunched a little. "Hey, you're the one who killed them all. Maybe they brought us here because of *you*. Have you been here before?"

His cheeks hollowed, jaw hardened. A sign of defiance? Anger?" No. A vampire's powers are greatly reduced in their world. Witches kept us apprised of where the portals were and we avoided them. Occasionally a vampire disappeared into the Fey realm." A lengthy pause. "Rarely did they return."

Valerie turned to Rachel. She didn't trust her. Couldn't believe she'd want them here on purpose but felt the need to ask. "Why didn't you feel it, then? You're a witch. Shouldn't you have noticed?"

She scowled. "Yeah. And I probably would have if I'd ever felt Fey magic before. Or if I hung out with other witches and swapped trade secrets. I just didn't feel it." She shrugged then leaned in towards Val a little. "But next time, I'm on it! Won't fool me twice." Her words were vicious somehow and Val turned, stalking away.

She wasn't going to fight with Rachel right now. *Maybe later.* Jack reached out, put his hand on Rachel's arm for a brief moment, getting her attention. He shook his head at Rachel, telling her without words to settle down.

Rachel rolled her eyes.

Val gasped. "Is that *snow*?" In the distance, white clouds were rolling in, a massive storm coming towards them.

"We need shelter. We are here and we are at the mercy of the Fey for a reason. To assume they don't wish us harm is folly. Let us go."

"Shouldn't we try to find a castle or something? Seek refuge there?" Rachel asked.

"If they had wanted us at the castle, we would be there. They would have brought us there. This location was chosen for a reason. Survival is everything now," Lucas said.

"My instincts tell me we should stick together and not give the Fey a chance to separate us. However, we could find shelter faster if we roamed ahead and tracked back, Rachel said to Lucas.

"You're a witch. You may be more valuable than I to their survival at this point. But I will not leave her undefended...and I imagine they want us separated." Lucas sighed, a frustrated sound. "We stay together. It is not worth the risk. Do you know how to send out your will?" he asked Rachel.

"Yes," she said hesitantly.

"Do it."

"I need to lay down to do it. Lay down or fall down."

"Would you rather be carried?" Lucas asked.

"*No.* No, thanks." She seemed nonplussed and Valerie wondered at the byplay. Whatever the reason was for her not wanting to be in Lucas' arms, it was clearly something that she had a strong reaction to.

Rachel was many things, but afraid of Lucas didn't seem to be one of them. She back-talked and seemed to relish being insolent.

Rachel lay down on the ground, propping her back against a tree trunk. She laced her fingers in her lap and then looked up at Lucas. "It takes a lot of energy," she said quietly.

Lucas nodded, faint lines bracketing his mouth. Valerie knew she was missing something, but she didn't know what.

Rachel closed her eyes, taking a deep breath. Then another. Val and Jack exchanged a 'now what? ' expression. Two gray wolves appeared out of thin air, taking shape beside Rachel.

The shape was right, but they were like ghosts, their bodies see through. They leapt off, each of them going in different directions, bounding silently through the forest.

"Jesus Christ," Jack muttered, pacing away from Lucas and Val.

Rachel stayed propped up against a tree trunk with her eyes closed, but it didn't look like she was sleeping. There was no one home. The spark of vitality was gone, and her skin was chalky and lifeless. She looked dead.

Minutes passed, and Valerie could see the storm moving closer to them. As if a giant was dropping a white sheet over everything and blanketing the forest in sections. They needed shelter before the storm hit. The temperature began to drop, and she could see her breath fogging in front of her, felt her hands go numb. Val jumped in place, trying to get warm.

Lucas was almost as still as Rachel while they waited. Val had the urge to throw a rock at Lucas or do something to get him to move. Looking at him when he became statue- still creeped her out. It wasn't hot. She closed her eyes and thought about him, what he might be feeling.

Nothing. But when she opened her eyes, Lucas was watching her. Had he felt her reach out to him? She gave him a small smile, almost apologetic, and then turned back to Rachel.

Rachel's skin was gray, the flesh under her eyes sunken and the greeny-blue quality of her veins more pronounced. As though her flesh had thinned and the trace amounts of fat that kept her skin young-looking, and healthy, were gone.

Her eyes flicked open as she stared sightlessly into the distance. It reminded Val of a doll that would open its eyes when she turned up-right. She'd had one of those. It had blinked on its own and scared the crap out of her.

Rachel gasped. Like her soul was thrust back into her body, and the only way to keep it there was to lock it in with air.

"Where?" Lucas instantly asked.

"That way." She pointed to the left, almost horizontal to the storm. Her voice was grating and rough, like she'd been searching for water for days and only found more sun.

"What is it?" Lucas asked.

"A cottage."

"Inhabited?"

"I don't think so. But I couldn't tell because the doors and windows were covered. I can't go through something closed."

"Can you walk?" Lucas asked.

Rachel's eyes were very wide. And she looked like hell. She licked her lips quickly, before turning away. "I need time."

Lucas dropped to his knees beside her, arm extended towards her, palm up so that his wrist was before Rachel's face. Val could see his back, knew he'd positioned himself on purpose—to keep Val and Jack from seeing some of what they were doing. A hint of privacy.

"The time for hiding is done. You are what you are," Lucas said quietly.

Rachel's expression was almost sad. And Val wondered at their relationship again. Rachel nodded, watched the wrist Lucas extended towards her with banked desire.

"I can bite? I mean, you don't want to—" She seemed uncertain.

"Would you prefer me to make the wound?" he asked, almost surprised.

She flushed.

His wrist was to his mouth in an instant, and then it was back, blood glinting in the light. A look of longing crossed Rachel's face. Her head bowed over him like prince charming about to kiss sleeping beauty—A kiss of adoration without knowledge.

Her hands came up, cupping his wrist. Then her lips touched his flesh, clamping onto him. His arm was stretched out towards Rachel, and her body still rested against the tree. Neither of them making any effort to get closer to each other. It was as impersonal as possible.

As clinical as sucking someone's body fluids could be. *Which means really fucking personal.*

Rachel swallowed and made a low, almost sexual sound, deep in her throat. A sound so unequivocally of pleasure that it made a flash of jealousy tear through Valerie like lightning.

Rachel's shoulders slumped, and her grip tightened on his arm, trying to pull him closer to her. Her skin changed almost instantly, restored to the state it had been before the invisible wolf business, but better. Her hair was smooth and perfect, and when her eyes flashed open, they sparkled like jewels in the sun. She was not only restored, but amplified.

"Enough," Lucas said, and Rachel instantly quit drinking, her head dropping back to the tree, eyes closed as she licked her lips.

Val looked to Jack, but he wasn't watching. He was staring at the snow in the distance, arms tight against his chest, a muscle in his jaw jumping. He seemed as uncomfortable as a priest in a sex shop.

Lucas stood, extending a hand to help Rachael up. She took it and glided off the ground, her body as flexible as a flower in a storm.

"This way," Rachel said, her voice husky, and they set off into the woods.

CHAPTER 27

The temperature had plummeted. Their breath fogged, and Val's legs were tired from the punishing pace. She was also thirsty and hungry.

Really thirsty and hungry. The storm was almost on them, and everyone was silent as they hurried toward the unseen shelter.

And then they came to a little clearing in the woods where a cottage stood. It was quiet, and there was something about the little home that made it seem uninhabited. It also looked like it belonged in a fairy tale. "Who's inside? The witch who cooked up Hansel and Gretel or the big bad wolf?" Val said, teeth chattering.

Lucas gave Valerie an odd look under his lashes. "As though we would be lucky enough to find food."

Val recoiled a little. *Is he joking?"* Was that a joke?" Val asked.

"I don't know," he said vaguely, attention fixed on the front door and the wooden shutters that covered the windows, "Was it funny?"

Yeah, kind of.

"No, it wasn't," Jack said, almost vibrating with anger.

What is he so pissed about? Sure, they were all irritated, impending doom seemed to have that effect on a person, but the rest of them were *trying* to stay upbeat.

Val felt a slight sting on her cheek. *Snow.* They'd only just made it. Val hoped the cottage was empty, because she suspected that Lucas was going to get them in there whether someone put up a protest or not.

"Give me your scarf," Lucas said, hand extended.

The question was unexpected. "Why?"

"The metal on the door handle is silver. It will burn my flesh if I touch it without a barrier."

She unwound her scarf from her neck and handed it to him. Lucas wrapped it around his hand and reached for the door handle. The door opened easily.

"Why does that seem ominous? I almost wish we'd had to break in," Jack said quietly.

Lucas stepped into the cottage, gesturing for them to wait while he checked it out. Jack stepped towards the door, a knife in hand, but Rachel caught his arm. "What do you think you're doing? If there is something in there, he can deal with it."

Jack's jaw was tight, his arm rigid. "I can help."

"No. *You'd* die," she said firmly, grip tightening. "I am stronger than you will ever be, and he makes me look like a child. You leave the dangerous things to us, or it'll be aone-way trip to the land of Tinkerbell for you."

Jack jerked against Rachel's grip, but she didn't let go. He stepped in towards her, crowding close instead. "Don't underestimate me," he said with quiet, angry intensity. Rachel let go, as if she wanted to keep some distance between them.

"You may come in," Lucas said from inside the cottage.

"The vampire invites us in. Now I've seen everything," Jack said, moving out of the way to let Val go first. Rachel cut in front of Jack, going in ahead of him, and Val thought she could hear Jack's teeth grinding in irritation.

It was dark inside the cottage. Dark and small. There were two rooms. The main room had two wooden chairs, a hearth with a kettle on a black spit, some logs next to the fireplace and a few folded blankets, presumably for sleeping on.

"Rustic," Rachel said tonelessly.

Lucas was kneeling down next to the hearth, building a fire. "I saw no flint," he said as he tucked pieces of straw carefully into the arranged wood.

Rachel looked around. "Nope."

"What's in the other room?" Val asked.

"Hansel and Gretel," Lucas said, barely pausing as he rubbed two sticks together, inhumanly fast, his arms a blur. There was a curl of smoke, and after a few more seconds, a flame. He touched it to the straw, blowing on it for long moments, tucking in more straw as the flames caught. As if he was tending to a sick child. His movements were slight and careful.

"Jack. Can you keep the fire going?" Lucas said, not turning away from his task.

"Yes," Jack said, a small amount of anger leaking through.

"Good. I shall find more wood. If we are trapped here for a while, we'll need it. And do not go into the other room until I return." And then he was out the door and gone.

Ominous. Maybe it is Hansel and Gretel.

"What about food and water?" Val asked. "Should I go get snow or something?"

"Wait for Lucas."

"I'm thirsty. I can just put some snow in the kettle, get it melting."

"You need to wait."

Val walked to the front door, ignoring Rachel. She was thirsty. Rachel moved, appearing in front of her and with a click of her tongue said, "I told you to wait."

"What will Lucas do if he comes back and you've laid a hand on me?" Val said, beyond irritated. She'd push past Rachel if she had to.

Rachel smiled. "I can keep you here without violence. And he'd certainly be mad at me if you went out there and—"

"Enough." Lucas was back, standing behind Rachel as she blocked the door, his arms filled with firewood. Snow dusted his shoulders and sparkled in his hair. Valerie looked at him and felt a sharp pang in her heart. There was something so human about him carrying firewood. Maybe because he'd carried firewood for centuries, before electricity, and so his comfortableness with the task went deeper than the modern man's. When doing the task well meant the difference between living and dying.

Or perhaps it was just the primal knowledge that a man was providing for her and protecting against the elements to keep his woman safe. Now that she had slept with him, she was trying to make him more human. *I think I've made a huge mistake.*

She remembered telling him she'd fall in love with him, throwing out that awkward piece of information, like having a pair of underpants in the middle of the living room when someone came to visit. Painfully awkward and inexplicable. *You will get your heart so broken if you keep this up.*

Jack was frowning at her hard. *And Jack might slap me upside the head. Best case scenario.*

The fire was crackling and close to a blaze. Heat spread out into the room, making her muscles thaw. Val sat in one of the chairs, watching Lucas arrange the firewood into a neat pile for later.

"You're really settling in," Jack said flatly.

"Caution is appropriate."

"I'm thirsty," Val said. *If in doubt, don't let Jack and Lucas interact in any way.*

Jack walked over to the kettle and peered into it. "I don't know how clean it is, since there doesn't seem to be anything here invented after the spinning wheel, but I suppose it will have to do."

Lucas put his hand to his head, pressing his hand over his eyes as though he was thinking hard or trying to be patient. He stood, and stared at Rachel steadily.

Val felt lost. What was the problem?

Rachel shrugged. "I don't know."

"I hate it when you two have these big conversations with a look and keep me in the dark," Val said.

"Could fire burn the magic off?" Rachel asked tentatively, as though Val hadn't said a word.

"The risk is too great. And since the enchantment spreads to food, cooked or raw, I would assume not."

Val feared she understood. "Are you two conversationalists saying that we can't eat or drink anything because we'll be stuck here?"

Moving closer to Val, Jack crossed his arms, as though on the alert, ready to protect her. *Good luck to him.*

Lucas nodded.

"I'm lost," Jack said, unhappy since he was usually the guy who had all the answers. Now he was out of his element. He'd been put in his place by Rachel questioning his physical strength, and now he was behind on the situation. And at the mercy of Lucas.

"Traditionally, the Fey take people to their land. They can return home on their own so long as they find an exit and do not eat or drink anything enchanted. If they do, they are bound. Water is out. Any food from the land, all hunting, everything," Rachel explained.

Val crossed her arms. "How did humans make it out before? If they didn't eat or drink anything?"

"We need to find a portal," Lucas said.

"I'm already stuck here and bound, right? That was what the dreams were all about. So, how come *I* can't drink anything?"

Val asked, knowing there was the smallest truckload of whine in her voice.

Lucas said, "No, you have been claimed through blood, and you are at one Fey's mercy. Eat or drink from something another has created, and you shall be bound to them as well. But if you drink, you will certainly be at their mercy. Rachel, can you send out your will and locate a portal?" She looked down at the ground and back up, her expression a bit tortured. "I don't think that will work. I need to be able to feel the portal's energy. Sending out my consciousness—it's like a shadow. I can't touch or feel anything. I'll try it, don't get me wrong, but I really don't think it will work. And it leaves me weak. Even with your blood, it's the witch power that gets tapped out."

"What range could you cover?" Lucas asked.

She hesitated. "Three, maybe four miles."

Lucas shook his head and sat on the floor, legs outstretched and crossed at the ankle. Watching him sit on the ground made Valerie look at him a little longer. Every time he did something human, or normal, she became fascinated by him. Why was that? Because she wanted him to be normal? Or because he was so beautiful that when he did something normal it exacerbated that beauty, made it stand out in contrast. Like giving a black and white TV color.

"I doubt that would help," Lucas said. "We were taken here because it's undoubtedly the farthest from any exit."

"So who brought us here?" Val asked, moving to stand closer to the fire.

Lucas raised both eyebrows as though slightly surprised. "I assume Cerdewellyn brought us here, or his Queen, perhaps. Someone powerful."

Rachel went to the door and opened it. The snow had come unnaturally fast, and was waist high. "Well they did an excellent job. We're not going anywhere anytime soon."

A few minutes passed where they all thought about their impending doom. And pizza. *But that might just be me*, Val thought.

Jack squeezed the back of his neck with one hand, a sign of his rising tension. Val realized he was staring at Lucas. Jack took a step back, moving closer to Valerie as though to protect her. What? She looked at Lucas, and he had the cold reptile vibe going on, as though he were conserving energy. One could throw a blanket over him like they'd done to Aunt Edna in Vacation, and no one would know the difference.

Then Lucas breathed, blinked, and his eyes were suddenly aware again. "This must be related to Valerie. She is the target."

"No, she's the one who bled out. If you'd bled all over the ground maybe you'd be dreaming of flowers," Rachel said.

Jack stood beside Valerie, his hand behind his back. Was he touching his gun? She pretended to sneeze, turning a little to see behind him. Sure enough his hand was on his weapon. What the fuck was he thinking?

"This is fucking fantastic. So what you're telling me is we have no food or water, we can't leave because we're buried in snow, we may never get home again, and some Fey creature is toying with us until we are too weak to fight? Is that it?" Jack's voice was husky.

Lucas looked to Rachel as Jack talked, "Do nothing," he said to her, before turning back to Jack, who was still talking. "And yet the two of you are just fine, is that it? Got the food problem all worked out because of Valerie and I?"

Jack drew his gun, the small click of the safety being turned off loud in her ears. Jack pointed the gun at Lucas and shifted closer to Valerie, trying to move her behind him. Lucas watched patiently, making no overt gestures.

He's one cool cat.

"I suppose I can't kill you, but what about her?" Jack said.

And the gun swung to Rachel.

Rachel looked genuinely worried, and her gaze flicked to Lucas as though asking him what she could do to defend herself. Lucas had known what Jack was about to do. So why hadn't he stopped him?" There is another option. And if you attempt to kill Rachel, you will be dead before you can hit her twice."

Jack's jaw was clenched tight, sweat on his brow.

"Jack, no," Valerie whispered to him.

"No! You were right, you make bad decisions around him. I am *not* food. If we're going to die, I'm taking one of them with me."

"I'm not dying!" Val said loudly.

"The other option," Lucas said, voice even, "is to share blood. Your lives are sustainable for a month or two if you drink my blood. In turn, Rachel can survive without feeding more than once or twice in that period. Any additional needs she has shall be supplemented by me."

Jack laughed angrily. "You're a real fucking saint, you know that? You think I'll drink your blood or hers? *Never.* No one will *ever* feed on me. Tell me you fucking understand?"

"Let me be clear on my priorities," Lucas said, voice low with anger. "I want Valerie out of this land. I will do what needs to be done to accomplish that. I'll keep everyone alive as long as it doesn't affect my ability to keep her safe."

"And if we're still sitting here in the snow, like the goddamned Donner party when that starts to happen, what's your priority then?" Jack said, fingers white from gripping the gun so tightly.

"I am unwilling to indulge that conversation," Lucas said, tone final. He stood, like a puppet master had pulled him up off the ground. Jack swung the gun back towards Lucas and pulled the trigger. Sound exploded in the small room.

Valerie screamed and lunged forward, towards Lucas or Jack, she wasn't really sure.

In the blink of an eye, Lucas held the gun in one hand, the other wrapped tight around Jack's throat. Lucas leaned in, so close that no matter how quietly he spoke Jack would hear him, lips bared in a feral smile. "I fear Valerie would be rather put out if I killed you. Or else I would." He shook Jack lightly by the neck, and Jack's hands tore at Lucas', scrabbling to get air into his lungs. "And that would benefit me greatly. How long need I wait for her to mourn you, if you push me? One year? Perhaps two? I cannot fathom that it would be more."

"Let him go!" Valerie shouted, pulling on Lucas' immobile arm. But trying to force Lucas, no matter how hard she pulled on him, was like pushing against a concrete building.

Finally, Lucas released Jack, pushing him away, but keeping the gun. He stalked away from Jack, his gaze landing on Valerie and burning her like a spark of fire. "Come here. *Now*."

"She's not going anywhere with you. Stay here, Valerie," Jack said.

"I'm not a fucking dog, Jack. Now sit down and try not to get yourself killed," Val responded, disgusted with him. It just wasn't smart. And Jack was smart. So what the hell was he doing?

Lucas went to the door and opened it, extending one hand back as though Valerie might take it. His eyes were almost glowing, his whole body so tense and coiled that she didn't recognize him.

Cool, aloof Lucas. This wasn't icy and contained, it was a man on the edge.

She went towards him, and he took her hand in his, his large one swamping hers. He cast Jack a look that could only be described as malevolently possessive. She felt sick under everyone's attention and the deathly excitement.

She could feel Jack looking at her and Rachel, too, the combination of one burning gaze and a frigid one having a visceral effect on her, like a little patch of ice on overheated skin right in the middle of her back.

Val's voice was thin. "Just a minute. Can I... No, I'm not asking, I *need* to talk to Jack for a minute. Can you give us a minute? Please?" She begged him with her gaze not to get mad.

Lucas ran a hand through his hair and looked at Valerie for a long moment, intent on her face, then her hands as though he was looking for some tell-tale expression or gesture.

He nodded stiffly, and Rachel stepped around her and stalked to the other room, Lucas following her and closing the door behind them. The room felt huge now that he and Rachel were gone.

Jack walked to the chair in the corner and was about to sit down. "No, wait," Val said. He turned to look at her, a blank look on his face, like he had already closed down. Like he was a dead man walking. She went up to him and hugged him, wrapping her arms around him, her head on his chest. Her throat burned with tears. This was a bad situation, and Jack was going to get himself killed if he wasn't careful.

"It will be alright," she said. He was so familiar. His smell, his warmth. But not his body, or standing with him and being held. She had never hugged him enough to be familiar.

"I'm sorry," he said, voice rough. She pulled back to look at him but his palm came to the back of her head, holding her in place so she couldn't see his face. "I didn't listen to you."

"Why not?" She knew the answer, but she wondered if he did.

She could tell he was shaking his head, feel a slight tension in his shoulders. "I knew best. That's how it's always been."

She tried to laugh but it sounded more like a huff. "You've always known best? No, you've always been the one with the most conviction. The hero complex. But this isn't a question of who's right or wrong. It's a matter of survival. How important is living? To me...it's *really* important. You might have picked up on that," she said with a tremulous smile, trying to lighten the mood a little.

He was quiet for a long time. She knew what he *expected*—to die a la vampire. And what he thought he *deserved*—more a la vampire. But she didn't really know what he wanted. If he even wanted anything. Maybe it wasn't something he ever let himself think about. "I want to get you out of here. And I want to go back to when we were in Hawaii and you told me this would happen and I decided I could keep you safe."

"Keeping me safe is no longer your responsibility."

His arms tightened around her, giving the hug a Boa Constricter vibe. What, he was going to squeeze her feelings for Lucas out of her? Her voice was muffled in his sweater. "You *were* right. What we want and what we get are two different things. I want a normal life and it's not happening. I get that. It's also pretty irrelevant since we might die here. But please, please try to get out of here with us. You can't give Lucas the satisfaction of killing you. He's ruthless."

"How can you say that to me and still go to him? He's compelling you, Val, I know it," Jack said.

"I'm not compelled. That's not how it works. Compulsion is only effective in small doses, and it has limits. I just have a thing for emotionally unavailable men," she said, chuckling uncomfortably.

He let her go, and she stepped back, crossing her arms over her chest and moving back towards the fire.

"I need you to survive this. I always understood you and why you did things and now...I have no idea what the hell is going on with you. Honestly, you're either being a total jerk or you're behaving recklessly, and I just don't get it. It's not like you."

He gave her a smile that held nothing in it. Not vacuous, but desolate. Happiness had checked out long ago. "You don't know me, Val.... *I* don't know me. But, you're right. We have to get out of here. Just... promise me... promise me you won't let him feed off you."

Val wanted to lie to him. Just promise him she wouldn't, and then do whatever she wanted. She could even make a case that lying was the best course of action, considering how trigger happy Jack was. But he already didn't trust her. And truthfully, he needed to let her go. She wasn't his responsibility anymore. He needed to find something else worth living for. She wondered what he was thinking and what he saw when he looked at her.

"He's not going to drink my blood," Val confessed. *Hurray for the truth.*

"What do you want, Jack? Dad is gone. And I'm gone, too, right? Is that what this is about? I'm one step away from being a lost cause?"

"No," he said harshly. "You're not. I'll get you out of here. I'll save you, I swear."

"Please, Jack. Please try to not give him a reason to kill you."

"He already has a reason to kill me."

"Okay. Well, try not to give him a reason to act on it." She walked to the door and opened it. Rachel was leaning against the wall. She came forward and jerked her head back toward Lucas.

"Boss man wants to talk to you," Rachel said and slunk past her, closing the door behind her.

The storeroom was small, no more than a few steps to pace in either direction. Val stepped inside and took a breath, feeling bewildered and in shock. She was also sad and a little bit angry. That was how Jack always made her feel, it seemed like.

He'd been her friend, but she knew when that had ended. It had ended the night they almost had sex on a million dollars of Monopoly money.

Then they'd been lovers and that had been so brief and stressful that it seemed unreal. Like something she'd imagined that had never happened—déjà vu, maybe? And it shouldn't have happened, because now things were worse.

If she could go back, would she undo it? Sure, it made her miserable now, but at least she could move on and wouldn't spend her whole life pining after him. Now she could move on. *To the dead? Nice trade-up.*

Lucas was leaning again the wall, arms crossed, ankles crossed, looking very relaxed, but then he stood, as if to ready himself for an attack. Valerie felt her heartbeat change, speed up a little. The confined space, his declaration that she was his priority, his rage and jealousy. ...It *totally* turned her on.

He seemed closer, bigger, harder, in this small space. Desire flowed over her, like water in a dry creek bed, soaking up her will— welcome and wanted.

Compared to the snow and the frigid environment outside, he looked warm. The dark blond strands of his hair looked like the sun, the blue of his eyes like a warm sky. He was warm here in this freezing environment. When Lucas was cold, he was appealing, but Lucas warm? Warm she didn't want to resist.

She could hear little echoes of his voice in her mind, the promise in his words to Jack and to her—no matter what he was getting *her* out. Everyone else might die. But not her.

Wasn't that what she'd always wanted? To be chosen first? To see death as an option, something looming in the distance and creeping closer, and yet have someone love her enough to try to keep it at bay?

He was going to speak, but she really didn't care what he was going to say. Thoughts of Jack, of the unknown danger they were in, of Rachel the Bitch, all of it disappeared at the sight of him. She saw him and could only remember his body over hers, the things they had done. Snd hanging over all of that was the glowing notion that he would protect her. No matter what. It was enough to make her breath stutter in her chest.

She threw herself at him, arms wrapping around his neck, her mouth seeking his hard lips. And they were *hard*. There was no softness, no humanity in them. He wasn't pretending to be human for her. Not willing to make it easier. Like he was angry too. At what? Her wanting to talk to Jack? Jack shooting at him? Being here?

Her lips met his and she shivered at the contact. His arms went around her back, enclosing her in a huge hug that meant he bent his knees a little, hunched his body around hers slightly as though he would protect her from the elements, cover her, expose himself so that she might live.

Opening her mouth she touched her tongue to the seam of his lips. He groaned and kissed her back, kissing with abandon, plunging her tongue into his mouth with fervor, wanting to reach deep within his body, meld them together on a new level, not just fucking, or even making love but beyond that, something that would recognize that commitment— that he would harm for *her*, kill for *her*, even die, just for *her*. A little bit of Val was ashamed, too, wanting something so selfish. But a primal part of her thrilled at the notion.

Her hands went to his face, sliding down the cool hard planes to rest along his jaw then slid to the back of his head, tangling into his hair, loving the thickness and softness of it. He closed his eyes, brow slightly furrowed.

He moved her against the wall, pressing his body flush to hers, mouth to mouth, chest to chest. But then it didn't work, he was too tall. So his hands went to her thighs and lifted her, picking her up so that her legs wrapped around his hips, holding her where he wanted. She could feel him— hard and ready. He adjusted her a little so that she settled on him like a blanket over a sleeping lover, the folds of her flesh surrounding him as best they could with all these clothes between them.

She blushed, aware of how he moved against her, mimicking sex, his breathing fast, kisses frenzied and then she felt a small sting on her lip. Lucas jerked back from her and his hands tugged lightly at her waist, indicating that he wanted to put her down. She tasted blood in her mouth.

"I am so sorry." His tone was odd, like a boy caught in a lie. She tried to keep him holding her, wrapping her arms a little tighter around his neck and her legs around his waist, wiggling closer.

"I'm not sure if you sound sorry or not," she said, watching his gaze flash back to her eyes, her lips, then away again. *Tempted.*

"I feel like a fool. I did not mean to cut you. It should not have happened. I apologize."

She wanted to laugh. "Isn't it the sort of thing that happens all the time? Vampires have fangs. And they are pointy."

He sighed and tugged at her waist again, still trying to put her down. She squeezed him, wrapped her arms and legs tighter, refusing to let go. He could obviously pull her off of him and she wondered if he would, heard the quick, shallow breaths he was taking as he decided what he was going to do with her.

She felt him give in, relax a little, tension easing from his shoulders as he wrapped his arms around her to keep her close.

"You are very stubborn," he said, his voice so low it vibrated through her.

"It's endearing. What does it matter if you cut me a little? You just said you were willing to drink my blood if we were stuck here."

"Actually, I said you could drink mine. I do not remember the last time I cut someone while kissing. It has been..." he paused, clearly trying to remember. "It does not signify."

"Embarrassing, huh?" she said teasingly, her head angling back to his, wanting to kiss him again. "Then how come it happened?"

He turned his head away and her kiss landed on his jaw. She opened her mouth on that section, could feel the raspiness of his beard on his jaw bone. She nibbled him lightly, swiping her tongue across his flesh in a wet stroke.

His voice was hard with desire and weak with longing, coming out thick and quiet, the words guttural, "Because I want you." She thought that was all he had to say and that he'd summed it up succinctly. But then he continued, "more than anything. Because I lost control and had to taste you," he said, his head descending to hers slowly. His nostrils flared as he was an inch away from her, as though breathing in the smell of her blood.

He kissed her again and her back hit the wall, breath leaving her in a whoosh as he surged inside. She was so hungry to have him fill her body, feel his cock sink into her while his fangs pierced her neck. She wanted him to be in her twice, have him taking and giving at both ends, knowing that he was connected to her more than anyone else could be. He'd drink, drink and she'd come, shattering again and again as he took her, came in her.

Her hands were on his shoulders, kneading his skin through his shirt and then lower, slipping under his shirt, touching his stomach, feeling each delineated muscle of his smooth flesh. She sank her fingers into his skin and he stilled-head tilted to the side as he listened intently.

"What is it?" she gasped.

"Jack is arguing with Rachel. He says I may hurt you."

"Oh, I'm hurting," she murmured and he responded with an urgent press of his hips.

Lucas laughed and she looked around, startled, like the snow should melt and birds should sing at such a joyous sound. The sex was incredible, their chemistry explosive, but happiness.... He wasn't capable of it and she'd spent her whole life trying to find it. Hearing him laugh made it seem like happiness was not just a fantasy but *here*.

"There was a reason why I wanted to speak to you."

"Yeah, and I like it," she said, disappointed to be distracted from sex, relieved to not think about what he couldn't give her.

"You need to talk to Jack. If we cannot convince him to drink my blood voluntarily...." The sentence trailed off, hanging out there like Wile E. Coyote after he's run full-speed off the cliff before plummeting to the ground.

Oh crap. "Alright, you're going to have to finish that sentence. Let's get it all out in the open. No misunderstandings."

He nodded. "I will do it involuntarily, if that's what you wish."

"You'll force him to drink your blood?"

"I'll compel him with my gaze, yes. If that's what you want. It will be your decision."

She wanted to protest. *Me? Why is it my decision?"* And if I say no?"

"You know the answer," he said implacably.

She huffed, "So then how is it my decision?"

"It is your decision whether we ask him or whether I take the liberty to do what needs to be done on my own."

"Is that *really* the only option? Can't we wait a bit and see if we get out of here?"

"Optimism is not typically a successful strategy." He set her down, crossing his arms. "I do not know. If I leave you here while I go look for a way out, it will weaken me to wade through this much snow. It is at least a yard high."

"You mean three feet?"

"It's an abominable unit of measurement, but yes. Three *feet.*"

"How far could you get, before you would need...blood?"

He acted like her saying the word was a slap. *What, is the mere word a turn on?*

"The way things are now, I can go for a month without feeding. Even feeding you, Jack and Rachel, I still would not need sustenance for a few weeks. If I go into the wild and look for a way out once or twice, that time frame could drop down to a week, perhaps less, before I would need food."

"Right now we have no way to go anywhere. Let's say Rachel sends her will out, isn't it possible she could find *something* and then you could check it out? Then your trip would be focused?"

"We would both need blood if we did that." He crossed his arms, like he was settling in for an argument.

"I feed you and you feed Rachel."

"I cannot feed from you. I do not know what would happen. "His voice was implacable.

"You're not being reasonable. You've already had a few drops. What's the worst that could happen?"

"Slaughter."

She scowled. "Concise."

She watched as he lifted his hands to his mouth, blowing on his fingers. Did that work since he was a vampire?" Oh! I get it. You'd need to drink from *Jack*." She laughed. She couldn't help it. The hilarity of the situation was overwhelming. Not only would Jack *freak* out but it would be quite the picture. She stopped laughing. Lucas piercing Jack's neck and drinking his blood. In a twisted way, she suspected that would be super-hot.

But Jack wouldn't allow it. No, that made it sound trivial. As though Jack wouldn't eat a meat-lover's pizza because he was a vegetarian. His parents and the way they had died. What he had seen over the years.... Feeding Lucas would really screw with his head.

"There must be some way to ensure you have my blood without you becoming violent," she said. "Besides you *always* say that, and now you've had my blood twice and you've been fine. I think the lady doth protest too much."

His hands gripped her arms lightly, trying to rub warmth into them. "My luflych, thou cannought quoth Shakespeare to me."

His hand cupped her cheek, and she leaned in to him. *My love*, he'd said. It made her warm inside, the silly term of endearment that he rattled off simply to show that his Middle English was better than hers.

"If you were a full blooded empath who knew her powers, maybe. That would change things. Then it's a matter of trust, not violence."

"Why trust?" she asked, her voice soft.

"Trust you wouldn't harm me, kill me... permanently enslave me." His words were a bare a whisper before her, like the air would carry them away just as they reached her unless he kept close.

She felt the world narrow down to the two of them, an odd shimmery thing between them, an idea, just a kernel that was there for only them to see. Almost a dream, or a wish, to be so close, so connected that he'd trust her, and she'd trust him.

What was deeper than that? More seductive than giving yourself to someone because you knew they wouldn't hurt you? Because hurting the one you love would be just as bad as hurting one's own self.

Then he smiled and took a step back, his hands coming up to his face, coveringhim for a moment so she could only see his eyes. Like the connection was too much and he was erasing any outward display of how he felt, making himself a perfect blank mask again.

His hands came down, his arms folded across his chest and he said, "The evil glint in your eye makes me glad that is not a possibility or else I would be doing dishes and cleaning for the rest of my life."

She felt a slow smile spread across her face. "I'm not sure I had anything so domestic in mind, actually. A man of your skill and looks, I'm not sure you'd ever make it to the kitchen." She leaned in to kiss him and then pulled back, chastising herself. *Serious shit first, flirting later.*

"Is there any other way, besides drinking from Jack?" She bit her lip in agitation, but it hurt because of where he nicked her, and she reached up to touch the cut. Lucas walked away from her, all the way against the wall—putting distance between them.

If Jack was the only option, she'd have to decide if she was willing to allow that, let him take away Jack's will, violate him and then what? Pretend it never happened? Hope he'd forgive her if they made it out of here alive and she came clean in a Geraldo Rivera kind of way?

"If Jack allowed Rachel to drink from him and I drank from her immediately after, that would sustain me."

It killed her to say it, brought images to her mind that she hated. "Then why don't you drink from Rachel and leave Jack out of it?"

"We both need live blood. We cannot survive on vampire blood alone. It is power yes, but we are creatures of death. We need life to sustain ourselves. He is the only human. It must be him."

She shook her head and felt the need to pace, not just because it was fucking freezing but because there were too many bad options and she wanted to leave them all behind and pretend they didn't exist. Also, it really creeped her out to talk about Lucas being a creature of death.

"I'm telling you now, there is no way in *hell* Jack would let Marion's girlfriend—the woman who killed his parents while he watched— drink his blood. He'd rather die."

Lucas shook his head. "I think you are wrong."

Her mouth dropped open. "Are you fucking crazy?" Her heart started to pound, and Lucas shook his head, like shaking off a blow. Could he hear it?

"No, I am observant. And that is why we are in here discussing this. Because I think he will let her, and you need to be prepared for that."

"Me? Why me? He hates vampires. You heard him. He'd rather die than let one feed off of him!" She almost spit the words at him, she was so angry. "If you let her roll him with her gaze, it will be over between us, do you understand? I don't want her near him. Promise me that the moment we get out of here she won't go near him again."

"I do not police her."

"Bullshit. You can. You *should*. I don't want her with him."

"Jealous?" he said, the words barely audible.

She felt nauseous. "She's toying with him. It's sick. This isn't about jealousy, it's about not wanting someone I love to be tortured. You're talking about letting her feed on him, and it would break him." She could barely speak through the choking sensation in her throat.

"Listen to me. Stop. Listen." He was trying to make eye contact with her, wanted her to understand, his hands on her shoulders, leaning forward so that their faces were close together.

She looked at him, and his hand went around her nape, possessively, his fingers lacing through her hair. He kneaded the back of her neck, like forcing a comatose person to swallow water— forcing the knowledge down into her whether she wanted it or not. "He is drawn to her, the same way you are drawn to me. It's a very fine line between love and hate. He wants to kill vampires, and in that is a desire, almost as strong, to master one."

She tried to shake her head no, but his grip tightened a little. She didn't mind, didn't feel like pulling away, just noticed it, and allowed it because she needed him to understand too. And the connection, his hands upon her, his face close to hers, meant he'd understand her, too. "That's fucked up and wrong. I can see how that could happen, but not with him." Tears filled her eyes, coursed down her cheeks before she could blink them back.

He swore, not in English, something with lots of harsh consonants, and then he pulled her to him.

Why am I crying? Because he's mine. He's always been mine. Or was it because he'd always been a beacon of goodness, and Rachel was not good, but evil. Jack was the standard she was always supposed to have lived up to. The one she failed.

And if he'd go to her, let her drink because he wanted it, then she didn't know him after all. If that was true, she'd only known the *idea* of him, and she'd been wrong for years.

She was the weak one, the fucked up one who wanted a vampire despite what one of them had done to her mother. Jack was better than that. She felt her legs give out, but Lucas supported her.

That wasn't fair to Jack. To put that responsibility of moral perfection on his shoulders. Had she done always done that? And had she always felt like he was so much better than her? How could anything have worked between them if she really felt that way? *Duh. It couldn't.*

"You need to leave this alone," he said persuasively. Not with vampire powers but with a sincere conviction. "You must be prepared for him to allow her to feed from him. Do not interfere or else I will take away his will and give him to her. Do you understand? We could all die here."

She felt a touch of power that he put into the words. She pulled back from him, kicked at his shin as she jerked her head to the side, but his grip tightened a little, not letting her go.

He shoved her body flat against his, so that she'd have a harder time kicking him. She felt like a mummy, she was wrapped so tight against his body.

Her head was pressed to his shoulder, close to the crook of his neck, and she was angry, furious that he was telling her these things, and that he'd dared to use that touch of power on her. Had it worked? She tilted her head upwards, the only part of her that she could move, and bit him, determined to hurt him, make him let her go. She'd leave him and this awful conversation behind.

Because he was wrong. He didn't know a damned thing. And he'd tried to roll her. That was not part of their relationship. It was a betrayal.

The bite was harder than a press of lips or a kiss, harder than a nip or a love bite. So hard that he groaned and shuddered, his legs collapsing, taking her to the ground.

As they fell, his hands adjusted her legs so she straddled him. His cock became steel and he threw back his head in pleasure.

His blood hit her tongue like nicotine, suffusing her, cocooning her mind and body, sweeping down her like heroine and she cried out. His arms wrapped behind her keeping her in place as he thrust against her from below.

The blood tasted like wine with echoes of metal. The barest trace of dark magic, heady and powerful. Her body remembered it, shuddered in response, spasming in reflex and she bit harder, wanting to savage him. The small traces she was getting not enough to quench her sudden, rabid thirst.

"Wait," he breathed, the words agony as he rocked his hard length against her.

She pulled back and looked at him, breasts heaving against his solid chest. He reached up to his neck and she barely saw the knife. He shifted her slightly, aware of how squeamish she was, masking his movements.

When he turned back she could see the tiniest wound on his neck. Blood slid down into his shirt, a tiny crimson line against his smooth, white flesh. Her indecision was plain. What she

wanted—to gorge upon him. What she should do—get the
wiggins and bolt.

"I need you strong. I need you to survive this. Let me give it
to you." His eyes were intense, almost vulnerable or defiant, but
not quite either. She should go. She might need his blood, but
she didn't need it yet.

And then he cheated.

He slipped his hands around to the front of her body,
cupping her breasts, lifting them, pressing his palms and fingers
flat against her, then stroking his thumbs across her nipples
gently. His hands traced down, one going around her hips,
settling on her buttocks, the other slipping between her legs and
the seam of her jeans, where a hot ache spread from her in
waves. His hand pressed against her clitoris and she closed her
eyes, leaning forward and swiping her tongue against his neck
like he wanted.

She locked her lips onto his flesh, let him feel the dull edges
of her teeth as she sucked. His hands moved, one on her lower
back, pressing her close, the other in her hair, holding her
against his neck as he groaned and hissed out a breath of
desperate want in her ear. Making sure she didn't stop. He was
thrusting lightly, so that the friction of him pleasured her,
mimicked what his fingers or tongue would do to the pulsing
center of her body if he got her out of her clothes.

The blood filled her mouth and she swallowed. She knew he
could feel it by the way his hands convulsed as she took that first
gulp. Her name fell from his lips like a litany. The vowels

accented, the usual blandness of his words gone, voice filled with the sound of desperate passion.

Her teeth sank into his flesh again, wanting to coax more blood from him. Lucas liked that, gave a low cry. The blood blazed through her, hitting her stomach like whiskey— smoky, hot, and then burning.

She felt her body changing. A soul deep realignment as her blood vessels swelled, reacting and making her wet. And beyond that, somewhere deep inside, was that locked box of power. Like a treasure chest lost on the bottom of the sea, his blood found it, pulled it to the surface, smashed it open, releasing power into her body.

She needed to do something with it. She was *supposed* to do something with it. But what? How?

It was as if there was a gun pointed at her head, but she couldn't find her dammed wallet to give to the thief.

The urgency of it was there and she realized Lucas was talking to her, had been talking to her for a while now and she'd been so in her own head, her own body, turned around in her own raw power she hadn't heard a thing he said. "Make me come," he said, over and over again.

How the hell did she do that? The power was like a mudslide, coating her, sweeping her away, dragging her under, unhappy that it was directionless. Could it turn on her?

"Think it, channel the power to me. Think of your desire, think of what you want from me. You can bring me with it. Valerie, you-" And then he kissed her hard and the blood was back, copper and gold in her mouth that he drank down, the a drop of blood coming from the wound on her lip.

There. That was what she'd needed. She made her thoughts sharp, focused on Lucas. All her will, all her energy on him. How she wanted him, wanted him to come—

No.

That wasn't what she wanted. She dredged up all of her memories where she felt her own happiness and pushed it into him—A hug, a kiss, a funny movie, knowing someone loves you, laughing with a friend, doing something well and achieving a goal. All those things she wanted him to feel. Remember.

The magic was like a leviathan, slow to turn and follow, hard to make it go where she wanted to, but then she caught it, held it, focused every single part of her on that goal. She felt each vibration and pulse going from her to him, like waves sloshing in a pool, the energy bouncing off on one side and back again.

When he released her, his head dropped down to her shoulder, his breathing unsteady. Finally, he looked at her quizzically. "What did you try to do?"

"I tried to make you happy." She knew she was blushing.

"Why? I thought you were going to bring me."

"I can do that anytime," she said saucily, snapping her fingers to show how quick it was.

His brows raised but he didn't challenge the statement. Then he turned his head away from her, giving her just the strong profile of him as he smiled, chuckled lightly.

"I wanted you to be happy. I guess it didn't work." She tried to shrug like it was no big deal. He stood, lifting her away from him and she felt alone, not just sexually but because she had thought she was on to something.

He shook his head and looked back at her. "No," a really long pause, a shaky breath, and then quietly, like a secret, he said, "No. It did work. I was simply surprised."

"Maybe your idea of happy and my idea of happy are two different things," she said. *So why don't you tell me about it!? !*

He nodded his head very slightly and clasped her hands in his, raising her hands and twining his fingers through hers. "I thought you would give me the pleasure of sex and I suppose over time, the fleeting ecstasy of release is as...close to happiness as we get."

He blinked rapidly for a moment and stepped away from her, letting her go, putting his hands behind his back. "But that is not happiness. I had forgotten. Thank you."

Her throat was tight with unshed tears. What did he mean? What had he felt?" So it was happiness?"

"It was... a memory from very long ago. I didn't feel the happiness of it, so much as the moment...." His smile was real and human. "I remembered my daughter learning to ride her horse. It was like I could feel the horse's mane under my palm, knew the heft of the leather bridle. She'd hold out her arms at the end of our lesson, and I would always smell the sun on her hair. Anyway, I was reminded of that."

"You felt that?" she asked, hope in every syllable.

His brow furrowed, like he was thinking of lying or something. "As a young boy in my father's keep, I always knew when it was a feast day. The men would stay up late, drink a lot, and everything was very loud. Rowdy as the night wore on. I would be sent to bed with the other children and yet I could hear them through the walls. I was not in on the joking nor was I part of the festivities, but it was a comfort to know it was there. The feeling was like that, not something I was involved in, but it was...good to have it so close."

He tucked her hair behind her ear almost reverently. "Your power is wild and unused. The more comfortable with it you become, the more you can alter it. Emotions can be less or more. You can give pain, take away pain, even steal memories. Your power is a strength. And given time, you could wield it like a weapon."

"Would you like that?" she asked, unsure what answer she wanted.

"I want you safe. I want you to know how to protect yourself and to have defenses. And maybe, one day, I would like that." He gave her a light kiss on the lips, so soft and warm that it was like the first day of spring. Her heart melted, leaving the surrounding snow temporarily forgotten.

CHAPTER 28

Jack watched Valerie go 'talk' to Lucas. He was the grim reaper and they were all at his mercy. Waiting for him to pick them off, one by one.

He still couldn't believe he had tried to shoot him. He knew with every fiber of his being that a bullet—even a dozen bullets— would have no impact on Lucas, but he just had to.

He'd snapped. Panicked. Been overcome with rage. Killing Lucas accomplished something. Shooting him did nothing. *I'm a fucking idiot.* He was lucky Lucas hadn't killed him. A small part of him wondered if he'd done it on purpose, egging Lucas on.

Val had warned him, just about begged him, not to send her to him. To leave Lucas alone, and smug asshole that he was, like his prick was made out of diamonds, he'd told her she'd be fine. He'd actually believed he'd be able to keep her safe. Why? What kind of track record did he have for keeping anyone safe? Not his parents. Not Nate. And now Val.

He needed to hit something. Was stuck taking a deep, unsatisfying breath instead. *Yeah, really not that great. Like some yoga bullshit is going to be enough to erase this rage.* The rage of failure, of looming disaster, sat on his chest like a Mack truck.

And the rage of goodbye, because that monster would take her from him if he could. And that was Jack's fault. *Fuck!* He punched the wall, pain chasing away the despair and anger so he felt—not better—but different.

"He won't hurt her," Rachel said from near the door. He'd almost forgotten about her. Turned his back on a vampire. *Christ.* He was fucking worthless.

His voice sounded pulverized. "He's already hurt her. It's his fault she's here. That we're all here. We're going to die here because of this hare brained scheme." Then he turned, stalking towards her. She didn't move overtly, but there was *something* that made him think she was on her guard.

Why? An unarmed, puny human that she could kill whenever she wanted to. Another glaring example of how stupid he was. How weak. Since the day his parents had died he'd been cautious. He had always double checked everything. When the odds were impossible and death was likely, one was damned careful. That was the only reason he had lived for so long.

Now he was out of his depth. Not acting, but reacting. And failing.

Jack caught that almost imperceptible flinch on Rachel's face, and it made him brave. *You like her being afraid of you.* And that fucked up thought rekindled his anger so that he continued towards her, watching almost hungrily as her back pressed harder into the door. He boxed her in.

She took a shaky breath.

His hands slapped the wood on either side of her head. He looked into her face and let the anger—his only constant friend—boil to the surface.

More anger, more disgust for himself and this *thing* with her. Her eyes were wide. As if she were afraid. And he wondered if she was mocking him. Pretending to be worried before she laughed at him.

Her lips were smooth and full, her eyes vivid, cheekbones almost sharp. She looked like an actress. Not a model, who would take beautiful photos from one angle and look odd from another, but icy perfection from all angles. And that brittleness that lurked under the surface.

Vulnerability.

But for what?

His instincts as a hunter, as a killer, honed in on that weakness, like a cheetah finding the sick gazelle in the herd. *Isolate her. Take her down. Easy prey.* The closer he got to her, the easier she was. "Do you think we're going to die here?" he asked her with a lover's tone. Gruff and intimate, searching for the smallest sign of trickery on her porcelain face.

"No. I think we're here for a purpose," she said. Too loud for how close he was.

"What's that? So he can drink her blood and kill her? So you can have mine?"

She ripped her gaze away, and he felt the victory of that. Like he was right, and acknowledging it made her weaker.

"The Fey will come for us. When the Fey want you, you don't escape. There is no running from them."

He stepped in a little closer. Close enough to see a tiny freckle on her neck. "You say that like you're afraid." A whisper.

"I am. We should all be afraid of the Fey. Lucas especially. They're the bogeymen, the monsters under the bed that made vampires frightened," she said, staring over his shoulder.

He couldn't help but see the rise and fall of her chest. "And you're afraid. You're worried, is that right? Every time I see you, you're different. One day you're confident. One day you taunt. The next day you burn. And now you're afraid." *Is there anything real about her?*

She bit her lip.

His anger coalesced, had a target now. Her response to him and that he liked it made everything worse. Made him feel dangerous. The flip side to self-loathing. "Every day is different, and every day is false. Why would Lucas come here if it's so dangerous to him?"

"I don't know."

"That's bullshit. You *know*," he said, hand smacking against the wood, right next to her ear. It sounded like a gunshot and she reacted the same way—jumped, trembling with a desire to run away.

He lifted his hand and he could feel her terror and indecision. His hand cupped her jaw, holding her in place, trapping her with her own desire for him. The barest touch and she froze. He didn't need to be a vampire to compel her or beat her, all he had to do was touch her and she crumbled before him.

If it's real.

She made the faintest sound, almost of despair, her body trying to sink further into the wood, as she let him overpower her.

Because that was the truth, and they both knew it. She could kill him, escape him, hurt him with her physical strength. And yet she seemed paralyzed. Weak. Like he was the one with all the power.

She was tall. So tall that her mouth was perilously close to his.

"He hates us," she said. A bare breath of sound.

Jack put his hand on her neck.

"He hates vampires. Hates them all. And I think, at first, he wanted the Fey back so that they would kill us for him. But Val is a wild card."

His grip tightened when she said Valerie's name and she jerked her head lightly, as if in pain.

Jack let go, saw white marks from his fingers. Had he hurt her? Did he hurt women now? No, he hunted and killed monsters. *Just because she plays nice now and again doesn't change what she is.*

She turned her head, looking away from him to the far wall, sucking her body in even tighter against the wood—but not escaping.

"He only wants her because she's an empath," Jack said.

Rachel looked back at him, and a flash of pity crossed her face. "No. He wants her for more than that."

"What?"

"Everything." She gave a sad smile, like he'd have no concept of what she really meant.

"I'll kill him if he tries to turn her."

"And her too? You'd kill her too?"

He pushed away from her angrily. He saw her shoulders relax, her hands tighten and loosen, then her arms crossed over her chest as she straightened. Still standing in front of the door.

"Don't be stupid, Jack. You *know*, you must understand how strong he is. You can't be so foolish as to-"

"Die for love? Die at his hands to keep her from him? She wouldn't love him then."

"No. I understand dying for love. I understand sacrifice for pleasure, when devotion turns to anger. But you have to look at this clearly. Lucas won't turn her into a vampire. He *hates* what he is and he wouldn't do that to her. She'd be different. She'd probably break. Having to take life to survive, that's not what he wants for her. That's not his goal. The only reason I'm alive—" she broke off.

Wait. His head cocked to the side. "Why is he keeping you alive?"

Her words were quick. "For this. To help with the Fey."

No. She'd given something away. He just had to find it.

"What else? What could his goal be, that he would leave you alive? Why would he need a witch?" He seemed to be thinking it over, trying to find the pieces, and then he gave her an evil smile.

A smile only one person had ever given her. Dark knowledge, a smile of pain and bitterness. Marion's smile. And it had the same effect it always did. It made her hot, made her want to surrender.

Dammit, she wanted to move away from this door. She'd run outside, run away screaming, bury herself in the deep snow until her blood became as sluggish as an Alaskan stream. Anything but this terrifying heat.

Jack came towards her again, stopping in front of her.

Too close.

She was in her own personal horror movie. The villain sneaking up on the unsuspecting woman, knife raised, while his victim watched it all happen.

Let it happen.

She was transfixed as he prowled back towards her, settled his arms on either side of her body, hands on the smooth wood.

Oppressing her.

She could smell him. Smell his skin, which smelled like the sun. His blood, which smelled like cotton candy and would dissolve on her tongue. And then there was the scent of his anger— smoky and woodsy. And under that, *deep* under that, but rising to the surface, was the perfect scent of lust.

His voice snapped her back to the present.

"You tried to kill him. And he's killed others for less. But not you, and not Marion, solely so he has a hold on you. I want you to tell me why."

And then she almost moaned in frightened lust, bit her tongue to keep herself quiet, as he lifted a finger and traced it down her cheek. The warmth of his skin seeping into her. There was blood on his hand. Almost dry, from where he'd punched the wall and split the skin that covered his knuckles. He scared the hell out of her. The temptation of a good man brought low.

She'd do anything to kiss his hand, lick it better. To have his blood inside of her and have him take her in return.

Her mouth filled with saliva, her body already liquid desire. And he *knew*. His hatred for her and for himself was clear. And that shook her back to herself. As though he was the vampire and she was breaking his compulsion.

Well, Fuck Him.

He hated her, was manipulating her in a pathetic and obvious way. She knew it. And yet, she was still vulnerable. Still wanted him badly enough that he had the upper hand.

"That's not my secret to tell," she said. Then she leaned forward, so her breath hit his lips, "And I'm a lesbian, so the odds of you being able to fuck the answer out of me are pretty low. And the chances of you being able to beat it out of me are non-existent. Now get the fuck away from me or I'll rip your dick off." She raised her body off the wood, bringing it closer to his, almost certain that if her body pressed up against his, that she'd feel his cock, hard as a steel bar.

Jack jerked away from her and she had to hide a tremble of joy and loss that he'd left her alone.

He could own her. He'd hate her, fuck her, hate himself and they'd both be destroyed by it. Their rage and despair was like a river of golden honey before her. She could eat that negativity, feed her abilities forever on all the fucked up misery they could make come out of each other.

And all she had to do was be herself.

Lucas and Val eventually returned. Jack looked them both over from head to foot and had to look away. It was possible that the cold had put that flush on her cheeks. Possible, but unlikely. Yet, she was still alive. What the fuck was he going to do?

Lucas held the door open, inclining his head and Rachel followed him. Leaving him alone with Valerie. The fire crackled and Valerie jumped a little. What could he say to her? *I'm sorry I'm such an asshole. I'm sorry I've failed you. I fucked up.*

"Did he hurt you?" he said instead, hating the sound of his own voice.

"No." She blushed.

Jesus Christ. And it was his own fucking fault.

CHAPTER 29

The night was tense. The fire was steady, the only sound it's faint, periodic crackle. There had been a moment of confusion when they all had to decide where to sleep.

Lucas and Rachel didn't need to sleep, and that was part of the problem. Knowing that they were there, looming over them while they were at their most vulnerable. Well, the truth was that Jack was worried— Val felt safe enough and knew she'd sleep like a baby.

A hungry baby.

When Valerie had come in with Lucas, things had been weird. Tension so thick it wouldn't cut with a knife. Tension like resilient Jell-O. Val knew she had problems with Lucas, but, she wondered if maybe Jack really did have his own problems with Rachel.

Lucas had said as much.

And so she'd watched them. Watched how they *didn't* look at each other. At least not when the other might have the faintest chance of seeing it. But as soon as one of them turned away or was distracted, the other looked, absorbed the other's form with the intensity of a desperate prospector sifting for gold.

Did it hurt? Hell, yeah, it hurt. But how much? That was the question. The answer was somewhere between a little and a lot. She wanted to throw Rachel out—okay, no. She wanted to *kill* Rachel. There was a time and place for pacifism. Rachel didn't deserve a stay of execution. She also wanted to make Jack notice her, keep his devotion on her and yet....

Was it stupid to say it was like a purse? A purse she'd wanted forever and ever but then had finally gotten and found that maybe the opening was too small or it slid off her shoulder when it was supposed to stay put. *Reality wasn't as good as the fantasy.*

And now she was here with Lucas, in this tiny space, with his blood coursing through her body. And those tiny molecules of her own blood in him. She felt different, slightly disconnected from herself, like part of her soul was dangling in front of her, an umbilical cord to Lucas so that her own person was no longer just her own.

She would swear her heart was beating differently, too. Almost more pronounced. The thud was a little more resonant, as if she was in perpetual meditation or that moment before one faints—a second before everything goes black.

And so she found herself looking at Lucas when she knew she should be looking at nothing. She watched him and everything he did. When he put wood in the fireplace and wiped his hands. When he stood in a smooth gesture and absently ran a hand through his hair. And occasionally he rolled his shoulders, like he was tense.

He watched her back. Not obviously, but she was aware of it and suspected he wanted her to know that he was thinking of her. She'd see him watching her under his lashes, or he'd give her a brief smile, a quick flash, a quirk. And then once, when he seemed to be very distracted, he'd blinked back to himself and given her a nod, as though he couldn't remember quite who she was or why he was here.

No conversation, no talk about food or drink. They'd just laid down and pretended to sleep. She wanted to lay next to Lucas, curl into his body or put her head on his thigh as he satleaning back against the wall, but couldn't. Jack was unpredictable and she worried about setting him off again.

There had been a moment where they'd made eye contact and she'd remembered Hawaii. The few nights they'd slept wrapped in each other's arms.

It made her sad on a fundamental level and that wasn't only because something had been lost during those few days, but because of the futility of it all. They'd held each other so tight, not even a sheet could slip between them.

Every morning she'd had a crick in her neck because they'd clung to each other so tightly. Her heart seized in her chest a little. There was no reason to bullshit herself. She knew why they'd clung to each other so desperately. Because their relationship was fleeting. It wasn't something they were going to get comfortable with and she'd hoped that if she'd slept close enough, grasped him tight enough in the midnight hours, that she'd always be able to remember what it felt like to be in his arms.

Or that maybe it would have worked.

She felt a tear splash on her hand and a handkerchief instantly dangled before her face. She looked up through a glaze of tears and saw Lucas, his golden hair blurred so that it looked like a halo.

She took the cloth and pressed it to her eyes, turning away from Jack and Rachel in hopes they'd leave her alone. She knew they'd notice. She never got away with tears when she really needed to.

The cloth was fine, ironed and pressed, made of linen that smelled like rosemary and sandalwood. Just a hint of a pleasurable smell from another time. And really, when was the last time someone had used a handkerchief anyway? 1960?

Lucas slid down the wall and sat beside her. Not moving towards her or doing anything to rile Jack, which she was grateful for. But his hand was open and beside her, a bare inch from her thigh and she knew she could take his hand, that he was offering a hidden comfort. A way to be touched without the others seeing and she wanted to— so much that for a moment she felt a ghostly handshake on her palm.

But she left it alone. Turned her head away and stretched out, laying on the ground. Pillowing her head on a little cushion that had been left behind.

By who?

CHAPTER 30

Valerie knew she was dreaming. She was back at the pond that Lucas had dragged her out of, but now he was nowhere in sight.

"Will you go in now?" Cerdewellyn asked her, gesturing towards the water.

"Why?" Val asked.

"You must go to the island and get the flower, then bring it back here to me."

"Which flower?" In the middle of the pond was a small island, a single tree and some scrub bushes crowded together. She didn't see any flowers.

He inclined his head and she looked again. A beautiful flower, like a bird of paradise was there, all on its own. How had she missed that? Val walked towards the water but he stopped her with a word.

Had he called her name? She couldn't remember what he'd said, as though he hadn't said anything aloud. His hands were on her back, undoing the laces of her long gray dress. His touch was impersonal, so light and quick that if she hadn't felt her dress sag she wouldn't have noticed it at all.

"The dress is too heavy. It will pull you under the water. Do you understand?" he asked.

She nodded and the dress pooled at her feet leaving her in a shift. She wondered if she should remove that too, but didn't want to and she *felt* him tell her 'no. '

Was that right, she'd felt it?

"Where is Lucas?"

The hands on her back stilled. "He will not interrupt again. Not here. Although, his connection to you is stronger. You must stop taking his blood or you will never be free of him. The more you drink from him, the more you will want it. And it is the same for him. With each exchange he will crave you more and more until he devours you. But now that you are here I can protect you."

The meaning of his words slipped off of her as she stepped into the water and stepped deeper. The cold murky water licked up her body, almost parting for her, caressing her as she swam to the little island.

It didn't take very long, twenty strokes, maybe a few more, and then she could touch the bottom near the island. The ground squished unpleasantly, mud and sharp rocks poking at her. One of the stones embedded in her foot and she yelped, hobbling to the shore. She sat down on the bank, cradling her foot in her hands. A small white rock protruded from her heel.

She pulled it out, blood dripping all around her and studied the rock. It was odd. A brilliant white, tiny sharp ends on one side. Her hands trembled. It wasn't a rock. It was a human tooth. Val dropped it and scrambled onto the island, her feet sliding in the mud.

Why would there be a tooth on the bottom of the water? What else had she stepped on? All those hard sharp things, which she'd assumed were sticks...what if they were bones? Her toe had slipped inside a shell and she'd ignored it, but...what if it had been a skull? What if the thing she'd stepped on that had cracked had been a jaw bone?

She wanted to throw up, felt bile rise in her throat as she thought about the slippery things that had touched her. Not seaweed. She had an image of skins, wet and slick sliding past her in the water.

Who had died in this water? No, that wasn't the right question. How *many* had died in that water?

Her stomach heaved and she gagged, but her stomach was empty, dry spasms wracking her body. She almost wished she had eaten something, just to blunt her body's clenching as it tried harder and harder to purge itself of nothing.

She collapsed on the ground, hugging her knees and looking out at the brown water. Brown and bloody. The only way out was back. Through that clinging stew of water, the bottom filled with jagged bones and a muddy layer of death. She couldn't do it. She just couldn't.

There is no other way.

She looked at the shore and Cerdewellyn who stood there, watching her.

Waiting for her. He stood proud and tall, his hands clasped behind his back as though he were patient. A gentleman with all the time in the world. But there was more to it than that. An intensity and a focus was in his gaze that made her hesitate. He didn't gesture to her or call out, but she expected him to urge her on, or ask her why she was waiting, even tilt his head in inquiry, but he remained motionless.

Pick the flower and get back to shore. This can all be over in a moment.

Val picked the flower, the bloom detaching easily. The stalk shriveled and died, like a salted snail, decaying before her eyes.

Her heart sped up. She turned back to the water and waded in a few feet. *I don't want to go back in there.*

She was being ridiculous. It wasn't a human tooth. She had no reason to think that. There was nothing at the bottom of that pond except sticks and mud.

But her body was clammy with revulsion. She had goose bumps on her skin and dreaded each step in the cold, dark water. It swirled around her waist and she dove in, swimming as fast as she could to shore, lunging forward before she could think better of it and change her mind.

If you hesitate, you shall never go in.

Water licked at her lips, went into her nose and her eyes. She wanted to scream and give in to the horror but if she could just keep it together for a little longer—five, four, three more strokes she'd be there.

Her foot touched down on the bottom, standing and wading to shore.

Run. Her feet touched and scraped things, some of them warm, a few of them viscous and one terrible thing that was round and small. When her weight shifted forward it exploded.

It wasn't an eye.

She emerged from the water on the verge of panic. Cerdewellyn's hand was extended, waiting for her to put the flower in to his waiting palm.

It was bright and beautiful, a perfect juxtaposition to what she had just swum through. She looked at his outstretched hand. Elegant fingers, smooth palms that looked like he'd never done a day's worth of manual labor.

Too perfect. She blinked. A feeling of tightness surrounded her, like she was in a summer storm, the ozone heavy. The breeze caught her hair, lifting strands towards him, reminding her of snakes writhing.

"Just take it," she said on a hunch, her hand poised above his.

He shook his head. "I cannot. You must give it to me."

"And then what? What do I collect next?"

"Nothing. This is the final piece. I ask nothing else of you." There was a smile on his face. Gentle, and yet for some reason she thought of little red riding hood. She suspected that with the outdated outfit he was rocking, making a joke about sharp teeth or big eyes would be lost on him.

"But you must give it to me." The words were not forceful, nor were they begging but there was a hint of urgency in them. As though he wasn't sure he could convey how important it was— and didn't know if he wanted to.

"What will happen? When you have it?"

"I do not know. I have things I would like to do, but am unsure if I have the means to accomplish them."

She nodded, the reason somehow good enough and put the flower in his hand, the tips of her fingers touching his warm palm. The sky went dark and the wind picked up upon contact. Val had a desperate urge to take the flower back.

Too late.

Bits of leaves and twigs began to swirl around her, pelting her, like she was close to the center of a tornado but had just missed the calm center.

His dark hair blew in the breeze, an eager smile making fine lines appear at the corner of each eye. His response reminded her of Lucas. He knew things, didn't plan on telling her anything and had a stock reaction—a smile. It was unreadable and she had no idea if it was sincere or not.

Cerdewellyn wore the smile like armor.

But Lucas didn't smile. His response to surprises, bad information, or questions was a perfect blankness. Impenetrable because she never knew what was important and what was trivial. Everything got the same response.

But they both had reactions they'd cultivated over the centuries.

They are both so damned old.

He looked at her palm, tilting his head to the side a little, brows furrowed. "The bloom harmed your fair skin." She looked at her hand, at the blood dripping to the ground.

The sky turned black, so dark that it was like an eclipse was slicing through the land. He took a step closer, his hand cupping her face, and he tilted her face up so she looked into his grave-dark eyes.

"Do you want to see?" he asked her.

"Yes."

She'd always been too curious for her own good.

CHAPTER 31

Valerie changed, felt like she evolved and lost corporeal form. She was above the land and part of everything. From the trees to the air. From the twigs flying around to the water in the pond.

Her consciousness flew upwards as though she was watching a movie play out below her. She was no longer part of the earth but as insubstantial, and uninvolved with the world below as the clouds that surrounded her.

Cerdwellyn was beneath her, walking through the meadow filled only with perfect blooms. But the color was gone and the flowers were black. The grass chrome gray. Darkness was everywhere, roiling towards him, the ground buckling upwards.

The end of the world.

Thunder boomed, lightning slashing through the sky as far as she could see. Twenty, thirty strikes at a time. Veins of fiery illumination brightening the sudden gloom.

There was a breath, as though everything in nature was expectant and ready for this moment. Pressure. The energy from the lightning and the sound from the thunder built. The sky lit up, bright lightning slamming to the earth, twelve huge bolts of it across the land that sizzled and flared, leaving fire in their wake.

This is hell.

The places where lightning struck continued to glow and burn. The vortex descended upon Cerdwellyn, consuming him, As if the world had devoured him.

Lightning struck, slamming into the vacant space Cerdewellyn had left behind. Then the storm was gone. The fires died and there was nothing but charred earth.

Slowly, the darkness wandered away like fog before a rising sun.

Cerdewellyn was back.

Cer was pleased that she looked at him without fear. As though he resembled himself. He still had enough glamour to trick a half-mortal. If she saw him as he really was, she would run away screaming, perhaps even die from fright. He looked down at his nude form and the pieces of himself that he had been able to force together.

She had brought him his arms and his legs, his torso, his head, even his manhood. A dozen pieces the Queen had cut him into. This mortal had picked them all up, believing them to be flowers and returning them to him without hesitation.

He knew he looked akin to a ghoul. One of the misshapen creatures who had previously walked the earth and been under his dominion. Blood leaked from his wounds, all the pieces stacked on top of each other, held together by will alone.

One more piece. His heart. Then he would be whole. Able to fuse himself back together and start the long process of regaining his strength.

She swam back to shore and he wanted to scream at her to hurry but he waited. Regal dignity. Unending patience. A vendetta that could keep a moment longer.

She came out of the water, water and blood streaming down her form. She still believed it to be an ordinary pond—*good*. He did not want to deal with the theatrics she would have if she knew just what things clung to her hair and dripped from her skin.

The pond was a graveyard for creatures both fantastical and common. All of them moldering away in the deep.

His heart at the very center of it all.

Give it to me, he wanted to shout at her. So he smiled, instead. *Patience.* It meant he knew every contingency of his revenge. After all, he had plotted it out for centuries. This woman held his heart in her hands and gave it to him gladly. Her own hand was bleeding and he was pleased with the way her blood joined with his, absorbing the essence of her vitality like a midnight fiend.

As soon as she handed him his heart, he began to heal. Power rushed to him, flowing from the land, through the air and the water, coalescing inside him and remaking him.

Whole.

Free.

Virginia.

Cerdewellyn knew, *knew*, she was dead. That he'd been away for a small eternity and that she was lost to him. But he had to look for her. Couldn't help himself. He ran towards the water, where her body had been discarded so cruelly and waded into it, looking for her. He screamed her name and dove under the water. And all the time he wondered why he did it.

To help him grieve?

Because he had imagined doing it, even as he lay in a dreamlike comatose state, for so long that he could not imagine doing anything else?

He didn't know how long he looked for her but when he'd awakened the sun had been high and now there were long shadows everywhere. The sky was pink and orange with the setting sun and it was time to go.

Virginia was gone. Slaughtered. And for what purpose? What did his Queen think she could accomplish with him out of the way? He was King. *He* was what mattered. She had been nothing but a glorified brood mare. All her power and glory had been a gift he had bestowed upon her. She was nothing.

And to try to kill *him*?

His castle was in the distance and he walked towards it, his boots squishing with pond water and his breeches cold and soaked. He pushed his black hair back from his eyes and walked up the hill, using a touch of power to force the water from him, feeling the muck and water slide away, leaving a dark trail behind him. He was dry within steps.

He would kill her. The faux-Queen bitch. Walk up to her, put a hand upon her chest and take all the life he had given her back into himself. Put an end to her and whoever defended her. Every guard and subject who had been loyal.

Even his people. If they were not happy to see him he would take them too. Nothing but blathering apology after apology would assuage his murderous rage. Then he would fix things—*if* he could.

Virginia Dare was dead. The girl they had all needed. The one who held the magic. Let him see what his witch thought could be done this time. He could not fathom a solution.

The main castle was on top of a hill. There were others spread throughout the land. Holdings several weeks away by horseback, but this was his home and where the court had always been.

He passed cottages and workshops, finding them abandoned. As if they had been empty forever. Once upon a time there had been tens of thousands of Fey. Ones that appeared human. Ones that looked like monsters. Some were impish. Some were small and yet others were large. As many varieties of Fey as one could imagine.

But the decline had started thousands of years ago. The rise of other gods had taken its toll, left him weaker and weaker as fewer people believed in the fierce dreadedness of *Him*.

By the time Lucas had come along, his own world looked as though it had been struck by the plague. People abandoned their homes to move closer to his court. Fields were empty, forests deserted.

The drawbridge was down. Cer frowned, looked up at the portcullis and was shocked to see that no one was present. Was there a feast? Would he take them all unawares? The most peculiar thought went through him—what if they knew he was back and were all here to curse his name? Awaiting him in order to ambush him, again?

Try. Let them. He did not cower and would not retreat. *Not again.*

He had fled Lucas.

He had been patient with Virginia.

He had allowed his Queen to live out of sentimentality.

And in the end he had learned a terrible and priceless lesson— Kindness is a fatal mistake. He should have been ruthless.

He was King.

He was a God.

And he was vengeful.

He walked up the drawbridge and the the silence heavy. Despair was thick and cloying in the air. It clung to everything. The keep was dark. No torches to light his way. Not that he needed the light. He walked confidently into the pitch black castle, knowing every step and uneven stone.

To him, even the castle had a pulse. At least it had. Once upon a time. Now he felt disconnected. As though everything around him was a vision he had seen a hundred times before but had never experienced in reality. Cer went into the great hall.

And stopped dead.

The table was set with crystal and gold plates. Food was on the table, and his people were seated, ready to partake of a meal that had never begun. In the dark he could see them covered in gray dust. His Queen sat at the head, her bright blond hair and elfin features—so beautiful that mortals had gasped in adoration when she appeared—were shriveled and old.

Her hair looked like someone had shaken flour over it, no luster but brittle and pale. She was slumped back in her seat, lips open, eyes wide and sunken, dried up in the sockets like plums. Fifty of his followers sat at the table. The velvet and satin of their clothes decaying upon their halted forms.

He walked around the table, heard his boots echo on the floor, saw the wolves transformed in front of the fire—as though they were idle and waiting for their master to come home. They were still as death.

Were they dead? He went up to his Queen, peering at her, feeling slightly anxious. As if she might lean forward suddenly and scream at him. A nightmare fairytale come to life.

Was he scared of her? No. But he could not allow himself to touch her or he would kill her in his fury. Cerdewellyn backed away. He went to the other end of the table and touched Verica, one of his lovers, instead.

A spark of life was still there. It was as though they had all sat down for a meal and then, for some reason, they had never gotten up again. Cer laughed miserably. There was only him. Trapped in a world of his making. Alone in an empty realm.

But not for long.

CHAPTER 32

Valerie awoke with a gasp. She jerked up, taking a deep breath and looking around her. Jack, Rachel and Lucas were standing. Lucas threw the gun he'd taken from Jack back to him. Jack caught it, looking confused. Lucas pointed at the front door and said harshly, "*That* is more dangerous than me. You must be armed to defend yourself and Valerie."

There was a terrible howling sound outside and it was growing louder, closer. So sinister that it raised every hair on her body and made her throat go dry. "I feel like I'm in the Blair Witch Project. What the hell is that?" Val asked.

"It is the Wild Hunt," Lucas said coolly.

"And that means *what*? Christ, just tell us the damned information," Jack said angrily, taking a step towards Lucas.

"Legend says that when the Wild Hunt rides by, all must be in their beds, must close their eyes tight, for even to catch a glimpse of the Fey as they pass by is to put oneself in the greatest peril. One must not draw their attention."

"Are they looking for us?" Jack asked.

Lucas said nothing for a moment. "I have seen no one else to look for, but we shall know soon enough."

"Stay inside," Lucas said and picked up his sword, going to the door.

"Wait! Why are you going outside? You said we were supposed to stay hidden," Val said, reaching out to him.

He looked at her, an almost fond look on his face. "No, I said it was legend that one would be harmed. I did not say it was fact. This is nothing but a parlor trick, simple Fey Glamour. I'll meet them, discuss terms and then, when I tell you, you may come out."

He turned away from her, took a step towards the door and stopped. There was only silence outside. She strained to listen and heard nothing. "Maybe it's gone," Val whispered.

"No. It is here. He has come to us," Lucas said.

And then there was a knock at the door.

CHAPTER 33

The door swung open, the hinges squeaking from rust and sounding ominous—just like it always did in the horror movies. *Crap.* The man from her dream stood at the threshold. Beyond him was sunshine and, in the quiet, she could hear the dripping sound of melting snow splashing onto the ground.

"Cerdewellyn. Well met," Lucas said gravely.

Cerdewellyn's gaze slid over Lucas briefly and then beyond him, to Valerie. "And there is the woman who set me free. You have done me a great service." He looked back at Lucas. "I intend to return the favor."

Lucas stepped in front of her, blocking Cer's view. "She is under my protection. We sought you of our own volition and wish to put the past behind us."

Cer laughed darkly, looking at Rachel and Jack in turn. "You have unusual travelling companions, Lucas. You come traipsing around my lands with your horde nowhere in sight?"

"Most of those you knew are gone."

Cer raised a brow, almost mockingly. "A changing of the guard, is that it? Or has a smattering of justice finally reached out and wiped out your own kind, just as you slew mine?" He turned back to Valerie, apparently dismissing Lucas.

"Welcome to the Land of the Fey," he said evenly. Then he shook his head slowly. "You were always so careful, Lucas. After all this time, all the tricks and traps, we never managed to get you to our land, where the odds were even. And now, here you are. I look forward to extending you the same courtesy you have given me and mine. You are more than welcome to join us at the castle, as soon as you may."

Something grabbed Val around the ankle, and she stumbled backwards. Vines twined around her legs, sliding upwards towards her waist, binding her legs together and cinching them tight.

The dense green vines consumed her, covered her ears and her eyes, so she could hear nothing, *see* nothing, consumed so fast she couldn't even draw breath to scream. The green bands tightened across her stomach, forcing the air from her lungs, strangling her tight from head to toe.

She felt tugging, as though someone was trying to rip the vines away from her, even as they coiled more tightly. She was nothing but a spider's meal, wrapped up and ready to be devoured.

CHAPTER 34

As the vines twined around Valerie, Lucas burst into action, charging Cerdewellyn—and running straight through him. Cer laughed. "Really, Lucas? You are getting old. It is an illusion. I would not stay around here, waiting for you to take my head off as I free your victim."

Lucas was back to Valerie, ripping vines off of her body, before Cer had even finished speaking. The vines multiplied, grew sharper, so that each one he touched pierced his hands, shredded them. Jack swore and rushed forward, standing beside Lucas as they tried to get Val free. The vines were alive. Twisting and shifting away from their grasp. When one was pulled free, another grew back, stronger and more resilient. In seconds, the vines went slack, dropped to the ground, dried and blackened, then decayed. And where Valerie had been was only a small pile of earth.

"Where is she?" Jack asked, gasping.

Lucas was already up, strapping his sword across his back, looking at Rachel. "The castle is to the West. Go there as soon as you may, and I will meet you."

Rachel looked outside. "What about the snow?"

"It is melting. He has no purpose for it any longer. As soon as you can travel, come find us."

"Lucas, you should wait. He's not going to hurt her," Rachel said, coming forward and taking his arm.

Lucas stepped close to Rachel. "You do not know anything about him or what he might do. Come to the castle and, when you get there, we leave this accursed land. There is a way out at the castle."

"Wait. How do you know there is a way out?" Jack asked.

Lucas didn't spare him a glance. "Everyone knows." And then he was gone, disappearing in a blink.

Jack stared at Rachel sightlessly, thoughts whirling through his mind. Valerie was gone. They were trapped here. He and Val were nothing but food. *Assuming she is still alive.*

His fault.

I failed.

Rachel turned, watched him. "Let's go. We'll follow his trail. It'll get us there eventually." She walked to the door, and Jack took a step, tried to follow, heard the blood pounding in his ears, beating out accusations and blame. He'd pushed Val into this. She was here because of him. *Wasn't that always a price you were willing to pay? You knew it was dangerous and that she might die, but you wanted her here anyway.*

"Let's go, Jack. We have to move."

He stumbled after her, almost falling out of the cottage and into the snow. Lucas was right—the snow had begun to melt and was now hard and frozen, half the height it had been the night before. At this pace, it might be completely gone in an hour or two. *Impossible.*

Jack trudged along behind Rachel, lost to his own thoughts. Rachel stepped carefully, filling Lucas' tracks in the snow. Lucas was nowhere to be seen, using his super-speed to hurry ahead of them.

The ground was flat enough, but trudging through the snow was awkward and slowed them down. Every now and again, they passed through sections of forest. But there were no more cottages or dwellings, no other footsteps in the snow beyond Lucas' and theirs. Not even animal tracks.

One foot in front of the other. And so he did it. Stepped and stepped as his mind sluggishly rehashed everything that had happened in recent memory. *Nate. Hawaii. The fights.*

Eventually, Rachel stopped and so did he. She turned and looked at him, head to foot and then back, stopping at his eyes. "You're still back there, huh? I wasn't sure. It's been hours since you've said a word."

Jack licked his lips. God, he was thirsty. "What is there to say?"

She shrugged. "Fair enough."

She looked around, rubbed her arms like she was cold.

"Where is everyone?" Jack asked.

"I don't know. I've only seen pictures of Fey in books. And I've heard stories. Forests teeming with animals and creatures of all kinds. Monsters that live in lakes and in the skies. But this...I think...it feels like it's just us. It's like walking through an apocalypse. Let's keep going. Hopefully, we'll see it soon."

Jack looked at Rachel like he'd never seen her before. Had only just seen himself. "Do you know"—he took a breath and it was ragged, like he was breathing in grief, exhaling despair—"I have now failed everyone I've ever loved. When Marion came to my family's hotel, Nate said to hide. But I was afraid. I didn't listen to Nate. I had the right course of action in front of me, and I couldn't do it. I told my dad and he walked straight up to Marion and she killed him. If I had listened to Nate, listened to Val, she wouldn't be here." He rubbed his eyes. "It's all my fault. All of it."

She was very quiet. "You were really young, Jack. What? 10? 12? Don't rewrite history. You did the best you could." Snow crunched underfoot as she moved closer to him.

"My best is worthless."

"Oh for Pete's sake. What? Did you cause Cancer too? It's not your fault. And, I hate to tell you, but you were *never* going to be enough for Val. She wanted things from you that you could not do. You're a hero, Jack. A *hero*. How could you give that up? And how could she be so selfish as to ask you to?" she said, voice filled with scorn.

"She's not selfish. She's been through a lot," he said dully.

"Bullshit!" Rachel said, voice harsh and angry. "She's got it *all*. She had you and she didn't want you. She had Lucas and she threw him away, too. The girl is a fucking menace."

Jack shook his head slowly, crossed his arms. "She didn't have me. That was the problem. I couldn't do it. Couldn't be 'the guy'."

Another crunch as she took a step closer. But she didn't speak until he looked up, meeting her gaze. "You are 'the guy', Jack. She just wasn't the girl who fought hard enough to get you." Rachel made a slicing motion with her hand—conversation over. "Now stop your bitching and let's go. She's not dead yet."

She trudged away from him, and there was nothing left to do but follow.

CHAPTER 35

Val dragged in a huge breath, suddenly feeling weightless now that the vines were gone. She shook her arms and legs, trying to get her blood moving again. That pins-and-needles feeling was everywhere, from her feet to her hands, radiating down her arms and legs.

She turned in a circle, looking at where she was. A castle straight out of a fairy tale or the Princess Bride. Huge stone walls that were made of sand-colored stone, torches that lit every corner, making the room feel as inviting as a castle was ever going to.

Colorful rugs were on the ground and massive tapestries were on the walls. The countryside, a hunt, and some satyrs mating with some less-than-willing women. It took a long time to make those tapestries, potentially years. Women working around the clock, getting arthritis just to make this beautiful piece of art. And it was of a gang-rape? People were so weird back in the day. Like having a public disemboweling event for family entertainment.

Goosebumps rose on her skin. She might as well be in another time. And she just knew that couldn't be good for her.

Call it a hunch. And against the backdrop of this huge majestic room was Cerdewellyn.

He advanced towards her, hands clasped behind his back, standing tall, looking severe in black velvet and satin trimmed with gold thread. He made Lucas look current. Even when Lucas wore his 'old' clothes, there was something slightly modern about him. She hadn't realized that until she saw Cerdewellyn, a man who was *really* stuck in the past.

This guy was gorgeous—make no mistake—but it wasn't his looks that made her jerk her gaze away from him but his intensity and charisma. It was an almost *touchable* force. An electrical charge that went before him.

Cer was handsome, but she *could* find fault with him. His lips were wide, nose slightly large.

Whereas, Lucas was too perfect. He was almost hard to look at. She looked at Lucas and couldn't stop, her eyes roaming his face like her brain was trying to find something out of balance— people didn't look like him. It made him almost freakish in his beauty.

"Miss Dearborn, I owe you my thanks. We are in your debt."

That's a good start. "We who?" she asked, crossing her arms nervously and glancing around the empty room. She was so thirsty her head was pounding. There was no one else in sight. Certainly not Lucas or Jack. Shoot, even Rachel might be welcome about now.

He smiled sharply. "'We' as in the royal we. *Me.* "He stepped up close to her, eyeing the length of her dispassionately. "Your companions are on their way here. But I wanted a chance to thank you in person. You did me a great service. And, of course, I will release you from him. It is the least I can do."

Hewalked a little ways away from her, as if to give her a break from his scrutiny. "How long have you been with him?" He turned back to her, his knowing gaze taking her apart. She stared down at the ground, feeling uncomfortable. He wasn't scary, just.... He watched her like he knew her every thought. As if she was a simple puzzle and he almost had her figured out. It was disconcerting and creepy.

"We will start earlier, perhaps. Something less personal. How many of your kind are left? The Empaths."

What? Is it tattooed on my forehead? She tried to think what the harm would be in telling him she was the only Empath left. Well, *probably* the only one left. Could it make things worse?

If anything, it probably made him less likely to kill her. Unless he decided to keep her here forever. *That* would be worse. But why would he want to? Lucas had told her that the Fey were uninterested in Empaths. That they had done nothing to protect her kind when the vampires killed them all—at Lucas' direction.

"Not many," she hedged.

"And your wolves?"

Her hands were clasped tight together, nails digging into her palms. *I'm so ridiculously out of my element.* And the way he said 'your wolves' was odd. Like there was a story there. Or as if he might have said, 'where are your shoes? 'That the notable thing was their absence.

"Did he kill them? Do they know where you are?" He seemed genuinely concerned for her.

His gaze narrowed. "Lucas is your *companion*? Is that what you said?" He seemed almost as confused as she was.

"'Pleading the fifth' isn't going to mean anything to you, is it?" she mumbled, breath coming fast.

He stopped before her. "May I?" he said, his hand extended towards her.

"May you what?" she said, and took a step back. "Let me go? Buy me a pony? I'm good with either of those."

"Touch you." He looked down at her hands. They were clenched tightly in fear, his eyebrows rose at the sight. "Tilt your head up, so I may see you," he said gently.

"No. I mean, I'll look up, but you, uh, don't need to touch me." *Dude is going to get a serious frown line if he isn't careful.*

"Asking was a mere formality. I ask to touch you, and you say no? Why?" He didn't like that. She felt like she'd just told Henry VIII he couldn't marry Anne Boleyn. *It's never a good idea to tell a King no.*

"I'm not the touchy-feely type," she muttered, looking around, for an escape route. She forced a smile. Not a door or a window in sight. *What kind of room has no door or window? A Fey cell?*

He straightened, expression suddenly foreboding. His words were quiet. "I am the King of the Fey. I have offered to put my hand upon you, and you say no. You come to my kingdom with no protectors. No wolves, no Witches, not even another of your own kind. When we left Europe, there were some who refused to come. Presumably your ancestors. If I asked you their names, would you know? Do you know your history at all? Do you know the value of my touch for one such as you?"

Oh shit. This sounded like some kind of mumbo-jumbo crap that was about to bite her in the ass. "I'm sure you have an... *awesome* touch. Really. But...I'm...okay without it. Not to be mean or anything, I just have no idea why I should want you to touch me." She swallowed hard. "I'm ignorant, like...peasant, sign-my-name-with-an-x-because-I'm-illiterate ignorant."

He scowled. Her valley girl speech might be a bit confusing to a guy like him. She tried to clarify. "But I can read. That was just to illustrate my point."

"You can read?" he said, seemingly pleased with the idea.

"Yup."

"Then come. Let me take you to my library. I will acquaint you with your history, provide you with food, and we will speak again."

"No! No food. I've heard all about the food!"

He waved a hand negligently and walked out of the room. She followed, assuming she was expected to and not really seeing another option.

He waited for her and then said, "Food in the realm of Fey is enchanted. So are drinks. To imbibe or drink from them can bind you here." They walked down hallways, her boots making light clicks on the stone floor. His shoes made no sound. Because *he* was graceful, and *she* stepped like a drunken Clydesdale.

Everything they passed was clean and perfect. Oiled tables and vases, huge gold and silver urns. There was a faint smell of lemon and beeswax as though things had just been polished. And yet, something was off. Out of the corner of her eye, she saw things that weren't...right. Tapestries that were faded and black, curtains in rags, but when she'd turn to examine the item head on, they were whole and unblemished.

They passed a huge dining room and Val stopped, looking inside. A fire burned in the fireplace, and the table was empty and cleared. Impulsively, she closed her eyes, and the sound of the crackling fire disappeared. The pleasant smell of wood smoke and lemon vanished, replaced by a heavy throat-clogging smell of dust. She opened her eyes and caught a flash of something different.

The dining room table isn't empty. That doesn't make any sense.

Cer was there beside her, his hand coming towards her arm.

She jerked back, almost stumbling. "Don't touch me."

Now he looked angry. "What do you presume I intend?"

"How the heck should I know? You've kidnapped me. Separated me from my friends. I know nothing about you. Why *would* I trust you? I'm starving, thirsty, exhausted. So yes, I *do* trust Lucas more than I trust you. And all this cryptic crap about touching me and truth...I may be 'young', but I have spent enough time with Lucas to know the *uselessness* of words. Words are easy. I'm judging by actions. You've done nothing to show me you are sincere. In fact, you've manipulated me and used me." *Plus you scare the living shit out of me.*

He threw back his head and laughed. It made her feel warm, like the sun had just come out on a cold winter morning. "I can see magic. See a vampire's compulsion. He has not compelled you. And yet... you do *trust* him." He said it like she'd just told him she believed in the Easter Bunny. "I can tell that you do not know how valuable that is. Trust. Loyalty. You are so...*young*."

Telling me how naïve I am won't make me like you more.

"The Fey do not make idle promises. We are bound to them. Do you know this?" He stood straighter, looked more arrogant and kingly. *Actually, this guy makes Lucas look relaxed. Huh.*

Yeah, she knew the Fey were bound by promises. She nodded.

"I swear to you—I *promise*—that I mean you no harm. I acknowledge that I owe you a great debt for helping me, and I will only speak the truth to you while you are here. Ask me for a boon and, if I may grant it without harm to me or my people, then I promise to grant it. The truth is that Lucas is a murderer. A slaughterer of every creature he meets." He was close, his presence even closer, as if it rolled out before him. And there was that feeling again: Electricity. It wasn't sexual, just charismatic.

"But no one is in more danger from him than an Empath. Trusting him, looking to him, stripped from every ally you should have is...." He shook his head, almost speechless. Then he gave her a look of such sincerity that she forgot to breathe, dreading, and yet desperate to hear, what he was going to say. "He will kill you. You have no concept of the things he has done."

She felt a buzzing in her ears. Felt sick at his conviction, the disgust he felt for Lucas, the pity he felt for her. A part of her believed him. She spoke on auto-pilot, towing the party line. "I know what he did. He does too. He regrets what he's—"

"No, he does *not*," Cer cut in sharply, lifting a finger. "Regret is an emotion. A part of remorse, a shard of grief. That is not something he feels. The vampires killed Empaths because they did not *want* to feel and saw no need for a conscience. You do not know what he has done, or you would run to *me* for help and fall upon your knees in gratitude!"

The words were like a punch. "He's changed," she said. But she felt like Bill Clinton saying he hadn't done anything with Monica Lewinsky.

His voice was almost hypnotic. "The number of deaths he has been responsible for is incalculable. Lucas Tiberius Junius, slayer of Gaius, the King who had ruled in a time before the Christian God's birth. You have no inkling of the number of your kin he killed. If you did, you would seek shelter from me. You would kill yourself rather than go to *him*. When I walked the Earth with him, he was a King so mighty, no one dared usurp him, no matter how depraved he became."

He paused as if giving her time to digest what he was saying. Like bitter medicine, the truth could only be given in small doses or her body would rebel. His eyes searched her face while he waited. "His own kind viewed him as perverse, child. Vampires were wary of Empaths. All of them were—except for him. He was a *glutton* for them. He could no more abstain from devouring an Empath than a dog could keep from mounting a bitch. *Instinct*."

She wanted to scream. Do anything to make him stop. To keep the words from burning into her brain.

"In my time, the Empaths and the Wolves lived together. Rarely, one would be seduced into a vampire's embrace. The draw flows both ways. Empaths are drawn to vampires—it is part of your nature. And every now and again, a vampire was curious to know what an Empath's embrace was truly like. Similar to seeing a tall mountain and having to prove to one's self that one can make it to the top, it is a contest—one's *self* against nature. But that was a sick abomination, the mating of the two. Because it always ended in death. Always. Lucas has taken the liberties that all victors do—he has rewritten history to suit himself."

He was close enough to her that he might have kissed her had he chose. So close she couldn't see anything but the truth of his words. No escape. "You may be rare. You may even be the very last of your kind, but that doesn't mean he will protect you. Lucas will treat you like all the rest."

A beat passed. A moment where she noticed her own breathing, tried to keep her expression unmoved, and finally had to move away from him. The room was too silent. As if they were standing in a mausoleum buried deep under the earth, and any conversation was a sacrilege. Would wake the dead and bring them near. He turned away from her, walked to the door and she took a step, following him.

She couldn't give him anything—no indication that his words had made an impact. He hated Lucas. He'd kill him given a chance. This could all be a lie. *Be brave.* She smiled and followed him. Emptied her mind so she didn't think, tried to pretend she couldn't still hear Cerdewellyn's voice in her head telling her that Lucas would treat her like all the rest.

Because he's right, isn't he? After 1600 years, what are the odds I'm interesting enough to make him change? And the real *flaw in my logic? After 1600 years, could he change even if he wanted to?*

Val followed him down the hall. Half-hoping to catch a villainous smile of satisfaction on his face so she could discount everything he said. He glanced back at her—down at her because he was tall. She was going to go to one of those slutty shoe shops if she ever got out of here and buy a pair of seven-inch heels. Then she wouldn't be so short.

Good prioritizing.

"You do not have to believe me. Come and read your history. The history of the Others. See what he has left out. I promise to bring you food and drink that will not bind you to my world. And I promise that after we have talked—to my satisfaction— that I will let you leave."

"I want them to come with me. Rachel, Jack and Lucas."

He stiffened, picked a piece of invisible lint off the forearm of his jacket. "I will release the human. The female vampire I will release as a gesture of my goodwill. But Lucas…. I cannot let him go. I can think of nothing offered, nothing to gain, that would make me release him after what he has done to me and mine."

"You said you would grant me a boon."

"Yes, and the caveat was that it must not harm me or mine. There is no force or power on this earth that has brought more harm to my people than him."

Was he gauging her reaction to his words? *A millennia is an awfully long time to do evil.* She couldn't leave here without Lucas, could she? No. She couldn't. Not even after all the terrible things Cerdewellyn had told her. But there was no use arguing with him now. Especially when she didn't have all the information.

Val didn't know what to think. She knew Lucas. Knew him intimately, had welcomed him into her body and anticipated doing it again. But knowing him physically didn't translate to knowing *him*. Unfortunately. Sex should be like osmosis. All that time pressed up against each other should allow her to know him without having to wait six months before finding out they had mommy issues or unpackable baggage.

But he'd never denied what he'd done to the Fey.

He'd admitted it. Admitting what he had done did not minimize it. *But he knows it was a mistake.* What if Lucas were a regular person? If she'd met him and he told her he'd killed a lot of women but realized the error of his ways—and, hey, would she like to hit the sheets? What would she have done? She'd have run away screaming and called the police.

Why did Lucas being a vampire give him a free pass on evil? Make it more acceptable? Because she knew going into it what he had done and how he survived?

They stopped in front of a library with twenty-foot ceilings and rows upon rows of books. Every single one was incredibly old and beautiful. Even their bindings were eye-catching. Leather and suede, brilliant dyes and gold lettering. These were books made for the super-rich centuries ago. When owning a book was not only a status symbol—like owning a fancy car would be today—but a piece of art.

Even as he pointed to a shelf, she could still hear his words ringing in her ears—that she'd be like all the rest.

"Here is a history of your people. Read through this, and then I will come find you and we shall eat. This one—" He pulled a book off the shelf, the pages crackling as he turned them, his face transforming into an expression of killing rage when he found the page he wanted. "This is your savior, is it not? Read this while I am away, and then we can speak again, when you know the value of my words and the true nature of Lucas."

He held the book out to her and saw a drawing of Lucas in the heat of battle. Long hair, the tall, heavy form, drawn by a master in black ink. Lucas was in a burning city, bodies were all around him, his sword held high as villagers fled from him. The script was old and almost unintelligible.

Cerdewellyn probably hadn't collected a book since 1580. She'd taken classes on Middle English, had read Sir Gawain and the Green Knight as well as Chaucer in the original text, so she could slog through this even if it was six centuries old...but, she didn't want to. Because this was the truth.

And she didn't want it.

CHAPTER 36

Val couldn't have said how much time passed in that library. There was a fire in the fireplace, and she'd sat down in a huge chair, looking at book after book until her eyes strained and her brain was fuzzy. Lucas had never given her histories. Never a complete text.

He'd given her folders and copies of carefully selected pages. At the time, she had thought it was because the books were so rare they needed to stay protected. But now she feared it was because he wanted to control how much she knew.

She could find guilt in almost everything he had said and done. He'd taken her to the British Library, one of the few libraries where there might have a book old enough for her to discover something about him, and he had stayed with her, hovering.

She'd assumed it was because he wanted to be with her. But that wasn't the reason. He'd stayed to ensure her ignorance. *Which makes the the ass in assume.* He was beautiful and compelling. So far out of her league that when he'd paid her any attention, she'd been pathetically eager to be with him.

The guy had supernatural massacres named after him! And some of the things that she read about him, what he'd done after killing a whole bunch of Empaths.... they were not the sort of things one could overlook, sugarcoat, or whitewash in anyway. Evil was evil. And this was some *serious* evil.

If she had not known him, but had only read of him, she'd be scared shitless of him. In a choice between him and Marion, knowing what she now knew, she'd choose Marion as a safer option. How the fuck was *that* possible?

And what really sucked was how desperate part of her was to ignore all of this. When Lucas came for her—which she knew in every fiber of her being he would—she wanted to run to him, have him hold her and act like all of this was a lie.

Which was pathetic. It turned her into 'that' girl. The girl who went out with some shithead guy that everyone said was a mistake and she blindly ignored because *she* was different. And, this was the part, she could change him.

Yeah, fucking right.

She looked down at the book, but couldn't see the words. *Oh great, here come the waterworks.* Her lower lip trembled, her throat closed up, and she felt a sob welling within her.

Seriously, how could she get it so wrong? And what would she do when she saw him again? How could she pretend she didn't know? And once he saw how much she knew, what would he do? Best case scenario was that he would apologize. But is an apology sincere when one doesn't feel regret?

Would he kill her? Make her forget? She heard the door scraping open and dashed her tears away, setting the book down and standing by the chair.

"Come. I have food and drink," Cerdewellyn said, waiting in the doorway.

"When will they be here?" she asked, voice a little raspy but not too bad.

"A few hours."

She nodded. Followed him back to the dining room they had passed earlier. He led her to one end, away from the fire, but the room was so warm and well-lit with torches along the walls that it didn't matter. And on the table was food. It made her stomach growl and was a little embarrassing. Cerdewellyn ignored it, pulled out a chair for her like a gentleman, and walked around the table so that he was sitting across from her. He poured her a glass of red wine, and Val looked at the assortment before her.

"*Wow*. That's a whole pig you have there." Her stomach flip-flopped. "Eyes and all." Did she sound as disgusted as she felt? She couldn't help but stare at the empty sockets. The eyes had cooked away and...Oh, it was so gross. Its tail was burnt to a twisty crisp, and an apple was shoved in to the animal's outraged mouth. The pig looked vaguely angry. As if he knew things had gone bad for him and was pissed about it. *I feel for you, buddy.*

She looked away from the animal to the ceiling. Cer must have seen her revulsion because he snapped his fingers and the dish was gone. In its place was a silver platter with some sort of meat and Jell-O concoction on it.

"What is that?" she asked, giving up on keeping the horror out of her tone.

"Larks tongues in aspic. It is a great delicacy."

Val wasn't hungry anymore. "So, the jelly stuff is the aspic, right? And probably made out of actual hoof. And when you say Lark's tongues, you mean tongue, literally, and from...a bird. That's...uh...what I'm looking at?"

He frowned. "Well, it *was* a great delicacy. This is not going as I had hoped. Explain to me what people eat in your day, and it shall appear. Do you still eat cheese?"

There was something vaguely amusing about the situation and Val couldn't help but smile. "Yes, we eat cheese. And fruit. And bread. But there is no point. I'm not going to eat it. So thanks." This place would be a dieter's dream. No eating or there will be serious consequences.

"So, this food, it's real?"

"Yes," he said, as if he'd told her everything she might want to know.

Oh shit, another guy who doesn't talk. Is this what makes women lesbians? The desire to have a good conversation?" And?"

He arched an eyebrow. Something that all poor conversationalists seemed good at it. In this case it meant, 'What do you mean? ' or 'What else would you like me to say? ' or even, 'I've given you an answer so why are you still banging on about it? '

"And it comes out of the air with a snap of your fingers because...."

He looked up at her, brows furrowed. "Because I am the King of the Fey," he said as if he were talking to a child.

She shrugged. "Okay. Thank you," she said sarcastically.

"You are welcome," he said sincerely.

Fabulous.

"You will not eat, then? Regardless of my promise that the food is untainted?"

"No, I won't eat. But thanks." *I think.*

Cerdewellyn stood, clearly expecting her to rise as well. "Come. There is something you should see."

It's not a dead body, is it? Val knew she was getting better at biting her tongue because she didn't say the words out loud. But that was a pretty ominous phrase. Wasn't it what they said on CSI and all those murder shows? Val didn't watch a lot of murder shows. She'd seen it—not pretty. She'd rather take a good comedy any day.

He inclined his head towards the other end of the room, and she wasn't sure what she was supposed to see. They walked parallel to each other, the huge dining room table between them. She passed chair after chair, maybe forty all together before reaching the other end.

There, laying on a red and blue Turkish rug in front of the fire, were two wolves. Gray, silent and massive, they were larger than any animal had a right to be. They also looked very, very dead. *Maybe I should have said that dead body comment out loud after all.*

CHAPTER 37

"You can help me," he said, startling her. She'd been so absorbed in looking at the Wolves that she'd forgotten he was standing there.

"How?" Val asked, *really* not wanting to know.

"You are an Empath. You have power. Together we could begin to restore what has been lost."

There were so many problems with that idea she didn't know where to start. "I'm only half Empath. And I don't know anything about it. It's like asking someone to do Tae Kwan Doe just because they're Korean."

He looked at her blankly. *Dammit*. Couldn't she talk with someone from the 21st century? If she ever made it out of here, maybe she should teach high school. Deal with people more on her level.

"I mean, I haven't been trained. I don't know anything about it— power, energy, channeling, wolves. The whole enchil— *thing* is new to me."

Cerdewellyn shook his head. "You have power. It does not matter if you know how to use it. Magic *is*. Unless one is a witch, the training is minimal."

"Okay. The next problem is that I'm weak."

He smiled at her. "You may be...diluted, but the abilities I would call upon will be strong enough. Let us try. See how compatible we are. It will not hurt. Nor will it weaken you. But it would give me some idea if you can help me and my people."

Truthfully, the fact that it wouldn't hurt made her more willing to give it a shot. "What would we do?"

"We will try to wake up the wolves."

Her mouth dropped open, and she looked back to the huge beasts before the fire. They really looked like big dogs. "What kind of wolves are they? They're huge."

"They are Werewolves." He gave her that look again—the what-the-hell-has-the-world-come-to—look. At least that's what she thought it was. "You have never even seen one?" He sounded very sad.

"No. Sorry. Are these the only two left?" she asked.

"No. There are more. But these two lead the pack. If they awaken, hopefully the others will as well. Do you not want to help them? Look at them. They are alive but unmoving. Their hearts beat, and yet, they are unaware. Your natural affinity for them should draw you to them. If you told me you didn't want to help them, I would know you for a liar."

Val chewed on her lip as she looked at the Werewolves. "So, there are people in there?" She crouched down next to the wolf, looking at its closed eyes, the long snout and its soft coat. She wanted to touch it. Her heart beat picked up a little, the desire to touch the wolf growing, as if acknowledging the desire gave it strength.

It was decision time. Her instincts told her that Cerdewellyn wanted what was best for his people. And they were here because Lucas wanted to make amends. He'd told her humanity was better off with the Fey back in the world. So perhaps she should help Cer a little. A show of good faith.

And you know what? I really don't think Lucas is going to kill me. Even if he was, it was not going to happen here, in Fey. So, if she could make a bargain here, she should. "I will try to help you if you promise not to kill Lucas and to hear what he has to say. We sought you out. You've been stuck down here for centuries and everyone thinks you're extinct. I understand that you want vengeance...but I don't think you're in a situation to ask for it."

"Beautiful and demanding. Now I know why you still live."

"Flattery will get you everywhere. Oh! That was a joke."

Cerdewellyn crouched down too and put a hand on the wolf's neck. The animal seemed to sigh, a fleeting expression crossing its face. She'd never thought of a dog as particularly expressive. Not beyond 'food' and 'out, ' anyway.

"They are people. With families and wives, a life dedicated to protecting your kind. To killing vampires. I—" His voice faltered a little. "I failed them. Lucas is their enemy, too. If I agree to keep Lucas alive, it would be another failure."

"Promise to hear him out and not kill him for 5 years, then I will help you." *He's Lucas, if he can't talk this guy into giving up his vendetta or escaping in 5 years, I'd be shocked.*

"I promise to 'hear him out' and not kill him for a period of 2 years, But, if you ask me of your own volition to kill him before then, that promise is nullified."

Damit! I don't know if this is a good deal!

"He responds to your touch," Val said, almost expecting the wolf to open its eyes and wake up. Now *that* would be a good distraction.

"The wolves are dependent upon my magic. They abandoned the mortal world and came with us hoping to start anew. Fey magic and sustenance kept them alive. But now my kingdom is so weak that there is not enough energy to keep them awake. It is as though my entire world is hibernating."

She reached across the wolf and touched Cer's hand in sympathy. He met her halfway, his warm hand clasping hers. The contact was hot. As though they were two electrical wires sparking off of each other. Val tried to let go, pull away from him, but he gripped her tighter.

"Your power is based in life, instinct and emotion. My magic comes from life as well. So our power feeds each other, you see? We can give it to the wolves, and it will bring them back to us."

Val wanted to ask lots of questions, but the words wouldn't come out. She couldn't speak or move, her focus narrowing down to the small contact with his hand. Her flesh was inconsequential, merely a container for her energy. The *real* her was a calm pool of power.

Cerdewellyn was the waterfall, pouring his own energy into her, breaking the still surface inside of her and churning her magic around, forcing it to overflow and spill outwards.

Her magic suddenly made sense. It was a revelation. Val knew, on an atomic level, what separated her from a normal human. It crystallized in her in a way it never had before.

He pushed her hand down onto the wolf's back and the damn burst, power flowing from him, swirling in her and then out again, down into the wolf. Its coat was soft. An almost odd texture, like it wasn't quite hair, but had the smoothness of skin as well.

The animal called out to her, not in words but in emotion. The wolf spoke to her soundlessly, and she wanted to listen, like a song she had once loved and then not heard for years. She wouldn't try to move away again.

Cerdewellyn let go of her hand and stood, walking around her and the wolves slowly. Then he lifted her up into his arms, shifting her down between the two furred bodies, snuggling her close and tight between them.

Sweat slid down her temple, and she wanted him to both stop and continue running his power through her. Cerdewellyn's energy was overwhelming.

Stop fighting and the hurt will go away. He said, and she didn't know if he said it aloud or if she heard his voice in her head.

He was right, she was fighting it, trying to control the influx of energy from Cerdewellyn, rationing it out to the wolves. She needed to be open, let it pass through her instead of trying to control it.

She relaxed, stopped clenching her muscles and let the energy rush over her instead. The moment she did, the pain disappeared. The wolf was with her, his mind and thoughts close enough to touch.

"My wolf...my wolf I call you," Cer said.

Why is it *his* wolf, she wondered. What did that mean? The animal tried to tell her, offering up the story in pictures, memories, scents and feelings. Willing to let her see the memory of how the wolf became bound to Cerdewellyn.

Snippets of the wolf's past rushed by her, like riding in a speeding car and looking out a window. A village. A hut. A fire. A woman in homespun garb. A baby. A pup. Wolves around a fire. The vision slowed down, rotated around her like the world was spinning. It slowed and finally stopped. She could smell the forest as the wolf did, hear people speaking through the wolf's ears...feel the wolf's fear.

She and the wolf were one. She knew his name— Ajax. That he had a wife and children and that he did not expect to survive the night.

Ajax padded into the dark night. He could hear the paws of other Wolves beside him as they went towards the glowing orange light. A clearing had been made, and a fire was shifting in the wind, the flames flickering high.

Friends and family were here, the children more subdued than usual as everyone waited anxiously around the fire. The women chanted, and those that were of breeding-age were stripped naked, dancing around the fire while the young girls and the old women made a circle, hands clasped, heads bent as they invoked Cerdewellyn's name and begged him to come to them.

The fire blazed, and a black shape appeared inside the flames. As if someone had been burned at the stake and was now being rebuilt from the inside out. The flames parted as he solidified. The wolf's heart stuttered at the awesome display of power.

He is strong enough to keep us safe, Ajax thought.

Cerdewellyn was in the fire, whole and unblemished. As he stepped out of the flames, the women scattered, giving him a wide berth.

The wolves leader dropped down onto one knee. "My Liege. We have summoned you here in order to seek your protection. The horde is near. Villages in all directions have been wiped out. Will you shield us?"

Ajax heard the fire crackle, saw the women shuffle, all of them waiting with baited breath to know if Cerdewellyn would save them. And at what price.

"I will take you from here and claim you as my own," *Cerdewellyn said.* "But you must bind you and all of your people to me. Know that you are given my name and shall work for my will alone from this day forth. Do you accept?"

Their leader licked his lips and made eye contact—not with the men but the women. Were they willing to offer their children up to Cerdewellyn? Safety in exchange for binding to the Fey King? The women nodded, clutching the children tight. Cerdewellyn or death.

Their leader opened his mouth, ready to agree when Cerdewellyn spoke, "I hear them—the horde. He has come.

Does Lucas know you have called me? For his vengeance will be twice as harsh for those that remain."

"He will kill us all anyway, should we still be here by the time he arrives. It makes no difference."

Cerdewellyn laughed. "The difference is in the means of execution. The length of time it takes to die and the horrors he can make one endure before he finishes playing with you and yours. I demand the binding first. It is the only way to take you through the fire. He is close now. Be quick."

Ajax turned and looked into the dark beyond. He couldn't see the vampires coming, but could smell blood and death upon the wind. His leader sent the strongest wolves into the night to meet the horde, trying to delay them until the women and children were safe. Howls rent the air as Ajax and his brothers dashed into the night.

The smell of decay and iron grew. Rot and corruption coming closer.

The vampires stalked down the streets, dipping into houses, searching everywhere for the villagers. At the head of them all was their Dark Lord. He didn't stop and he didn't hesitate, but moved steadily forward, not looking for those that hid but for the group.

His hair was dark, coated in blood. Ajax had been told that the blackness was not the Dark Lord's natural color. That his hair changed from the brightest gold to the dark of the dead when he went to war. The blood stained him and he gloried in it—kept it to inspire fear into the hearts of his prey.

The face of an angel and the soul of the devil.

He wore armor. An armor so black it absorbed the light and a cape of pelts that billowed out behind him. His steel shoes rang through the night, a chime of death approaching with each step. His sword was out, the blade dull with gore. And in his other hand was an axe, the head massive and weighted so that it could break through an opponent's shield from a distance— taking any advantage away before the fight began.

For Lucas, the Dark Lord, fighting was not about honor, conquest or faith. It was not even about the heartless joy one could find in proving one's strength against another. His purpose was carnage. How many dead in how short a period of time. That was what spread his name in dreaded whispers from village to village. No mercy. No pity. No desire beyond unending slaughter. Ajax growled and felt his hackles rise.

He knew the moment his leader bound them to Cerdewellyn. The cool, detached strength of the Fey, filled his mind like a tangible shadow. The wolf's natural blood lust and urge to rush forward and attack Lucas receded slightly. The calm intellect of Cerdewellyn tempering the beasts' basest instincts.

Ajax knew he only needed to bide his time, delay the horde so that their loved ones could get to Cerdewellyn's realm. They would all walk into the fire, a portal to the Fey realm. The children first, walking into the fire and vanishing to the Land of Fey. Then the women. Stay in the shadows, do not encounter the horde.

One of the wolves snapped. Emotion overcoming him, and he rushed forward, out of the forest's safety, charging Lucas, unable to control his animal instincts. A vampire ran up beside the wolf, appearing out of nowhere, pulling the wolf down to the ground. They wrestled, the vampire laughing as it tried to sink its teeth into the wolf's neck. The wolf snarled, foam gleaming from its maw as they fought.

The vampire screamed as the wolf burrowed into its chest cavity. Lucas continued forward, ignoring his subject's desperate cries, focused only on locating the villagers. He passed the outermost edge of the village. Moving silently towards the forest, as though he could hear the villager's hearts beating in fear.

Return to me, Ajax heard Cerdewellyn say. And it sounded like the wind sighing.

Cerdewellyn's call was impossible to ignore, and Ajax heard whines of fury in the air as the wolves tried to disobey and follow their bloodlust. They did not want to go back. Did not want to escape. Calm rationality slipped away from Ajax as the wolf's rage unfurled inside of him. The Dark Lord would pay for his sins.

A few of the Wolves turned, running back to Cerdewellyn, not strong enough to resist his call now that the pack was bound to him. But Ajax held out, waiting a moment longer, desperately wanting to attack Lucas. He moved a paw forward, then stumbled as blinding pain ripped through his skull.

Cerdewellyn's commands coiled inside of him, contracting tighter, the pain growing, and he knew it would only get worse until he obeyed. With a furious howl Ajax turned, sprinting through the forest as fast as he could. The pain disappeared and he felt a gladness inside of him, pleasure at obeying Cerdewellyn's will.

Cerdewellyn urged Ajax into the flames, and he ran straight towards it, felt the heat of the blaze on his muzzle, the blinding light of the fire searing his eyes as he stepped close. Fear made him want to stop but Cerdewellyn urged him onwards and Ajax gave in, kept running, closing his eyes at the last moment and prayed to survive the flames. Not to God. Not anymore. Now they prayed to Cerdewellyn.

CHAPTER 38

Lucas saw Cerdewellyn's castle up ahead and stopped running, slowly approaching the edge of the tree line that gave way to a cleared area before the high castle walls. It was beyond aggravating that he could not teleport himself from location to location. Another manifestation of his weakness in the Fey realm. The castle walls were thirty-feet high and, if he had to guess, four-feet thick.

He crouched low to the ground, staying hidden for a moment and examining everything around him. Closing his eyes, he listened intently, blade out and ready. The snap of a twig, a rustle of an animal, the steps of a man as he tried to approach undetected.

Nothing.

This was nothing like the land he had heard of. Centuries of encounters both mysterious and fantastical, told that deadly and seductive creatures lurked around every corner.

But this place had an air of emptiness, a loneliness so complete that, if he had emotions, he might have wept for the sense of loss around him.

Desolation.

This was a failed civilization. Everything gone. But for whatever reason, Cerdewellyn had managed to survive.

That was going to change.

Valerie was here because of Lucas' mistakes. He'd tasted her, felt the gentlest *hints* of emotion, and decided he wanted things that were beyond him. Things that turned a man weak and made a vampire an easy target.

He could not afford to be vulnerable. She was his only weakness. So what did Cerdewellyn do? He took her. Cer had been out of the game for 500 years, back for less than twenty-four hours, and already he knew Lucas' weakness and had exploited it, reducing his strength and power by bringing him here.

Lucas felt a pang, almost like a splinter of emotion at the thought of what the future *needed* to hold. Get Valerie out of here. And no more blood. He would never drink her blood again. If he had not been so desirous of it and her, he would not have left her alone in that wood back in Roanoke. And she wouldn't have bled on the ground, allowing Cer a way to control her.

If Lucas had not imbibed her blood, he would not have cared about seeing her with Jack. Would not have orchestrated Jack's appearance to judge their relationship—because sharing her would have meant nothing to him.

But he *had* drunk her blood, and it had made him careless. She had called him a monster, compared him to one of the vilest men on Earth, felt her revulsion ring through his body like a pike slamming into armor—painful and crushing. He was now useless and susceptible to sentimentality.

Pathetic.

He was not a man. He would never *be* a man. Happiness, family, the simple pleasure of a summer day. And in truth he could not even remember what that had been like. He had put all of them in danger for a ridiculous quest.

Never mind. The mistake was done. He would go in, get Valerie out and they would start again. He was a vampire, a murderer. Unconscionable. He would embrace that, and she would obey or else.

No more compromising.

Lucas looked at the top left turret of the castle, which was at least a hundred feet in the air. Lightning struck the roof repeatedly, clouds churning like an angry sea. They were gray and unnatural. That was the portal back to the mortal world, and it was only accessible via the roof. Plus, he would have to find Cerdewellyn and sever his link to Valerie before she could leave. Cer would not want to let her go. Centuries of hatred for Lucas would be focused on her as part of his revenge.

At least, that is what I would have done.

Cer thought to control *him*? Lucas knew what he would do to Cerdewellyn. He remembered. There were means of torture that universally broke people. Those were boring. It was not the common things—splitting a tongue, removing an eye, or slicing off a penis that caused bone-deep terror.

No, he wanted Cerdewellyn to be so afraid that he would piss himself with fear. Lucas was going to find him, rip his stomach open with his bare hands, take out the Fey's heart and eat it before his very eyes. And if that wasn't enough to make Cerdewellyn release Valerie, he would become creative.

Satisfied that no one was lurking nearby to attack him, he made his way around the castle, looking for the entrance. He walked further, further, until he returned to the spot where he had started. There was no entry.

Of course there was a way in. *Illusion.* He could not see the entrance, but it had to be there. He walked up to the wall, checking above him periodically to make sure no one would attack him. It was habit. Never walk below an enemy's walls. Sliding his hand along the stone, he searched for the slightest difference in texture, temperature or sound, looking for any variation to show where the illusion ended—ideally a big hole that he would be able to walk through with ease.

He was conscious of time ticking by as he circled the castle walls again. He was back where he had started—again. Lucas stepped backwards slowly, surveying everything around him. He scrubbed his hand across his jaw as he contemplated another way to approach this.

This was easy. It had to be. There was an entrance. *Somewhere.* He went back to the tree line and stared at the wall, looking for patterns in the rock. There were none. He looked for any places where the color was too uniform. *Nothing.* No well-worn paths that led the way. Nothing.

He looked at the sky and was shocked to see that it was almost dark. How long had he been here? He'd arrived at noon, had walked around for no more than 30 minutes, yet it was almost nighttime. He swore. This was what happened in Fey. He was at Cerdewellyn's mercy. All these spells, all this glamour and illusion, time out of balance.

Someone was coming. He pulled himself up into the boughs of a tree and out of sight, hiding his sword so there would be no glint to give his location away as he waited for them to come into sight.

Jack. Rachel. He jumped down and both of them whirled.

"What are you doing?" Rachel asked, surprised by his sudden appearance.

"There is no way in," Lucas growled. "I cannot find it."

Jack looked at him like he was an idiot. Perhaps the day would come when Lucas would kill him anyway. Despite his promise to Valerie. It would improve his mood.

"It's right there," Jack said, pointing directly behind Lucas.

"Truly? You see the way in?" Lucas asked.

Jack nodded.

"And you?" Lucas asked, looking at Rachel.

"Nope. He's human. Fey glamour is harder to work on humans than it is on Others."

"Why? That doesn't seem very likely," Jack muttered, clearly disbelieving humans could have any advantages. Until this moment, Lucas would have agreed.

Rachel shrugged. "Don't know. It's one of the very few advantages humans have. Be happy about it."

Lucas turned and saw nothing. "I have touched every section of this wall and looked everywhere. If you see it, lead us. But first we must discuss the plan. We go inside. We find Valerie and Cerdewellyn. I will convince Cerdewellyn to allow Valerie to leave, and then we will depart from this beleaguered land and never return."

"I like that plan. Its beauty is its simplicity," Rachel said, looking around unhappily. "Man, this place has got some seriously bad mojo."

Lucas addressed Jack. "I want her out. I want us all out of here. Take direction or be left behind. Do you understand? Now go." Lucas nodded towards where Jack had pointed.

Every thought Jack had was on his face, painfully predictable. So earnest and passionate as he looked daggers at Lucas. Such a fool. He may as well have said: *Give me the chance. Just one chance to kill you and I will take it.*

Was it this...*passion* that drew Val to Jack? Or perhaps it was his simplicity. Jack wanted to kill Marion, but his desire to kill Lucas was almost equal in its intensity. Perhaps it was even worse, because Jack was a man now and might actually be able to prevent Valerie coming to harm. Jack must know there was nothing he could have done to forestall Marion. It had been vaguely difficult for *him* to stop Marion. Although he preferred to think that apathy on his part was what caused the trouble.

It was hard to maintain a killing rage for decades. Lucas knew that all too well. There always came a point where that flame of rage ran out of oxygen. Became a smolder and then nothing but black smoke.

Jack managed to bite back his pathetic death threat. *Good.* Lucas was not in the mood to coddle him.

"Yeah, cause the two of you at my back is going to make me feel safe," Jack said, moving towards the wall.

Lucas called him to stop. "Before you go in, take Rachel's hand. If the magic allows you in, we do not want to get separated as we pass through the barrier."

Jack snorted. "What might happen if we got separated? You wouldn't die, would you?" he said sounding hopeful.

"I have no idea what would happen. Potentially nothing. But how do you think you would get Valerie out of here on your own? What purpose does it serve to antagonize me?"

Jack gave Lucas a feral smile, a baring of teeth. "No purpose, it's just cheap entertainment." Then he held out his hand and took Rachel 's. Both of them wearing pained expressions, attempting to convey just how much they did *not* care that they were touching each other.

Childish.

Lucas took Rachel's other hand as Jack led them to the wall and through it. They emerged into an empty courtyard, opening their eyes to a new backdrop. There were troughs for horses and a smithy. Carts, long disused, the wood split from weathering, lay abandoned on the dirt ground.

Plague. The thought flashed though his mind again. But even when a whole village was wiped out, there had at least been animals. There was an impressiveness to nature's reclaiming of what man had stolen from her. Here there was nothing.

The drawbridge was down, and they made their way forward, silently. The only sound was their footsteps, Jack 's breathing, and their heartbeats. The keep was dark except for lit torches embedded in the walls. There was something nostalgic about a torch. The heft of it, the sense that *anything* might be just out of sight. Lucas breathed deep, tried to sense where Valerie was.

Lucas let Jack take the lead, knowing the human would be the only one able to see any tricks or traps. After several moments, they came to the first room.

Jack gasped, frozen in the doorway.

"What do you see?" Lucas asked, staring at a boring, but grand, dining room. There was nothing here to elicit such a startled response as far as he could see.

"You really don't see it? The table is filled with...*bodies*. Corpses. And there are bones everywhere. Jesus. A whole pig carcass is there. Just... bones on a plate."

"This guy needs to hire a cleaning crew. Dirty dishes are one thing, but to leave it for so long that all the meat rots away? That's some nerve," Rachel said. She bit her lip, looking around the room and then hard at the table. "Shit. Still looks like an empty table to me."

"She is here," Lucas breathed deeply and knew Valerie was somewhere in the room. Her smell— sunlight, femininity, and something sweet and delicate that was attributable solely to Empaths. He went forward, around the table, finding Valerie on the ground, unconscious. She was fully-dressed and lying on a dust-filled, decaying fur in front of an empty fireplace.

"Jesus, Valerie!" Jack said and tried to rush past Lucas.

No.

He'd had enough. Lucas shoved Jack back, sent the man flying so that he landed several feet away. "You will not touch her," he snarled and bent before Valerie, feeling his heart pound. *Emotions. Still.* Losing control when Jack was the only one who could see anything in this godforsaken place. He picked Valerie up, felt her warmth and the soft weight of her in his arms.

Still alive.

Lucas felt a burning, almost choking, feeling in his throat. The press of tears. Relief to find her whole and unharmed. *A terrible distraction.* "She is alive. We need to get to the roof. To the portal. If Cerdewellyn is here, that is where he will be."

"Give her to me," Rachel said.

His grip tightened, ready to say no.

"You're the brawn. If something comes at us, you need to be ready."

He felt himself nod jerkily. Not smooth but as though his bones had rusted together—a tin man.

He held her out, watching as Rachel took Valerie from his arms. Jack stood, shaking his arm, apparently having landed on his elbow hard. *Good. Maybe now he will stay out of the way.*

CHAPTER 39

Jack's arm was killing him. That fucker had barely touched him, and yet he'd almost broken something. Jack started backing out the door—he couldn't get out of this hell hole fast enough. The bodies at the table creeped the shit out of him. They looked dead, but they weren't. He didn't think so, anyway. They had a light in their eyes. A weird, golden glow that made him think someone was still home in there.

Or something.

Not his fucking problem. They went down the hallway to a set of stairs, Jack leading the way up, Lucas a step behind and Rachel a few paces behind that, carrying Valerie effortlessly. Valerie was at Rachel's mercy, unconscious in the vampire's arms. It hit so many of his buttons, made it difficult to do anything but resist the urge to fight.

His mind was dragging him into the past, to Marion. How she had picked him up, carried him down the hall, ready to keep him for her new pet. He remembered his mother's screams as she followed them. How they had stopped when Marion snapped her neck.

Howls pierced the air, the sound of massive feet thundering behind them.

"Wolves. Perfect," Lucas said in a low tone that conveyed both boredom and understatement at the same time. "Put Valerie down on the ground, back to the wall. Jack guard her— get your weapons out. Rachel, guard both of them. You are the second line of defense. I will take them first." He drew out a huge vicious-looking sword that couldn't have weighed less than fifty pounds.

Show off.

The wolf came around the corner—the hugest damned animal Jack had ever seen outside of a zoo. Lucas made short work of it, feinting one way, drawing the animal to the side and then lunging forward, his sword skewering it neatly. The wolf squealed in a high-pitched tone, then lay still on the ground.

That was surprisingly easy, Jack thought. Then Valerie started screaming. She was awake, her eyes open wide in fear, transfixed on the sight of Lucas' blade as it slid out of the wolf's body.

CHAPTER 40

"No! No!" she screamed. Val knew him. *The Dark Lord. Murderer. Killer. His hair was gold when it should have been black, but it was him.* She could smell the blood from the Wolves Lucas had killed, smell the smoke from the fire she had leapt into. Her hands still felt like paws, her last clear memory was being something else, of fleeing *him.*

He's coming for me. He'll kill me. He'll never let me go.

She leapt to her feet and ran, running as fast as she could when his hand suddenly snaked around her, jerked her backwards like a safety belt pulled tight.

His hard chest was against her back, his breath in her ear. "Do not struggle. Do not fight. Calm down so we may leave. You must be calm."

She laughed hysterically. "You did this. You killed them all!" Val struggled, and he gripped her harder. He put her down, and she turned to run again. Faster, farther away so he'd never catch her. Never kill her.

He had her within three steps, whirling her around to face him. He grabbed her chin, forcing her to look at him. "*Stop.* Do not scream. Relax. I will not hurt you," he said, the words rolling over her, slamming her down and stripping her bare.

She exhaled. Breathed deep. *Again.* Her body relaxed at his command, swaying forward so that he caught her up in his arms, and she laid against him heavily, enjoying the fact that he was in charge. He would take care of everything. Because he loved her. Right? He wouldn't hurt her. Right? Why would she scream in the first place? The thought drifted away from her, only an echo now...*scream...scream*....

Scream!

Valerie began to pant. Huge breaths and sounds like little sobs coming from a primal part of her very self that should have died out with the cavemen. She tried to shake off his will, saw him look down at her with a frown.

Lucas cursed, knowing he would have to wipe her memory. This was not working. She was not responding to his compulsion. He had tried to be gentle, had hoped to use enough force to subdue her long enough to get them out of here. Something he could later explain and have her forgive. *That is not how it works, remember? You do not* ask *for forgiveness. You tell. She will be the one who changes.*

He had to get Valerie out of here. Had to get her to trust him or else she would flee, run into the Werewolves and be attacked. Or alert Cer to their location. Although Cer probably knew where they were anyway. What was his reason for not attacking? For leaving Valerie for him to find? And what had he told her?

Later.

If there was another option, there was no time to figure it out. He had to take away whatever Cer had told her. Take it away and get her out of here before Cer could interfere. *Later.*

After they escaped, he would talk to her, tell her why she was different from the other Empaths he had known. Why Cer was wrong to frighten her, explain that he was not the monster Cer had undoubtedly told her he was.

He could not claim that he was here for altruistic reasons. The truth was that he had come here to get something from Cer. That goal had failed. Now he just wanted to leave.

He could come up with *something* to win her favor after they were free.

Lucas opened a random door, finding a bedroom and taking Val inside, ready to shut the door in Jack's face. Valerie's struggles were growing. Any moment now she would start screaming again.

"Let me go! Let me go! You killed them all! You did! It's a lie! You'll kill me too, I know it. I *know* it!" She shrieked like a banshee, clawing at Lucas, shredding his face as he tossed her onto the bed. Lucas straddled her, grabbing Valerie's hands and pinning them to her side.

Jack tried to follow them into the room. But Rachel got there first, shut the door, blocking it with her body.

"Not so fast my little ravioli," Rachel said and instantly regretted it. Val's screams became louder, more grating as her voice started to give out. *Not the best time for whimsy.*

And then, everything was as quiet as the grave. There was a seemingly endless moment—one of those moments Rachel knew she would never forget, no matter how long she lived— Jack was so close to her, so angry, but there was a tiny scrap of trust or camaraderie between them. *Choose a side*, his gaze said.

All she had to do was get out of his way, let him go in there and get killed by Lucas. And if by some miracle, Jack managed to escape, he'd what? Throw her a pity fuck? She gave him an ugly smile.

She snapped that moment of trust like a puppy's neck. Grabbed his shoulders and swung him back, shoving him into the wall. She pressed his hard shoulders flat against the wall, and he struggled, surprising her with the force of his response.

"Don't speak. Stop fighting," she said desperately, compelling him with her gaze. Her cold fingers clamping on to his warm, rough jaw so he couldn't speak. She locked his body against the wall with hers, pressing him tight, leaving him powerless. "Don't move your arms," she said. He stopped trying to push her away.

Jack stared at her with murderous fury. Her body weighed against his, keeping him still. He kicked her hard, scraped his foot down her calf, and she hissed. "Don't move your legs, either," she growled and he stopped kicking her.

"God damn it!" she said harshly and looked at Jack, two inches from her face, murder in his eyes. He had been so fucking trusting. He'd looked her in the *eyes*! What the hell was wrong with him? It's Vampire Rule Number One—don't look them in the fucking eyes. *He knows better!*

Trust.

Shattered.

Her body was draped over his as she caged his body against the wall with her own. Even now she wanted him. When all she could feel was his misery and anger, blazing from him, hotter than the sun. His helplessness was an emotional smorgasbord. She could take it from him. Suck him dry and feed her magic. Like she'd done with Marion.

She swayed slightly, her forehead pressing against his. The steady rise and fall of his chest pulsed through her. Each breath pressed her breasts flat to his chest. And then, every time he exhaled, the faintest gap appeared and she missed his heat and skin.

"Don't speak," she commanded him again, in a thready whisper. It was very important he didn't speak, but she couldn't remember why. Her thumb slid over his full lips, and she was dimly aware that there was still no sound from the other side of the door.

"Ignore them," she said. "Focus on me." And he did. "There is nothing wrong. You're happy here." *Oh, Christ. I can't do this to him.* His features smoothed out, his gaze sliding down to her mouth, and his brow furrowed in confusion as she continued to touch him. She felt his body relax against hers.

And he was growing, getting harder against her as she pressed him into the wall. "Oh fuck, I am so sorry," she said, feeling him against her core, knowing herself empty, desperate to fix both of those things.

Rachel bent her head to his, kissed his lips lightly. Once, then twice. His lips firmed under hers, and she could feel his mental struggle as he tried to move. Closer or away, she didn't know. Suspected it was away. She pulled back from him, looked into his eyes.

Another moment where there could have been trust between them. *Just let him go. You can come back from this, if you let him go right now.* Why? He'd never be hers. Never want her.

And she'd never deserve him.

"Open your mouth for my kiss," she said instead. He licked his lips slightly, lips soft and willing, her tongue sliding into his mouth with a moan. She learned things about him in that small taste—learned his rage and misery, his unwelcome lust for her, even his self-loathing.

It made her wet, open...vulnerable. He kissed her back, his tongue in her mouth, kissing her angrily, a harsh noise coming from his chest. She felt the vibration of it in her own and became dizzy, almost *unknowing* as her fingers slid down his chest, across his flat stomach to the waistband of his pants.

No.

He'd never forgive her.

She pulled back and looked into his eyes to compel him. "You will be able to move soon. As soon as I have finished speaking." Her voice trembled. She used her normal voice this time, no compulsion, extending an olive branch to him. Putting her trust in him.

"When I release you, you are not going to attack me or Lucas. You're not going to remember Valerie screaming and fighting Lucas. I'm going to release you from my compulsion, and you're not going to attack. He won't hurt her. We need to get out of here and we can't do that with her freaking out. The Fey did something to her."

Rachel looked into his eyes, tried so hard to will him to understand and play along. To not fuck this up. She leaned closer, right next to his ear. "I want you to trust me. He will kill you if he figures out I didn't wipe your mind. Don't make me regret it."

She looked back at him, could see his emotions warring within him. "If I had, you wouldn't remember Valerie screaming. Wouldn't remember Lucas using his compulsion on her. Tell me you understand." She released him, felt his body go rigid as it came back under his own control.

His first impulse was to throw her away from him in disgust and hate. She could see the battle on his face. But he didn't. His head went back, hitting the wall so hard it must have hurt. He was breathing fast, nostrils flared in anger.

"I understand," he said, gutturally.

She could see him swallow. Wanted to lick the flesh at the hollow of his throat. She nodded and took a step back. "Take my hand."

He looked at it furiously, like touching her would contaminate him on a fundamental level. Cell-deep revulsion. But he did it. He reached out and took her hand, grabbing it hard and then relaxing, making his grip soft on hers. Holding her hand like he *wanted* to be with her.

And all the while she could see the desire to kill her in his eyes. She pulled him away from the door, stepping backwards, tugging him along as though she were about to take him to bed. They went down the hall a little to wait. She let go of his hand, but he held her fast, pulled her in closer to him.

Her mouth went dray, knees weak, not understanding what he wanted. Why wouldn't he let her go? He made a gesture with his head, and she knew he wanted to say something, was asking her to come closer to him again. He was inviting her deep into his personal space, so he could whisper in her ear.

Her heart pounded.

It was dangerous. Lucas might hear. But Jack was going to say something, his breath would be on her body, his voice quiet and intimate. She'd never hear it like this again. She couldn't say no to that.

Wouldn't.

She stepped closer and he waited patiently, relaxed against the wall, the faintest smile on his lips. His hand came up, cupping her jaw tenderly, pulling her closer so that his lips brushed her ear. She shivered, exhaled shakily. He spoke softly, and she moved closer yet, so that she felt each brush of his lips as he spoke to her. His voice snuck inside her, pierced her, left her soaked and wanting.

Flesh, blood, him.

Darkness.

Sex.

She wanted all of it from him.

Then his words registered and she pulled back, met the rage in his gaze, absorbed the promise on his hard, unyielding features. "Touch me again, and I'll fucking kill you," he'd said.

With a slow nod of understanding, she stepped back.

CHAPTER 41

The door opened and Lucas came out, Valerie walking beside him, looking up at him with a smile. Rachel's stomach churned, adrenaline arcing through her body like lightning. She felt almost as sick with foreboding as she had the night of the Challenge. Things were going to end badly. Jack couldn't keep his cool around Lucas. She'd acted irrationally.

Was it sad that she'd assumed he could lie well? Didn't everyone compartmentalize their emotions while they waited for the perfect moment to strike? It was second nature for her to smile. Smile until it was too late and her victim looked at her with surprise. But Jack was too *good* to lie well. Too heroic. Considering who he palled around with, it was a big fucking problem.

Lucas closed his eyes for a long moment, as though he was composing himself. "We cannot leave until Cer releases his hold on Valerie. I believe he is in the North tower, where the portal is."

"Why?" Jack asked, only a hint of anger in his tone.

"Because it is the only exit available to us, and he does not wish us to leave," Lucas said, his gaze intent on Valerie. She cast a look up at him and blushed.

Ah, young compelled love.

"I will go there, make him release her, and then we will leave."

"You want to leave us *here*?" Jack said, gesturing around the empty corridor.

"No. I want to leave you in a room. Barricade the door. You will be safe. Cer will not waste his energy on you, and the Wolves cannot get through the door."

"I'm coming with you," Jack said.

"No. You will stay." Lucas reached out, brushing the back of his hand along Val's cheek.

"The hell I will. I'm going."

Lucas dropped his hand from Val's cheek and turned to Jack. Absorbing every detail of him, Rachel thought. *Oh god*. He would know she hadn't done it. Why the fuck hadn't she done what Lucas told her to?

A big conversation transpired in that one look between Jack and Lucas. They sized each other up, exchanged death threats, could have talked about sports, the stare lasted so damned long. Lucas turned those pale, cold blue eyes to Rachel, and she got chills. *I see you and what you've done*, the look said.

"Fine," Lucas said, tonelessly. "We will return as soon as we may."

Jack walked out of the room and Lucas followed, closing the door behind him, the sound reminiscent of a sarcophagus lid shoved into place.

Valerie was just standing there like a bump on a log, looking at a tapestry on the wall. She blinked and frowned. Hopefully, she'd come out of it now that Lucas was farther away. Rachel wondered if she even knew her own name, she was so whacked out.

Dammit. Rachel would never say she knew Lucas well enough to predict his actions. No one did. But she knew with a certainty in her bones that Jack wouldn't be coming back. And it was her fault. But if she went after them Lucas would...kill her? Stick her in a coffin like Marion? Leave her behind? She felt sick with the weight of what was to come.

Hadn't Lucas always planned on killing Jack? Her mistake meant that it was just going to happen a little sooner. Rachel valued her life. She had to get out of Fey. Save Molly.

The cards were dealt, she'd pushed all her money to the center of the table, and she was still sitting there, unaware she'd just been conned, waiting for the house to throw her out. Or for Jimmy Hoffa to take her to the desert to see the sunrise. Rachel paced back and forth for a few minutes, thinking furiously.

I'm evil. Just do what you are supposed to do. Just stay here and wait until—

"We have to go. We have to catch them, now!" Rachel said, grabbing Val by the hand and rushing down the hallway. Val stumbled as she tried to keep up with Rachel's breakneck pace, but Rachel couldn't stop to help her, just tugged a little harder as they skidded around the corner.

CHAPTER 42

Jack followed Lucas down the hall— knife out. This was a special knife. Half silver, half wood. It would get the job done if given the opportunity. He didn't doubt that it was the right decision. The Fey hated Lucas. That's why they were here. Lucas couldn't find his way out of a paper bag over here, so he was useless. Their chance of survival did not improve with Lucas being here. And he knew Lucas was gunning for him too. If the chance came...yeah, he'd take it.

And then he heard them. Wolves. They came out of nowhere, barreling down the corridor, snapping and snarling as they launched themselves forward, taking Lucas to the ground. One clamped its razor-like jaws on Lucas' thigh, blood gushing out of him as the wolf unerringly sank his canines into the femoral artery.

Another wolf landed on Lucas' chest, jaw locked on his arm, trying to get to the vampire's vulnerable throat. The wolf let go of his leg, bloody spittle dripping from its mouth. The wolf bit into Lucas' ribcage, head and shoulders thrashing from side to side as the wolf tried to gnaw through him. With a wild roar, Lucas used his free hand to attack the wolf attacking his arm. Lucas stabbed upward, deep into the wolf's gut.

Where the fuck did he get a blade from?

Both wolves jumped clear of him, eyes focused on the blade—a sign of intelligence that was unnatural. Lucas pushed himself up, using the wall as leverage to get himself standing. Desperate for a more defensible position. There was a pool of blood underneath him, black blood pulsing from his leg, oozing from his side and also his arm. The wolves waited, ignoring Jack, intent only on Lucas who was pale, shaking, and breathing hard.

If only Lucas had been weaponless, the wolves would have killed him. Jack was sure of it. Lucas raised his arm, trying to reach behind him into his scabbard to draw his sword, the better to keep the wolves at a distance, but his arm collapsed, hanging limply at his side, blood gushing out of his side from the aborted move.

The vampire's attention was focused solely on the wolves in front of him, his back toward Jack. This was *it*. Jack's one and only chance to kill Lucas. Jack waited, felt the rush of anticipation he always felt before a kill.

With a curse, Lucas reached up again, agonizingly slowly, groaning in pain as he tried to make contact with the sword. The wolves darted forward, attacking with snarls, claws slashing as they tried to keep Lucas from reaching his blade and getting the advantage. Lucas drew the blade, hand adjusting on the pommel, as though he couldn't grip it as tightly as he wanted to.

Jack pulled his gun, sighted carefully and fired, the bullet slamming into Lucas' hand. The sword clattered to the ground, and Lucas stumbled into the wall, clutching his hand to his body instinctively. The wolves launched at him, and Lucas put his arm out, swinging wildly at one with a yell, making contact so that the wolf smashed into the opposite wall.

The distraction cost him, the other wolf reaching Lucas before he could recover The wolf stood on its hind legs, mouth close to the vampire's throat. Lucas fell forward, using his weight to push the wolf backwards—and giving Jack his chance. He drew the wood and silver knife, then lunged forward, shoving the blade deep into Lucas' side, just beneath the ribcage, angling the blade up, searching for Lucas' black fucking heart. Lucas staggered forward, a shudder going through him as he collapsed to his knees. Jack followed him down, but Lucas turned, rolling onto the dagger and crying out as he pulled Jack over him, using Jack as a shield to protect himself from the wolf.

Jack threw his hands outwards, trying to keep the wolf at bay, its long claws slicing into his stomach, catching on something so that the claws didn't slide all the way through him, from one side to the other. The wolf jerked back, and Jack knew what the claw had gotten tangled on—his spine.

It should hurt more, Jack thought as he wrapped his arms around himself, trying to keep his intestines inside his body. White, blinding pain sliced through him as Lucas shoved Jack off of him and onto the floor. A moment passed, an eternity. Then there was a yelp, a crunch.

Silence.

Dimly, Jack hoped it had been enough. That the attack on Lucas would prove fatal. Jack sank into the shadows and had a moment of perfect clarity. As if it was a final parting gift from

God, telling him the truth of his life just before it ebbed out of him completely: He would have died for his parents. He would have died for Nate. But it felt right that, in the end, he died for Val.

CHAPTER 43

Valerie came around the corner and didn't understand what was in front of her. Lucas sat on the ground, covered in blood, his head in his hands, a dark pool spreading beneath him. He was pale and looked up at them sluggishly, blinking slowly. Two dead wolves lay on the ground and beyond that was...

"Jack!"

He was on the ground, unmoving, bloody ropes of intestine surrounding him. *He needs those*, she thought stupidly and rushed to him, trying to stuff them back into his stomach. His blood warmed her hands. The intestines were slick and elusive. Soft. She called his name and, when he didn't respond, didn't even move, she shouted. He needed to hear her. He *had* to answer.

Rachel was beside her, saying something in a low hurried tone, her hands over Jack's heart. The air was suddenly warm, like the first day of summer. His skin, blood and organs grew hot under her palms, and Val jerked away from his body, which was now suffused with a golden glow.

"Stop! It's too late," Lucas called hoarsely, stumbling towards them on his hands and knees. Val looked at him, shocked. His wounds were healing, though slowly, the one on his side still a bleeding gash, his thigh dripping blood.

Rachel didn't look at him as she stayed leaning over Jack, her hands still on his chest. "No it isn't. I can save him!"

Lucas swore, kept his gaze on Valerie for a moment before turning his attention to Rachel. He spoke quickly, his accent thicker than she had ever heard it, the words running together. "He is dead. It is done. Cease *now*."

"No!" Rachel said frantically, shaking her head, "He'll live. I can do this. It's not over, give me a chance."

Valerie reached for Lucas, her hand sliding down his face, scanning his injuries. Lucas ignored her, every fiber of his being riveted on Jack.

She put her arms around Lucas, her cheek resting in a patch of blood on his shirt. He was soft, not as hard as he was at his full strength. The impenetrable exterior gone, so weak that his flesh was almost mortal. Red lines that dripped black blood marred his face where a Werewolf had slashed at him.

Jack might by dying but Lucas... She couldn't look away from him, couldn't stop touching him, needing to reassure herself that he was alright. *Isn't that kind of fucked up? Jack might be dead. Gone forever.* Val knew she should care more, be worried for him. And then the thought slipped away and she looked back at Lucas, feeling compelled to touch him again.

"To what end?" Lucas called over Valerie, angrily speaking to Rachel. She'd never heard him sound so human. So angry and impassioned. *Cruel.* "You think he would thank you for it? Forget what you are? You do this and you only give him the power to kill you. Do not Rachel. It is Marion's life, and more, if you do it."

But even as he said the words, Val heard Jack gasp and cough. She turned, keeping her hand on Lucas' chest, as though he might disappear at any moment. The shimmering glow was fading, and Jack lay on the ground, clothes still bloody but skin healed.

"Why is he still unconscious?" Val asked.

"Tell her what you've done," Lucas said darkly.

Rachel bit her lip as she slumped to the ground, her head in her hands. Her voice was muffled. "He'll survive. But... not as a human. He'll become a wolf. But he'll live." She looked up, her face pale, with that dehydrated look that she'd had before, when she'd made the wolves out of thin air. Whatever she'd done had taxed her.

"If we are going to bind him, it has to happen before he wakes up," Rachel said tiredly. She got to her feet, hands braced on her knees as she took deep breaths.

Valerie felt her own breath hitch, her ears ring a little. "What? What do you mean *bind* him?" She had a flash of an image—a wolf and Cerdewellyn, children walking into flames. She blinked.

Rachel was looking only at Valerie, ignoring Lucas completely. As if Val was the one with the power. "Werewolves are no better than animals. Mindless and driven by animal urges unless they are bound to another. They need a pack. Jack won't have one. If there is no pack, he needs the emotions of someone else to restrain his beast."

Lucas stood, and she felt his presence behind her. She turned to see him, his facial expression so cold that Valerie knew he was furious.

Would he have let Jack die? Was that what she'd just seen? Her heart pounded. She thought she knew the answer but wasn't sure. Had to do *this* first, then she would worry about Lucas and whether or not he would have let Jack die.

Are you stupid? He totally would have let Jack die!

Valerie remembered her history and what she'd read, "Empaths! An Empath was bound to a Werewolf! You can bind him to me, right? How do you do it?"

Lucas took a few steps forward, walked around Val and Jack, and stopped before Rachel. Her head went back, and she swallowed, looking up to him. He reached out a finger, gently placing it under her chin, forcing Rachel to look him square in the eyes.

Rachel flinched, blinking through tears.

"Take him to the room, Rachel. We will meet you there." Val could barely hear him as he said, "I know what you love. Do you hear me? It is not Marion, and it is not him. I know of *her*."

Rachel nodded jerkily, tears coursing down her cheeks as she stumbled backwards, dropping to the ground. She scooped Jack up in her arms, turning and walking down the hall, opening a door and disappearing inside.

Lucas turned back to Val, enveloping her in his arms. She buried her face against his chest, letting him comfort her, enjoying his solidity and strength. Had he tried to kill Jack? Had he? She knew it mattered, but it felt unimportant.

"Why did you threaten Rachel? She was trying to help."

"Do not trust her. The wolves are not dead. They are healing too. Do you see them?"

She pushed away from him and looked at the animals, saw their chests rising and falling, their wounds shrinking. One of them had its eyes open.

"They will attack again. They are Cerdewellyn's, and he is healing them. Listen closely to what I must tell you and then go into that room and wait for me. You cannot bind yourself to Jack, Valerie. The tie must be strong. Only the strongest Empaths could bind themselves to a wolf. You are half Empath at *best* and have no notion of your abilities. You cannot bind yourself to him. It would not work."

She pulled away from him, not touching him at all. "What do you mean, it wouldn't work?"

"I mean, that if the wolf was stronger than your ability, he would be no better than a feral animal. If his anchor is strong enough, he will be Jack. Perhaps a little quicker to anger. Stronger and more intense, but the urges will not rule him. He will only succumb to his instincts and change at the full moon. If he binds to you and you are not strong enough, not only could he harm you, but he'd be gone forever."

"What's the other option?" she said and felt like she already knew. Her mind was screaming a warning at her that this was a bad, bad idea. She took a step back. One and then two. Distance. Like she could take a few more steps and go back in time too. How far back would she go? Before Roanoke? Before Hawaii? Before London?

"Me," Lucas said.

Valerie laughed—a rattling sound. "Yeah, right. Jack bound to you. How bound would he be? You know how much he hates you. I mean, you *have* to know. It's really frigging obvious. Like he'd rather stab his eyes out than have a connection with you. It would destroy him." She looked at the ground. Saw her hands fisted, shaking, felt like she needed to sit down. *No, I need to get to Jack.*

"Being bound to me does not need to affect him negatively. I am strong enough to shut down the connection. He would not feel it. The advantage is that he would not try to kill me anymore. He would be stronger and less likely to die by a vampire's hands. As long as I live, so would he."

He'd be at your mercy. She shook her head, felt like her head was filled with sand. "Wait. You're making it seem like this is not a big deal and it is. It must be."

Lucas looked at her as if she was naïve. *I hate it when he does that.*

"There is no other option. It needs to be done immediately, or he will die from his wounds. I can leave him unbound, but if I do, he will be lost to you. He already hates me, nothing of that will change. Would you rather he died? Or bind to you and become feral? Aside from the physical toll it would take on you, would Jack want to live as a beast—unknowingly acting depraved? Committing the sins he's always fought against? That is your decision. He binds himself to me or he dies."

Valerie looked at him sharply. That sounded like a threat. "No...but there has to be another option. How do you know I can't—"

She heard a growling sound and turned. Two of the wolves were coming to their feet, stalking closer.

"Go. I will follow in a moment," Lucas said, already turning away from her as he went to finish off the wolves. Val hesitated for a moment, looking at them. They were evil. Had almost killed Lucas and Jack. Attacked them. And yet, she looked at them and felt a connection. *That doesn't matter. Jack matters.*

Val opened the door to the bedroom and saw Rachel inside, standing over Jack. Rachel's backpack was on the bed, her hand dripping blood, Jack's lips red with it.

"Shut the door," Rachel said agitatedly, throwing her a brief look. "Where is Lucas?" Rachel asked, pouring some herbs into a bowl positioned next to Jack's head.

"He'll be here soon. He said the wolves were still alive."

Rachel stroked the back of a finger down Jack's cheek familiarly.

"He wouldn't want you to touch him," Valerie said, even as she knew now was not the time to worry about that.

"Oh, please." Rachel rolled her eyes. "There are bigger priorities here. For example, this Werewolf binding is a big fucking problem."

"Go on, tell me what you really think," Val said sarcastically.

"Okay. Listen, fast. Lucas wasn't straight with you. You can totally bind yourself to Jack. He'll be fine, you'll be fine. Lucas just doesn't want you to have that connection with Jack. It's intimate. You'd spend more time with him, care for him, be drawn to him. And he would be drawn to you. You know that's the last thing Lucas wants."

If felt like a physical punch. "He's lying to me?" She knew she was shaking her head. "He wouldn't do that." *Yes, he would.*

"Yeah. He would and he is. I can get the procedure going. I just need some of your blood. You need to distract him for a while, and then you can come back, finish it and, voila, you've got the pet you never wanted."

"Wait. Why do you care? Lucas will kill you if you do this."

Rachel looked worryingly at the door. "I'm sort of counting on you making my continued existence part of your demands. Cause yeah, he is definitely thinking of killing me. If Lucas binds himself to Jack, it's over. Jack will be his bitch for eternity. This is your last chance, and it has to be now. I need ten minutes, tops."

"What am I supposed to do? How do I distract him for ten minutes?" This was stupid. There was no distracting Lucas unless she what? Tried to fuck him in the hallway as they rolled around in a pool of cold wolf blood? *Man, I wish I hadn't thought that.*

Rachel grabbed Val's hand, and she caught the glint of a knife, felt a sting of burning pain as Rachel cut her flesh open, shoving a cup under her hand to catch the blood. The cup filled quickly— she'd cut deep.

"Gee, your blood *does* smell really good," Rachel muttered, eyes focused on the gushing blood. "How do you distract him? Are you kidding? You're an *Empath*. He's desperate to get into your artery and you're *dripping* with blood. Give him a taste. I can guarantee you that will distract him for more than a few minutes."

"What? *No*. He said it's dangerous."

Rachel set the bowl of blood on the wooden table next to the bed, then closed her eyes, taking a deep breath as she turned back to Val. "You want to know the truth and how much he's been lying to you, don't you? *This* is your chance. Maybe your only chance." Her eyes burned into Valerie's, trying to convince her of her sincerity—and it was kind of working. Val made sure to look at Rachel's forehead, rather than her eyes, so she wouldn't be compelled.

"I need a distraction or he's going to bind himself to Jack. Nothing except your blood—which is dripping on the floor, by the way—will keep him occupied."

Val looked down. Shit, she'd bled through the towel. How fucking deep had Rachel cut? Rachel grabbed Val's wrist, swiping blood from Val's palm and slapping it on Val's injury-free hand, then her neck, even her lips before Val could do much more than swear. "I look like fucking Carrie at the prom! Get off me!"

Rachel licked her lips but took a step back. "Yeah, you've got a definite birthday cake vibe going on. Go! I need ten minutes, that's it."

"Wait, wait." *This is happening way too fast.*

"He's coming. Now or never!" Rachel went back to the little bowl, stirring the ingredients with her pinky as she started speaking in Latin.

Val opened the door, stepped outside, and shut it behind her. Blood. Her hand still dripped. She wiped her palms together like a satanic version of Patty Cake, noticing how tacky the blood was. Her stomach roiled as if she were on a ship in a choppy ocean.

Lucas came down the hallway and froze. His gaze sweeping her bloody form from head to foot.

I am a birthday cake!

His clothes were ripped, his hair matted with blood. Dark with it. His injuries were almost healed, and she wondered where he'd been. The wolves were in the same spot, but their heads were chopped off in a clean strike. So why was he coming from down the hall?

"What happened? Are you all right?" His gaze was riveted on her hand. She knew the moment he breathed in the scent of her blood because he staggered backwards a step. His nostrils flared with desire, and he made a sound— half despair, half longing, then he slapped his hand over his mouth and nose like that would keep him from ripping into her jugular.

This is a big mistake. WWJD? What would Jack do? He'd keep going. Risk death for what was right. Dammit!

"I'm binding myself to Jack. Rachel is getting it set up," Val said, studying him carefully.

Lucas looked her over, his gaze roaming her from head to toe. "No. You cannot."

"She says I can do it."

"She is wrong. Get out of the way. Or I cannot be responsible for my actions. "The words were a growl.

She pushed back against the door, blocking it as he took a step towards her. "You'll have to go through me," she said, the stupidity of her statement obvious.

Lucas must have recognized the ineffectualness of her comment, because he smiled at her indulgently. Like a man who was about to take his lover to bed and who would not be stopped for any amount of gold or reason in the world.

His head tilted to the side as he took a step closer. "What *are* your intentions?" he murmured gently. And she knew this was an amusing game to him. He wasn't afraid of her. He trusted himself and his ability to resist her completely. And *that* pissed her off. What was it with these men? If he stripped off his clothes, she'd have a hard time refusing!

He was *going* to drink her blood. There was no other option. He wasn't binding himself to Jack. .

"Look at me," he said urgently.

"Why, so you can do your mind-Voodoo on me? Hell, no!"Val said unhappily and pushed her fingers deep into the wound on her palm. Tears welled in her eyes, and she looked away so she wouldn't be sick or faint.

Blood poured out of the open wound and she wiped it over her again—neck, hands, lips. If he wanted into that room, he'd have to go through her. He was going to drink her blood, and she would know if he was lying to her. Jack 's life depended upon it. She wouldn't fail.

This is a stupid fucking plan.

Lucas looked around the hallway like the walls were closing in on him.

Maybe not as confident he can resist as he wants me to believe.

He swallowed hard.

"Get out of the way, or I will harm you," he said, voice gravelly, eyes fixed on hers before dropping to her hand and the blood that dripped from it. Watching it fall. It was odd to be wanted for something so unusual. Her blood. Like being a kidney donor or something. The stress, fear and surrealness of the situation combined within her, making her feel jumpy.

She licked her lips nervously, tasting blood on her tongue. His shoulders straightened, his whole body hard and angry. She felt his energy change, could see his decision in the slight readying of his posture.

Lucas stalked towards her, slowly watching her and her hands. Almost casual, belying the importance of the moment. Trying to lull her into thinking he was relaxed. His voice was smooth and deep, as though he were going to tell her a secret. A look similar to a condescending sneer crossed his lips. "The trick to combat is in watching the center of your opponent's body, looking for the shift and tension so one knows where they will move. Are you watching me? Can you even move fast enough to make an impression?"

Okay, definitely condescending.

"Tell me, my little Valkyrie, what do you think you may accomplish? Make me drink your blood, and then what do you want? A declaration of love? To have Jack and I both? To be my Valkyrie in truth and lead me from the field of battle into the gates of hell?"

He was trying to distract her, make her mad. Why didn't he just back down? Jack wasn't his concern. "I want the truth. And I don't know if you've been giving it to me."

He licked his lips. "There are other ways. *Ask* me. Trust me of your own volition," he said, the tone of his words soft and coaxing. He'd closed half the distance between them but waited several feet away, like he didn't want to come closer if he didn't have to.

Lucas was breathing rapidly, his pupils wide as he watched her. He was hard and huge with desire, looking from her lips to her chest, absorbing all of her.

"I have to know that you will tell me the truth!" She held out a palm towards him, like warding him away. Her breath was shaky, and she shifted on her feet.

His hands fisted at his sides and he took a step back. "I will," he said. A promise.

What if it's a lie?" Drink my blood. Let me inside you, so I know you're telling me the truth."

He shook his head slowly back and forth. "No. After all the time we have spent together and what I have explained to you— what this may do to *me*— you want to force the issue now? When enemies surround us? When Jack is vulnerable? Who will protect him if I am insensible? Rachel? She will kill you as soon as look at you. She is not loyal, Valerie. No one else is strong enough to see us out of Cerdewellyn's realm. This is not the time. If you need answers, I will give them to you, but not here or now."

"I think you wanted him dead. I think I can bind myself to him and that you're lying to me because you don't want the competition. How can I trust you?" she whispered, determination wavering. He looked to the side and somehow that gesture gave him away—he was not going to let her be with Jack.

He rushed her, but she saw it coming, had a bare moment to guess how he would try to get past her, and reach the door. He was afraid to let her touch him, she knew it. *Right or left?* She had to decide.

She threw her palms up in front of her, stretching her arms out like anticipating a hug, while throwing her body forwards, jumping outwards to meet him, in a split second, deciding he would come at her from the left.

He moved at full speed, but he was weak, slower than usual, so she could almost catch everything that was happening. Her chest slammed into his, her forehead cracking against his jaw, hard.

He made a harsh sound at the contact, and she twined her arms around his neck desperately, gripping him hard around his neck with all of her strength, tilting her head back in an effort to reach his lips. His hands reached up, clamped on her arms, pulling her off of him. Her lips slid along his, brushing, her tongue pushing at the seam of his lips, begging him to kiss her. She arched closer, forcing him to take her weight, trying to push him off balance.

Keep him close for a moment longer. Each fraction of a second like an hour of temptation. How long could he resist when each time they came together, the need grew? When it was what they both wanted.

Please. Everything seemed to pause as she waited to see if he would break. Always. He could always resist her. And she feared he would do it again. He would jerk back, move away, toss her aside, maybe even laugh at her, then go in to see Jack and change all of their lives forever.

Please, she thought again. Desperately, like that painful declaration of love when one didn't know what the response would be—a moment of endless waiting and yearning that was filled with hope, terror and an openness to devastation.

The only action was the slow slide of her bloody lips on his. He was frozen and cold. On the outside and the inside, both his heart and his body. *What did he want?* What did he *really* want from her? To be warm? To love and feel? Excitement? Or was it just control? If he could walk away from *this,* she'd know the answer.

He trembled, hesitated...broke.

His arms closed around her, and he jerked her hard against his cock. She gasped against his lips, and his head tilted to the side, mouth opening under hers, taking her blood inside him greedily. She knew the moment that he swallowed, felt it like a door banging open inside of her, her power sliding into him, pouring down his throat and into him. He kissed her hard, sucking her lower lip into his mouth as he swallowed, tasting her lips again and again, seeking more of her.

The blood on her lips was cold, but his kiss became hot. The fire of their connection blazed between them. The kiss softened, wasn't as frenzied but became an exploration, an end in and of itself.

Lucas didn't just give in but surrendered. The urgency left him. His kisses turned languid, and he moaned in a way that made her body spasm in desire.

His legs collapsed, and he sank to the floor, breathing hard, like he'd just sprinted to her from the depths of hell. His head bowed before her, like a knight before his Queen, forehead resting on her stomach, his broad shoulders slumped in defeat.

He looked up at her, and she caught his gaze, caught the hungry look in them, felt like *she* was compelling him. His hands were on her hips and his fingers clenched as she raised her hand, extending her palm towards his parted lips.

She saw the fight in him— it was still there, after all— a little flicker of fire in a snowstorm. His eyes were vivid. A deep, dark, blue like the ocean after it had claimed a ship full of men.

A hundred things passed through his eyes as they stared at each other, like she was looking into a small window of his soul. He cradled her bloody palm in his hands, brought it to his lips like a cupful of water, his tongue swiping across her flesh. His fangs pierced her hand. He bit deep, and she cried out at the pain.

Blood welled into his mouth, and he swallowed it in quick gulps, pulling so more blood welled out of her, like she couldn't bleed fast enough. As though he would gulp it all down no matter how fast it pulsed out of her... and he would still want more.

She hadn't seen anger in his surrender. Nor defeat. No love or tenderness, either. There was no room in him to feel anything else besides need and desperate blood lust. Obsession and self-absorption coalesced into the gravest, most primal hunger possible.

Maybe he hadn't even *really* known it was her. *I could have been anyone.* Val looked down at him, watched the way he worked her, then swallowed audibly, cradling her hand flush to his mouth. There was nothing but instinct there. An instinct so long denied that he was now lost to *it* and no longer himself.

He was desire. Desire for blood. For feeling. For everything that had been gone for hundreds of years and that he had never thought to see again.

She was on his tongue, sliding down his throat in spurts as he drank and drank, wishing it would never end. She slid inside of him and hit his stomach, radiating outwards like a tsunami hitting land, into his veins and bloodstream, riding his blood as it pumped through his body and worked its way to his heart.

Yes.

She knew the moment it hit—transforming him into something new. He gasped and fell forward, collapsing to the floor, arms too weak to catch himself, his shoulders and head hitting the ground hard. Lucas closed his eyes, looking like he had survived the most draining passion.

And that was exactly how he felt. She was inside him and she knew. Val smiled darkly. He was the princess who'd touched the spinning wheel. He had avoided this moment for what seemed like all of his life, and now that it was here, it had sucked him under.

Utterly destroyed him.

Her *soul* was in his mind, twisting through the little pathways of his brain, broken images like white noise coming back to her as her blood made a circuit through his body. She was so deep within him she ached.

It was hard to orient herself inside of him. Val forced her energy to pump through him, past his heart which was filled with chaos— like a bar at midnight. Emotions carousing inside him before she reached the quiet peace of his mind. She knew what she wanted to know and called the information forth, '*Tell me about Jack.* ' She left the question open-ended. Not wanting a filter, unsure *why* it would work, but certain it would.

She saw a silent movie of his intentions and what had occurred in the hallway before she and Rachel had arrived.

Jack attacking Lucas and the moment he decided to put Jack between himself and the wolf. His relief when the wolf ripped Jack apart and inflicted the mortal wound so he wouldn't have to.

She could bind herself to Jack, that knowledge was there. How close it would bring them and how much he didn't want that to happen.

Wolves. A memory drifted towards her like a ribbon on the breeze and she caught it. Examined it. She was screaming and Lucas carried her into a room, tossed her onto a bed, straddling her, grabbing her chin, compelling her to forget all that she had learned in Cerdewellyn's castle—what he had done to Empaths, to the wolves.

He told her not to be afraid of him, to trust him, made her believe it blindly. And then there was another pause, a hesitation as the ribbon slipped away. She tried to grab it again—he was struggling. Didn't want her to see the next part—

They were still on the bed and she was looking at him blankly. He stared at the ceiling for a moment and then looked back down at her, *'forget what he told you, what you learned, trust me, know that I will get you out of here...and you will love me for it.* 'He finished the compulsion and she saw herself through his eyes, how beautiful he thought she was, the way she awoke, innocent of his treachery, her kissing him, not wondering why they were in a bedroom or how they had gotten there.

Nothing had mattered except him.

He told me to love him.

Val felt sick and angry. Wanted nothing more than to get out of his mind and leave him here, but there was something else. A dark area, like a shadow. She willed the darkness away, like pulling aside a curtain, and reached inside, reading the events of her life through his memories.

The vampire, Roberto, had returned to Lucas after killing her mother. Lucas, as he drank her mother's blood from Roberto's neck. Collapsing in joy. And then—something she never knew, never even suspected—Lucas coming up to her at eight as she played outside, as he dulled her grief and took it away, wiped the image of Roberto and that day from her mind.

So that when she thought of what had happened, she wouldn't be too sad, couldn't see it clearly or know exactly what had happened. He'd taken that from her, and she had never known.

It was like a bullwhip stripping off her flesh, peeling open her skin down to her beating and vulnerable heart. Her mother's death had brought him more pleasure than he'd felt in hundreds of years. And in that moment, Val's fate was sealed. He would have had her, pursued her, taken her willingly or by force once he realized the pleasure she might bring him.

No matter how ugly, boring or awful she might have been, he *still* would have wanted her. Being near her was the most exhilarating battle he'd fought in a millennia: him versus himself, the desire for her blood at war with his determination to abstain.

She tried to pull out of his mind, disengaging from him, but it felt like they were tied together with Saran Wrap. She pulled, and the connection stretched but it was too thickly wrapped to break. She wanted out and imagined herself stumbling away from him, putting distance between them. Tried to bring forth the wall of her mental shields but couldn't remember what a wall looked like.

Valerie screamed, the sound severing the connection between them. She fell down onto the floor and looked at his unconscious body. His features were soft in sleep, a slight frown between his brows like he was having a bad dream.

I hope to fuck he is. Would he be different when he awoke? It didn't matter. She didn't care. She couldn't care. Everything Lucas had ever done had been a manipulation and a lie.

Everything.

She stood and opened the bedroom door, leaving Lucas on the floor in the hallway. She hated herself for hesitating and looking back at him, knowing how he had used her and what he was capable of, the man he really was, but she did look back.

One last time.

He was peaceful and harshly beautiful as he lay on his side, unconscious on the floor. Something glistened on his cheek. A single tear that slid down his face and disappeared into his bloody, golden hair.

Her hands clenched, and she almost went back to him. If she touched him, she could know what that emotion was. Remorse? Grief for losing her? Despair that she'd found out what a monster he was?

She closed the door behind her.

CHAPTER 44

This was a time to compartmentalize. Her hands were tacky with blood, and her palm felt like a dozen rattlesnakes had taken a chomp out of her. Emotionally, she felt ripped open, as if her nerves were on the outside of her body and even the air was too abrasive.

Jack was lying on the bed. He was pale and sweating, his hair mussed up. He looked like he had a fever. But a seriously fatal one, maybe Scarlet Fever.

"Did you find Lucas?" Rachel asked.

Val whirled around and saw Rachel in the corner, sitting in a chair. Val nodded, momentarily unable to speak.

"Where is he?"

"Unconscious. On the floor in the hallway."

"I guess you pack a punch after all. Jack is coming out of it. He'll be ready for the binding in a few minutes. I got it all set up. I'm just waiting for him to wake up. He needs to agree, you know."

"Then what?"

Rachel stood, moving casually towards Valerie, a small, almost pitying smile on her lips. "Then he's going to need blood, and the blood he ingests will bind him. *Forever.*"

Val nodded jerkily. "Do you want to keep an eye on Lucas, make sure he doesn't wake up, while I... donate?" She shrugged, at a loss for a better word.

"Oh, Lucas won't wake up for a while now. His system is in shock from all those emotions he's no doubt full of. Just think, when he wakes up, he'll be a whole new man. You know he's vulnerable right now, don't you? What do you think Cerdewellyn will do to him? Kill him straight away or torture him for a year or two?"

Val held back a whimper, her heart seizing painfully. "I don't owe Lucas anything." She shook her head, cutting off the remnants of feelings she had for him. He was a monster. He'd used her. He didn't care about her. He wasn't capable of it.

Rachel was close, and Val gave ground backing up. *This is Marion's girlfriend. She almost killed me once.* Funny how that came to mind every now and again. *You never forget an attempted murderer.*

Jack moaned from the bed, beginning to wake up.

"That's your cue. Exit stage left. It's time for you to go," Rachel said and gripped Val's arms hard, so hard Val knew she was instantly bruising. Rachel carried her to the door, lifting her feet off the ground, arms straight out in front of her, like Val was a small dog that had just peed on her rug and was going outside for the night. Val kicked at her, struggling, trying to break Rachel's grasp.

"What are you doing? Let me go! I have to help Jack!" Val cried.

Rachel made a tsking noise. "No, *you* don't. You're done here. Thanks for getting Lucas out of the way. Jack really would have had a problem with that."

Rachel threw her out the door, and Valerie's back slammed into the wall. The blow knocked the wind out of her, and she couldn't drag air into her lungs, that feeling of drowning overcoming her for a moment as her mouth opened and closed like a fish.

"Jack is mine," Rachel said, hand on the door, ready to close it. "Turns out, I wasn't very trustworthy, after all," she said with a shrug, before slamming the heavy wooden door shut. There was a scraping sound inside as Rachel shoved furniture against the door.

I knew I couldn't trust that bitch!

Val threw herself at the door. She pounded on it, pushing with all of her strength, desperate to find a way in. She looked down at Lucas. Still out. She kicked him absently, hoping he'd wake up and open the door for her. He didn't move.

Jack bound to Rachel? It isn't going to fucking happen!"Cerdewellyn!" she screamed at the top of her lungs, over and over as the seconds ticked by.

Cerdewellyn was suddenly next to her, appearing cool and collected. He looked down at the ground, at Lucas unconscious on the floor, and blinked as if surprised.

"I have to get into that room. She's in there! She's going to bond with Jack! Help me! *Please*, help me," she said, still pushing hard against the door.

"You ask me for a favor?" Cer said, his voice quiet.

Oh shit. "Yes!"

"And do you understand that when I give a boon, I ask for something in return? Something of equal value?" His gaze went down to her mouth and back to her eyes.

"I don't *care*! Just get me into that room!" He could have her first born child if he wanted, she just needed to get to Jack.

He listened, head tilted towards the door. "By taking you into that room, I change the course of several lives. Do you understand the gravity of your request?"

"Yes!" *No! Why is he still talking?* What was he waiting for?

"The bargain is made." He snapped his fingers, and the door disappeared. Val ran into the room and Rachel turned towards her, a look of fury on her face.

"I will kill you if you touch her," Cerdewellyn said to Rachel. Rachel froze, then nodded unhappily before turning back to Jack. He was leaning against the wall on the other side of the room, a feral look in his eyes as Rachel held a bloody palm under his nose. Cer waved a hand, and Jack disappeared, reappearing on the other side of the room, away from Rachel. Between them both so he'd have to choose who he went to.

Val dug her fingers into her palm again, the pain blinding, as blood welled to the surface. *If the Staff infection I'm going to get in my hand is the worst of my problems, this will count as a good trip.*

Jack saw her and shook his head, as if really loud music was playing in there. "Val?" he said, confused. He was breathing hard, like it hurt to pull air into his body.

Cerdewellyn stood near the door, his arms crossed, body tense. He was looking at the blood on Valerie's hand. *Oh great, another junkie.* She turned back to Jack.

She stuck out her palm and took a step towards him. Jack looked at Valerie hungrily—not sexually but like she was a Milk Bone. He looked different—bones sharper, eyes wild—but still human.

Val stood a few feet away from him and spoke to him gently. "Come on Jack. Let's finish this. Just drink my yummy blood, and we can go home."

His gaze flicked to Rachel, raking her in from head to foot, a look so hot it could have burned her where she stood.

What the fuck?

Jack moved towards Val slowly. One step and then another.

Rachel called his name and he swayed. His gaze stayed fixed on Valerie's outstretched hand.

"If you go with her, she will give you happiness and peace," Rachel said, voice raspy. "We both know that isn't what you want."

Valerie dared a glance at Rachel, saw her slightly bent forward, palm out. Rachel's lower lip trembled, and she sounded like she might cry.

I can make that vampire bitch cry! Val thought angrily, looking around for Jack's knife.

Jack was breathing heavily, the sound of it echoing around the stone room. The bitch started talking again. "If you choose me"—her voice broke a little—"I'll give you revenge. I'll keep the fire going so you can kill them *all*, Jack. Come with me, and I will give you the triumph you seek, the pleasure and the violence. I *know* who you are," Rachel finished, sounding sweet and so sincere Val wanted to barf.

Val snapped, "Who the fuck do you think you are? You *know* him. You don't know him! You just want to screw him and have a pet. If you cared about him at all, you'd want him to be happy and you would let him go." Val said, then turned her attention to Jack. "Everything will be alright. Everything will be okay. I love you! We are family. It's been me and you forever. Come on, Jack." She stopped herself from saying, 'come on boy. ' But it was close. "Now come over here. Don't be an idiot!" Her voice sounded desperate and pleading. But she couldn't lie to him, couldn't make the promise that she would be willing to let him die just so he could have his revenge.

"Lucas will kill you," Val hissed at Rachel. "I'll get him to kill you, unless you leave now, "

Rachel didn't even look at her, as if Val wasn't worth the effort of turning her head. "Wow. That is one empty threat. You blew it, sweetheart. You chose wrong. If Lucas gets out of here, you might be in deeper shit than I am."

Jack strode towards Rachel, a look of killing violence on his face. Rachel backed up until she bumped into the wall. Jack boxed her in, putting his body closer to hers.

"I like it that you run from me," he murmured to her.

Oh brother.

Rachel said something faint in response, and all Val heard was the word 'blood. '

"I don't want your hand," Jack said and dropped his head a little, pressing his lips to Rachel's neck. He was dark and dangerous. Pure violence and animal. Different. *Other*. No sign of softness or restraint in him. The control that he lived by was gone.

Rachel's hands went to Jack's shoulders, and she pushed at him a little. Away or closer, Val couldn't tell. And then Rachel let him go, and a moment later she held a knife in her hand. Jack watched her with the blade, saw it inches from his face and didn't react.

She laid the blade against her neck lightly, but Jack made a shushing noise and took it from her. Rachel's hand dropped back to her side limply, and she turned her head, exposing the long column of her neck. She closed her eyes, breathing fast and shallow, hands fisted. He touched her neck with the blade, and she cried out like he'd just shoved himself deep inside of her body. He didn't break her skin, letting the moment build like this was some kind of sick foreplay.

"Do I drink a little or a lot?" Jack growled.

She gasped, words shaky. "A little. You only need a drop or two."

"I don't want to cut you there," he said, his voice a deep, deep rumble of sound. The blade slid down her neck, not leaving so much as a pale mark on her skin, until it stopped on the juncture of where her shoulder met her neck.

Somehow the spot seemed even more vulnerable than her neck—more intimate. He nicked her very lightly, so lightly that hardly any blood welled to the surface. But Valerie knew when it happened because Rachel's eyes squeezed tight, her lips parted, breath changing to harsh pants. Jack moved, dropped his head to her neck, sucking her there, kissing her, the lower half of his body grinding into her.

Rachel twined her arms around his neck, pulling him closer, spreading her legs wider to make space for his hips. His hand went to her thigh as he twined her leg around his waist, adjusting his stance so he was lower, could notch his erection in the vee of her legs. They both moaned at the same time, as though he'd found the right spot for them both. His other hand went to her ass, hauling her closer as his mouth stayed latched at her neck.

Cerdewellyn had moved next to Valerie, and she hadn't even noticed, was so dismayed at the sight before her that she wouldn't have noticed if the whole damned castle was burning to the ground.

Tears blurred her vision.

"Come. There is nothing for you here," Cer said, and he took her hand, just as Jack lifted Rachel up, turning, carrying her to the bed as he kissed her deeply.

Val blinked and felt a bone-deep displacement as Cer shifted them from the room, taking them outside, wind whipping her hair across her face. Her eyes stung, adjusting to the harsh light of day.

"How could this all have happened? It's everything...upside down and wrong." Her voice was crackly, and she was staring into the distance with glassy eyes. Where were they? The castle was in the distance, and she could hear the pounding of the ocean around her.

"Your day is not yet done. I must insist upon collecting my debt," Cerdewellyn said calmly.

She laughed, a tinge of hysteria making it loud. "*Now?* Really? And what do you want, O Mighty king."

"My people are dying and you can save them," he said.

"Are you kidding me? Everyone wants something from me. And, okay, your reason for wanting me is particularly compelling, but— I really, *really*, just want a normal, boring life."

He frowned. "There are so many people in the world. And yet, no more than a few are actually needed on a fundamental level."

"That sounds like a compliment," she said.

"Only you can save us. Be glad you are needed. There are people who would kill to have what you are born with. In fact, there are many of my kind who would sacrifice everything one could name to have your gifts."

"Huh. No chance you can give *them* my gift, is there?" she said waspishly, knowing she was hanging on to her sanity by a thread.

Cerdewellyn looked into her eyes, tilting her chin up so she could see into his black depths. "I can give you the power to defend yourself and start anew. I can make Lucas and Jack rue the day they chose other than you. Can make revenge your toy, laughter and pain your coin. But perhaps most importantly, I can take away your naiveté, grant you immortality so that you need never fear again."

"Immortality and power?"

He nodded.

She grimaced and shook her head. "That sounds like the sort of promise that includes some seriously fine print at the bottom. But, thank you. That's super nice of you." Val looked around, needing to get off this rock. No, not a rock. A cliff. *I'm on a fucking cliff?*

He acted like she hadn't spoken. "No more fear, no more bumbling about in the dark. You will know the answer to every question you have. I can bring you into the light."

An alarm bell went off in her mind. He sounded pretty fanatical. "What's the catch?" she said, squinting.

He looked at her in confusion.

"What's the downside. Why *wouldn't* I want to do this?"

He smiled at her radiantly, then laughed. It made the ground tremble and some scraggly bushes that were growing out of the rock, bloom, the flowers opening and stretching towards his voice.

"This could be the last time you ever ask someone that question and not know if you are getting an honest answer."

Now *that* was tempting. No one ever told her the truth. For a moment she took his offer seriously. "I won't die, and I'll have lots of power? People won't be able to lie to me and, with these gifts, I probably won't be afraid or naïve anymore?"

"Yes," he said and gave her a gentle smile.

"I want to think about it."

He shook his head. "I am afraid that is not possible. You promised me that you would grant my favor, despite the fact that it would change the balance and alter lives. This is my favor, a gift you *must* accept. To become my consort, a full Empath, and help my people thrive again."

She took a step back, a gust of wind, pushing her back into Cer's arms.

"Another step and you will fall." He held onto her. "Accept," he said quietly, his words carried away on a gust of wind.

"Will you kill me if I say no? You just said you needed me!" she said, desperately gambling that he wouldn't kill her and was bluffing.

"I do need you, and you are now in my world. Look around you, look at the barrenness. The hard desolation. Below us is the magic sea and, in it, you will find your power. You shall go in no matter what. I am a King first. You will obey. The only question is whether you obey and enjoy it, or obey and have it break you to pieces."

She tried to struggle.

He took a step backwards to the edge, dragging her with him. She couldn't think, was afraid to fall, knew she wouldn't survive the drop. She could hear the ocean pounding far below.

"It will hurt if you are unwilling. I will not ask you again."

She was deathly afraid and didn't care what she promised, just didn't want to die, would find a fix later. She wanted to accept. *I always say yes. That's what gets me into this bullshit.*

"*No,*" she said and then louder, her conviction growing.

He took a deep breath, his grip on her arms relaxing. He shook his head as if her answer created a problem he had not anticipated. "Never say I did not warn you." His arms wrapped around her, her chest to his as he took one step, then two. The ground fell away and she was falling, screaming, as they fell towards the raging sea.

Extras

Want more Love is Fear? I had to remove a sex scene because it just didn't further the plot. Yeah, really! But I'm going to be sending it out as an Extra to anyone who writes a review of LIF. Write a review, send me the link and your email address and I'll send you the scene. It's Val and Lucas and occurs before they get taken to Fey.

I love to hear from fans, and respond to everything. If you sent me something and have not heard from me, it means I didn't get it. Please try again! I can be reached at:

CHcarolinehanson@gmail.com

@Caroline_Hanson on Twitter

http://www.facebook.com/pages/Caroline-Hanson/205847429481635

Made in the USA
Middletown, DE
14 August 2015